Lost Daughter of the Stars

ShennonDoah Rivière

RhetAskew Publishing
United States of America

Cover Illustration and Interior Design

© 2023 – Flitterbow Productions

All characters, settings, locations, and all other content contained within this book are fictional and are the intellectual property of the author; any likenesses are coincidental and unknown to author and publisher at the time of publication.

This work and its components may not be reproduced without the express written permission of the author and Rhetoric Askew, LLC.

ISBN-13: 978-1-949-39882-3

© 2023 — ShennonDoah Rivière

ALL RIGHTS RESERVED

This book is dedicated to

JoAnn Wagner

Brent Bills

Collette Bills

Alex

Amanda

& Aiden.

Always Believe!

CHAPTER 1

More of the Same

A NEW TOWN, OUR new home, where we'd create a better life together. Wait—could I make it through this space? I hefted my favorite chair, almost through the entryway...

"Tell me you did not just scuff the wall when you turned that stupid, oversized chair of yours!" Nick restrained his clenched fists in the presence of his buddies. Thank goodness they were here, a few of his co-workers organizing our "moving brigade."

"Relax, man." Joe clapped him on the shoulder. "We're sure to bump a few more walls before all of your furniture's off the truck. You don't need to be so hard on Jen."

"Besides," I added to further appease him, "I still have a couple of weeks left before school starts. Plenty of time to touch up the walls."

"We painted them before moving to avoid having to 'touch things up,'" he grumbled, leaving to fetch the next item.

Alone in the living room, I caressed the dark brown chair Nick despised—my favorite possession. I yearned to curl up in it, tucked away in a fuzzy blanket. I'd purchased it after graduating college and moving out of the dorms. It had comforted me during winter weather, offering relaxation on unending summer afternoons. It had coddled me during illness, refreshing me whenever I needed a catnap. My chair was the one thing I refused to let Nick throw out.

Our move to North Dakota provided a great excuse for him to eliminate many of my possessions. Nick detested clutter. He didn't understand that my so-called excessive knickknacks and stuffed animals, yearbooks and blankets, and old clothes I might wear again, kept me grounded each time I relocated.

I'd moved so much as a child. Sometimes to a new city, sometimes within the same town, but always in the state of Nebraska. Possessions helped me remember who I was and where I'd been. I trailed my hand along the back of my chair, grabbed a box marked "living room," and ripped off the packing tape.

"Ah-choo!" A violent sneeze tore from my body.

"Damn it, Jen. You're not getting sick, are you?" Without the cursing or the harsh tone, I may have believed Nick was concerned about my welfare.

"No worries, silly goose. It's just my allergies."

"I thought you said those would clear up when we moved up North."

"But Nick," I pleaded, "we've only just arrived. Plus, I'm sure it was just some cardboard dust from these boxes."

Although we were newlyweds, I hoped Grafton, North Dakota provided a permanent residence. Many of our wedding gifts remained in their original packaging because of Nick, who complained about his bachelor pad shrinking after I moved in. With all this space, we should have more than enough room to truly grow.

"If you didn't have so much crap," he began the familiar tirade, "that wouldn't be a problem, either. At least you're not getting sick." His tone brightened when his friend handed him a domestic bottled beer.

They strolled into the family room, where a baseball game blasted from the oversized flat screen. I sighed, resolved to get as much put away as I could while the Kansas City Royals played.

A flutter of curtains by the small corner window in the living room, combined with a hint of burning incense, sent a shiver down my spine. My pixies, it appeared as if they had followed me all the way from Nebraska. I called them my pixies to make them seem a little more beautiful and a little less frightening. Whatever physical form they embodied—pixies, fairies, brownies—they'd been watching me for years.

Not that I'd ever seen the creatures I suspected of haunting me, but I often sensed a disturbance in my aura—like the fluttering curtains—as if someone, or something, had been watching through the window before rushing away. The sudden departure of something large enough to cause such a movement filled me with a sense of foreboding.

Did my pixies have a message to share about my future? Was this greeting a sign of hope or an omen of something more sinister?

I shook the productivity-inhibiting daydreams from my head, continuing to unpack in the living room and kitchen for the rest of the afternoon.

Around five thirty, I offered to make a beer run for the moving brigade and picked up ingredients to make pizzas—including blended cheeses and my specialty spices. I preferred to cook when possible, and the guys raved over my homemade pizza. Although deserved, such high praise embarrassed me.

"Yeah, my Jen is an amazing cook. I think she's trying to fatten me up so I won't leave her for anyone else." He swatted my ass, rougher than necessary, when I walked by with an armload of empty beer bottles.

"Ow, Nick!" Tears sprang to my eyes as I scurried away.

"Don't let her fool ya," he laughed to his friends. "She likes it rough."

I cleaned up from supper, retreating to the dining room to unpack until my exhausted body demanded I drag it up the stairs to bed. Nick ought to be happy with all the completed cleaning and unpacking, although many hours of work remained.

After one o'clock the front door crashed shut, followed by his noisy trek up the stairs. Unlike nights he worked at the club, Nick often enjoyed using his free nights to binge on alcohol until he passed out. Tonight was no different, inspiring me to seek comfort elsewhere. Echoes from his loud snores followed me down the stairs. I set a pillow on my armchair and curled up in a lush, white blanket.

* * *

I awoke to bright sunlight warming the walls and carpet. I snuck back into our bedroom to grab a cotton summer outfit along with my hairbrush and a washcloth, dressing downstairs where I wouldn't disturb Nick.

While he slumbered, I figured I'd venture out. I should head over to the school and assess my classroom. After, I could stop by the school and office supply store that served communities as far away as Devil's Lake and even Fargo.

Grafton High School was a straight shot, nestled into a hillside little more than a half mile away. Early morning shadows from monstrous black walnut trees offered some respite to the wilting grass. Temperatures threatened to climb toward 100 degrees again today.

"Weird," I muttered, "being this far north and getting this hot." However, I had done my research; despite the current warmth, within three months temperatures would dip below freezing.

At the high school, I parked beyond the expanse of grass that stretched to my classroom. They had not yet set up my outdoor key fob, so I entered the school through the front doors by the office. I contemplated telling someone I was in the building, but decided the security cameras were more effective at announcing my presence.

Shadows consumed the hallway leading toward my classroom. Desks on each side piled on top of each other, smashed flush against mustard-yellow lockers. A shiver skittered across my neck and down my back as I imagined myself in a haunted school in a Goosebumps book.

I sorted through my keys, trying to remember which one on the bulky key chain opened my room. I discovered the door wasn't shut tight. Dim light poured through a quarter inch slit between door and frame. I yanked the handle, revealing a gloomy room. Sunlight muscled its way past the boundaries of generic white blinds on six windows. I pulled and released the cordless blinds to allow full penetration by the sun. Seconds after releasing the third blind, the fourth flew up of its own volition.

I jumped back, laughing at my edginess. "Looks like I've got a classroom ghost. Thanks for the welcome, Señor Fantasma."

I contemplated my room for a few more minutes. When I took a step toward the door, a large shadow appeared on the wall I faced. It looked like the leg of a giant. I spun around to see who stood outside my classroom. No one stood there! Certain I'd seen that shadow—and that some rambunctious juvenile laughed at my expense—I bounded to the windows, peering across the lawn of fresh-cut grass.

Still no one.

Gusts of wind, shadows, and burning incense—the scent my pixies often left behind. I'd been right. Not only had they followed me to this new town, but they also asserted themselves more so than before. Why try so hard to alert me to their presence?

In a hurry to reach the classroom door, I glanced around my garden-level classroom one last time and suppressed a shiver.

* * *

Once at the store downtown, I lost myself in classroom daydreams for the better part of an hour. I made my way out, arms laden with several books. I glanced up the sidewalk, shocked to see my sister about half a block away. She faced me, and I gave her a halfhearted wave, but then she turned away.

"Arana! Hey, Arana, come back! What are you doing here?" Despite the books in my arms, I managed an awkward shuffle-jog after my sister.

"Arana!" I shrieked after her retreating figure. What was my sister doing in Grafton? And where were my parents? Surely, she wouldn't visit alone. "Arana!"

Finally, I caught her attention.

"Hey Arana, I love what you've done with your hair." I lavished the breathless compliment, but she stiffened and pulled away from my awkward hug.

"I don't know who you think I am, but you've got the wrong person, lady."

At first, I thought she joked with me, but her hard eyes weren't playful. "Arana? C'mon, quit teasing."

"Look, lady: my name is Kali, and I've never met you before. Are you crazy or something? Never mind. I'm outta here."

With those words, she pushed into a trendy jewelry and trinket store, leaving me gaping. I must've been confused, although I could've sworn... I wanted to follow her, press for more information, but I needed to get back home for Nick.

I made my way to my car, curious and excited at the thought of a surprise visit from my family. We weren't very close. I held the rank of oldest child, my parent's only natural-born among several adopted children. I wanted to see them as I was proud of my new house and eager to share the plans I'd made for our new life.

But what if they'd gone to my house already? I sped up, remembering I'd left Nick sleeping in bed. I couldn't allow any unannounced visitor, even my family, to ring the doorbell and wake him without warning. Any guest, other than someone he'd invited, seemed to aggravate him.

With a slight tinge of disappointment and an overwhelming tidal wave of relief, I spotted no vehicle other than Nick's white diesel pickup in our driveway. I left my purchases in the car since they belonged in my classroom. Nick would not appreciate my extra "crap" cluttering up the house.

I'd tested the silence factors of our new front door on my way out of the house, so I applied them upon re-entry. First, I turned the knob all the way before pushing inwards. Once the door opened far enough for me to slip through, I reached around, grabbed the knob on the other side, repeating the same actions in reverse. Excellent! This door squeaked even less than the one at our old house.

I crept toward the kitchen to fix a pot of homemade oatmeal for Nick. He loved his hot breakfasts. He also stressed that I get him up by 11:00 a.m. on mornings he could sleep in. I glanced at the red Graff Floral Tourbillon knockoff on my wrist, a Christmas present last year from Nick; minutes after 10:30, I should be safe.

Misfortune continued to dog my steps. Rounding the corner into the kitchen, Nick stood in a direct path between me and the stove. "Where the hell have you been?"

"Look, Nick," I placed my hand in the middle of his chest and backed away. "I just went to school and the school supply store. I got back plenty early."

"Except," Nick glowered, "I woke up at 9:30 and was starving."

"Okay, okay," I tried to scuttle past him. "I'll have some apple-cinnamon oatmeal ready in about ten minutes."

He grabbed me by the upper arms, clamping down. "I didn't know where you were!"

"Okay, sorry."

"And I already ate."

"Oh." My struggle to get past him stopped, but he wasn't through with me. He shoved me with such force that my lower back smacked into the center island. I sensed a welt and bruise forming. He took my right elbow, spun me, and threw me into the wall. My left shoulder took the brunt of the encounter.

I slid down in defeat, hoping he was finished, which infuriated him further.

"You coward!" he bellowed. "Look at me when I'm talking to you."

Nick seized the material of my blouse above my right shoulder and gave another tremendous shove, causing my face to hit the refrigerator handle. I sank to my knees, holding outstretched hands to catch the blood spewing from my nose.

He walked by, tucking his foot under my butt and dumping me onto the ground. My damaged face hit the floor first.

"Nick, why?" I whimpered.

"You're so stupid." He laughed as he walked toward the stairs. "If you had just stayed at home, none of this would have happened."

Naturally, his argument made sense. I never should have left home this morning. My anticipation to decorate my classroom outweighed common sense. Our house came first. I'd wasted countless minutes better used unpacking boxes. Nick was right. Good decisions, especially those relating to prioritization, often escaped me.

After a few minutes, I dragged myself to my feet. I located the 409 and some paper towels to clean up the mess I'd made in the kitchen. This extra mess hindered our ability to become settled.

In the main-floor bathroom, I pried open the box of hand towels. Blood trickled from my nose, and my right cheek swelled, blocking my vision. With tender strokes I wiped the blood, lightly blew my nose to expel any remaining blood clots and searched for ice.

Damn, but that ice stung my cheek. Though I deserved this pain, it handed me another issue to deal with today. If Nick could be a little calmer, things wouldn't get so messy. As I entered the living room, holding the ice pack to my face, a large shadow whisked away from a window not yet shut to prepare for today's heat.

"Alright, pixies, I get it. I know you're here. So unless you're going to make yourselves useful and help me unpack, you can leave now!" I yelled, more frustrated than afraid.

"What the hell are you yellin' about?" Nick called down from upstairs.

"Nothing, sorry."

"Keep it down then!"

"Stupid pixies, getting me in more trouble." My face crumpled, a few salty tears stinging all abrasions they encountered.

At that moment a refreshing, gentle breeze swept through the room. Maybe my little tag-alongs accepted their guilt and asked for absolution?

CHAPTER 2

NEW FRIENDS

NICK'S HANDIWORK KEPT ME at home for the next couple of weeks. He confessed he regretted marring my beautiful face. As an apology, he eagerly completed every shopping list I compiled, no matter how extensive.

Also, during my homebound phase, I unpacked most of the remnants from our move. Any remaining boxes I tucked deep into the closets where Nick would never look. Our new home appeared uncluttered and adorned with love... perfect.

I hadn't forgotten to call my mom after encountering Arana, waiting until Nick departed for work. I demanded to know if they drove to North Dakota, and if so, why they hadn't stopped to visit? Part of me fervently prayed they hadn't stopped by during Nick's outburst, deciding to leave based on what they heard. However, Arana, along with my parents, insisted they'd never left Nebraska.

"Well then, honey," I informed Arana, "I found your identical twin! I'm not even kidding you. This girl thought I was a mental case, and I was getting so mad at you—I mean, her—for not acknowledging me."

About a week and a half after the episode with Nick, I sneaked back to my classroom with the supplies I'd purchased after he left for work. The infamous first day of school loomed two weeks away, and a handful of cars scattered along the street and in the adjacent parking lot. This time, fluorescent bulbs illuminated every hallway locker. All desks found their way back to their respective classrooms. A janitor, small of stature with curly gray hair, scrubbed at the grout along the sides of the hallway floor. He glanced up at me.

"Hello, Mrs. Adesco. Welcome to Grafton High School."

"Umm, thanks." Though reluctant to stand under the glaring overhead lights with my still-puffy face, I needed to ask, "Do you know if there's a key fob I can pick up for access to the school building?"

"Yes, ma'am. It should be in yer mailbox in the office."

With another thanks, I scuttled back toward the office door. My heart dropped when I saw the pert secretary perched on a stool behind the counter. During my three encounters with her—once when I interviewed for my position, and twice on the phone—she'd launched into full-blown Spanish conversations. Not that I couldn't hold my own, but I exuded extreme self-consciousness concerning my accent—not North American, but European Spanish. My Zs and soft Cs came across as THs, which didn't resemble South American informal chatter.

My junior year abroad in college taught me invaluable lessons in the culture and language of Spain. Madrid also educated me on big-city street smarts, applicable worldwide. I braced myself for the barrage of questions I sensed crouching behind the solid wooden door.

Luck sided with me today. No sooner had I pulled the heavy door backward, than the phone rang. The eager receptionist reined in her Cuban accent. "Allo? Grafton High School, thees ees Cohnie Chavez."

With no desire to waste this opportunity, I gave Connie a quick wave, grabbed the key from my mailbox, and darted out the office door.

"Got yer key then?" At my nod, the janitor continued, "Just finished shining everything up in there for ye. Good luck this year, ma'am."

"Thank you, ummm..." I glanced at his denim button-down shirt for any sort of name badge.

"Elliott, ma'am."

"Well, thank you, Elliott."

"At yer service, Mrs. Adesco."

I passed him but hesitated when I reached my room. "Umm, Elliott?" I called halfway down the hall where he still worked. "Wasn't my room supposed to be locked?"

"Yes, ma'am. We locked 'er up when we finished in there. Not all teachers lock their classroom doors but, until we know what you prefer, we lock 'em up."

"Okay, that's what I thought. Thanks again." I grasped the handle of my door that stood ajar by about three inches. Certain it was a fluke, I entered my classroom and flicked the overhead lights.

Everything looked in order and smelled like the kind of cleaning supplies ordered in mass quantity—not overly pleasant, but the sanitation appeared thorough. My classroom boasted two closets, both along the same wall. One was beside the windows adjoining the science teacher's room. The second closet sat beside it, originally intended as a grade-school coat closet before being transformed into a dark room for photography. An "in use" sign rose above this closet, and the current status of the light glowed green. I crept toward the closet, wondering if someone waited inside and meant to scare me as a prank. Perhaps one of my new students, resentful his former teacher had ditched him?

Easing toward the dark room, my knuckles about to graze the shiny silver handle, I prepared myself for confrontation when I heard,

"Hi. I'm Alice Ann Swanson. Your neighbor across the hall. One of the English teachers. Wow! Sorry. Didn't mean to make you jump. And…" Here she offered a rueful grin; "I need to stop speaking in staccato sentences."

I honestly thought my heart bypassed my ribs. Clutching my chest as if coaxing it to stay put, I shot a feeble smile at my new acquaintance.

"Hi, I'm Jen Adesco." Her firm handshake shamed mine when compared. "I suppose we'll be seeing a lot of each other."

"In theory, yes. But after our teacher workdays at the beginning of the year, it'll mostly be quick waves through open doors and an occasional passing in the hallway. Don't worry, though. Administration has assigned me to be your mentor, so I'll check in with you as frequently as time allows. Look at me, doing all the talking again. Do you have any questions?"

Now that my turn to talk arrived, I contemplated several brewing questions. But before one formed, Alice Ann grabbed my left arm between the elbow and wrist. "Wow! Did you get into an accident or something?" She gazed in keen awareness at my face.

Great. An observant, verbally expressive English teacher and mentor. I'd believed the amount of makeup I gooped on concealed the remnants of Nick's anger, but maybe I needed more.

"What? Oh, you mean this." My hand hovered over the slight swell and scab near the bridge of my nose. "I fell into the tub while hanging the shower curtain in our upstairs bathroom. Got a little too tangled up to catch myself."

"Wow. It appears tender. No worries, it'll be gone before school starts." Her phone pinged. "Oh hey, I'm meeting up with a friend for coffee in about fifteen. Do you want to come?"

I hesitated but remembered a five-dollar bill I'd tucked into a side pocket of my purse. While plenty of tasks remained in my classroom, having some friends in this new community constituted a good thing. "Sure, that sounds great. I'll just unload the supplies from my car, and I'll be ready."

"Okay, I'll come get you in a few." Alice Ann's perky, infectious voice promised. I found myself smiling in anticipation as I hung verb conjugation posters.

We left soon after. Alice Ann, her friend, Nakayla, and I spent the better part of an hour at Patsy's Café Express. Nakayla held the title of executive director at Sunset Gym. Her sparking brown eyes, shoulder-length brown hair, olive skin, tall stature, and laid-back demeanor contrasted Alice Ann's perky, petite platinum blond curls and deep green eyes; yet both women equally captivated me.

While heading home, I was proud of the day's accomplishments. I had gained two new friends and a better outlook on Grafton.

CHAPTER 3

Kitchen Floor

I CREATED A ROUTINE to maximize my free time before school started. Mornings focused on settling into our new house, afternoons at school, and evenings performing household chores.

Soon enough, school began without a hitch. My class sizes ranged from five to fifteen students, which suited me. Either my students behaved well on autopilot, or I interjected enough sternness to intimidate when necessary. After the first week and a half, I'd adjusted to my schedule and figured out how to motivate students and plow through lesson plans.

My spirits soared when I skipped through our front door on the Friday afternoon before Labor Day. Even with Nick's white pickup still in the driveway, my mood hadn't dampened. I assumed he'd begin work a little later than usual to compensate for the longer hours of a Friday night.

Nothing prepared me for Nick marching to greet me with several letters clutched in his hand. At six-foot-four inches, he towered over me. My gut began to quiver. I didn't know what upset him, but if he deemed it my fault, this would not end well.

"Can you explain all this?" he shouted.

"Nick," I placated, "I can't even see what you're holding."

He thrust a pile of bills and bank statements in my face. Bewildered but meek, I flipped through while he trembled with growing rage. "I guess I'm not sure what the problem is."

"The problem is income versus expenditures!"

"But Nick, you knew we'd be a little short until my first paycheck came from the school. I haven't been spending that much, and we had some extra set aside."

"This isn't acceptable!" His voice rang out, making my ears pulsate in immediate pain. The act of covering them to cease the throbbing put Nick over the edge. He yanked my hands from my head, throwing the collection of papers to the ground. Pulled flush against his chest, he yelled into my left ear. Sharp pain, followed by a sensation of fullness, consumed that side of my head. No longer able to concentrate on what he said, I squirmed back with every ounce of force I could muster.

"Oh, you wanna dance?" he roared, inches from my face. Spittle hit me, dripping from the long strand hanging out the side of his mouth. He morphed into a rabid animal—eyes that wouldn't focus, slobber flowing over his jowls, unkempt hair, and a low snarl emanating from his lips.

I sank to my knees, limp as a rag doll, hoping he'd storm off. No such luck. He jerked my lifeless body upwards, smacking my left elbow into the ornate marble frame encasing the fireplace. In anticipation of more yelling, I pulled my head back and closed my eyes. But my feet were whisked out from under me, and he cradled me in his arms. With my cheek flush against Nick's shoulder, I guessed that remorse coursed through him, and he planned to cart me to the bedroom for make-up sex.

My mind switched gears regarding his intent when he lifted me higher in the air. Then he dropped me, my body toppling away from him as if rolling down a hill. At first, I didn't register the muffled thud my left elbow made on the granite hearth. Pain blossomed down to my fingertips then up, shooting past my shoulder.

I retched a couple of times, facing the dark hole where we had yet to light a fire. Holy shit! most of the pain seemed confined to my left side, but so much of it ravaged my body. I rolled onto my right hip, half scared that Nick's foot poised there, ready to kick me into the cast-iron grate.

He'd disappeared, inspiring a deep sigh of relief that was cut short by the pain rising in my chest and arm. Tears streamed from my eyes. I struggled into a cross-legged sitting position to inspect the immediate area for blood but found none. Relieved at less mess to attend to this time, I couldn't ignore the pain at my elbow, pulsating like a neon sign.

Damn that Nick! Didn't he understand his violence added unnecessary complications, or was he indifferent when overwhelmed by emotion?

As if on cue, Nick clomped down the stairs, rounded the corner, and stood in front of me.

"Oh, by the way, babe, I'm heading up past Winnipeg to fish and unwind a little. They're shutting my part of the club down for major renovations next week, so there's nothing I can do around here." His eyes narrowed. "Why don't you see if you can figure out this money thing while I'm gone."

He set his bags down and stepped closer. I was inclined to cringe but remained immobile. Nick squatted in front of me, using the back of his index finger to wipe the tears from my cheeks. "Then," he murmured, pressing a gentle kiss to my lips, "we can get back to the business of having fun and enjoying our new life here."

Nick's tender smile bathed me before he stood, collecting his bags as a chorus of obnoxious honks sounded in our driveway. "That's Joe. He's driving us there. I'll call you once we get settled if I have reception. I'm pretty sure we'll be camping somewhere around the lake. Bye, babe!"

What the hell just happened? My head spun with Nick's final words, and my stomach lurched again. I needed to get this pain under control before whatever remnants of my undigested lunch made a second appearance.

I gingerly walked up the stairs and toward the master bathroom to inspect the new damage to my body. Large steps bumped my arm around, further aggravating it.

Once there, I fumbled with a bottle of pain reliever. I moved my elbow as close as I could to the right-side mirror. The counter space narrowed between the two sinks, so I angled my body into the gap, perching my left butt cheek beside the bathroom window. This window filled a space twice the size of both bathroom mirrors combined. Ruefully, I wished that it was a mirror. It would be easier to assess my injuries if it reflected, rather than offered transparency.

As I suspected, a massive bruise formed above my elbow on the back side of my upper arm. The spot where I'd thunked into the side of the fireplace. And there, on the side and front of my elbow, discolored pools of blood seemed to manifest before my eyes. No bones protruded through my skin, but the pain! Even my light ministrations produced more free-flowing tears.

A low growl and a huff sounded outside the window. I thought I saw an image of something furry, but what? Wiping at tears with my uninjured arm, I thought about the image I'd viewed. It resembled...a yak? Like a fuzzy yak head. Except I lived in north-central America, and yak habitats flourished in south-central Asia. But what animal could it have been?

Then I froze, remembering I stood in the master bathroom. On the second floor. No yak, dog, wolf, or anything boasted such a height! Did giant pixies exist?

Fearful shudders wracked my body until I forced them to quit by squeezing my left shoulder with my right hand, creating a tight self-hug. New waves of pain inspired more nausea.

Somehow, I made my way back downstairs to fetch ice. In hindsight, I should have grabbed an ice pack before heading upstairs the first time. But this worked, allowing me to lock all doors and shut the first-floor windows. All the better to keep out furry, growling creatures, my mind reassured as my body suppressed another involuntary shudder. I trekked back upstairs to the king-sized bed I shared with the person I'd once deemed the man of my dreams—who I still wanted to be the man of my dreams.

Fresh tears flowed. "Damn it, Nick!" I cried out to lavender walls. "Why do you make it so hard to keep loving you?"

Of course, he loved me. It radiated from his eyes when he crouched before me earlier, wiping my tears away. Only... I wished he wouldn't hurt me.

What a sniveling, pathetic mess. Curled up in bed when many hours of daylight remained. The clock on the nightstand next to our canopy bed (which I still couldn't believe Nick let me choose) read 5:34. Not even supper time yet. As my eyelids lowered, easing me into oblivion, a large cloud blocked all sunlight from entering the bay window, rendering it quite dark.

* * *

Through the night and all of Saturday morning, I drifted in and out of consciousness. Throbbing, incessant pain roused me after two in the afternoon. Reluctant to seek medical attention—we were short on money, anyway—I needed to figure something out if I wanted to make it to work on Tuesday. The prospect of a shower or even a change of clothes seemed unlikely in my near future.

More bad news greeted me when I perused the internet. Grafton had no Urgent Care facility, and doctors' offices closed at noon on Saturdays. My lone option for medical attention involved a trip to Unity Medical Center's emergency room.

I announced to the emergency room attendant that I slipped while scrubbing the kitchen floor. He asked routine exam questions as he prepared me for the on-call doctor, so quietly I longed for a volume-control button. When he completed my debriefing, I inquired how I might expect to wait until the doctor arrived. I couldn't understand his muffled response. How rude!

Minutes later, when a balding man in wire-rimmed glasses and a white lab coat pushed aside the curtain, a scowl still marred my face.

"Good afternoon, Shenandoah." Kind, murky green eyes crinkled at the edges. In a delicate and professional manner, he took my right hand between both of his. "Tell me about your injury."

Dang. This guy was soft-spoken, too. Or maybe... I shook my head to clear the fog settling around it. An image of Nick screaming in my ear brought back the probable cause of my impairment. Turning my right ear toward the doctor, I posed my question.

"Sorry, what did you call me, Dr...?" My eyes scanned his chest for a name badge, rising to his face when I found none.

"Oh yes, right. I'm Doctor Bisbee. Are you having difficulty hearing from your left ear, Shenandoah?"

"Am I being that obvious?" Trial and error warred in my head, but I realized I'd contorted my head at an awkward ninety degrees to test my theory. "And I just go by Jen now."

Another prime example that William and Monica Decker graced this planet about twenty years too late. They embodied perfect 60s flower children. As their first child, they named me after a traditional American folk song with a melody they considered beautiful. I drifted through life with this cumbersome name until I met Nick. On our second date, he protested.

"Whoa, babe. I really like you," he'd said, "but your handle is way too long. I think I'm just gonna call you Jen."

"So, Jen," Dr. Bisbee's mouth quirked into a smile. "Suppose you tell me about your injury before I start poking and prodding."

I launched into the story I rehearsed. Dr. Bisbee stroked his beard, a thoughtful gaze in his eyes as he listened, afterwards ordering the attendant to take me to X-ray. After he reviewed my internal damage and manipulated my arm to the extent that I threatened to vomit again, he gazed at me with kind eyes.

"Are you sure you just fell on a wet kitchen floor?" At my nod, he continued. "Because, quite honestly, if it happened in your kitchen—and you were by yourself—the only way I could envision someone of your stature gaining enough momentum to inflict such an injury is if you stood on a kitchen counter, then fell directly onto a bent elbow."

I cringed internally but remained calm. "I guess it's a fluke, then."

Dr. Bisbee didn't press the matter. Instead, he suited me up with a sling over a cast, even though he harbored concerns the cast might exert too much pressure on the bruising around my fractured elbow. He collected pain medication from the hospital pharmacy and sent me home with a paternal smile.

The bank thermometer reported a high of 73 degrees for the afternoon. Despite my recent long stretch of sleep, the prescription pain medication spun foggy tendrils along the corners of my eyesight. Too tired to trek upstairs once I got home, I grabbed a blanket from the couch and headed out the back door.

Nick strung a hammock between two trees on our first weekend in Grafton. With great care I climbed into it, butt-first, doing my best to spread out the blanket with one hand. I flipped over the waterproof pillow and fell asleep, despite continuous throbbing in my left arm.

I awoke to loud sniffing noises intermixed with growling yaps. It took a moment for me to regain my senses. I laid on my side, with my arm flung up and over the thick, woven strands of twine. For a few brief moments, I thought the muffled noises were from the neighbor's dog and willed him to shut up, but I'd pressed my right ear into a pillow. Maybe the dog was closer than—

Something sharp raked across the back side of my hand.

CHAPTER 4

Hvezda

"**OW!**" **I SAT UP** in a rush, throwing my weight off balance. In an attempt not to eject myself, I swiped at the far side of the hammock with my left hand and cried out again at the ensuing pain.

"Son of a bitch!" Tears pricked my eyes as pain reverberated up and down my arm. I imagined a percussion player in a marching band, pounding the bass drum with a mallet. Already small beads of blood formed in three or four spots on my right hand. Miserable seemed like too mild a word to describe my present state.

My eyes gradually focused, and I searched for the offensive sharp object. Nothing came into view. But seconds later, a furry bundle darted between my swinging legs. It stopped, turned about face, and sat on its haunches. Reddish-brown eyes gazed at me, and an apology smile lingered on its lips. How freaking cute was this little fox? Or was it a dog? I concluded a dog. Foxes presented too skittish a nature around people.

"Hey, buddy." I used my good arm to propel myself from the makeshift bed. "What's a little guy like you doing off on his own? Isn't there anyone looking for you?" As I patted his head and scratched behind his ears, I swore he shook his head.

"No, huh? Well, I guess you can come with me then." My words were halfhearted, certain the foxy dog would neither follow nor comply. Except that he did. All my life, despite my love of dogs, most of them treated me like the mangy neighborhood cat. With this one desiring my company, I instantly fell in love.

After I redeposited the blanket on the couch, I fixed a frozen dinner to quiet my growling stomach. For my new friend, I reheated some leftover pork chops—minus the bones.

The foxy dog lay at my feet while I ate, and we watched a chick flick on Nick's big-screen TV. I took advantage of the proximity to confirm this critter sported male parts. A stubborn boy, I soon discovered.

When I opened the back door, ready to let him return to his wild ways, he wouldn't budge. This delighted me more than upset me. The rooms in our house stretched wider with Nick gone. Still, was this a wild animal? An abandoned puppy? Or someone's pet that they'd searched for all afternoon? In my condition, I wasn't capable of removing my new friend, so I let him stay.

The strange thing about this foxy dog: instead of acting like a puppy, he acted like a mature companion dog. He followed me everywhere, without getting underfoot, and gave me privacy by laying outside the bathroom door. He didn't bark, chew on things, or pee on the floor. These coincidences were comforting instead of unnerving.

When I climbed into bed, I cast a rueful glance at our wedding picture before shifting to the fuzzy red puppy curled at my side. It wasn't like this little creature could tear into me any worse than Nick already had. As the pain pills worked their magic, dragging me into a deep slumber, I thought the foxy dog winked at me.

* * *

I awoke Sunday morning before nine o'clock to a soft tongue lapping my hand.

"Good morning, Hvezda," I murmured, scrunching my forehead at the name that rolled off my tongue. In my dream, I'd owned a dog with that exact name. It wasn't English or Spanish; I didn't know what it meant, but it seemed to suit my new little pet.

Most of my time Sunday and Monday I spent grading papers, watching TV, and napping. The potency of my pain medication knocked me out. I'd need a milder drug for school days, or risk passing out on my students.

Hvezda provided excellent company and required minimal bathroom excursions. The perfect pet!

I fell asleep Monday night wondering where to keep Hvezda during the school day, and how to convince Nick to let me keep him. Tuesday morning, while struggling to clip my earrings, I glimpsed Hvezda in the mirror and decided a one-syllable nickname appropriate. "Okay, Vee, whatever will you do without me today?"

Vee followed me all the way to the porch, laying down with his head on his paws. I scratched him behind his large, red, upright ears. White tufts of fur overflowed from the front side of those ears. This feature—along with his bigger, black nose—softened his foxlike appearance. I needed to research his breed of dog. Leaning down, I kissed him between the ears before I left—sweetest puppy ever. I sure hoped he stuck around until I got home.

* * *

Once I arrived at school, Alice Ann swooped in on me the second she heard my key fumbling at my classroom door.

"Holy guacamole!" she gasped, eyeing the contraption on my arm. "Do I need to hire you a bodyguard?"

Trying to make light of the situation, I smiled at her. "How about renting me a padded suit? This new house and I are off to a rough start."

"The house did this to you?" Skepticism laced her tone.

"Nick took off on a fishing trip. When I was deep cleaning the kitchen floor, I spilled the mop water and then slipped. I think I even passed out from the pain for a few hours. It was hell trying to get in to see the doctor Saturday afternoon."

"You had no one to help you?" A hint of tears glistened in the corner of Alice Ann's eyes. "Give me your phone!"

After depositing my belongings on my desk, I acquiesced. She made a production out of punching in her contact information.

"Mrs. Adesco!" One of my favorite first-period students looked stunned when she entered the room.

"Hola, Caterina. Está bien. I just had a little accident in the kitchen. The doctor says I'll be good as new in a few weeks."

"In time for the Homecoming Dance? You're coming to the Homecoming Dance, aren't you, Mrs. Adesco?"

I laughed, enjoying her enthusiasm. "I believe that I'm one of the sponsors for the dance. So yes, I'll be there."

"My dad's a sponsor, too." Catherine didn't wait for a response but ambled over to her desk.

"And he's hot," Alice Ann whispered as she handed my phone back. "But we're both married and all that. Speaking of which, will your husband be joining you to chaperone the dance? Spouses or dates are allowed. I'll be there, too, with Bryce. Dance sponsorship seems to somehow fall in the laps of the liberal arts teachers."

"Nick isn't into the social scene. Unless he's hanging out with his buddies." I added, "I doubt he'll want to come."

"I'll have to meet him another time then." Alice Ann flitted toward the door when the first bell rang. "And if your house ever attacks you again, call me." She pretended to hold the phone.

My elbow throbbed by the end of the school day. I fixated on getting home, taking some medicine, and relaxing. I'd almost forgotten about the furry beast who looked thrilled to see me when I pulled in the driveway.

"Hi, Vee!"

He jumped off the porch and came running to the car, offering a proper escort to the house. Vee waited while I scuttled around the house, joining me in the hammock. Without realizing I'd fallen asleep, I woke up to the incessant jangling of my cell phone.

"Oh hey, Nick," I mumbled.

"What were you doing, sleeping in the middle of the day?"

"No, it's just..." Did he even remember that he'd hurt me? "I fractured my elbow this weekend, and the pain meds kinda knock me out."

"Geezus, Jen! A doctor's bill and a cast? We can't afford shit like that!"

I didn't bother telling him about the ER visit or that he'd been the one responsible.

"Damn it, Jen." Nick's anger reverberated through the tiny speaker. "I'll be back on Sunday. You'd better have something figured out by then. We need more money!"

I pushed the call-end button, noticing Vee regarded me during this whole discussion as if privy to both sides of the conversation. I offered him a weak smile, massaging one temple at a time with the first two fingers on my right hand. Now I had to devise a plan to fix this mess.

CHAPTER 5

A Second Job

I SNAPPED MY FINGERS. Alice Ann's friend, Nakayla. I could check with her for any openings at the gym. I could manage a part-time gig on top of my teaching job. Glad that Alice Ann programmed herself on speed dial, I faltered at her unexpected dismay.

"I'm here for you, Jen. Are you okay? What can I do?"

I laughed despite her serious tone. "Well, if you'd let me get a word in edgewise."

She sucked in her breath, following it with a relieved chuckle. "Again, with the babbling. I know. I apologize. I was just picturing you laying on the floor, trapped by a door that had fallen off its hinges."

This time laughter consumed me. "No, silly. I wondered if I could get your friend Nakayla's phone number. I'm thinking about picking up a few extra hours on evenings and weekends."

"Sure, but won't your husband mind?"

"That's when he works, anyway. He won't notice if I'm home or not. Besides," I joked, "with a little extra cash, maybe I can buy some expensive artwork and make a peace offering to the house."

Far from sounding convinced, Alice Ann gave me Nakayla's number. Nakayla said she was thrilled to hear from me and in the process of hiring people to staff the front desk. My experience as a guest services employee at a large hotel should complement this position. I agreed to come in late Friday afternoon for an interview.

* * *

As the week wore on, the pain in my elbow diminished. Each night brought sweet relief when I unfastened the sling and allowed my neck and shoulder to relax. My new puppy became a constant presence during my time at home. Vee and I adapted well to each other. He dispensed my loneliness and gave me something to look forward to each afternoon.

On Friday, my interview with Nakayla transpired more like a meeting of old friends. She agreed I'd fit in well at Sunset Gym.

At the conclusion of our interview, a knock on her office door announced one of the facility's board members. Charles Newman, a fine specimen of a man, who could pass as Shemar Moore's younger brother, was preparing to give a speech at a national convention of independently run fitness facilities. He wanted Nakayla's input; unfortunately, right after she introduced us, a minor crisis elsewhere in the building demanded her attention.

"Sorry, Charles. This may have to wait a bit." Her last words carried in the air on her way through the outer office.

"Hmmm." Despite Charles' perturbed air, his murmured interjection was sexy as hell.

"Umm, if you don't mind my being a stranger and all, I'd be happy to listen to and critique your speech," I offered. "I was originally an English major in college, and I competed in speech tournaments in high school."

In the brief minute Charles spent appraising me, I detected each feature of mine which his gaze lingered on. A flush tore across my cheeks, threatening to increase exponentially if his perusal continued. When he broke away to look into my eyes, my entire body tingled. No man had ever evoked such a response from my body, at least not without touching me. I stared back at him, not willing to let him see how much he'd affected me.

"Yes, I think you'll do fine." Charles drawled. He meant as an audience for the practice run on his speech, but it sounded like he meant something else. Holy hormones! I needed to calm down.

"Have a seat." His voice, his eyes. My mind raced again. I pictured myself sitting in his car, at his dining room table, on his lap, in his bed.

I sat back in the chair in such a hurry that I almost fell off the other side of it. Nice job, I congratulated myself. Way to play a fool.

Charles launched into his speech, delving into the facility's mission statement, and highlighting several successes. These stories weren't limited to individuals losing weight, but also about children gaining confidence and older adults learning new skills. His agitation over giving this speech was obvious and also endearing. Guys who looked like freaking models shouldn't seem shy about standing in the spotlight.

"It's very good." I commented after clapping. "The only thing that might make it better is a little less fidgeting."

"You're right. I just want to represent the facility well."

I rose and walked over to Charles, placing tanned hands over his dark brown hands, where he'd dropped his notes on Nakayla's desk. "You'll do great."

"Thanks for the vote of confidence. I'm sure you're right." He moved the thumb of his upper hand over the top of my hands. "I'll let you know."

I caught both the meaningful look in his eyes and the promise in his voice.

Nakayla walked back into the office and confirmed I could begin next week on the front desk. I would work Tuesday, Thursday, and Friday evenings or Saturday afternoons, leaving me enough time to make supper and clean the house.

Elated at having another job with extra income, I couldn't wait to tell Nick the good news. He'd be so happy. In my distraction, I didn't notice that Charles waited for me until he fell into step beside me.

"Would my lady care to join me for dinner this evening?"

"Oh, sorry. No, I can't. I'm married." And flustered, apparently.

"It doesn't have to be like that. Just wanted to say 'thank you' and get acquainted with our newest employee. As a board member, it's important I connect with both staff and members." He struggled with his next words, "Bring your husband along, if you'd like."

"No. That is, he's out of town until Sunday."

Charles put a hand on my good arm. "Then I absolutely insist. You can follow me in your car."

What choice did I have?

He led me to downtown Grafton where he parked half a block from Shenanigans, a cozy Irish pub offering authentic Irish cuisine and ample Guinness. An outgoing host seated us at a snug booth for two (I didn't even realize they made such things), and I soon relaxed in the upbeat but dim atmosphere.

Surprised at the hunger clawing at my stomach, I ordered a shepherd's pie and a pale ale. Like me, Charles also avoided the fish dishes but opted for a stout. We both enjoyed the ambiance in silence until our food arrived. At this time, we punctuated the background music with quiet moans of rapture at consuming dishes cooked to perfection, their taste augmented by microbrewery recommendations.

As our stomachs filled and the chewing slowed, conversation picked up.

"So Jen," Charles remarked, savoring a bite of his rosemary pork medallions, "Tell me a bit more about yourself. Are you new here in town?"

"We're barely out of the unpacking stage. We moved here in July."

"Interesting." He perused my face over the rim of his mug. "Now answer me this. What kind of man leaves his young, beautiful wife alone for days at a time? He must be on a business trip."

His statement sounded more like a question. I thought the likelihood was small that I'd run into him often, if ever again, but the beer relaxed me enough that I sensed I could open up to him.

"No, he left for a week already on a fishing trip. He enjoys his adventures with his buddies. Oh, and here's a bit of trivia for you—my name's not really Jen."

"No kidding?" I noticed I'd piqued his interest by the forward lean of his body. "Are you going to share this secret, or remain the gorgeous yet mysterious fishing widow?"

His words caused havoc with my insides. He kept calling me pretty, and his eyes gave every indication he wasn't throwing out compliments with indifference. With the term 'fishing widow,' he made me sound like someone available for the taking.

More excited than I thought I'd be to share this information, words poured from my mouth. "Well, the name of this establishment is close to my given name."

"Shenanigans," Charles pondered. "So, Shannon, then?"

"We're going to lean away from the Irish, and more toward American soil. Native American, that is." At his puzzled look, I continued. "My parents were both born to '60s flower children, and they both grew up loving that era and its ideals, including the music. They named me after a traditional folk song. They loved the melody and lyrics, and even visited the inspirational river before I was born. My name is Shenandoah," I confessed, suddenly shy. "It's Algonquian. It means 'Daughter of the Stars.'"

"Wow." Charles breathed. "That's beautiful." He put his hand on top of my hand, which still gripped my beer mug. "You're beautiful. A beautiful daughter of the stars."

I swallowed a nervous lump in my throat. Even though I was having fun, things seemed to progress more rapidly than made me comfortable—that they were progressing at all alarmed me. I picked up my second mug of beer, a movement successful in removing his hand, and slammed the rest of it.

"I should get home. My puppy will be waiting for me."

Charles stood before I did, maintaining eye contact when I also rose. His sparkling brown eyes mesmerized me. I was still staring at him when wooziness filled my head, and I caught myself on the back of the booth to keep from falling.

"Oof. Two drinks with my pain medication wasn't such a good idea." All indications led to the possibility of me staggering around, completely hammered and more than a little embarrassed.

Charles understood the meaning of my gesture, and he didn't attempt to help me. He only watched, intent on lending assistance if needed.

"Look, Jen," he chose his words with caution, "I can certainly drive you home in your car, then walk back here to fetch mine. Grafton isn't that big a town. Unless you live miles out in the country, I think that would be best."

"Thank you, Charles. Dinner was absolutely amazing, much nicer than another meal alone, but I'll be fine in a couple of minutes. Besides, like you said, Grafton's not that big. I only live a few blocks from here."

He grasped my arm with a firm hand, a gesture I accepted with reluctance but remained grateful for at the same time. He escorted me to my car with no further protests. Once there, he lifted my right hand to his lips, pressing a lingering kiss.

"And thank you for agreeing to accompany a thirty-year-old bachelor to dinner. I'm glad you'll be working at Sunset Gym now. You'll make a wonderful addition. Perhaps I'll see you there from time to time."

To any onlooker, Charles' behavior appeared chivalrous with a hint of flirtation. I thought I read innuendos behind his actions but took time to rationalize. After all, I was a nobody, a married schoolteacher in a sling. The thought that any other man would be interested in me was laughable.

Still, I worried that any of this would get back to Nick. In the future, I'd ensure that encounters with the opposite sex happened in group settings to combat potential jealousy.

After I sat in my vehicle for a few minutes, the alcoholic fog lifted somewhat and returned confidence in my driving abilities. It did not escape my attention that

Charles' sporty silver car pulled from the parking lot and followed at a distance, most of my way home. He rounded the corner once he saw me turn into a driveway.

I should have been creeped out, since he followed me in stalker mode; instead, I felt comforted and protected. What a sweet guy to make sure I safely arrived home.

Upon opening my car door, something else that exuded comfort and safety bounded up to me.

"Vee!" I reached down with my good hand to scratch him behind his ears. It still amazed me how calmly he acted for a puppy. He didn't jump on me or bark in excitement, only running to accompany me into the house. I needed to look into getting him vaccinated and licensed, but first I had to win over Nick.

However, Saturday and Sunday came and went with no sign of him.

CHAPTER 6

More Shenanigans

AFTER SCHOOL ON MONDAY, I pulled up at the house with some fresh groceries, happy to see Nick's pickup back at home. I figured after eating a lot of camp food, I'd surprise him with a gourmet meal. What I had forgotten about was Vee.

"Oh shit," I muttered, not seeing my puppy on the porch or coming to greet me. "This was NOT how I wanted them to meet."

I rushed into the house, thrusting the groceries on the countertop, calling for Nick. I found him in the backyard. With a rake raised above his head, he stared down at Vee, who stood—alert and wary—with his backside to the garden shed.

"Nick, no!" I screamed.

He swung around so quickly I thought he'd hit me instead. "Get back, Jen! It's a wild animal. It could have rabies or distemper or Lyme disease. Go back in the house. I'll protect you."

"Wait, Nick—please! It's okay. I know this animal. And it's not a fox, it's a dog." I edged my way between the two of them.

"What? Are you sure? Does it belong to the neighbor or something?" Nick lowered the yard tool, uncertainty etched in his features.

I used his hesitation to scoop up my cute little defenseless foxy puppy. "He's homeless, Nick. And he kind of adopted me."

"Geezus Jen, we can't afford a dog. We don't have time to housebreak and train a puppy."

"Actually," I countered, "he's already housebroken and perfectly well-behaved. He's been here for the past week and hasn't caused me one bit of trouble. Plus, he's great company for me when you're gone. He'll be a good protector when you're working nights."

This claim held importance for Nick. He preferred to keep me safe himself, loathing the idea of me spending time with other people. A puppy, though, was hardly a threat to him.

Nick appeared to consider my request. Seconds later, he snapped his fingers. "If this dog is house-trained, he's got to belong to somebody."

"But what if he doesn't, Nick? Can I keep him then?" I kept my expression hopeful and added some information meant to sway his vote. "Oh, and I got a part-time job at Sunset Gym."

His face lit up. "That's awesome, Jen." With this information, he relented. "Okay, look. You need to find out if someone is missing this guy. If he's a lost pet, he goes home. If nobody claims him, I guess you can keep him. But," Nick warned. "he'd better stay out of my way and not cause any problems."

"Thank you, Nick!" I stood on my tiptoes to kiss his cheek and rushed to the house. I wasn't about to let him change his mind.

On my way there, I glanced down at Vee, who peered over my shoulder. My grip fumbled when I saw the menacing snarl on my puppy's face. He directed this at Nick, who turned his back to hang the rake in the shed.

Once inside, Vee appeared to understand Nick's words. Any time Nick entered a room, Vee minded his duty and trotted out. When Nick carried me to the bedroom to, in his words "ravish me," he kicked the door shut behind us. Although he said he was being careful, he jostled my sore arm much more than I preferred.

When he collapsed in exhaustion, I grabbed my pain meds and padded down to the kitchen for a glass of milk. Vee rested outside the bedroom door and joined me in the kitchen.

"Don't stare at me, accusing and all that," I begged Vee. Tears of pain and mental exhaustion threatened to spill. "He's a nice guy once you get to know him—well, for the most part."

I brought the glass of milk with me to the living room, then snuggled in my favorite chair. Vee jumped up, nestling himself between me and the back of the chair. His head nuzzled its way under my left elbow. The comforting warmth lulled me to sleep.

* * *

The next evening, I started at the gym. My shifts lasted from 5 to 8, and this week I trained with experienced staff members.

On both Tuesday and Thursday, Charles stopped by the front desk to visit for a moment after his workout. I had to admit his impressive physique caught me off guard each time I saw him—even more so when glistening with sweat. Friday, he did not show up, which was a bit disappointing.

The following week I worked solo, confident I'd gotten the hang of my new job. I worked extra hours, even with my progress hindered by a fractured bone, and the ensuing week slid by in an endless blur.

A routine seemed to establish itself. Catherine came to class early each morning and returned after school every day. She did not participate in sports and cast a shy demeanor. Through chats with her, I learned she and her dad moved to Grafton ten years ago after the unexpected passing of her mother. Her dad worked long, hard hours to make sure they maintained a comfortable life. However, he attempted to be available most nights and weekends to spend time with his little girl.

I spent my evenings either at the gym or at the house. I continued to work on personalizing our home, and despite the fact that only two of us lived in this huge house, endless chores awaited.

On the nights that Nick didn't eat with me, I left a home-cooked meal in labeled Tupperware containers as lunch for the following day. When he worked at the club, he ate at the club. We both recognized this as a temporary phase, agreeing not to let this get us down.

At the end of two weeks, since no one had claimed Vee, I made an appointment to take him to the vet for a check-up and shots.

When Friday evening rolled around, I headed to my second job, relieved that the week finally ended. I settled at the front desk, adjusting my sling with an impatient sigh. Two more weeks in this cursed contraption.

I greeted gym members when they entered and asked them about their workouts when they left. A few of them I knew by name without glancing at the computer check-in screen. Nakayla left a couple of small tasks for me, which I completed in less than half an hour. I surmised that a home football game in Grafton slowed business to a crawl.

In the middle of wishing that I'd brought a book to read, none other than Charles stopped in front of me. "Hello, gorgeous."

"Hi, yourself." I flirted from the safety behind the counter, flattered by the attention.

"So hey," he leaned toward me, his arms folded on the countertop, "I've been wanting to tell you about my speech at the banquet. Are you free for a bit this evening when you get off work?"

"I don't know if that's a good idea," I stammered.

"Oh, c'mon. Please? Just a little thank-you dinner for letting me use you as a sounding board."

"I thought that's what the last dinner was for."

"Ahh, yes, but now I've actually made the speech. Besides, what else do you have going on? Planning to head over to the football game?"

Even with sweat stains on his tee shirt, the magnetic pull Charles exuded won me over. We agreed to meet at 8:15 back at Shenanigans. This time, I vowed to avoid all alcoholic beverages even though I no longer took any form of pain medication.

As before, we both ordered, enjoyed the ambiance, and fed ravenous appetites after the waitress served our food.

"How's your arm doing?" he asked, popping his last bite of sirloin into his mouth.

I had gone with the safe option, no cutting utensils required, ordering shepherd's pie again. I did a lopsided shrug in response to his question. "Just a couple more weeks and I should be as good as new. At least I'm hoping to be. I've got an important dance to chaperone soon."

"Not the infamous Homecoming Dance?"

"Is it really infamous? Why? What happened in the past?" I didn't mean to let my gullibility reign, but I also didn't want to appear like the unarmed newbie teacher if a repeat performance occurred.

Charles laughed at my earnest questions. "It's nothing. My bank is one of the sponsors of the dance. I've been known to tear up the dance floor a time or two."

"So, you go to the dance?" I both anticipated and feared his answer.

"Not always but, if I'm available, I like to at least stop by. Now, back to the subject I started with. How did you hurt your arm in the first place? I'm only asking because you didn't freely offer an explanation at our last meal together. I know you a little better now," he drawled.

"I slipped on the kitchen floor when I was cleaning one weekend. Nick had left town, and I wasn't able to get in right away, so that slowed recovery a bit."

"Why couldn't you get in right away? No open appointments? You do know that you need to specify if something is an emergency," Charles chided.

"I, umm, kinda passed out from the pain."

"What?" He looked absolutely aghast. "Give me your cell phone."

Not this again. "No, it's fine." I pulled it out to show him. "I've got my friend's number in here now."

He slipped it from my fingers, messing with the device before handing it back. "And now you've got mine. But why didn't you call your husband?"

"Oh, he...well, he'd left on a fishing trip, and he doesn't like to be bothered."

"I wouldn't think a serious affliction to a spouse's health would be troublesome. Was he mad when he found out about the accident?"

"Just mad that I got hurt," I muttered, instantly appalled I'd said those words aloud. What was wrong with me?

Charles regarded me. Crap. He heard what I said.

"Shenandoah," he breathed.

My heart flipped at his quiet utterance of my given name. It sounded so pretty when he said it. I swallowed against a suddenly dry throat but didn't respond.

"Are you afraid of me?" His voice remained unbelievably soft, as if we shared an intimate secret.

Fear? Lust? I had no idea how to describe this inner turmoil. I didn't think he wanted me to fear him. "No." My voice didn't waver, but something betrayed me.

"I don't believe you," he whispered back. He rose in a sudden, gallant movement. "I've kept you late enough this evening."

Charles waited for me to rise, escorting me to my car, where he gave a stiff bow. "Thank you once again for being a delightful dinner companion." He bowed a second time, let his full lips wander over the back of my hand, and grinned from ear to ear when he stood. "Until we meet again."

On my drive home, I realized that ever since our last meal together, he refrained from touching me until we parted. Not that I expected him to. Anger swelled in my chest. In fact, far better that he didn't. No need to propagate inappropriate feelings. Still...

A worry crossed my mind that someone had seen us and reported it back to Nick. Sure, every witness could attest that nothing happened between us, and Charles served as a board member at my place of employment—technically making him a boss, of sorts. Sadly, Nick's temper sometimes got the better of him, impeding the clarity of reason.

CHAPTER 7

CAST OFF

THE WEEKS LEADING UP to the removal of my cast and sling teemed with questions from everyone.

My students bombarded me about Homecoming: Was I coming? Who would my date be? Would they get to meet my husband? I'd come to the game to watch them win, right? Did I like to dance? Could I even dance? Would my arm be healed by that time? I also received the offhand question. "Mrs. Adesco, if I bring a bottle of rum by your house, will you spike the punch at the dance?" Never in my life did I recall basking in any depth of popularity.

Alice Ann's questions echoed those of my students; however, hers honed in more on my husband. Meanwhile, Catherine quizzed me with impressive thoroughness about my likes and dislikes, presumably to report back to her dad. I hoped the inquisition hadn't stemmed from his suggestion.

Charles, too, bounced question after question off me. How was my arm today? Did I like my job at the gym? Was the teaching gig going well? What made me decide to enter the field of teaching? If both my husband and I worked full-time jobs, why work extra? He also posed similar questions as Catherine. In his case, I suspected the questions related to small talk more than anything consequential; however, I reconsidered upon hearing the pièce de résistance: "Will you save the last dance for me?"

Not just any old dance of the night, but the last dance.

And then there was Nick. He demanded to know when my arm would be better. This injury slowed me down in the kitchen and interfered in the bedroom. He also appeared irritated that I planned to attend both the Homecoming game and the dance. I explained that, as one of the sponsors, they expected me. I welcomed him as my date, but incredulity sprang from his eyes.

"Babe, you know I have to work."

"But couldn't you take off for an hour or so? Over your supper break? Everyone wants to meet you. Plus, then I'd have a dance partner."

"Not my scene, babe. I already did high school once. And," he warned, "you'd better not be dancing with any other guys."

"No worries." I forced a laugh. "Teachers can't dance with students, and I'm sure any other men there will be other teachers or husbands of teachers."

I pushed away the thought of Charles sauntering toward me, his hand extended as an invitation to the dance floor.

* * *

On a crisp fall Saturday morning, six weeks after I checked myself into the hospital emergency room, the same doctor removed my cast. The relief of cool air hitting exposed skin overloaded sensory receptors. Although self-conscious of the smell, Dr. Bisbee didn't seem a bit phased. He nonchalantly washed it off, examining it between my intermittent scratching. My poor itchy skin!

After a follow-up x-ray, Dr. Bisbee ushered me to the physical therapist who instructed me on some stretching and strengthening exercises.

"Make an appointment with my receptionist to come back in three weeks. Otherwise, great healing! Take care when performing those household chores in the future."

Even though the air carried a chill this fall morning, I slung my jacket over my right arm rather than wearing it. The formation of goosebumps on my left arm meant that air touched it, and I relished in the sensation. I never wanted to break another bone again!

Nick, of course, bounded to my side at the sight of my unrestrained arm. He insisted we celebrate with a round of wild, animalistic sex before lunch.

That afternoon, I took Vee in for his checkup. He didn't seem thrilled to enter the veterinary clinic, but acquiesced.

"I've never seen this species of dog before. What did you say it was?" Dr. Lavinsky asked while checking out Vee's paws and looking for dew claws.

"I honestly don't know. It was a stray, and we never located an owner."

"I'll have my assistant research it while we finish the exam."

Ten minutes, one blood sample, and three shots later, Vee sat ready to go. The assistant's investigation revealed that Vee's breed, Dhole, derived from a pack animal from Asia. How Vee arrived in a small town in North Dakota mystified us all.

By the time we got done, Nick would've already left for work. I wanted to buy a new dress for the Homecoming Dance but wasn't sure I should spend the money. Still, looking never caused any harm. If something special caught my attention, I'd consider making a purchase.

While my car idled and I contemplated my afternoon, a furry head pushed itself under my hand, demanding attention. "Hey, Vee." I scratched him lovingly behind the ears. "I should probably take you home first before I go window shopping."

The vehement nuzzling of my hand and the way he shoved against my side indicated his desire to stay with me.

"Okay, okay." I laughed. "It's cool enough out that I can park in the shade and leave the windows part way down. You can come with me." I kissed his fuzzy snout before putting the car in gear.

My first leisurely trip to downtown Grafton. I noticed it resembled the original hub of activity where most towns began. However, like many small towns—thanks to the internet and lack of a need for face-to-face contact—it appeared on the verge of dying out. Most buildings stood short of stature with nondescript storefronts and either slight awnings or none at all.

I found some wall art painted on the side of a building next to an empty lot across from the Chamber of Commerce, which intrigued me. Most prominently, a huge RIP painted in red, outlined in black, and ensconced in purple. Several painted names lined one side. I wondered if some tragedy occurred in Grafton, or if perhaps these were fallen war heroes? I made a mental note to ask Alice Ann on Monday.

Speaking of Alice Ann, her suggestion motivated me to peruse the downtown city blocks today. She told me about two clothing stores which prospered in the heart of the city, situated side by side and owned by sisters. One sold modern clothes, with moderate to upscale prices. The other offered elegant trends from the past. At a large social event in Grafton, one might be hard-pressed to discern current fashion styles with the popularity of the two shops.

My first stop was Chez Monique. An adorable petite, plump woman offered her assistance. She directed me to her selection of tea-length to mid-calf length dresses. I walked from rack to rack, my fingers caressing the material of each dress. One caught my eye, coming in four different colors—all in my size. Short-sleeved, with a rounded neck, and sewn with pleated lace, its slimming style would brush my knees. Deciding which color to try on was no deterrent. I selected blue, my all-time favorite color. This particular shade of blue fell somewhere between admiral and azure. I loved it.

As I pulled it off of the rack, a frigid voice from behind made me pause. "Ooh, yeah, if you're thinking of getting that for Homecoming, you just might want to reconsider."

"Excuse me?" I peeked over my shoulder, recognizing the voice but unable to place it.

"Well, you probably don't know—since you haven't been here before—but Homecoming is a rather classy event," Adrienne Norris, the Home Ec. teacher at Grafton High, said.

"But wouldn't this work?" I held up the dress for her inspection.

"Well," she said with care, "I'm just not sure you could pull it off."

What the hell? Just what did Ms. Snippy Bitch mean by that?

"It's just that it's obvious a more subdued style fits you. You're suited to something more comfortable and just a little less flashy."

I glanced from her to the dress, and back again. Her name-brand clothing indicated she kept up with trends. After all, she was the cheerleading sponsor. One of her offspring graduated, a former head cheerleader; her next daughter was up for head cheerleader the following year. If that didn't qualify her as a fashionista, I didn't know what would. Back in high school, I'd always watched the cheerleaders and dance team in awe. I'd wager Adrienne Norris represented her school as head cheerleader back in her day.

"It's just," I emphasized her repetitious word of choice, "I thought this was so pretty." Lame! That's not the way to talk to popular girls. "I'll look around some more." With deep regret, I hung the dress back on the metal rack.

"You know," Adrienne aired a peevish quality, "There is another store right next door where you might find something more suitable."

"Okay, thanks," I mumbled, shuffling away. My original plan included stopping at both stores, anyway.

Vee whimpered when he saw me but remained calm. "I'll be back soon!" I hollered at him.

Chez Brigitte overflowed with eclectic accessories and oozed a homey atmosphere. Fancy teal and violet armoires filled with clothes lined the walls, shoes peeking from underneath, while jewelry and handbag displays adorned any open wall space. A pink chaise and purple chairs with large pink polka dots invited patrons to sit and enjoy their surroundings. I almost succumbed to the temptation when a tall, stately woman with dark feathered hair and a bold nose swooped in to check on me.

She gave me a once over before commanding, "Follow me!"

I jumped up from a near-sitting position and trotted after her. She led me to one of the violet armoires. "These," she said with a flourish of her hand, "are all size 8." She waved toward both hanging items and others stacked on tables in the general vicinity.

"How did you know?"

"Countless years of experience, my dear." Her demeanor was off-putting, but I detected kindness in her eyes.

"Thanks for your help." Bestowing a warm smile, I searched for appropriate sponsor attire.

My eyes lit on a sleeveless tea dress, belted at the waist with a blue floral pattern and ample greenery. I tried it on and walked into the main store area to the three-way mirror. This more subdued dress suited me better. I spun a couple of times, noting it did not twirl around me the way I imagined the other one would. The pretty hues brought out the green in my eyes, but did it work for a dance?

"To what event are you planning to wear this? And might I add, it looks lovely on you." The tall lady walked up behind me with silent footsteps.

"Thank you. I'm helping sponsor the Homecoming Dance next week, and so..."

"While this dress is beautiful—and I can tell you think so, too—it's more for a garden party. Are you planning to dance? Wouldn't something with a little more flare be preferable?"

"I saw one next door that I liked."

"Then what stopped you from getting it? My sister has exquisite tastes and the latest fashion trends. Was the price too high?"

"No, I... You know what? I think I might take this dress another time. I could use some new panty hose, though. Then I'll stop back next door. I never even tried the other dress on, and you may be right."

"Thanks again for your help and honesty." I bundled my purchase under my arm and pushed the door open into bright sunshine.

Vee jumped in the car seat, thinking I joined him when I walked to the car. His ears drooped when I set the parcel in the back seat and told him to watch over it. I promised to return soon and spend the rest of the day with him. He settled back down at those words, as if he understood.

My courage diminished when I peered in the windows of Chez Monique. What if Adrienne loitered inside? Was I brave enough to not back down and try on the dress if I still wanted to? I took a deep calming breath, something I'd learned from Tai Chi, and pulled open the glass door.

The same plump, middle-aged woman glued herself to my side again, welcoming me back to the store. Try as I might, I could not fathom how this lady and the one next door were related, let alone sisters. I interjected a polite smile and told her I just couldn't stop thinking about one of the dresses and wanted to try it on. Using the word "just" made me smile, even more so since Ms. All That no longer lurked on the premises.

Slipping the blue lace dress over my head in the fitting room, it conformed perfectly to my body. The dressing room in this store came equipped with four wall mirrors, allowing me to enjoy seeing the material waft away from my body, before settling back around my legs when I finished spinning. This dress mirrored the description of perfection. A little more than I wanted to spend, but so worth it. I'd show Adrienne I could pull off this outfit!

CHAPTER 8

Homecoming Preliminaries

THE NEXT FEW DAYS enlightened me. During my stint in a cast, I'd forgotten how efficiently I performed my chores and completed my schoolwork. Everything seemed like a breeze, and I loved it. Not to mention the anticipatory atmosphere at school. With everyone getting ready for the big game and subsequent dance, I found myself anticipating it more than I should have.

The last time I entered a football stadium, I carried the title of student rather than teacher. I treasured the few high school games I'd attended. My dad always thought the rough behavior of crowds would encroach on my enjoyment, and his protective nature prevailed. He told me once that a babysitter more or less kidnapped me as an infant, resulting in him and my mother becoming the textbook definition of overprotective parents.

And a dance! Those also were scarcities in my teen years. Of course, we'd hosted a large wedding reception. There, Nick danced the obligatory first dance, the dance with his mom, and also the chicken dance. He'd even led a conga line. But my feet missed the dance floor. I didn't know for certain I'd get to dance on Friday night, but the possibility existed.

* * *

Spirit week capers made each school day an adventure. Although ironic, Nick was gung-ho over the idea of me dressing up for each themed day. I, however, wanted to kick back and observe the festivities this year. What better way to prepare myself for the following year?

Monday's theme involved tourism, so I added a pair of binoculars around my neck to a Hawaiian shirt and khakis. Tuesday was cartoon character day, and I found a Mickey Mouse headband from a box of high school keepsakes to wear. Wednesday welcomed color wars, and teachers were assigned orange. The color contrasted with my skin tone, so I wore a piece of hideous costume jewelry, an oversized orange flower brooch.

Thursday's sports hero day was easy. Mary Decker Slaney had long been my idol, perhaps because my mom idolized her, too. I'd grown up watching video footage of the Olympic qualifiers' races, often gazing upon a poster of her on the back of my mom's sewing room door. Wind pants, tennis shoes, and a t-shirt completed my look and made for the comfiest outfit of the week.

Friday's theme corresponded with the football team we supported, and I wore my maroon school spirit polo. A sensible choice given the activities planned for the day.

That afternoon, the entire student body headed to the larger of two gymnasiums for a pep rally. First, the cheerleaders performed a dance routine. Following that, the senior football players imitated a dance routine. Next, various student groups enacted a couple of amusing skits, poking fun at the coaches.

"And now," Lily, the head cheerleader held the microphone again, "we'll have a relay race!" Cheers followed her announcement. "Participants will be drawn randomly. You've been warned." She reached into a bowl, a mischievous smile curving her lips.

I figured they'd draw participants from a pool of student body names. I half listened, enjoying the tangible energy of the crowd. I heard more cheering and the shop teacher sitting on the bleacher behind me slapped me on the back.

"Yeah, Mrs. Adesco!"

"You've got this, Señora!"

Shit! Had they called my name? I rose, cautious of the upcoming activity. Not that the crowd bothered me so much but doing something I had neither planned nor prepared for irritated me. I joined other staff members and parents on the gym floor. Apparently, this constituted an adult activity for the students' amusement. Awesome.

After calling 25 names, cheerleaders grouped us in teams of five, lining us up in rows. They handed the first person in each row an orange. The entire object of the game consisted of passing the orange from person to person, down the row, then back again—the catch, no use of hands or teeth. We could only pass the orange by holding it under our chins.

The guy in front of me stood well over a head taller than me. When the whistle blew and he turned to face me with an orange under his chin, my jaw dropped. Holy smokes, this guy was hot. His bearded face aimed toward mine with a distinct purpose. How would I do this? It was almost like making out in public! Spontaneous perspiration dampened the hair on the back of my neck.

"Relax," he whispered, and somehow, I heard him over the noise of the crowd. "Stretch your neck out like you're wanting me to kiss it. When the orange gets situated, bring your chin in like you're having second thoughts."

I nodded and complied, not wanting to hold up the relay. Damn, but he smelled good, too. I forced my concentration to turn to the orange, successfully removing it from his neck. Turning to the person behind me, I saw a woman about my height. We passed the orange with ease. However, the next transaction miscarried. When the fruity round ball thudded to the floor, the cheerleaders informed us of another snag—we had to start over.

Not again, with Mr. Hottie and I necking in front of half the community.

This happened several times until the orange reached the fifth person in our line. The operation reversed as we started passing it back to the front. The woman behind me and I messed up once, returning the orange to the back of the line. The second time I captured it and turned to pass it to the number one guy. The process did not work as effectively in reverse. We dropped it the first time, tapping our toes and drumming fingers, waiting for it to work its way back up the line.

The next time, he stooped and put his head on my shoulder. I tried not to dwell on his soft beard tickling my neck as I rolled the orange from my neck to under his chin. He turned around, and the crowd went wild. We won!

"And for being such good sports," Lily announced, "a bag of oranges for each of the winners!"

Applause surrounded us as we returned to our seats with the fruit. The pep rally finished with a couple more enthusiastic routines by the cheerleaders.

* * *

As always, Vee leapt in delight upon my return home. I played fetch with him in the yard for a few minutes, a skill he'd adapted to and understood. I fixed shrimp scampi with linguini for Nick to eat later, one of his favorite dishes. I tolerated it and every other kind of seafood but opted to eat a salad instead.

They scheduled this Homecoming game to start at 6:30, a half hour earlier than usual. Even though daylight savings time had not yet begun, and the sun still shone low on the horizon, late fall in North Dakota meant temperatures already began dipping for the evening. I wore my winter coat to the game and brought a blanket to place across my lap.

Once there, I presented my activity pass and set off to find Alice Ann. A loud whistle brought my eyes straight to her grinning face. She and her husband reserved seats clear at the top of the bleachers. I trekked up the steps to join them.

"Thanks for saving me a seat."

"Of course, chica." She threw some gratuitous Spanish my way. "Hey, nice job with the orange relay race today."

"Thanks," I mumbled.

"The what?" her husband asked.

"The orange relay race. Here, I'll show you a picture." She dug in her purse for her phone. "Oh, wait. I forgot you guys haven't met. Jen, this is my husband, Bryce. Bryce, this is Jen. She teaches Spanish across the hall from me. Okay, here we go." She located a bejeweled rectangle and showed Bryce something on the screen.

"Wow!" he approved. "That looks like an activity we should try at home tonight after opening a bottle of wine."

Alice Ann giggled. "Have you seen the pictures yet?" She handed me her phone. "Go ahead, scroll through them."

About a dozen shots of the relay race glared back up at me, but I paused on one. There, in my hands, an incriminating picture of me, my head bent backward, appearing to expect ravishment by the dark head descending toward my exposed neck. Involuntary shivers wracked my body. If Nick saw this picture, he would kill me!

I rubbed my left arm in remembrance of my most recent injury. "You're not planning to post these anywhere, are you?"

"Me? No. The yearbook students took these, so I'm sure that's the only place they might end up. Why?" she teased. "Are you worried your husband will get jealous?"

"I'd get jealous," Bryce piped up.

I swallowed, nerves drying my throat. "I just don't think he'd be too fond of them."

Seeing the look on my face, Alice Ann assured, "Hey, I'm sure it will be fine. Besides, it's not like you were necking somewhere in private and got caught."

"True," I whispered, trying to immerse myself in the game and forget about the picture.

The Spoilers won the game by a score of 31-7, an impressive Homecoming victory. Alice Ann told me about a meeting for sponsors at nine o'clock, before the dance's official start at 9:30. We parted ways with a little less than an hour before reporting back for dance duty.

I drove back to a house that wasn't empty anymore, thanks to Vee. "Hi sweetheart!" I greeted him with as much enthusiasm as he welcomed me. Vee followed me upstairs, and I continued to chat with him. I told him all about the game, minus the part about the picture. It seemed taboo to even mention it in this house.

As I donned my gorgeous royal-blue dress, I gushed to Vee about the dance. I enjoyed the carefree ambiance at the game and looked forward to more of the same tonight. Happiness amidst groups of people often eluded me.

I wore small diamond studs in my ears and a dainty silver chain for a bracelet. The round neckline of my dress didn't lend itself well to wearing a necklace, so I went without. Two-inch silver strappy heels completed my ensemble.

I splashed my face with water and patted it dry. Before I put the towel down, I swore that either my overhead light flickered or something large blocked it for a moment. When I spun around, a woodsy scent drifted over me, but nothing was there.

I touched up my blush and eye shadow, adding a hint of black eyeliner. My hair gathered in a bun at the nape of my neck. Several tendrils escaped on each side to soften my appearance. When I stepped back to view the final result in the mirror, one word came to mind: fetching.

"What do you think, Vee? Do I look fetching?" Vee, who stretched out on the bed watching me with his paws tucked under his chin, sat up and barked in approval. "Thanks, boy." I scratched him behind the ears, taking one last look in the mirror.

Part of me wished Nick could see how good I looked. But the other part of me rejoiced in the thought of not falling under his scrutiny. In fact, that was the real reason excitement clung to me. At this social event, I could look good and enjoy myself without his judgment—within reasonable limitations. It was still a school event, after all.

CHAPTER 9

Homecoming

WHEN I WALKED INTO the gym at school, the lights had already dimmed for the upcoming dance. I walked over to the small group assembled by the stage. With no spotlights turned on, I struggled to distinguish Alice Ann from the others gathered for instructions.

The school administrator gave us simple yet effective directions. Basically, we existed as watchdogs. Keep a lookout for kids who may have been drinking alcohol, watch for kids trying to sneak in or out, prevent fights from breaking out. If we noticed any problems or potential conflicts, we did not need to intervene. We were to report to our principal or the athletic director. Otherwise, he instructed us to have fun. We could dance, enjoy the refreshments, and visit with each other.

Students began rolling in after our meeting concluded. Standing by Alice Ann and her husband, I listened to her commentary on who dated whom, which couples arrived as friends, and her opinion on students' clothing choices. So far, she hadn't squealed at the sight of anyone's outfit, except mine. I beamed under her approval of my taste.

At nearly 9:30, she gave a low whistle. "It looks like someone else is decked out in a version of you, only in red."

I turned my head to see Adrienne walk in, just a smidge too late for the sponsor meeting. Her eyes glowed with resentment, if not outright hatred, as she walked over to me.

"Cat fight!" Bryce whispered.

"I thought you took my fashion advice," she spat through gritted teeth.

I shrugged in an offhanded manner, trying not to show fear. "I changed my mind."

"Ugh!" she huffed and stalked away.

Although brief, the encounter shook me up a little. I detested confrontations. I leaned against the wall for a few minutes before meandering through bodies engaging in excited chatter or mindless gossip. Amidst my tour of duty around the gymnasium, a body planted itself square in front of me.

"Mrs. Adesco!" Catherine's usual timidity appeared hidden this evening. "This," she tugged hard on the elbow of a nearby man, "is my dad."

The mystery man turned, and I uttered one word as my jaw dropped. "You."

Standing before me was the man whose simple directions when under duress led our team to win the relay race this afternoon. Catherine grinned broader than any Cheshire cat replica before backing away, leaving us alone.

My face flushed deep red, but I wasn't sure how noticeable it was in a darkened room with fake lighting. His intense perusal flattered me.

"I guess you've already heard of me. I'm Jen Adesco."

"Not only have I heard of you," he clasped my dainty hand in both of his larger ones. "I could have sworn that we had a relationship in a past life."

If possible, I turned redder.

"My name's Jason...Wolfe, obviously, since Catherine is my daughter. It's very nice to meet you officially."

Since the pressing matter of juggling fruit no longer consumed me, I allowed myself to study Jason's face. A good, solid look at someone revealed a lot about their character. Not to mention, gazing at a man so easy on the eyes was always enjoyable. He had a high forehead, dark brown hair flowing into a well-kept moustache and beard, and sparkling blue eyes...

"I've been hearing that I needed to meet you." I murmured but shook my head to clear the cobwebs. I was married, for goodness sake.

"Well," he drawled, bowing as he released my hand, "the pleasure was definitely mine both times."

I meandered around the gymnasium a bit longer, returning to my place as a wallflower next to Alice Ann.

She greeted me with a smile and a teasing voice, "So, single hot dad takes a shine to the new Spanish teacher. Maybe you were more right than I thought about safeguarding that picture. Especially if your husband is the jealous type."

I ignored her probes for information by commenting on the unusual floor-length dress one of the senior girls chose for tonight.

About an hour later, the constant music relaxed the attendees. More and more of them stepped onto the dance floor. The DJ, amazing at his job, encouraged kids to get up and move. When he demanded that everyone make a circle around the center of the gym, a warm hand grabbed mine, urging me forward.

How could I resist doing the Hokey Pokey with Catherine? It wasn't until I put my left hip in that I noticed who was grooving on the other side of Catherine. None other than Jason. Of course, she'd want her dad out here, too. I recognized their tight bond. Catherine had confessed before that her painful shyness prevented her from asking anyone to the dance or even accepting an invitation from a boy.

When the song ended, I laughed and clapped along with everyone else. I planned to return to my spot along the wall but, like a young persistent child, Catherine pulled on my hand again.

"C'mon, Mrs. Adesco! Everyone's dancing in groups. Join us!"

I glanced around to verify her statement. Most students and sponsors danced to the upbeat tune vibrating from four large speakers. Some couples isolated themselves, but most groups consisted of three or more, sprinkling themselves across the dance floor.

"Why not?" I gave up trying to keep guard by monitoring my behavior. Other parent, student, and teacher groups existed, so why was mine any different? Abandoning myself to the music, I smiled, laughed, sang along to the lyrics, twirled in my fancy dancing dress, and shook what the good Lord gave me.

When that song ended, we stayed out for three more songs. But when the music slowed, I tried to beat a hasty retreat. I was not oblivious that several pairs of male eyes watched me, including those of some high school boys.

Light pressure on my shoulder made me turn back around.

"May I have this dance?" Jason looked so earnest and sweet that I couldn't refuse.

I let him lead me back to the middle of the room. He stopped by Alice Ann and Bryce, who snuggled close but still maintained an appropriate distance. I placed the standard right hand in Jason's left hand and my left hand on his shoulder. In turn, he clasped my one hand loosely and slid his other hand around my back. We chatted with the Swansons for a bit until they seemed more engrossed in each other.

Jason continued to hold me in a loose grip. "Sorry if I made you uncomfortable when I dictated directions for the relay this afternoon. I'd been certain my method would work. And it did."

A second slow song began. Jason pulled me a little closer, our bodies a respectable distance, but only just. He confessed, "You know, the reason I dropped the orange when you were passing it back is that I was distracted by how unbelievably close your lips were to mine."

Red. Instant red. My face flamed with heat from his admission.

"Hey," he soothed, "I'm not trying to make you self-conscious. I mean, I can see you're married and all that. It's just that you're very pretty, and I guess I feel like I know you well because Catherine talks so much about you."

My heated face and Jason's proximity covered my body in an uncomfortable cloak of warmth. I craved a drink and an exit from the dance floor. I gave a slight tug to his hand. In response, he gripped mine tighter.

"Please stay. I promise I'll be good and won't ever try anything. I'd like it if we could be friends—for Catherine's sake, at the very least. Agreed?"

"Por el amor de Catarina, sí." I finally replied.

Jason smiled and inched a tad closer when the third slow song in a row began playing. As I'd noticed earlier in the day, Jason smelled amazing. Had I been in a backroads country bar and not in a relationship, I would have rested my head on his shoulder, looping my arm around his neck, and inhaling the mixture of cologne and sweat. Even from a slight distance, this heady combination played tricks on my senses.

Too soon, the tempo increased, and another Top 40 hit rocked the gym. Catherine joined us, intent on the three of us dancing together again. She grinned while looking back and forth between us. I made a mental note to share with Catherine a polite reminder of my marital status while assuring her that her dad and I were friends and planned to continue our relationship on that level.

After dancing two more fast songs, I begged for a reprieve. I used the ladies' room, then selected a piece of chocolate cake from the serving table. I'd savored the first bite of cake and sipped some fruit punch, when a figure blocked my line of vision.

"Hello, my lady." Charles took my plate and cup from my hands, depositing them on a nearby table. "Let's get this party started. Do you know how to polka?" he inquired once we wedged into the middle of other dancers.

"Every summer when I was a kid, we visited Wilber, Nebraska—the official Czech Capital of the USA—for Czech Days. I think I've got the polka down."

"Excellent."

We proceeded to polka in and out around the other dancers. Many of them performed awkward pretzel maneuvers while attempting to country swing to the fast-paced beat. The polka proved a more appropriate dance for keeping up. We, and one other couple, were the best able to execute it.

Exhilarated when that song ended, I anticipated dancing some more with such a great partner! A slower country tune washed over me. Charles slowed our steps to a standstill, before asking, "Two-step?"

"Of course." I grinned at displaying another skill obtained by growing up in Nebraska.

This time he followed the perimeter of the dance floor. I loved it every time he spun me because my dress twirled around my legs. Somewhere in the middle of the two-step, my eyes connected with Jason's, where he watched from the sidelines. He seemed interested and a little perturbed. I couldn't quite read his expression in the dim lighting.

Close to midnight, the DJ announced the last song of the night. "A nice and slow one for all you lovebirds out there."

Charles continued to hold me, altering the quick step we performed to a slow and languid one. Something about a slower two-step, even with the separation points when he twirled me, felt erotic. After a couple of spins, he brought me a little closer into his body. Heat radiated off him. Damn. For the second time tonight, I was as horny as a teenager for men who weren't my husband.

Although mentally relieved when the dance ended, my body pined for the intimacy it thought it needed. I offered—along with a couple of other sponsors—to stay and help clean, but the principal refused our offer.

"That's what the janitors are getting paid extra for tomorrow."

I ambled to my car, the cool night breeze refreshing on my overheated skin.

"Good night, Mrs. Adesco. See you Monday!" Catherine called.

"Buenas noches, Catarina. Hasta el lunes! Buenas noches, Jason." I waved to him, as well.

I heard a noise to my left. In anticipation of Charles, I turned toward him with a polite smile. Except he wasn't there. No one was. A shooting star caught my eye, but instead of perceiving luck, either fear or the late October air shook my body in an involuntary shudder.

Right before I reached my car, Charles pulled up alongside me in his sporty car. "Don't fret, my lady. I've been watching you from afar. A gentleman never allows a lady to walk to her car unescorted."

"Well, how nice of you to see to my safety. So," I remembered the noise I'd heard, "I was never in any danger?"

"No one even got near you as you strolled through the moonlight and artificially lit parking lot. Inside you were close to a dark-haired, perfectly harmless man. And then you were also next to me."

The noise I'd heard earlier I chalked up to imagination, or a sound further away than I'd thought. "So, Jason is safe for me to be around, and you are dangerous?"

"Nah, I don't think I care for you hanging around him. Also, no, I would never be a danger to you."

His hand rested on the door of his car. I covered that hand with mine. "Thank you so much for the dances this evening. I haven't had that much fun in a long, long time. Thanks also for ensuring my safety. It's kind of nice to have a bodyguard. I know it's not the first time you've done it."

"Guilty. And you're welcome. Good night, Shenandoah." With that, he kissed my hand, released it, and backed his car to the side so I could get in my vehicle. He'd follow me home once again, and that comforted me.

* * *

My beautiful foxy dog greeted me at my car door when I pulled up in the driveway. On our way to the front porch, I thought I heard the same sound I'd heard in the school parking lot. However, I saw no one when I looked around the yard, and Vee didn't seem concerned.

My foot hit the third porch step when I heard a distinctly evil laugh echoing down the darkened street. Fear froze me in my tracks. Vee stood, a serene fixture by my side, waiting for me to open the door.

"What in the hell was that?" I asked Vee, wishing Charles had escorted me all the way to the door. With senses on full alert, I kept listening while I crept the rest of the way to my front door. There it was again! That evil cackle. But this time, it was followed by less distinct cackles. More like... quacks.

"Shit! Ducks made that sound?" To quote my grandma, that scared the living daylights out of me. Why weren't the ducks asleep?

Sleep sounded like the perfect word. The more I thought about it, the sleepier I became. I fed Vee, got him fresh water, and jumped in the shower, all the while daydreaming about how much fun I'd had tonight. A permanent smile fixed to my face. Every time I walked by the mirror, it grinned back. After a warm shower, I brushed my hair out and realized I looked relaxed and happy. Tonight was a much-needed venture and something that would bear repeating soon.

As I drifted off to sleep with Vee curled by my side, I realized my lips were still curved upwards.

After two o'clock Nick came home with a couple of buddies. I heard them laughing and opening beer bottles before they meandered into the family room area. The clock read 4:43 when Nick collapsed into bed beside me. His snores rocked the poles of the canopy bed within minutes.

He'd come to bed much later than usual, a move which switched my brain to awake mode despite my body's fatigue. I repeated my nightly routine of padding downstairs to curl up with a blanket and pillow, deciding to read more of my latest library acquisition by Veronica Roth. Vee snuggled with me when I sat sideways across the chair, draping my legs over one side. Eventually, I succumbed to sleep again.

As daylight coated the interior of our living room, Nick woke me by stumbling to the kitchen. The fridge door clicked, and he unscrewed a bottle of some sort of alcoholic beverage. I released an internal groan. The days that Nick began hung over, and drank alcohol to cure it, never ended well. Hell, he probably wasn't even hung over yet. In all likelihood, alcohol still oozed through his liver.

I dozed back off but awakened to Vee's growls seconds before I catapulted to the floor. Nick screamed, "What the hell, Jen? Dammit, what the hell?"

When he dumped me on the floor, I landed on a tender elbow, still sore from its use the night before.

"You stupid, lying, cheating bitch. After all I've done for you... You're such a whore!" He took a swig from the Bailey's bottle, then picked my armchair up over his head.

"Nick, no!" I was so worried about my chair I didn't realize he meant to hit me and destroy the chair.

For a moment, something red caught my eye. Vee stood in front of me, looking more like a full-grown dog than a puppy: ears back and low, eyes squinted, and teeth bared. He barked and sent vicious snarls toward Nick, who gave him a drunken, sideways kick. He thudded into the wall with a whimper.

Pain crashed down, and my world disappeared in a shroud of black.

CHAPTER 10

Visiting Hours

FIRST, I NOTICED THE smell. Some sort of antiseptic or cleaning solution... repugnant. Next, I detected the pain. Everywhere. It hurt to breathe, it hurt to wiggle my fingers or toes, it hurt to swallow, it even hurt to move my eyeballs behind closed lids.

Where was I and what happened to me?

An insistent throbbing from my right hand prompted a slight squint at my surroundings. I did not recognize the room at all. My head tilted down until I spotted a cast on my arm. But I thought I'd gotten out of my cast. Had I reinjured my arm? I tried to remember, scrunching my forehead—a motion that cut like a knife. I allowed myself to relax, drifting back to sleep despite the increased pain.

All-encompassing suffering dragged me back to consciousness. Holy shit! I suspected my body had been the primary target for boulders in a landslide. My entire body seemed bruised and tender, broken pieces sloshing beneath my skin. How could a girl endure this much agony?

My low moan brought someone with quiet shoes to my bedside. Feminine perfume wafted across my face when she stopped at the bed.

"Hi there." She spoke in a kind voice, moving my hair off my forehead. "My name's Michelle. I'm your day nurse. I know someone who will be very glad that you're with us again."

Nick. It had to be Nick. He could take me someplace better, making all this hurt go away. But first, I had to ask, "Where am I?"

My raspy throat fought to produce audible speech. A dry mouth and scratchy throat, combined with an aching jaw I hadn't noticed before, began sinking me into utter misery.

"It sounds like Mr. Hoarse Voice could use a drink of ice water." Michelle must've been as French as her name, pronouncing it, "Mee-shell." She eased my bed into more of a sitting position, but each jostle during the increasing inclination jarred every cell in my body. I wanted to grab the sides of the bed to make it stop, but additional pain impeded the movement.

By some mercy, Michelle loosened her hold on the wheel of this reverse-rack torture device. My stomach, or maybe my ribs, began spasming. Michelle didn't seem to realize the harm she'd inflicted until I balled the blanket with my mobile fist. "Ahhh!"

"Oh! Sorry, sweetie. You've got so many internal injuries. I guess we're kind of touch and go on a lot of things for now."

"The rack" relaxed its grip and unfolded, slowing the spasms.

"Let's take a quick drink," she urged, pressing a straw to my lips. "You drink for me, then we'll check on Mr. Morphine Drip."

Since I wasn't a kid, and since my hurting body made me angry, Michelle's smatters of baby talk threatened to rip profanities from my injured throat. The descent into misery continued. My eyelids drooped as I forced two sips through swollen lips.

Michelle clicked her tongue, pulling the straw away. "Mr. IV will keep you hydrated, but Dr. Bisbee would prefer you consume your own beverages. Now let me check..."

I didn't bother to open my eyes as she read the numbers on Mr. Morphine Drip.

"Oh yes, I certainly can up the dosage. Only the frequency will remain the same." I heard a couple of beeps as she adjusted the monitor. "Goodnight, Jen."

Her last words disappeared in a wave of incessant babble. Would the voices that surrounded me ever shut up? Why wouldn't these jackasses let me rest? I refused to even open my eyes amidst all the cacophony.

Uncertain how much time passed since several male voices reverberated in my head, I sensed gentle fingers caressing the back of my left hand. A touch so light that it didn't hurt. In fact, it tickled. My hand jerked.

"Shenandoah." A masculine voice filled with anguish spoke my given name.

I cracked my eyes open, halfway expecting to see my father, but the image blurred. The blob in question patted my hand, light as a flutter of fine silk, before moving away.

"Wait!" I croaked, but silence greeted me for tangible seconds.

Someone to my left spoke. "Hey guys, I think she's up again."

The same annoying voices from earlier clamored around. I tried to raise my hand to massage my temple, finding I lacked the coordination.

I realized the loudest voice in the room belonged to Nick.

Nick!

Forcing my eyes open as far as they'd go, I scanned the room until I located him. He stood by two—no, three—of his buddies. I recalled that I must be in a hospital, but I still didn't understand why. Had I been in a car accident? How badly was I bashed up? Would I walk again? Would I ever get out of bed?

"Jen." Nick caught me looking at him. "Hey Joe, go tell the nurse she's awake." He turned back toward me, planting his face in front of mine. His anxious words rushed out, "Jen, I'm glad you're up. I was so worried about you. I know it looks bad right now, but the doc's report is that you should be fine. It'll just take some time to heal." He stared into my eyes. "You know I love you...right, babe?"

"I love you, too." My lips mouthed the words.

Nick sat back up, pleased and grinning. "That's right! We're the dynamic duo—Adescos forever."

By this time, the nurse came back to check my vitals. When finished, she turned to the mob in my room. "I've paged the doctor because he wanted to examine her once she woke up. When he gets here, you all will have to leave."

"These yahoos can go," Nick teased his buddies, "but I'll be staying right here with my wife. She needs me for support."

Michelle glared at him with tight lips, before stalking past him. "We'll see what the doctor says."

"Hey guys, why don't you go get some coffee or something? It might be easier for me to convince the doc if I'm here alone with Jen when he comes."

Nick's friends shuffled from the room. I didn't pay close attention to their interactions, but sensed that Nick, in all likelihood, got his way most of the time. Perhaps they dubbed him leader of their pack. Words to the old 60s song flooded through my mind, lifting the corner of my mouth in a mock smile.

Nick sat back down beside me and appeared pleased. Maybe he thought the smile, lopsided and all, was for him. It was, indirectly. He squeezed my left hand with too much pressure and spoke in earnest.

"So Jen, do you forgive me?"

I looked at him with half-opened eyes, croaking, "For what, Nick?"

He expelled a huge breath of air that he held and relaxed. "For not getting to you in time after you tripped and fell down the stairs."

"I did what?" My mind raced to replay the incident, but the ordeal wiped it clean from my memory—an accident so bad I repressed all of it. Geez. People died from falling down stairs. I was lucky to be alive! I needed to be more careful. What a stupid mistake.

A light rap on the door alerted us to the doctor's presence. Nick jumped up and stretched his hand toward the doctor, pumping with all the enthusiasm he could muster. "Great job stitchin' up my wife, Doc. She'll have her smokin' hot body back in no time. I owe ya one."

"About that." Dr. Bisbee looked grim. Was there something horribly wrong with me? He walked to the door, shutting it with business-like firmness. What bad news lingered behind his lips? He ignored Nick, continuing to my bedside.

"Hello, Jen." His smile invited trust.

"Hi." My voice wouldn't cooperate; upon vocalizing that syllable, my bottom lip cracked in the middle and warm blood trickled out. Dr. Bisbee pulled a tissue from the box on the table next to my bed. He dabbed at my mouth, holding it with slight pressure. Next he picked up the small jar of Vaseline next to the Kleenex box, smearing some across both of my lips.

"Now Jen," he said in hushed tones, setting the jar back down. "How are you feeling?"

"I hurt." Tears welled in my eyes. "I hurt all over."

Nick piped up. "It'll be okay, babe. You're already on the mend."

"Do you mind?" Dr. Bisbee turned toward Nick, I assumed to shoot him a glare.

"Jen," Dr. Bisbee returned his tone to calm. "Tell me how you sustained your injuries."

My throat ached like never before, but I felt compelled to answer him. "It's so crazy."

"What is?" he prompted.

"I was so stupid. I tripped and fell down the stairs." My voice broke.

Dr. Bisbee offered me ice water, which I drank greedily through a straw. "Is that what you remember or what you were told?"

"Hey now!" Nick yelled from behind the doctor.

"Shut up!" Dr. Bisbee yelled back. "I'll address you in a moment."

What did I remember? Of course, I recalled the moments before my fall, and the actual act of tumbling down the stairs—didn't I? But the pain...that I'd never forget. The pain still reverberated through my body.

"No, that's what happened. It was horrible."

"It's okay, babe. I'm here for ya."

Dr. Bisbee whirled to face him. "You!" he roared, much too loud for my head and for a hospital environment. As if realizing this, his voice dropped to low and menacing. "We've thoroughly examined and photographed her. If I ever find out you were in any way responsible for this, I will have you prosecuted to the fullest extent of the law!"

"Hey, whoa—relax, pal." Nick's temper shimmered, but he held it in check. "The girl can't help it if she's a bonafide klutz. It's one of the things I love about her."

I attempted a feeble smile through cracked lips. Nick loved me; he was here, and soon everything would be better. I pushed the morphine drip again. Time spent conversing and paying attention to conversation wore me out.

* * *

Sometime later I awoke, my parched throat begging for attention. I slanted my head to see if my glass of hospital-issued ice water remained within an arm's length. As I reached, I noticed that the door to my room rested wide open instead of ajar. The bright hospital hallway lights had all darkened. Had I missed a storm and subsequent power failure? But surely a hospital supplied backup generators.

A scraping sound approached from down the hall.

Both curious and horrified, I continued to stare into the shadowed hallway. A wheelchair creaked into view. The individual in the chair wore a metallic golden kimono with a hood. Something felt off about this person's aura. And that scent... I sucked in a gasp of air, choking on the fragrance of honey mingling with anesthetics.

My strained neck wanted to look away, but my body remained paralyzed. At its leisure, the chair backed to the side and pulled forward, facing my room. Terror gripped my throat at the dim visage with two dark orbs where eyes should be.

Holy shit! What the hell? Help! Help!

My brain screamed, but no sound emerged from my mouth. I feared this phantom apparition sought me out, hunted me, preparing to eat my brains. I waited for fight or flight to kick in, neither of which I could enact. Here I lay, immobile, doomed to die a ghastly death in an institution of healing.

Oddly enough, after a few more seconds the figure in the wheelchair retreated, rolling back a few inches and heading toward the opposite direction. Gone, as if he'd never been there.

My body, entirely contracted for the past two minutes, collapsed on the bed. The scratching and creaking subsided, the lights in the hallway came back up, and my eyes squeezed shut. Man, what kind of trippy drugs dripped into my bloodstream right now?

As if reading my mind, the morphine drip clicked, hummed, and clicked again. Whether due to additional pain medication or the anticipation of receiving it, all pain dulled in my lethargic limbs. A mercy, after seeing that vision.

CHAPTER 11

Unauthorized Visitors

THE NEXT TIME I opened my eyes, early October sunlight streamed through my standard rectangle hospital window. Although aware the nurses checked on me throughout the night, nothing except that creepy wheelchair woke me. Convinced that I'd hallucinated, I asked the food service girl who brought me a fruit smoothie if anyone on the floor had difficulty sleeping and roamed around at night via wheelchair.

"What?" the mousy young woman giggled. "On this floor? No, I don't think so. This is all critical care. We confine everyone to their beds."

So, a nightmare haunted me. Just what I needed.

Michelle came in shortly thereafter to check my vitals and bathe the parts of me not covered by bandages. "We should have you up and visiting Mr. Shower in a day or two." She beamed at me. "As soon as we get you walking, we'll move you to the second floor."

They thought I'd be walking in another day? Ha! Good luck with that. I couldn't move a single muscle without pain. Still, it occurred to me that I wanted to move. I wanted to get out of this bed, leaving these muted walls behind.

"Michelle," my throat didn't crack as much after consuming the smoothie, "what day is it?"

"Sweetie, it's Tuesday."

At my panic-stricken visage, she rushed to assure me. "It's okay. They placed you in a drug-induced coma for a couple of days to help with the swelling. Your cute hubby was worried sick about you."

Nick. Of course, he'd been worried—what a sweet guy. My heart warmed. But I remembered the reason I'd asked about the date. "My jobs!" I struggled to push myself up, but to no avail. Various casts, bandages, and aching ribs impeded my progress.

"Whoa! Slow down, sugar." Michelle's gentle hands pushed my shoulders back, pressing the lever to raise the head of the bed. "I can't put it up too much—doctor's orders. No undue pressure on the ribs while they mend themselves."

"But I was supposed to work at the gym on Saturday, and I should be at school now." I looked around until I spotted a clock to verify that statement. 8:42. Yes, I should definitely be in school—not only today, but also yesterday.

"Relax. I'm sure your hubby notified your employers. Now I've got to check on some other patients. Call the nurses' station if you need anything before I make my next round."

I spent most of the day falling asleep while watching mindless sitcoms and game shows on television. Nick stopped by for an hour before he drove to work. He munched on fries and a fast-food burger, all the while telling me how much he missed my cooking and couldn't wait for me to return home.

I asked before he left. "How is Vee? Are you taking care of him?"

A scowl crept across his face. "I haven't seen him at all. I think he ran off."

"Oh, Nick! Will you look for him? Please? He's still a puppy!"

"Sure, babe." Nick promised as he jumped up to go. "I'll have my buddies look for him, too."

Relief flooded through me. With so many looking, they'd find Vee. "Thanks, Nick. I love you."

"See ya tomorrow, babe." He leaned down to kiss me, or so I thought, but backed away and grinned, blowing me a kiss instead. "It's just that I don't want to hurt you."

I understood. He always considered my feelings.

* * *

Dr. Bisbee stopped by that evening. I got the impression he examined every single inch of my body for as long as he spent peeking under bandages, plying tender skin on different parts of my body, and examining bruises. It made me wonder how much of me sustained injuries. I wouldn't have thought carpeted stairs capable of so much damage.

He didn't talk much while completing his ministrations. He muttered the occasional, "Does this hurt? How much on a scale on one to ten? How far can you bend this?" And finally, "Would you like to try standing and walking a little tomorrow?"

"Do you think I can?" I asked, dubious about his sincerity.

"Surprisingly, your legs and ankles barely sustained injuries compared to the rest of your body. Quite odd, since I usually see a more even distribution of bruising. Your injuries are more indicative of blunt force trauma and defensive wounds. Jen," I looked squarely into his kind, probing eyes. "Are you certain you remember falling down the stairs?"

"Sure." I said in earnest but scrunched my forehead in thought. "Well, no...not exactly."

He kept looking at me.

I sighed. "No, not at all. I don't remember what happened."

"What about the time you broke your arm?"

Staring straight into his eyes, I replied, "Like I told you before, I slipped on my kitchen floor."

"But again, your injuries more closely resembled blunt force trauma than a slip and fall."

"What are you trying to say to me?" I didn't like what he implied.

Dr. Bisbee covered my hands with his in a fatherly gesture. "Jen, just seven and a half weeks ago you broke your elbow and weren't able to receive medical help for almost a day afterwards. This time, your husband brought you here in a comatose state with injuries that bordered on life-threatening. Now you may love your husband and may think you're protecting him. Maybe you even think you deserve it when he hits you."

I winced, hoping he hadn't noticed.

"But his violence seems to be escalating. Jen, he will kill you if you stay with him too long. However, because you are a consenting adult, no one but you can remove yourself from the situation. You must first realize that your life is in danger. Then you can have a restraining order placed on him. You can even press charges. Are you ready to take that step?"

Using anger for momentum, I jerked my hands out from under his, an action I regretted. Tears sprang to my eyes as pain ricocheted through my right arm, shoulder, and neck.

"Damn it," I whispered. "Why do you want to turn me into a victim? The only thing hurting me is my own clumsiness. Nick loves me."

"Okay." Dr. Bisbee moved away from the bed. "We'll leave it at that for now. But if you ever remember what happened Saturday morning, please consider telling someone. I'm also turning over the photographs I took of your injuries to the police and leaving copies in your medical file. This way any dispatcher will treat your phone calls with extreme urgency."

At my agonized look, he added, "I have to, Jen. It's my duty as a medical professional. I try my best to save lives, not to stand back and watch them be destroyed."

I turned my face away, saying nothing more to him than goodbye when he left.

* * *

True to her word, Michelle got me up and walking the next morning. My progress was slow, but we made it partway down the hall. Afterwards, they moved me to the second floor. I missed Michelle, despite her annoying mannerisms and superficial camaraderie.

My new daytime nurse had slaved at the hospital so long that she no longer wore her name tag. Michelle told me her name was Rachel but many of the inmates, she joked, called her Miss Ratchet.

Rachet's first order of business consisted of removing all wraps and bandages, covering casts, and showering me off. Although it was a painful experience, as she rewrapped my wounds, I conceded the experience refreshed me. She ticked off the list of my injuries while she worked, sounding somehow condescending.

—two broken ribs

—four broken fingers

—a broken wrist

—a concussion

—cut from the wrist to the elbow on the right arm

—bruising over the entire body

Geez, the damage exceeded what I recalled hearing the first time. I needed to slow down a bit more to avoid another massive accident.

Nick stopped by with his lunch, on the run again. But that afternoon, I received my first visitor other than Nick. Nakayla walked in; sheer concern plastered on her face.

"Oh my gosh, Jen! I had no idea you were in here until Alice Ann told me yesterday. I left messages on your cell phone and at your house when you didn't show up for your shift Saturday afternoon. You poor thing." She approached my bed tentatively. "Will you be okay? How long are you staying here?"

She informed me she'd cover my shifts at the gym for the rest of October, instructing me to call when I could return to work.

On Thursday Nick visited, like clockwork, and a surprise visitor arrived in the afternoon. During my nap, the sound of someone exhaling sharply interrupted peaceful dreams.

"My God!" Charles exclaimed, "You look like a smashed-up version of the girl I danced with less than a week ago."

I offered a weak smile, embarrassed at my presence in a hospital bed. No makeup, hair not combed well, a split lip. I had no idea how bad I looked, deliberately evading any mirrors.

Charles continued, "What happened?"

I replied with self-deprecation, "I was an idiot and fell down the stairs at my house."

"Wow. And what was it? Just a week after the cast came off your elbow?"

"Something like that."

"I'm so glad nothing worse than this happened to you, although this seems pretty bad."

Dr. Bisbee chose that moment to enter the room. He glanced at my guest, addressing him by name. Charles shook his hand then turned his back out of respect, busying himself with his phone while the doctor examined me.

He asked me how my new floor was treating me, and how far I'd progressed at walking.

"I miss Michelle," I lamented, "but I am happy to be mobile again, even though it's a laborious process."

Dr. Bisbee seemed happy with my prognosis. "Fantastic! This room will be your last stop before going home."

I grinned in excitement. "When will that be?"

"Not for a few days yet, I'm afraid. I want to make sure you're well on the mend before letting you go back to that house. A battered body will only heal as quickly as it's allowed to heal. If you, or anyone else pushes it too hard, relapses can easily occur."

At my puzzled look, he added, "You need time to mend. Will your husband be supportive and give you that time?"

"Of course, he will." But uncertainty laced my words. Nick held high expectations. Home-cooked, gourmet meals, a spotless house, sex on demand. I grimaced at the thought of having sex with my broken ribs. He'd been so aggressive with my broken elbow. Somehow, I'd have to figure out a way to keep him off me.

"That's what I thought," Dr. Bisbee nodded his head in confirmation. "I'll be keeping you here as long as I medically can. I'll see you tomorrow, Jen." He patted my left arm on his way out.

"Dr. Bisbee, a word?" Charles trailed him out of my room. A few minutes later, he reentered with something at his side. He pulled a chair beside my bed, lowering it until we shared unspoken words eye to eye.

"Shenandoah," he murmured, gazing at me. "a beautiful name for an extraordinarily beautiful woman."

My cheeks warmed. "I'm sure I've looked better."

He continued his intense gaze at my face. "I'm sure you have, too. In fact," he leaned in, "would you like to see exactly how bad things look right now?"

"No, not really." I protested, shutting my eyes when a hand-held mirror emerged from beside the bed.

Charles urged, "Look at your face."

I didn't want to. My backbone retreated, but he wouldn't let up. Over a mountain of reluctance, I peeled one lid then the other from eyeballs resigned to seeing whatever reflection the glass held.

"What?" I couldn't believe the face that stared back at me. A huge, peeling scab cracked my lips down to the middle of the bottom one. My right eyelid swelled into a large mass resembling an egg ringed with purple bruises. Cuts, more bruises, and abrasions littered the rest of my face.

"Ick," I commented, trying for humor. "Now I'm doubly sorry that you have to see me like this." I touched the mirror, trying to push it away.

"Beauty goes beyond physical appearances." Charles held the mirror up even closer to my face. "Shenandoah," he breathed, "you're safe in here, and you're safe with me. Tell me who did this to you, and I promise to always keep you safe."

I balked at his offer. I had to. No other recourse made sense. "Me. It was me who did this. How are you going to protect me from myself?"

"Okay, you win," he complied. "But remember, I am here should you ever need me."

* * *

Friday afternoon brought with it a host of new visitors. Alice Ann stopped by, and a handful of my students trailed in after her. Catherine even dropped in with her father. Mortification etched on his features, as it had on most everyone who visited. And to think I'd been healing for a week already.

Tears threatened to spill over Catherine's cheeks. She whispered something to her dad, he nodded, and she took off.

Turning back to me, Jason said, "Who did this to you?"

"Why does everyone keep asking that?" I complained.

"You look like someone beat the living crap out of you. What else could have done this? A car accident?"

I launched into my story for the umpteenth time. When I finished, the skepticism on Jason's face strengthened. "I don't buy it. Unless your stair railing was a broken apart, splintered wreck, no part of it would have cut your face and body like this. Bruises, yes. Broken bones, perhaps. But deep cuts and scratches? I don't think so."

"I guess I can't control what you think," I huffed.

With my lip set in a semi-pout, I pondered his words. Why did so many people doubt my explanation? Usually, when I got hurt, people believed whatever story I made up to explain the injury. Which meant that usually Nick inflicted my injuries, and I created plausible cover stories.

But had Nick done this to me? He told me I fell down the stairs. Was that the only thing he invented to cover his tracks? Did he have tracks to cover?

Catherine appeared in the doorway, flushed and breathless.

"What is it, honey?" Jason asked.

"Oh, nothing. I mean, a couple of guys from Spanish class are coming up here soon. They were in the gift shop, too. Umm, here." She handed me a beautiful white box covered in sparkles and topped with golden sprigs of ribbon. "This is from me and my dad." She whispered to her dad and handed him a pen. "This card is from us, too."

Poor, flustered Catherine's eyes wore a persistent trail to the door. I understood her shy nature and deduced she had a crush on one of the boys arriving in a few moments.

"I understand if you need to take off." My soft voice conveyed this understanding.

At that moment, Ethan and Lee ambled in. Catherine cast a nervous glance at them, sending pleading eyes toward her dad. Jason caught her unspoken message and rose to leave.

"Hope you're feeling better soon." He directed my way.

"Me too, Mrs. Adesco. I hope you like the gift!" With those words, they disappeared. Left in their place, two lanky teenage boys stood.

"We came to spring ya, Señora!" Ethan smiled at me.

Lee chimed in, "Yeah, your substitute sucks! She doesn't help us through homework like you do. I don't think she even speaks Spanish. When we ask her questions, she either says we should already know that, or tells us to look it up."

"So, yeah, come back soon." This came from Ethan, who aimed a shy kick at the baseboard. "Here's a card we got you."

"Aww, guys, thanks so much for stopping by. And thanks for the offer to break me out. Hang in there. I'm sure I'll be back in school before long."

The boys smiled, inching toward the door and eager for dismissal. "See ya later, Señora!"

My attention turned back to the gift from Catherine. From amongst layers of tissue paper I removed a beautiful stained-glass wolf—no, a fox head. A fox! An overwhelming sense of loss flooded over me when I realized I hadn't seen my precious foxy dog since last weekend. Nick hadn't told me if he'd found him, so I assumed Vee still roamed at large. I fervently wished for his safety. Incapable of more than silent prayers, I raised the suncatcher with bandaged fingers to better examine it from every angle.

Tall brown ears stood at attention, alert to any sound. Orange slits of eyes peered down a long snout, observing and guarding against evil. I loved it, and it couldn't have been cheap.

Catherine scrawled in the card, "A fox to watch over you when no one else can." My thoughts mimicked hers. She signed it, "Love, Catherine." Her dad added his own "Love" before he signed "Jason." Although sweet, I could not let Nick see this card under any circumstances. He'd be insanely jealous.

Who knew that lying in bed receiving visitors for several hours could exhaust a person? I barely acknowledged the evening nurse when she came to check on me around ten o'clock. At my nod, she turned out my light and pulled my door three quarters of the way shut. Plenty of light eked in. Once my eyes adjusted, I could still make out everything in the room. Like a child afraid of bad dreams occurring in a pitch-black room, hallway lights and the faint murmur of nurses at their station comforted me.

Except... I awoke before daylight to a dark room. The supper dining attendant fastened my suncatcher in the window. I saw the shape of the fox head, a soft glow illuminating it from behind.

But over there, to the side of the curtains...I stifled a scream when I identified—or rather, lacked identification for—the other head at my window. The cloaked head of an individual peered into my room, mystifying me as I resided on the second floor.

I discerned no distinct facial features, as if the man wore a morph suit with a hood. I could tell that his mouth stretched open in a farcical manner like Edvard Munch's "The Scream." This figure also placed a hand by his face but, instead of holding his cheeks like the character in "The Scream," his left hand cupped around his left eye, perhaps to better peer in my window.

What the hell should I do? Would nurses come running if I screamed? Turning my head to the left, I observed that—although my door still rested ajar—I no longer perceived any outside light. My breath came in short, frantic gasps; too late, I recognized the onset of hyperventilation.

The figure's left hand still circled his left eye, but a right hand and arm emerged, extending forward. It appeared as if the bodiless phantom reached straight through the glass. My eyes scanned the window one more time before sheer blackness encroached upon my vision.

I regained consciousness much like a drowning person during resuscitation—a gasp for air, slight choking gurgle, and an attempt to get up and run. My fight-or-flight reflex took over. With my injuries, in the hospital, I had nowhere else to go...but, at least, the window was empty again.

CHAPTER 12

"Get Well" Flowers

SUNLIGHT SPARKLED OFF MY suncatcher. "Stupid protective fox," I grumbled at it. "Where were you last night when I needed help? Oh, yeah, you were right there letting the creepy phantom from the undead access my hospital room."

I shivered, unable to imagine how that horrid creature reached my window. Did it find a way in after I passed out? Had it done anything to me? I checked my body over and glanced around my room but saw nothing amiss. Had it even been real? The morphine drip no longer catered to my needs so, unlike the wheelchair hallucination, this manifestation occurred without narcotic persuasion.

Still, shit like that just wasn't real. The incident had to be another nightmare, like in a movie. I'd seen one about a boy who also had nightmares. In his case, however, the monster was real and came after him even in the security of a hospital.

I decided not to mention the dream—or hallucination—to anyone. No sense making anyone suspect that I'd jumped on the crazy train and wasn't getting off any time soon. How awful, for instance, if the nurse had stood at my side when I saw the guy at my window. What if I'd pointed in frantic gestures at the window, begging her to look? I envisioned her eyebrows arching when she addressed me. "Sorry, but there's no one there."

Nick surprised me by arriving earlier than usual. Of course, it was Saturday. He often went to work early on Saturday to enjoy a game or two on the big screen with the guys.

Today, instead of strolling in eating his lunch, he carried seven red roses. "For you!" he announced with a flourish.

"Oh Nick, they're beautiful! Thank you so much." I laid them down beside me on the bed. It was typical of Nick to bring something special for me in my incapacitated state.

"So, when are they letting you go?" Nick plunked himself down at the foot of my bed. "I sure could use one of your home-cooked meals again."

"Thinking about your stomach when she can still barely walk on her own. You must be the husband."

I shifted my gaze in surprise to the condescending voice of Charles, who sauntered into my room.

Nick jumped up. "Who the hell do you think you are? Get out! We don't know you."

"Nick, this is Charles." My weak voice sounded pathetic to my ears. "He's a board member at the gym." I sensed Nick's good mood shift dramatically, and I didn't care to receive any of the backlash. "Charles, this is my husband, Nick. Look at these beautiful flowers he brought me." I glanced at Nick to see if my appreciation coaxed him back to a calmer place. His tense face revealed the opposite.

Charles' fingers ran across the tips of the roses. "Seven, hmm? What's the significance in seven?"

"You're a board member at the gym? So what? Get out!"

"Don't worry, I won't stay long." Charles' body language displayed composure, but anger burned in his eyes as he stared at Nick's face. "Why seven flowers?"

"You effin' jerk!" Nick yelled. "Seven, because it's been seven days since she got hurt!"

"Seven days since who hurt her?"

Thankfully, the heart monitor no longer tracked my progress, or both men would hear it racing. What the hell was wrong with Charles? Couldn't he sense Nick's anger? He needed to shut up. Or leave. Or something!

"Look buddy, I don't like what you're implying!" Nick stood in front of Charles, yelling in his face. With those words, he jabbed a finger into Charles' shoulder.

"I don't remember implying anything." Charles stood his ground. "And if you touch me again, I won't hesitate to press assault charges."

Nick's fists clenched and unclenched to a primal rhythm. I'd seen him in a fight once before when he got hammered on our honeymoon cruise. He'd never hurt me in front of anyone...but would that change today? He often refrained from anything too physical when I was injured, except for sex. He thought my body was readily adaptive and built for sex, no matter other physical limitations.

Well-founded fear inserted itself in my musings, causing me to wonder if he'd release his anger or wait until the day I returned home. Since he was more of a "react to the emotion of the moment" type of guy, I wondered if he could bottle things up for a few days. My body still hurt so badly. I didn't consider myself capable of enduring his anger in this state.

Nick resented people who challenged him. The demeanor Charles displayed hit like a physical blow to his masculinity.

"Who do you think you are to insult me? And in front of my woman!" Nick roared, pushing past Charles with his shoulders and knocking over a chair. Something about the overturned chair niggled some sort of memory in the deep recesses of my brain, but I couldn't get a complete thought to form.

I looked at the clock, then over to Charles. "He's probably heading to work. You shouldn't have said those things. Nick doesn't handle anger very well. This won't be good." I lowered my gaze to my hands, and to my chagrin, began to cry.

"You're not his possession, Shenandoah. You should not have to fear your husband." Charles picked up the overturned chair, settling in it after placing it by my bed. "Now please tell me, honestly, do you remember the accident that put you here in the hospital?"

"I'm sorry I'm crying. It's just that I had a nightmare last night..."

"And then another one today."

"No." I looked to him. "Nick loves me. He was in such a good mood today. He brought me flowers. He..."

"Flowers of guilt." Charles interrupted again.

I ignored the jab. "He misses me so much."

"He misses your cooking and cleaning," Charles corrected.

He was starting to piss me off. No wonder Nick got mad and stormed out of here. I didn't have that option.

"You're wrong!" I yelled with all the strength I could muster. Fresh tears fell onto my sheets.

"Hey," Charles' voice gentled, "everything will be okay. I'm on your side." He used his fingers to wipe large, balled-up tears off my face. "But I need to know if you can recall anything about the accident or the events leading up to it."

I shook my head in a forlorn stupor. We sat in silence for a few minutes. In the quiet room, I noticed a precise, insistent ticking. It came from Charles' wind-up watch. Focus on his timepiece prompted me to ask, "When was I admitted to the hospital? What time of day?" This information might help me remember my activities prior to getting hurt.

Charles jumped up. "I'll find out!" he said, excitement boosting adrenaline as he hurried to the door. "Don't go anywhere." He joked, disappearing from sight.

He returned moments later with Dr. Bisbee, who finished with his clinic patients and was making his hospital rounds.

"Hello, Jen," Dr. Bisbee's warm voice greeted. He consulted my chart. "It looks like they checked you into the emergency room on October 9th at 4:42 p.m. Does that help you place your activities last Saturday afternoon?"

I frowned. "Wait, Saturday afternoon? I was supposed to be at work at the gym by noon. Nakayla said she called the house when I didn't show up for my shift."

"My God!" Charles gasped. "He waited hours before finally deciding to bring her in."

Dr. Bisbee agreed. "I made notes attesting that her bruises appeared to be several hours old. Plus, blood had already clotted on her open wounds."

My stomach roiled. Wildly I looked for a trash can, locating it, and pointing at it using frantic gestures. Dr. Bisbee sensed my need and handed me a vomit basin. Luck sided with me. My breakfast consisted of minimal amounts of food several hours ago. Nothing but empty retching noises entertained the two gentlemen in my room. Mending ribs protested the spasms, echoing with contractions of their own.

When dry heaves subsided, I raised my head. My visitors were kind enough to step into the hallway while I humiliated myself. Why did everyone seem hell-bent on framing Nick?

Sure, he had a temper. Yes, he sometimes got a little physical. But it was always my fault. If I hadn't made stupid mistakes, he never would hurt me. It's not like he wanted to. And he always felt terrible afterwards. Besides, nothing happened last Saturday. At least not that I could remember. And even if I'd done something wrong, Nick never would have hurt me so much that I'd end up in the hospital. It made no sense.

"Do you remember anything yet?" Dr. Bisbee's kind eyes regarded me, but I summoned anger toward him. Did he play psychologist with all his injured patients? Try to assign blame when no guilty party existed?

"I think you both should leave now." I rallied a frigid a voice as an ally. Although I harbored a fondness for both of them, I didn't want to hear them trash talk my husband any longer. Forcing a yawn, I turned my head away from them. "I'm going to rest for a while."

Both men murmured their goodbyes. As my breathing slowed, I overheard their discussion in the hall.

"How much longer will she remain hospitalized?"

"At least a few more days. I'd like to make sure that when I send her home, it's a day her husband will be at work so she can rest. Luckily, she's young and mending quickly. Still," Dr. Bisbee paused, "in this weakened state she's more defenseless than usual."

Their voices died away, and I slipped into a mindless sleep.

Between Saturday afternoon and Sunday evening, a handful of visitors stopped by, including repeat visits from Alice Ann, Catherine, and Jason. It thrilled Catherine I'd already hung up the fox head suncatcher. Not one person made reference again about how I got hurt. They all concentrated on my recovery. Principal Haberman even made a brief, uncomfortable visit to my bedside.

The one person who did not show up over the rest of the weekend was Nick. He called early Sunday morning to tell me he and a couple of his buddies were heading up to Sky Dancer Casino and Resort in Belcourt.

"You understand, right babe?" he'd said. "After all, this is my day off, and I've been spending so much time at the hospital."

Dr. Bisbee scheduled me for release on Tuesday. When I tried to reach Nick, I received a text message stating his plan to return home sometime late Monday night. Although glad that Nick brought my cell phone to me last week, with numerous digit deficits, it proved difficult to use.

Tuesday, by mid-morning, I dressed and sat in a wheelchair, ready to go. I called Nick to see if he was on his way.

"Uh, yeah, babe, it's like this. We didn't get in until about three this morning. I've got one hell of a killer headache, and I gotta sleep it off before work. Can't one of those doctors give you a ride?"

"Never mind, Nick. I'll figure it out." I clicked my phone to disconnect.

CHAPTER 13

Welcome Home

SINCE MY ACQUAINTANCE BASE in Grafton consisted mostly of students or teachers, I thanked Nakayla for ditching work to drive me home.

The house sat in silence when Nakayla's Jeep Cherokee pulled up in the driveway. She lifted my bags from the hatch while I wrangled my way out the passenger door. If I refrained from accelerating my pace, the bandaged ribs faintly throbbed but offered support. Small movements caused my sore muscles to ache but didn't jostle mending bones.

We climbed up on the porch with a couple of steps to go before reaching the front door, when a welcoming bark sounded from the side of the house.

"Vee!" Tears poured down my cheeks at the sight of him. I'd worried so much about him for the past week and a half but always pushed bad thoughts aside since I'd been helpless to search for my runaway dog. Nick had been too busy to trouble with finding Vee. But here he was, safe and sound. And as much as I wanted to bend over to pet him, I shouldn't yet.

"Whoa! Cool dog." Appreciation clung to Nakayla's words.

"C'mon, boy." I unlocked the front door, cautioning Nakayla and Vee to keep quiet. "I'm sure Nick's still asleep, and since his head aches..."

When we walked past the staircase, my left hand caressed the ornate wood of the banister. I could not imagine how something so beautiful hurt me.

Nakayla escorted me to the family room, otherwise known as Nick's lair, and got me settled. She fetched pillows from the downstairs guest room and pulled a comforter across me. Since she insisted it was lunch time, she fixed a peanut butter and honey sandwich for me, cut into triangles, and plunked ice cubes and a straw into a glass of apple juice.

"Thanks so much. You spoil me."

"Someone should." Nakayla's sour tone soon brightened. "Hey, take care now and don't hesitate to call if you need anything else. No, no, don't get up. I'll see myself out." She grinned and waved.

I emitted an audible sigh. It sure was good to be home. Vee, who stood to the side watching my arrival with interest, approached, and adjusted himself on the couch with me. Somehow, he seemed to know and respect every injured part of me. Also uncanny, Vee's clean and well-kept appearance. Where had he been if not roaming the streets these past few days?

I scratched the dog I adored behind his ears and around his neck. He warmed me better than the comforter. As my mind wandered, my limp hand slid off

Vee's head. He shoved his snout under my wrist, flipping my hand back up on his head. I resumed petting him, mesmerized by his golden eyes.

Somewhere deep in my brain, a voice instructed me to use my inner strength to heal. It told me I could expedite the entire process if I concentrated on the goal I desired. I shook my head and blinked. Had Vee communicated with me? I smiled that I even contemplated such a thing.

I turned my smile toward a set of footsteps, which produced the sexy image of the man I loved. Nick appeared from the kitchen, hair tousled above three days' growth of facial hair. Oh, and also without a shirt. He was, without a doubt, one of the hottest guys I'd ever seen.

"Hey, babe. What's for lunch?" Nick grinned. "Naw, I'm just kiddin'. It's good to have you home, though." He ambled over and kissed my forehead.

A low growl emanated from Vee's throat.

"Oh." Came Nick's disinterested response as he eyed Vee. "You found the dog."

What was up between these two? The voice emerged again. Remember!

Wait—what? Did Vee know something about Nick? Something he'd done? Impossible.

Vee didn't take his eyes off Nick. Even when he retreated to the kitchen to fix himself a sandwich, Vee watched his every move. Nick stopped again to kiss me goodbye before he left for work and eyed Vee with distaste.

I'd never seen a dogs' eyes radiate such pure hatred before. After Nick turned his back, Vee allowed his lips to curl back, exposing his bared teeth. Strangely, this display of behavior didn't threaten me. Rather, it comforted me.

* * *

Nick pampered me for the next few days. He let me camp out in the family room, went shopping, and made simple meals. I ventured no further than the kitchen and downstairs bathroom, and my recovery progressed nicely. The weather grew blustery and cold, but I basked in warm comforters and Vee's fur. I couldn't remember the last time I felt so at ease in my house.

Perhaps this lackadaisical attitude got me in trouble. Alice Ann stopped by late Saturday morning to drop off some homemade soup. She and her husband were on their way to Fargo to watch their nephew play hockey in one of the Force's opening games of the season. Since she couldn't stay long, I stood in the doorway while she caught me up on a couple of issues at school. A brilliant sun shone in, so I wasn't terribly chilled.

Nick walked by, observed my partner in conversation, and—hovering unseen in the background—he hollered, "Shut the damned door! Do you want our heating bill to go through the roof?"

My face flushed red while Alice Ann's registered shock. "Oh, sorry." She stammered. "I'd better go."

I almost slammed the door after she turned away. Son of a bitch! Tears burned in my eyes. How humiliating for Nick to treat me that way in front of someone else.

I glanced at Nick, averting my head as I shuffled into the kitchen. But his vacant eyes showed no realization that he'd embarrassed me. Rehashing the incident would do no good. Still, how mortifying.

Bumping into the refrigerator, I braced myself with the back of my hand. "Ouch." Stupid static electricity. Now that winter had inserted itself into northeastern North Dakota, I'd have to implement my system of frequently discharging to avoid these large and painful jolts. I discovered this trick years ago. By touching as many metal objects as possible throughout the day, I did not allow electricity to amplify in my body. I considered myself a bit of an anomaly since I didn't know another soul with this condition.

While in the kitchen, I poured myself a cup of strong black coffee. Today marked the perfect day for a change of scenery. "C'mon, Vee. Let's soak in some sun in the living room."

Vee, always by my side but never underfoot, trotted happily along with me. While the family room resonated comfort, not much outside light filtered through its windows. In the brief time I stood at the front door, my body rejuvenated in the sunnier atmosphere.

A smile hovered on my lips at the thought of snuggling with Vee and a cup of coffee in my favorite chair, but dissipated when I turned the corner into the living room. A large patch of sunlight illuminated the spot where my chair should have been.

"Nick?" I backed at a slow pace from the room, searching around with wild panic in case he moved my chair to a new location.

"Nick?" my voice rose and became hysterical. "Nick!"

Something wasn't right. A hyperventilation attack washed over me. I set my coffee cup on the fireplace mantle, pushing against the wall to steady myself.

To his credit, Nick padded in an instant to my side on bare feet. He grabbed my elbow with a look of genuine concern on his face.

"What's wrong, babe? What can I get you?"

I shook my head vehemently. "My chair, Nick. Where's my chair?"

"Oh." His shoulders relaxed. "That old thing." His eyes moved to Vee. "The stupid dog peed in it, and I couldn't get the smell out."

I kept shaking my head. "No, no, no. Vee wouldn't do such a thing. He never did, not even as a little puppy first time in our house. Never. Besides, you said he ran off."

"Right, right." Nick rolled his eyes and grinned. "Yeah, I was actually a little drunk, babe. So were my buddies. One of them must've peed in your chair, thinking it was a urinal. I joked about blaming it on the dog, and he said it was a good thing I had a dog to take the fall." At my tear-stained look of devastation, he continued. "I couldn't get the smell out. It was impossible."

It was ridiculous to develop sentiment over fabric, padding, and wood. But I did. I had cuddled in that chair through so many emotions, naps, excellent novels, and hot beverages, mourning the loss as if a dear friend had died.

"Oh, Nick." I sobbed.

"Babe, look," he turned me toward him, placing his hands on my shoulders, "I know how much that chair meant to you. Hey, how 'bout when you're walking around a little better, I'll take you chair shopping? My treat."

I swallowed hard and nodded. Finding a replacement for the chair I thought I'd own my whole life was not a shopping trip I wanted to participate in, but I could tell that Nick thought it would cheer me up. And a cheerful Jen promised a balance of happiness in the house.

"Let's go back to the family room," Nick urged. "I'll let you have control of the remote."

I needed some time to grieve. "In a bit."

Nick shrugged and left me.

After retrieving my coffee cup from the mantle, the liquid now boasted a temperature of lukewarm. I needed to blow my nose, and a freshly opened box of Kleenex sat beside the coffeepot. Again, I returned to the fireplace.

As with all the house's woodwork, the fireplace carvings included intricate patterns. My unbandaged fingers traced the meticulous designs. I grimaced when my eyes honed in on the thick layer of dust that accumulated on the miniature slats of wood. Nick's recent preoccupations blindsided his neglect to this beautiful old house. He would have an absolute fit if he saw it.

Nick. My eyes dropped to the hearth. I recalled a vague shell of myself, a crumpled mass on this exact floor. In response to the memory, some ghost pains manifested in my left elbow. I thought I heard myself crying, reeling from intense pain and shock. Vee whined, drawing my attention. I looked down at him, grateful for his companionship.

More recent events clouded memories of that injury but standing in the exact spot it happened brought everything to the surface. I sipped my coffee, lost in deep thoughts as I backtracked to the balustrade accompanying the stairs to the second floor. Perhaps revisiting this scene would invoke a memory of circumstances leading to the accident.

Gazing up the steps, I wondered what my head collided with to render me unconscious. At what point had my fingers bent and snapped? And what caused the cuts to my body? Had I been carrying something?

As I contemplated this area, Nick emerged from the kitchen, heading upstairs to get changed for work. "I'm gonna go in early and grab some pizza with the boys while we watch the Broncos game. Is that alright with you, babe? You can handle lunch, right?"

I assured him I'd be fine.

"What are you doing hanging out at the base of the stairs, anyway?"

"Just trying to recreate memories."

"Okay. Weird, but okay."

Nick was right. What a strange way to act. Nothing came of it either. No vibes, no disquiet, nothing to alert me that something bad happened here. Distracted by my disappointment, I took another sip of coffee.

"Damn! It's cold again."

After another trek to the kitchen, I decided to at least stand and bask in the sunlight that would have melted over my chair like butter on warm popcorn. Tears pricked my eyes when I reached that spot, but I brushed them aside. Time to grow up already.

Vee stood beside me in the rectangle of sun on the living room carpet. Rays of sunlight fell further back than my chair had stood because the chair would have entrapped incoming light. I remembered the many occasions since Vee arrived that we'd cuddled in my chair.

Ow! A sharp pain stabbed through my head. What the hell? All I'd been doing was daydreaming of Vee and me, curled up in a blanket, getting dumped on the floor, and Ow! Ow! Ow! Strobe lights flashed behind my eyelids. Hammers pounded in all four corners of my brain.

Every memory I had of that morning, two weeks ago, came flooding back.

CHAPTER 14

Escape

I HELD MY HEAD, but it didn't suppress the pain. Nor did it prevent the realization of what Nick had done to me. To us, I corrected, peering down at Vee.

How could everyone except me have known that Nick's violent temper landed me in the hospital? If he was capable of beating me into unconsciousness and lying about it, what else he could do?

Vee sensed my distress. He rubbed against my legs to comfort me. I viewed the room the way a tornado victim might upon revisiting her demolished house. The shock and horror of what happened replaced the uncertainty and fear of what would come. My jaw still hung slack when Nick bounded down the stairs, talking into his phone.

He took one look at me. "Oh shit." He said into his phone. "I can't leave quite yet. Save a cold one for me." He deposited his jacket, phone, and wallet at the bottom of the stairs, moving in slow steps toward me, his arms outstretched.

My head still pounded, and as much as I wanted comfort, I wanted none from this man. Not right now. I backed away along the wall and around the corner into the dining room. Vee backed away with me, baring sharp, white canines.

"Jen," Nick pleaded, "C'mon, babe. You know I didn't mean to do it."

"You lied to me about my chair." My voice trembled, but I kept on. "You hurt Vee. And you hurt me."

"I didn't mean to. I just wanted to scare you."

"But why, Nick? What did I do that provoked you to break my chair and break parts of me?" Perhaps the reminder of his serious anger issues constituted an unwise move, but he at least owed me an explanation.

Nick's eyes darkened, and a scowl smeared his features. A tinge of fear tugged at the base of my skull. Nick had never hurt me when I was injured before. But then again, he'd never put me in the hospital, either.

"It was that guy. You were practically kissing that guy! It looked like you were ready to get an effin' room with him! God dammit, Jen!"

My heart sank. He'd seen the picture of Jason and me, reacting pretty much the way I'd predicted, but he never waited to hear my side of the story.

He advanced on me until I cowered and backed into the counter that opened up from dining room into kitchen, framed by a white wooden border. I contemplated pulling myself onto and over the counter, but in my state, he'd beat me to the floor on the other side.

"Nick, please." How rapidly this conversation turned from him to me being the one begging—him for forgiveness, me for mercy. Vee observed the unfolding events from the other side of the dining room table. He was poised, ready to attack should I need help defending myself.

I pulled a chair out from the table and placed it between Nick and me, continuing to inch back to the kitchen doorway.

"Nick!" I hoped he heard me. "It was just a relay race. At a very public pep rally. At a school event! For gosh sakes, that was the father of one of my students. They were taking pictures for the yearbook!" My ribs ached from yelling and taking deep, anxious breaths.

"I am the only man you should be necking with!"

Obviously, he didn't recall that I'd asked him to escort me to the Homecoming Dance and activities earlier in the day. He played the "no getting out of work" card.

He flailed his arms in anger and exasperation, connecting with the chandelier hanging above the table. Somehow his hand wedged in the contraption, causing him to hurl one profanity after another. I hustled through the kitchen, grabbing my purse and keys from the counter. This was my chance to escape.

As I pulled the front door open, I heard breaking glass. Nick screamed. Part of me wanted to go back, check on him, and fix whatever had gone wrong. The self-preservation side of my brain won. Wearing nothing but fuzzy slipper socks, cotton jogging pants, and an oversized flannel shirt, I darted to my car—despite the rapid movement causing my aching body parts to protest. Vee followed at my heels, jumping in the car before me and settling into the passenger seat.

I saw no sign of Nick when I backed out the driveway and pulled onto the street. I also had no idea where to go. Would he hurt me again? That sure seemed his intention.

This was the first time I'd ever run from him, and I already feared the repercussions. It was getting so difficult these days to determine what would set Nick off. Granted, this time the fault lay with me—most definitely. I should not have asked about something that stirred up such a violent reaction in the first place.

But where to go? I hadn't visited anyone's house yet, and I didn't want to go to the gym or school. We lived a couple of blocks from Leistikow Park, so I drove in as far as the pavement led me. With any luck, if Nick was already looking, he would think I'd gone further from home. I stopped in the parking lot at the head of the walking trail. I gained a good visual of both roads coming into the lot, confident that if Nick approached by one of them, I could jet out the other.

"What do you think, Vee?"

The puppy in the passenger seat regarded me with eyes that held the wisdom of a much older dog. He pushed his snout into my right hand, bumping one of my splinted fingers, insisting on access.

"Ow, Vee. I hurt this one worse today." I peeled off layers of tape, sliding the splint off a finger trickling fresh blood. The knuckle at the base of that finger swelled into a grotesque knot. "Son of a bitch." I stared at it, beginning to cry anew from the pain my body radiated and from my helpless situation.

Vee whined at me. I took my hand from the steering wheel, absentmindedly scratching his head. Vee didn't seem to want me to pet him, though. He shook his head a couple of times, flipping my hand and catching it between his two front paws.

I couldn't make sense of what happened next. Vee began licking my finger from below the bottom knuckle clear up to the tip.

"Ew, Vee. Gross, stop." I tried to pull away, but Vee's paws clamped about my wrist. Mesmerized, I watched his large, canine tongue bathe my finger. The blood disappeared. After a few more laps, the swelling ebbed. When he pushed my hand back to me, that finger was no longer distorted, swollen, or bruised. In fact, as I bent and examined it, I realized incredulously that it straightened in perfect shape.

"Vee! How did you..." my voice trailed off when I noticed he'd curled up on the seat and fallen fast asleep. The effort he expended in this healing ritual exhausted him. I couldn't get over it. My beautiful puppy arrived out of the blue one day, as if by magic. In a bout of selfishness, I wished he would heal all my hurting parts. Still, immense gratitude filled my heart for one less aching appendage.

A movement outside the car caught my attention. A white vehicle rounded the bend. I turned the ignition and shifted into gear, ready to flee when Nick pulled into the lot. It wasn't Nick. An SUV full of young kids drove past.

Possibly a family heading to the ice-skating rink north of town, taking the leisurely route to get there.

My breathing slowed. I turned the car off again and pulled my phone from my purse. Who should I call? Where could I go? Listed as my first contact: Nick. The last person I wanted to talk to. Second on the list: Alice Ann. No good because she left town. Third contact: Charles. He would take me in, but I also realized he'd seek a confrontation. He'd hunt Nick down and get the shit beaten out of him. Besides, that uncomfortable sexual chemistry between us might ignite. So, who?

I began skimming the Grafton white pages until my eyes landed on the name Catherine. Fervently, I hoped Jason and his daughter owned a home phone. I was in luck.

Without conveying the issue over the phone, I asked Jason if I could stop over. I needed to warn him that Nick might want to seek revenge on him. Jason informed me that Catherine's plans included spending the weekend at a friend's house, but I was welcome to stop by. Even better, I thought. This would be a messy situation to explain in front of Catherine.

The address Jason gave me belonged to a house on Griggs Avenue. I pulled into his driveway, reluctant to leave my car sitting in plain sight. The sun I worshipped earlier now shone too brightly as I scrambled in humiliation to Jason's doorstep. He opened the door before I rang the bell, a look of shock registering on his face. He ushered me and my dog in, holding my elbow while escorting me to the couch.

"What's the matter, Jen? Did someone hurt you again?" This was one of the things I liked about Jason. While he suspected that someone beat me, he never outright accused Nick. Now was the time to reveal that secret—although maybe not all of it.

"No, nobody hurt me today." My voice stayed low, and I couldn't meet his eyes. "In fact, it's my fault for bringing it up. I guess I didn't realize that by asking him why he'd been mad would make him angry all over again."

Tears seeking freedom spilled from my eyes, landing like water bombs on my lap and arms. "It's just that he saw the picture. Have you seen the picture?" At his nod, I continued. "He was insanely jealous. I knew he would be, and now that picture is everywhere!" I regarded Jason in desperation. "What should I do?"

"Is he out looking for you?"

"I don't know. He's supposed to work today, but he hadn't gone in yet. He loves his job, so I can't imagine that he'd skip. Even me being in the hospital didn't keep him away from it. But now he might try to look for you, too!"

Jason's face hardened. "Let him try," he muttered, then jumped up. He requested my keys, telling me there was room in his garage for my car.

Less than a minute after he'd gone out, a shadow covered the living room window—so large that it obliterated the sunlight for several seconds. Hair stood on the back of my neck, my entire scalp tingling, until it passed by and disappeared.

What had that been? Had Nick commandeered a hovercraft?

I ran to the window, peering at the sky. Earlier, it resonated with a brilliant hue of blue with not a single cloud in sight. When Jason returned, I asked if he'd seen any large clouds or if someone or something ran through his front yard. He suggested I lay down for a while, that the stress my body suffered today was not conducive to the healing process. He led me to a guest bedroom with mint-green walls, a single window too high for anyone to peer in, and a large bed covered by a snowy white comforter.

Once I got situated, Jason sat on the bed beside me, cupping my face with his hands. He leaned in, bestowing a light kiss on my lips. "You are perfectly safe here." He assured me. "Now get some rest, and we'll figure everything out when you wake up."

The care and concern I read in his eyes convinced me that sleep in a safe place offered some solace. Meanwhile, his proximity took my breath away. Once I nodded my consent, his soft lips kissed mine. My eyelids fluttered shut. One tender moment, then he was gone.

* * *

When I awoke, dim light filtered through the small window. Daylight savings time ended in one more week, so I calculated the time at about six o'clock.

Events of the day came flooding back, and I panicked. I found the bathroom in my search for Jason. I found him in the family room at the back of the house. Local news flashed across the TV but with muted sound. Although engrossed in his laptop, he noticed me the second I appeared in the doorway.

"You look much more relaxed," he commented. "Come. Have a seat."

When I walked over to the couch, Vee jumped from the recliner he shared with Jason. I'd forgotten I brought Vee with me, surprised that he warmed to Jason. He took his rightful place by my side.

Jason explained how he'd locked up the house, leaving Vee as guard dog, while he and a friend checked things out at Grafton Country Club. Nick had been there, working the bar with a bandaged right hand.

I listened anxiously to his story before saying, "I guess it's a good thing he's ambidextrous."

"That's exactly what he said when someone asked how the injury affected his job performance. And get this: he said he'd been changing a light bulb in the crawl space by the garage when he'd slipped and messed up his hand. I guess he had to get a couple of stitches at the emergency room."

I cringed at that news. Our medical bills have already spiked to astronomic proportions. I needed to get back to work at both jobs as soon as possible. Our financial crisis wrapped itself around my head until Jason's next question startled me, "Hey, are you hungry? I'm about to whip something up for myself, and I'll have plenty. Plus, it's so much more enjoyable to eat with someone than alone."

My stomach growled in response. I hadn't eaten since breakfast, and I understood solitary meals all too well. I graciously accepted.

Jason, it turned out, possessed exceptional culinary talents. He baked spinach lasagna, stuffed tomatoes, and served homemade biscotti with coffee afterwards. I sighed, pushing back from the table. "That was heavenly."

"My pleasure." Jason grinned. "I enjoy cooking, when I have the time."

"So do I."

"Something else we have in common." Jason walked around behind me to massage my neck and shoulders. His hands worked at the knots harboring along my spine. I closed my eyes and let my head fall forward for a minute. I knew what I had to do. I pulled away and stood up.

"I'm sorry, Jason, but I think I need to go home tonight."

Jason's eyes opened wide and his head kind of jerked to the side. "Okay, Jen. I'm trying hard not to ask if you're sure. Didn't you just come over here today half-dressed and out of your mind with fear for your own safety? What's going to happen if you go home? Will he hurt you?"

Jason looked so genuinely distraught that I walked back to him and held out my arms. We embraced, and I brought my mouth close to his ear. "The next two days are Nick's days off. If I'm not there when he comes home tonight, things will only escalate. My home was not safe when I left today, but I think he'll have settled down by the time he gets off work."

He swept a keen gaze over my face. "I'm not sure that's the right thing to do. I... I have to be honest with you, Jen. I care deeply for you," I tried to pull away, but he held me in a tight grip. "I know you're married and all, but he's not a good guy. I'm convinced he abuses you mentally and physically. I can't bear the thought of you going back to him and being hurt worse."

Aw shit. I liked Jason, too. In different circumstances, I'd likely crawl into bed with him without a second thought. But my life, the way I'd chosen it, did not adhere to that scenario.

"Jason," I searched into blue eyes, "I really like you. And I trust you. That's why I called and why I came over today. The attraction I feel toward you is unbelievable." That same attraction sprang to life where we stood, joined at the hips. I tried to fight the desire sweeping through me, "But the reality is, I am married. I know Nick well enough to realize that I have to be there tonight when he comes home. I'll keep my cell phone with me at all times. I promise to call if I need help." I gazed at him, pleading with my eyes.

"Do you have any idea how guilty I would feel if something happened to you?"

"I don't think it will come to that." I leaned forward, kissing him with a fierce intensity, and using much more tongue than appropriate for a married woman.

"Let's hope not," he whispered back.

Jason escorted me, slumber apparel and all, to his garage and my awaiting car. Once there, I pressed my body to his again for one last kiss. With Jason, protection surrounded me. I didn't fear what might set him off. Where I ventured, anything was possible.

CHAPTER 15

Back to School

I DROVE HOME THROUGH dark streets, getting confused on directions only once. For some reason, all the streetlights went out and forced me to guess what my headlights displayed.

At home I marched to the dining room where a mangled mess of a chandelier and a small puddle of blood awaited me on the dark-stained oak table. The chandelier weighed more than I should have lifted, but I carried it to the corner of the room, anyway.

My body ached anew by the time I fell into bed a little after eleven o'clock. As per his custom, Vee laid down at my feet on the bed. First, I couldn't get comfortable. I think Vee may even have resented my tossing and turning. My mind wouldn't allow me to sleep, either, racing with scenes from today and potential scenarios for later tonight. Had Jason been right? Should I have stayed at his place?

No! I firmly believed that being here would calm Nick back down. He always wanted to know my whereabouts. Who knew what type of havoc he might wreak if I stayed away? The punishment for such behavior would be atrocious. This made me nervous again. I glanced at my phone, charged and sitting on the bedside table. At Jason's insistence, I programmed 911 into speed dial. He tried to get me to promise to call if Nick so much as raised his voice to me.

I dozed off at some point, awakened by Vee nudging my leg, before jumping off the bed. I heard Nick set his keys down and climb the stairs with an unsteady gait. Floorboards creaked. I could scarcely breathe for fear of what might happen next. My entire body tensed in anticipation of needing to run. After all, the last time he'd awoken me in anger, he smashed a chair on my head.

Nick's breath filled an otherwise silent room with ragged gasps.

"Jen," he sobbed my name. "Jen. You came home to me."

More laborious breathing. He pulled the covers back on his side of the bed, sliding between the sheets next to me. He attempted loving ministrations, but he jerked me close with a little too much force.

His tears dribbled down the back of my neck along with his kisses. Moving the hair away, he whispered against my neck, "I'm so sorry, babe. I'll never do anything like that again. Please, don't ever leave me."

Nick's hand crept under the oversized tee shirt I'd chosen to wear over flannel pajama pants. The bandage on his hand abrasively scratched my skin, but I made no sign suggesting that the way he touched me wasn't entirely pleasant.

"Babe?"

"Yes, Nick?"

"Do you think we could have, you know, like make-up sex?" Besides feeling sad, Nick was drunk.

"I really don't think my body can handle that yet. I'm still mending bones and all."

"C'mon." he said gruffly. "I'll be gentle."

Gentle escaped his vocabulary and capability, but his entire sex act usually lasted a few minutes. I tried hard to make my grunts of pain sound like gasps of ecstasy.

When I descended the steps not twenty minutes later, I could've sworn Vee stared at me in disapproval.

"He wasn't always such a bad guy," I whispered in self-defense. "C'mon, Vee. I guess with no more chair, we're permanently on the couch now."

His sexual needs temporarily sated and his anger momentarily dispelled, Nick became a pleasant individual for the next two weeks. He either brought home some sort of carry-out food, or purchased simple meal ingredients that either he or I threw together.

Jason called to check on me a couple of times when he surmised Nick would be at work. He and his friend continued to spy on Nick at the bar when they had the chance.

Charles was brazen enough to stop over one snowy day, long after Nick departed for work. He commented on my beauty, asked if I remembered the accident, and kissed the back of my hand. He also kissed my wrist, just below the pulse.

Before he left, he asked again about the accident. I claimed I couldn't recall anything.

* * *

The day before the four-week anniversary of my accident, I kept an appointment with Dr. Bisbee. Like Charles, he questioned my memory. I realized he didn't believe me, but he chose not to push the subject. To my satisfaction, he gave me medical clearance to work half days the following week. If I deemed myself capable, I could try full days the week after that. He wanted me to wait a full two more weeks before I even considered returning to my part-time work at the gym.

Elated that I'd engage as an active, contributing member of society once again, I gave Dr. Bisbee a quick and gentle hug, promising him I'd be more careful. He informed me that from here on out, he only wanted to see me in the grocery store or at the park.

Nick seemed to take my medical release as an opportunity to return to his "good ole boy" ways. His supportive and caring manner never lasted, but it still disappointed me when he reverted to his carefree self. As long as he kept his anger at bay, I'd adjust.

My students greeted me in the hallway my first morning back, their demeanors ricocheting with enthusiasm. Those with afternoon classes groaned when they heard I'd work half days this week.

Alice Ann cornered me Tuesday morning, looking uncomfortable but determined to get an answer. Nick's behavior when she'd stopped by a few weeks ago disconcerted her, and she couldn't help noticing something amiss in our relationship. She'd texted me several times, alluding to that incident, but I always roses-and-rainbowed over her concerns.

Today no escape route circumvented her perseverance. I told her point blank that things were fine, that Nick suffered from a rough night and early morning. I found that by keeping eye contact with a person and not smiling when I lied, the typical listener believed my version of the truth.

Alice Ann's eyes narrowed, but she gave a curt nod before moving away. "Okay then." Her face relaxed, and she released a genuine smile. "Well, I'm glad you're here. Your sub is getting a little hard to handle. When are you back full time?" She grabbed my hands in earnest.

I laughed at her. "Doc says next week if I'm really good, and I've been trying to be so good."

Catherine came in extra early on Wednesday, excited to greet me. "Mrs. Adesco, I'm so glad you're back!" I loved this girl and her sincere nature.

"I'm having a hard time understanding these verbs we've been learning about. That substitute didn't explain things, and I'm so lost. Is there any way—I mean, my dad said that if you were available—you could come over tomorrow for a Thanksgiving brunch at our house. He said if you could help me with the Spanish verbs and learning how to work them, he would pay attention, too. That way he could help me out in the future if I get stuck. Do you think you could do that, Señora?"

It didn't take me long to ponder her request. Catherine was such a sweet girl. Her dad was also so, so nice, and very hot. "Claro que sí, Caterina. I'd be happy to."

I jotted a note for Nick in the morning, saying that I had left for a school meeting.

CHAPTER 16

Thanksgiving

JASON'S CULINARY TALENTS HAD impressed me the last time I visited his house, and my taste buds tingled on high alert before I even turned onto his street. He did not disappoint.

Catherine seated me at the dining room table by a window that looked out across their front yard and down the street. A little voice in my head told me this spot offered a perfect lookout post for Nick, so at least I'd know if he drove by. He'd never understand the innocence of me helping a student at the house of the same man he'd caught me with in a compromising position on film.

Like a waiter in a restaurant, Jason served the ladies in his house. Coffee and orange juice for beverages, quiche Lorraine, grapes, brie, and wheat crackers. While serving me, Jason whispered, "Would you like me to move your car?"

In response, I handed him my car keys. He'd shelter my vehicle in his garage and out of sight. After telling her I parked too close to her curbside mailbox, I distracted Catherine by pulling out some index cards with Spanish verbs written on them. I thought we'd start with definitions before moving on to conjugations.

By the time we finished brunch, she mastered the verb meanings. Jason suggested we move into the family room from there. I used a large sketch pad to demonstrate the formula for conjugating regular –ar verbs. I illustrated why Spanish verbs conjugated with greater ease than English verbs. Using my favorite analogy, I described it as a puzzle, showing how everything fit into place for proper completion.

Catherine asked an occasional question, but Jason sat in quiet observation. We practiced this process for the next hour until she conjugated, identified, and translated regular –ar verbs flawlessly. At length, she asked if she could check her texts. Afterwards she said that her friend, Shiann, would stop by in a few minutes on her way to a shopping trip at the mall in Fargo. She offered profuse thanks, convinced these verbs would have evaded her forever without my extra help.

Jason pondered the lesson and commented that he wished his French teacher had explained verbs this well. He suspected his journey with French verbs became arduous due to receiving the entire process in a quick presentation instead of a slower, more thorough explanation like the one I'd just performed.

He took my right hand, tracing up and down each finger with his index finger, an arts and crafts activity I had done as a child with crayons to make a Thanksgiving turkey. This was a thousand times more erotic.

When he finished tracing it, he started over. I licked my lips as nerves got the best of me, uncertain what to say.

Midway through the second trace, he glanced at my other hand, resting in my lap.

"Wow," He turned my hand over to peruse the entire thing, "didn't you have broken fingers on both hands? How did this one heal more quickly?" He turned it over a couple more times before continuing his caress.

How to explain that my dog wielded a magical tongue? You don't, or people think you're crazy.

Since Vee first showed me his abilities, I indulged a couple more times, letting him heal—one injury at a time—all the sore and mangled spots on that hand. If it didn't seem to exhaust him so much, I'd let him heal more of me. Each time he completed his magic, he fell into a sleep close to death.

"Perhaps the breaks were a little more complex on my left hand. I guess I don't know, I'm just glad to be healing. And," I stood, withdrawing my hand from his, "I should be getting home."

Jason rose, standing in front of me with no room to pass. "Are you sure you should leave? Won't he still be home?"

Every fiber of my being sensed Jason's proximity. My lust hormones surfaced and demanded satiation. I'd connected with Jason already, and I predicted he would be a sensual, thoughtful lover. Nick had been the only man I'd ever made love to and thoughtful rarely entered his vocabulary.

I peered up at Jason. Staring into his eyes, I rose on my tiptoes, falling against him as I pressed my lips against his eager counterparts. His body responded by eliminating any space between us. I ached with a need I could not fulfill.

But our kiss inspired a wave of guilt. I was a married woman, obligated to be more responsible. Just because a guy demonstrated kind gestures, cared about me, and didn't hurt me, did not mean that he wanted to get in my pants. Geez, if I started interpreting the intentions of every nice guy this way, I'd end up labeled the town whore.

When I pulled away and stepped back, he let me. Part of me wanted him to hold on, to stay with him. "I need to go home. Nick might want lunch before he goes to work."

"He hasn't..."

"He's been fine." I interrupted. "He hasn't touched me." My face covered in insta-blush because he had touched me in the bedroom.

Reluctance slowed my steps as I gathered my things, holding out a hand for my keys. Placing them in my open palm, he engulfed that hand and keys with both of his hands. "Stay."

"I can't." I shifted my feet and squirmed.

He released my hand. "I guess I understand. But know that you are always welcome here." He emphasized the word always.

I inclined my head in a mute nod. I let him carry my supplies to my car and waited for him to open the garage door. This time, daylight guided my progression home.

Surprisingly, at 11:36, Nick's truck no longer cast a shadow on our driveway. He'd placed a note on top of mine, saying that he went to work early to decorate for the huge corporate Thanksgiving Bash. The CEO from MacDon Industries in Winnipeg offered Nick's boss a hefty sum to open up late on a national holiday, using them as an employee and spouse corporate retreat. All club employees working it got paid time and a half plus a free dinner. His note suggested that we feast on turkey Friday at lunch. I sent him a text letting him know that I'd cook part of the meal this afternoon and the rest tomorrow morning.

"So, Vee," I gushed over the red canine at my side, "it looks like it's just you and me for the rest of Thanksgiving."

He responded with a happy bark, wagging his tail and licking the hand I'd used to scratch under his neck. He accompanied me to the kitchen where I pulled out the turkey along with necessary components to ready it for the oven. I assembled ingredients for homemade bread and cinnamon rolls. Each of these needed plenty of time to rise before baking.

While kneading the dough for honey wheat bread, I glanced out the kitchen window and froze in terror. Back by the tree line, in front of the hammock, stood a small child wearing an oversized green coat and a plastic Frankenstein mask. Not one of those new latex masks, but one with a piece of elastic going around the back of your head. One like I'd seen in pictures of my mom, back in the 70s, on Halloween.

My first thought, after the momentary shock, was that someone trespassed in our yard. Was that disrespectful child planning to use our yard as a shortcut to his destination? The flaw with this theory remained: the child stood motionless, staring right at me through our kitchen window.

What the hell? This defined super creepy and was disturbing on so many levels. Halloween occurred a month ago. Wrong holiday, young miscreant.

Also confusing, how Vee stood at the back door, peering out but neither barking nor agitated. How could the figure not alarm him? Usually even a squirrel running through the yard got him all excited. I appreciated his possessiveness and wary nature around strangers.

I completed the necessary three minutes of kneading my dough, most of the time keeping the stationary masked figure in my line of view. I covered the dough with a towel, washed my hands, and—while drying them—looked back out the window. I froze again. The figure was gone!

I hustled to the doors, locking them both, before rushing to various windows, half afraid to see the child standing right in front of one of them, holding a bloody hatchet. Curse my best friend in high school for making me watch a string of horror movies several summers ago.

After checking all the windows on the main floor twice, I returned to the kitchen. A jittery mess, my eyes kept darting to the kitchen window, but our backyard remained empty.

I dined on turkey and mashed potatoes that evening, offering Vee a few slices of turkey. After all, it was Thanksgiving, and I exuded extreme gratitude for the companionship of my puppy. Later, I enjoyed a slice of warm, fresh-from-the-oven bread and formed cinnamon rolls to bake early the next morning.

The night seemed blacker than usual, cloud cover that persisted all day obliterated every sliver of light from the moon and stars. Yet at one point, when running a glass of cold water from the tap, I swore a spot right beside the hammock was a little darker than the rest. Maybe my pixies were checking in? Or maybe not.

To take my mind off things, I relaxed in the family room glued to the first of many Hallmark Christmas shows I'd view this season. I always went in for happy, sappy romances. Nick hated these shows. If he caught me watching one, he'd say one of two things: "Don't you have something more productive you should be doing?" or "Isn't this the show where two people meet and are attracted to each other, but then there's a misunderstanding, then one of their exes shows up, but they get together in the end, laughing about their adventures?"

Due to his holiday work schedule, I planned on basking in many Nick-free evenings.

After 2:00 a.m. I heard Nick grumbling as he mounted the stairs. My body set itself on edge, ready to move in a split second if Nick harbored cruel intentions. As he kicked off his shoes and peeled off his skin-tight blue jeans, I concluded minimal amounts of peeved emotions drove him.

"Dammit, Jen," he muttered, pulling the covers aside. "Why'd you lock the deadbolt? Took me forever to find that key."

"Sorry, Nick. Someone was in our backyard this afternoon and it kinda creeped me out." The arm he threw across me in preparation for slumber tightened.

"What? Was someone stalking you? And trespassing? Dammit! Alright, that's fine then. Glad you're safe, babe." Moments later, his snores resounded in our bedroom.

On our nightly trek downstairs, I whispered to Vee. "See? He does care about me."

Although an impossibility, I imagined Vee rolling his eyes.

Even though I knew Nick wanted me to be safe, I still double checked the front door. Unlocked. Geez, Nick, my mind screamed. What if that scary child, or little person, still watched and walked right into our house? No, Vee would alert me to its presence.

Ultimately, I rationalized no person would go to the trouble of standing in the cold for the better part of twelve hours for the sole purpose of gaining access to our house. I nodded to convince myself that this made sense, but then stifled a scream when I walked by the closet door under the staircase. Expecting to see the scary child, I nearly woke my husband at the sight of myself in the full-length mirror.

I had no idea I was that scary, I joked to calm my nerves. Perhaps that's why the child stared at me today. Fear paralyzed him...yeah, right.

After that incident, sleep skittered out of reach. With no Christmas movies showing in the middle of the night, I set the TV to 90s sitcoms to lull myself to sleep.

* * *

The extended weekend continued with no further incidents and offered plenty of time to rest and relax. By Sunday, I'd almost forgotten about the costumed child in our yard. I texted my principal to let him know I wouldn't sign up for any marathons yet, but I planned to come back full time for the coming week.

By Sunday evening, I was ready to get out. Much as I loved the days of baking and cooking, I'd stayed indoors long enough. I rolled off the couch in the family room where Nick intently watched the Bourne saga. Intriguing, yes. Hot main character, also yes. But I became bored with the James Bond predictability of the series. My body, while still tender in many places, yearned for fresh air and exercise.

"C'mon, Vee. Let's go for a walk."

This registered with Nick, who wasn't sure he liked it. "Are you sure that's smart? I mean, it's already dark out."

Armed and ready, I responded, "Please, Nick. It's Grafton, North Dakota. Nothing ever happens here. Besides, I've got Vee for companionship and protection."

Nick eyed my canine friend, who bore an uncanny resemblance to a near-grown dog. "Yeah, I guess." He lowered himself back to his recliner. "But babe, can you bring me another beer before you go?"

I attached a leash to Vee's collar, even though I suspected he'd stay by my side without one. Grafton passed a leash law, and I thought it best not to tempt him with the ducks inhabiting the nearby lake. I decked out in ski pants, my winter coat, gloves, and snow boots. An inch or so of older snow coated the ground, and fresh powder still sifted through the clouds, enhancing streets and sidewalks with an even layer of sparkling fluff. Although unnecessary this evening, the boots kept my feet warmer than tennis shoes.

We headed to Leistikow Park through a veil of light snowfall. I'd walked around the lake a couple of times last summer, when I thought I could spare the time to enjoy the outdoors and explore. Before school started. Before Vee. And, sadly, before my body was broken into a mangled mess.

Dammit, Nick.

Tears pricked at my eyes, but angry blinks forced them back. Things would be better from now on. He'd finally learned his lesson. And I was so, so tired of always needing to coddle some part of my body. I also detested explaining away my injuries like the world's biggest klutz.

In silence, Vee and I walked a block to reach the park. Once we arrived, two options opened before me: I could walk the lake's edge, hugging a path most of the way around; or walk along the tree line by the road for a quarter mile until that path curved and merged. At that point it swept away from the lake, paralleling the road through the park, before dipping to a bridge that crossed an overflow point. From there it went uphill, passed a pavilion, curved left, following the lake at a bit of an elevation, through a meandering expanse of an arboretum, until it rejoined the trail head.

I opted to walk the tree line, avoiding the path by the boat ramp where the ducks flocked. Even with large lamp poles placed strategically around the park, the massive pine trees cast ominous shadows. Vee trotted beside me, sniffing with appreciation at occasional trees. After walking for a few minutes, he posed as if ready to lunge.

I took two more steps before something darted from the brush to my right and across the sidewalk in front of us. Vee spun me sideways, trying to run after whatever scared the shit out of me.

"Vee! Knock it off!"

He strained against the leash, wanting to chase... Two more steps and I saw the wary rabbit, wide-eyed and immobile. Perhaps he didn't realize his camouflage failed on the snowy landscape. I stomped, trying to make him run off. I'd pay better attention to Vee's cues so that I wouldn't be startled the next time we encountered a cottontail. Vee relinquished his idea of pursuit, adapting to my pace once again. We reached the end of the tree line and turned to reconnect with the interior path.

I enjoyed having the park to ourselves. Along this stretch of sidewalk, two paved parking areas adjoined. The first sat empty, but I spotted a stationary vehicle near the second one. No one had driven through the park since we began our walk. Perhaps it entered from the west side. As we approached the car, I squinted through large, wet snowflakes. No visible tire tracks patterned the fresh snowfall.

Someone must've parked some time ago. Were they hiking? Ice fishing? Were there two people making out in the car? How embarrassing. I averted my eyes in case that scenario unfolded. I gave the car wide berth, stepping into the grass at the other side of the path. A quick glance toward the car revealed no one in the front seat.

A movement drew my attention back to the car, something within a car seat in the back seat. I surrendered a violent shiver, not from the cold temperatures, but by what I thought I saw in that back seat. Was that a baby? Had some asshole left a baby on a cold winter night to freeze to death? My God! Was it dead? Did I smell smoke?

I backtracked to the car, horrified by what I might find. The relief washing over me when the baby moved turned to terror. Its head spun to look at me. It was no baby—a vicious clown with pointed teeth grinned at me from the car seat!

A scream couldn't even form in my throat. I tugged Vee's leash, but he didn't seem to want to leave. In fact, he wagged his tail in expectation.

"Vee!" I pleaded, pulling harder on his leash. "Let's go!"

The clown kept grinning, his ugly head lolling about in the car seat. I convinced Vee to come, and he plodded beside me. I ran in the pathetic, slow fashion of an injured non-athlete. Cumbersome boots landed at awkward angles. My ribs ached from so many deep breaths. I slowed, holding my chest to catch my breath, and looked back to see if the maniacal clown followed me with a cleaver. However, he remained in that car seat, watching me. The parking area light glinted off his sharp teeth.

I began running again. What the hell was that thing? Could it have been some kind of sick, battery-operated toy? But if so, why had it sat motionless until I came along? Way too creepy!

CHAPTER 17

Mistletoe

I CONTINUED ON THE trail, left with no recourse. The overexertion forced me to slow, and I recalled the spooky child I'd seen in my yard last Thursday. Were psychotic creatures stalking me? None of this made sense. When I got home, I'd tell Nick about the stupid clown. He'd come check it out and punch the prankster. Yes, I decided to take this course of action.

I comforted myself with that knowledge while I trekked through the arboretum. But the closer I got to home, the more I doubted my decision. First of all, Nick would burst into uproarious laughter. Second, he'd ban me from taking walks at night. Third, he might forbid me to go to the park at all. I loved the outdoors and nature, despite my horrendous allergies.

My parents took me to a specialist for allergy tests in the tenth grade. The nurse explained that they would introduce 75 potential allergens through tiny pricks on my back. Everything causing an allergic reaction would swell to the size of a dime.

Two nurses scratched and dropped for an eternity before leaving to let my allergies manifest. By the time the nurses reentered the room, I writhed from the itching. Even during a horrid case of chickenpox in third grade, I hadn't itched to that extreme.

By the obvious way their eyes bugged out, I presented an unusual case. They gave me a teddy bear and a lollipop, smoothing a soothing cream over my back while revealing the reason for my intensive itching. One nurse remarked, "Well, you are quite the anomaly. Usually, our patients are allergic to a handful of the most common allergens. You, however, are allergic to 72 out of 75. These things range from dust to pollen, to trees, to grasses, to mold—pretty much everything from the outdoors. You should stay inside."

"Oh, and not only that," she added, "Your reactions did not swell to dime sized. They are more like quarters or half dollars."

Well, hell, I'd thought. They need to fix this. I chewed fiercely on my lollipop, squeezed the teddy, and waited for the itching to subside. I found out later that they reserved the suckers and bears for younger kids, but they'd felt sorry for me after the massive swollen spots appeared. And the gimmicks helped. A little.

Nothing ever came from that appointment, though. Whether my parents had balked at the expense of allergy shots or simply wanted me tested to feed their morbid curiosity, I never knew. I comprehended I suffered an insane amount of allergies. Seasonal ones competed for the worst.

Exiting the park, I questioned again the wisdom of telling Nick about this encounter. By the time Vee and I mounted the front porch steps, I decided against it.

Besides, I rationalized in the shower that night, who would believe that a midget clown loitered in a baby seat in the back of a car? Seriously! Maybe I imagined the whole thing. My mom always told me I inherited her over-active imagination. I detested horror movies for that exact reason. Too often I recreated those scary scenes in my everyday life, kind of like the events from this weekend.

As I readied for bed, I smiled and realized this must be the case. My mind grew bored since I'd lived as a shut-in for so long. It manifested images to get me excited, to get my heart racing. I fell into a dreamless sleep; I was glad I'd return to work full time starting tomorrow.

* * *

I had spread out my clothes in the spare bedroom on the main floor, my routine whenever I worked or had an early appointment. Vee's ears drooped and his tail hung motionless. He knew that I'd leave him for the entire day once again. Before I left, I ruffled his fur, looked him in the eyes, gave him a big kiss on his head, and reassured him we'd play fetch soon. As usual, he did not stay in the house with Nick but disappeared somewhere outside.

My students were ecstatic, or so they claimed, to have me back full time. I missed Spanish immersion every day and bordered on overzealous while teaching new concepts. My first week back, more than one student told me I was crazy, to which I replied each time, "I prefer the word eccentric."

I related well to the self-proclaimed social misfits and outcasts at school. My whole life I'd never fit in with my peers, always on the outside observing social groups, subgroups, and loners. The isolation hit hard as my family moved almost every year. After a time, I decided to showcase my special brand of eccentric. What place could an adult display their eclectic tastes and not be judged? In a high-school classroom as a foreign language teacher, of course.

I spent that first full week back at school engrossed in lesson plans, grading, and evaluating students. I didn't give more than a fleeting thought to the bizarre beings I'd viewed over the extended weekend. In fact, I didn't contemplate them again until Friday afternoon.

Catherine stopped by my room after school. "I sure am glad you're our full-time teacher again, Mrs. Adesco. I really do learn best from you."

"Gracias, Caterina. You make me feel like a successful educator when you say things like that." I winked at her. "Don't worry, I'll try not to let it go to my head."

"Oh, Señora. You deserve more confidence." This coming from one of the shyest girls in all of my classes. Despite her uplifting words today, Catherine looked bummed.

"Hey, what are you doing this afternoon?" While I enjoyed my down time alone after school, I sensed Catherine wasn't ready to go home to an empty house to wait for her dad to get off work.

"Why don't you take a walk with me and my dog around the park?" With two of us there, we'd be safe from horror-show monsters. And if one dared to mess with us? Well, then I'd have a witness.

Her face lit up. "Mrs. Adesco, I would love that!"

"I've got some things to finish up here at school, then I could drop by your house to pick you up in about an hour."

"Sounds great. I'll text my dad."

When she left, the entire school fell silent. With December right around the corner, I figured my fellow staff members rushed home to get a jump start on Christmas preparations. Peering outside, I saw the weekend snow had all but melted. Icy crystals weighed down a few dead leaves, while others scurried past my window in the brisk breeze.

Bending to pick up the invariable pencil someone dropped, along with some paper fringes, I stood abruptly when a decent-sized object thudded into one of my windows.

"Oh shit." I spotted the twitching black feathery mass on the dried grass. I hated it when birds hit windows. Fervent wishes begged for this one to either fly away, or to die and end its suffering. As I moved closer, a large shadow covered the bird and three of my six windows.

Turning to see what obstructed the sun, direct solar radiation hit me full force. I gasped, throwing my hands up to shield my eyes. When I turned back to the befuddled and entirely miserable bird, all I found was an empty yard. I shivered and said a quick prayer of healing for the stunned bird. Deciding my cue to leave arrived, I gathered necessary items for the weekend and drove to Catherine's house.

Not a second after I pulled into her driveway, Catherine bounded from her house. She already appeared in better spirits. "My dad said he'd meet us at the pavilion by the flagpole at five."

"That sounds perfect." I glanced at my watch to see it was minutes after 3:30. Secretly, I harbored excitement that I'd see Jason again tonight.

Vee greeted me at my car like always, no matter the time of day. Catherine squealed when she saw him. "Oh my gosh! Mrs. Adesco! He looks just like the suncatcher I got you!"

"I know!" Sharing in her excitement, I introduced Catherine to Vee, who automatically took to her. "Now come see where I hung your suncatcher."

I led Catherine in the front door and around the corner to the base of the staircase. To our right nestled the hugest, most comfortable window seat I'd ever seen or sat on in my life. This window seat took the place of my all-time favorite armchair, the one I thought I'd still enjoy as a great-grandmother, the one Nick destroyed. I forced my thoughts to stop there. No sense dredging up memories of him almost destroying me at the same time. Besides, I had company.

There, high in the middle of the center window, sat the protective fox-head suncatcher Catherine had given me.

"It looks beautiful there," she breathed.

"I think so, too. You can stay down here with Vee, if you'd like, while I get changed."

Catherine agreed, so I mounted the steps in rapid succession, considering how many parts of me still sported tender muscles and faded bruises.

We started our hike alongside the tree line around four o'clock. As we reached the head of the walking trail, the point where both paths along the lake converged, we opted to enter the forested part of the park. Our choice became a virtual attribution; two females—braver together than alone—walking at dusk, in a wild and unprotected area, accompanied by one fearless, foxy dog.

The long dirt trail hugged Park River for about half a mile before crossing a bridge and delving into thicker trees.

"Wow! It really gets dark back here." Catherine remarked. "I guess I've never come this far. And I've never been at the park this late."

I hastened to reassure her. "It's not that late yet. We're almost halfway through the trail. We'll be out way before dark. Besides, we have our noble leader to protect us."

Vee helped us along the path by leading us, and he continuously sniffed the air, alert to any danger. Catherine was right. In this wooded area, darkness descended before night bathed the rest of the park. I shook my head, clearing images of little gremlins I swore I glimpsed darting from tree to tree to take cover. Why they caused no alarm for Vee, I couldn't fathom.

But no sense in divulging these hallucinations to Catherine. Instead, I spoke of my limited familiarity with botany.

"Leaves of three, let them be."

"Beware when walking, be not lazy. Stinging nettles can drive one crazy."

Catherine shot me a quizzical look. "Do they really say those things?"

I struggled to grin at her when I saw another creature scurry behind a large clump of nettles. "Not the nettle thing, no. But the ditty about leaves of three? That absolutely works for poison ivy or poison oak. I learned it way back in Girl Scouts."

"You were a Girl Scout?" she asked while we crossed a small bridge over an offshoot of the river that snaked along the north side of Grafton.

"I did it mostly for the cookies and the prizes." Joking put us a little more at ease in the ever-encroaching darkness. Soon we reached the northernmost point of the trail. From there it dropped sharply south, and into a well of darkness. Vee had not noticed the grotesque figures sprinting around in the woods. A scene flashed through my head of similar figures, scurrying about in urgency to protect or find something. As we headed south, they disappeared from my line of vision. Were these my pixies, manifesting themselves in a visual form?

In silence we jogged down the rest of the trail, Vee's happiness clear as he ran in front of us. At the trail's end, we broke into the remaining late-November daylight. At the far end of the parking lot, a vehicle sat next to mine.

Never had I been so thrilled to see Jason. "Dad!" Catherine broke away from us and ran up to him.

"Hey, guys." The warmth of Jason's smile slid over both of us. "Hi, Vee." He scratched Vee behind the ears. "Are you keeping these girls safe in the spooky woods?"

"Yeah," I said in way of an apology. "Darkness kind of crept up on us. After several weeks as a resting invalid, I guess I didn't realize how short the days were getting."

"Tomorrow's December already!" Excitement burst from Catherine's lips.

I contemplated this announcement. "You're right. Hey, if you don't have any plans for tomorrow, would you like to come to my place to help me decorate for Christmas? This klutz would appreciate any help she can get." My eyes roamed over to Jason. "It would be helpful if you could come, too, for heavy lifting and tricky hanging."

"Done. What time would you like us there?"

I smiled at his eagerness. "How about around four? I'll whip up a few holiday treats and feed you supper in exchange for your decorating expertise."

Vee seemed to nod in agreement to this plan. I gave them my address and rushed to my car. While I hadn't noticed the cold during our trek, the night air seeped through the dense fabric of my blue jeans.

In order to dispel the cold, I took a hot shower when I got home. Afterwards, I baked gingerbread men, spritz cookies, and some raspberry thumbprint cookies with almond glaze. Fully enclosed on three sides, and three quarters on the fourth, my kitchen retained heat well. Vee and I fell asleep that night to the pleasant aroma of vanilla, almond, and gingerbread. When Nick collapsed on the bed, filling the room with colossal snores, I tiptoed downstairs to the window seat. The scents of fresh pastries lingered in our house.

* * *

I roused myself early, prepared a grocery list, and headed to the store. Once back home, I checked the guest bedroom closet on the main floor for Christmas decorations. A mere couple of boxes surfaced, so I climbed the steps to check in the upstairs bedroom closets. Careful not to awaken Nick, I slowly turned the doorknob to one of the extra bedrooms, easing the door open far enough to slip in. I discovered daily more loose floorboards and creaky hinges, typical in an older house. Two such hinges groaned in protest after the swollen door frame shrieked when I tugged on the closet handle.

Holy hell! Nick would be furious if he caught me rummaging through boxes of worthless trinkets. In response to my noisy sleuthing, I heard Nick's loud yawn and simultaneous fart. Shit. I held my breath, listening intently to his activities. When he ambled into the master bath and turned on the shower, I expelled that breath. I closed both doors and scurried back downstairs. The day would not start out well if Nick discovered me sneaking around.

I walked into the kitchen and checked the timer on the stove, discovering the egg casserole I'd whipped up for brunch should be ready to pull from the oven soon. In perfect time for Nick's descent. Thinking he'd derive pleasure from the spotless kitchen and the timing of his entrance, Nick caught me off guard with his question.

"What the hell are you doing all this baking for?"

Quick thought came to my aid this morning. "I'm putting up our Christmas decorations today and wanted something to get me in the mood."

Nick relaxed a bit. "Well, as long as decorating doesn't last all day. You've fallen behind with the housework. I'm just sayin'." He let the words drop around my shoulders when he brushed me aside to get to the stovetop. "Hey, what's this? Yum."

He grabbed a serving spoon and shoveled a heaping pile of casserole onto a plate. When he walked away from the counter and sauntered into the family room, I wasn't surprised to see he'd slopped food outside the casserole dish. Nick liked things clean and orderly but didn't mind leaving his messes behind.

As I wiped up the counter, Nick's words dug deeper. I blinked back tears. Damn him. I reveled in how well I'd cleaned the kitchen. He always wormed his opinions into hours of hard work, undermining my accomplishments. His expertise lay in reducing my self-worth.

When he dressed for work, I arranged it so that I was "occupied" in the first-floor bathroom. Not twenty minutes later, I sighed in relief upon hearing the front door slam shut. Rounding the corner into the kitchen, I heard the front door click. Although frozen in place, I prepared to run back to the bathroom but a little too late. Nick loomed above me.

"That was pretty convenient timing. What are you doing sneaking around? What are you hiding from me?" His voice rose in suspicion.

"What? Nick, c'mon—I heard the door click, and I didn't know if it was you leaving or someone else coming in." My voice broke into a whine. I didn't desire sparring with Nick when company was coming in a few hours. "Remember the guy that was in our backyard last weekend?"

Nick's face clenched, then relaxed. "Oh yeah. Well, I came back because I forgot my wallet." My body twisted to the side to let him reach past me. His fingers snaked around his billfold. He transferred it to his other hand and clutched my forearm with bruising fingers. He spoke through gritted teeth, "There'd better not be anything going on."

My eyes widened, but I kept silent. As he let me go, he shoved me with forceful hips into the counter. Great. Another bruise. With Nick gone for the next eleven to twelve hours, my anxiety ebbed. I still had cookies to bake and decorations to locate. Vee, who disappeared when Nick came downstairs this morning, reappeared from his hiding place.

I pulled the sugar cookie dough out of the fridge, pressed several cookie cutter designs into the rolled-out dough, and baked them at a comfortable 350 degrees. I figured if we had time after setting up the Christmas tree, Catherine might want to help me decorate cookies. Next, I slid a ham into the oven to bake for a few hours.

With the oven occupied, I left the kitchen to haul boxes from the main floor bedroom out to the living room. The spot my armchair occupied would suit the tree. An oversized square window, separated on top by a narrow frame of stained glass, offered the tree an optimal street view. Raising the blind to let in muted gray daylight, I yearned for sparkling Christmas lights and tinsel to brighten the day and my house.

I trudged upstairs, back to the traitorous bedroom. Sure enough, beyond rusty hinges in the closet rested several more boxes labeled "Christmas." Maneuvering them from the closet proved difficult, but doable.

Beyond that, I thought it best to wait for Jason's assistance. Not that I didn't think myself capable of carrying the boxes downstairs. Of course, I knew I hadn't fallen down the steps. Still, the fantastic lie etched itself in my brain, creating subconscious fears of having an obstructed view when approaching the stairs.

A glance at my watch signaled that a couple of hours remained before Catherine and Jason showed up. I transitioned into house cleaning mode by streaming alternative music and pop hits from my laptop. For me, chores sped by when I danced from room to room while singing to a variety of tunes. Vee approved of my system for cleaning, following along to every room.

I tackled menial tasks that I'd neglected. After about an hour, I drew a deep lavender scented bath. No sense in opening the door as a dusty, sweaty mess when my company arrived.

When my doorbell rang, I presented myself in a clingy pale green blouse that made my eyes look huge and dark green in contrast. I wore a pair of dark blue jeans that fastened comfortably beneath my healed ribs. Vee barked in excitement until I opened the door.

"Mrs. Adesco!" Catherine rushed in and hugged me. "Dad! Look where she put the suncatcher!" She gestured with pride toward the window at the bottom of our stairs.

Jason nodded to Catherine but stared at the staircase. "So this is where it all transpired."

I realized what he meant but didn't want him dwelling on something that hadn't happened. Tugging on the crook of his arm, I pulled him into the kitchen. "C'mon, Catherine. Let's start with some hot chocolate to warm up."

I instructed them to sit on the two stools that lined one side of the island while I deftly prepared my specialty concoction. In less than two minutes, I served them mugs of hot chocolate topped with whipped cream, chocolate shavings, and a peppermint stick nestled along the side. It had been a huge favorite with my younger siblings, so I suspected Catherine would like it as well. And Jason? Well, I sensed Jason would be pleased with anything I offered him.

Once finished, I led them to the living room and showed them the spot I'd selected for the tree. By a stroke of fortune, one of the boxes I'd already brought out disclosed the artificial tree, so we began assembly. Between the three of us, the six-foot tree stood upright in minutes. Green, blue, and silver garland emerged from another box, along with multi-colored twinkly lights. I opted to leave the lights on steady rather than flashing. In my opinion, flashing lights added to the hectic pace of the season. I preferred the soothing soft glow.

"So, where's the angel?" Catherine asked.

I owned several angel ornaments, gifts from my grandfather who always referred to me as his little angel. But I couldn't imagine why Catherine would know or care about those. "What angel?"

"The one for the top of your tree, of course. Or do you have a star?"

"I do have a star," a light laugh escaped my lips. "No way, though. No way will I ever have an angel topper. My parents had one for a while when I was younger—the creepiest thing ever. The fabric over its wings, as they moved, sounded like something sinister hovering over us rather than a protective celestial being. I was never so happy as the day it fell, or someone knocked it off, and broke. My parents selected a star after that, and it's what I've always chosen as well."

"So where is it?"

"I have a few more boxes upstairs but didn't trust myself to carry them down." The awkward silence I anticipated slammed into all three of us. I chose to break it. "So Jason, could I use that massive strength of yours to bring the rest of the Christmas boxes down?"

"Anything for you." He swept his arms to the side, following me toward the stairs.

Catherine called after us, "Do you care if Vee and I stay down here and keep decorating?" She stroked his side with adoration, and Vee loved the attention.

Jason hauled down the additional decorations for me. We placed them around the main floor to a mixture of classic carols and contemporary Christmas hits. We hung an eclectic mix of ornaments on the tree, including those from my childhood and more recent impulse purchases. Catherine marveled over my collection of angel ornaments, agreeing that none of them classified as creepy.

By the time we'd picked through all the boxes, the star still hadn't been located. I headed upstairs again, past Catherine, who weaved garland and lights around the banister.

"Now where could that elusive star be?" I muttered to myself, searching first in the closet the rest of the boxes hid in, before seeking the contents of the other spare bedroom's closet. I rummaged around until I spotted a partial word 'mas' on the side of a tote.

"There you are, you little shit," I spoke to the inanimate plastic box, jumping at the laughter behind me. Jason leaned against a pole of the canopy bed, arms crossed on his chest, eyes twinkling like Christmas lights. "Umm, here it is." Embarrassment carried on my words. I didn't know he'd followed me upstairs.

We squeezed past each other at the closet entrance, so closely I absorbed the heat emanating from his masculine frame. That whole pass-the-orange game messed my head up. Any time I was near him, I anticipated him lowering his head to mine. Sweet mercy, this fantasy had to end.

In my daze, Jason already forged ahead toward the stairs. I scurried after him, admiring both his backside and Catherine's work on the railing.

At the bottom of the staircase, Jason stopped in front of me. He asked Catherine to take the tote and turned around to face me. Before I could ask what he was doing, he grabbed my upper arms and his mouth met mine, just the way I'd fantasized. Sweet mercy indeed! Jason's tongue probed the back side of my lower lip with expertise. His heat enveloped me. I clung to him, allowing further exploration. Until I realized that we stood in my house, that I was married, that this was my student's father, and that my student probably witnessed the entire scene.

He pointed upwards and shrugged. "I didn't have a choice. It was the mistletoe."

But our lips had no desire to separate, and we kissed once more.

CHAPTER 18

A Homeless Woman

RELUCTANTLY, AND STILL MAINTAINING contact until our heads pulled back far enough to render that impossible, we broke our mutual kiss. We stared at each other for a moment, our gazes lingering—closer than usual as he stood on the step below mine.

I stepped down to join Jason, not wanting but needing to move away. The winter chill in this old house penetrated my flimsy blouse once my foot left the bottom step. I backed up to the window seat and took in the entire scene. Almost picture perfect.

If only I could apply a different depiction. If Jason was my husband, Catherine my daughter, Vee still my trusty dog, and maybe a couple more children played together in the next room over...

A voice hollered from the kitchen, "Is that ham done yet? It smells delicious, and I'm starving!" Catherine bounded into the entryway, Vee on her heels. She beamed at us before leading him into the living room.

Jason caught my hand to hold me back. "I'm not sorry I did that."

"Me either." I confessed, staring hungrily at his lips. "But I should be. I mean, we should be. We shouldn't have done that. Do you think Catherine saw it?"

"I was too into you to notice anything else." I saw the longing in his eyes, an emotion I was sure also radiated from mine, but the moment had passed. And as Catherine was kind enough to remind us, it was time to eat.

Supper bordered on simple, with a hint of elegance; homemade honey wheat bread, homemade apple butter from the crock pot, green beans with almonds, a succulent honey ham, sparkling grape juice and wine for the adults. Both Jason and I began with juice before switching to wine. Jason's fantastic culinary skills did not intimidate me, but rather made me curious to see his reactions to my creations.

Over supper, we chatted about the month of December and upcoming festivities. Catherine informed me that the Saturday before Christmas Grafton held its biggest holiday event, and I needed to try to clear my schedule and attend. "In fact," she added, "Why don't you come with me and my dad?"

"I don't know. Sometimes I work at the gym on Saturdays. My husband always works on Saturdays, so he won't be able to go."

Catherine seemed pleased to hear this news. "Sweet. Well, it's December 22nd," she said after consulting her cell phone. "It's a date!"

"Okay, okay," I laughed, standing to clear away the dishes. "While I clean up in here, why don't you two see if you can locate that star."

By the time I came out of the kitchen, the rest of my team unpacked my Christmas village. They positioned everything around the fireplace mantel and stood, side by side, grinning at me.

"Hey guys, this looks great." I said, joining them by the fireplace.

"We also put all the empty boxes back in that bedroom closet. And look!" Catherine pointed out the large glittery star at the top of my tree.

"This view's even more magical." Jason turned me around to view the fireplace straight on. In the mirror that stretched the length of the mantel, the star and top portion of the Christmas tree released a brilliant sparkle. The soft glow from my village invited closer inspection. The reflection of three happy faces stood out, enhanced by the beautiful decorations.

I shook my head to clear the trance, then announced that the sugar cookies on the dining room table required frosting and sprinkles. Both Jason and Catherine saw the chandelier on the floor in the corner of that room, but neither of them said a word about it.

When I still lived at home, as an oldest child, I always took charge of icing the sugar cookies while my sisters and brothers decorated them. So, my inner child clapped with excitement when Jason said he'd frost and let us two girls decorate. Once nothing but frosted cookies stared back at us, we all partook along with generous mugs of milk. Jason and I each helped ourselves to another glass of wine, at which point Catherine excused herself to run around with Vee for a bit. We sat in silence, me fidgeting with the stem of my wine glass, Jason watching my fingers. Finally, he leaned forward and halted the nervous movements of my hands.

"We need to be leaving for the night." He told me in a low voice. "Because all I keep thinking about is how badly I want to kiss you again."

I feigned surprise when I glanced up at him, although I'd thought of little more than the kiss we shared ever since our lips broke apart.

Jason called for Catherine to gather up her coat and make sure she had her phone. Catherine protested having to leave but thanked me for letting her help with my Christmas preparations.

While shoving an arm through her coat sleeve, Catherine pointed at the sprig of mistletoe. "I wanted to make the stairs a happier place for you." Catherine blurted out. "I wanted to replace horrible memories with good ones."

"Well done, Catherine." I smiled in approval.

She hugged me goodbye and said, "See ya Monday, Mrs. Adesco!" She pulled open the front door. "Oh hey, it's snowing! Can I take Vee out quick before we leave?" At my nod of approval, she and Vee rushed out to the porch and down the steps.

A split second later, Jason whipped me around to face him under the mistletoe. "Clever daughter of mine," he whispered before crushing my lips with his. This kiss contained passion that led to desperation, as if we both feared we'd never have the chance to kiss again. We were both mature enough to realize that this wasn't right. Yet like teenagers sworn away from forbidden love, the taboo nature of our relationship—combined with mutual attraction—made the pull even stronger.

Then it was over. We walked to the front door, fingers intertwined in a loose weave, until Jason pushed open the screen door. I called for Vee. Jason and Catherine bundled into their car. I glimpsed both of them waving through the windshield as they backed down my driveway.

I returned to the living room, sighing in deep contentment. With the blind open behind the tree, I marveled at the peaceful snowfall. I also saw... deep, sunken, hollow black eyes.

I tried to scream, but a hiccup emerged. Struggling to pick Vee up, I faced him toward the eyes, ready for him to become enraged and begin ferociously barking. Vee looked right at them, cocking his head toward my terrified face. What was wrong with him? Why wasn't he protecting me? Was I... The eyes vanished. But where to? Could I have imagined something so horrible appearing amidst all this Christmas brilliance? Had I locked the door behind me?

I raced to the door, tripping first over my feet, then over Vee. He ran along with me thinking a game ensued, not rushing to my protection. Palpable relief washed over me when I realized I'd secured the door, but I jumped about a foot when a gust of cold air swept by me. I gawked about, frantic. An expectant Vee stood by my side, but I found no way for a draft to enter.

That was it! I marched into the kitchen and grabbed the bottle of wine. Between Jason and I, we polished off one bottle and started a second one. Collecting my wine glass, I considered drinking straight from the bottle, but a lack of coordination threatened that option. I moseyed back to the huge window seat.

Strangely enough, despite my recent creepy vision on the other side of a windowpane, my fear dissipated here. After pulling the curtains firmly in on all sides, I sat amidst blankets and pillows, ensconced in comfort. Afterwards, I did something rare for me. I drank to forget.

I drank to forget about conjured images. I drank to forget about undeserved pain. And most of all, I drank to sink all hope that I could ever be in a relationship where I was loved and respected.

Somewhere through a muddled fog I heard Nick proclaiming, "Half the lights in the house blazing, Christmas crap everywhere! Whoa! What have we here?"

My eyelids pushed back to find Nick grinning down at me. "What's this? My little lady let loose and had some drinky?"

He'd partaken in some "drink," too. I smelled it on his breath.

"C'mon babe." Nick pulled me from under my covers. "Let's make use of this. It'll be nice not to have you so uptight in bed for once."

Even through my drunken stupor, and even though he projected a good mood, I recognized the slam for what it was. Putting me down came so naturally to him.

Nick slung me over his shoulder in a hasty and aggressive manner, but numbness swamped my limp body. A peek at Vee as we ascended the stairs revealed the sparkle of Christmas lights on his bared teeth, yet he remained still and silent.

When Nick finished with me, I staggered back downstairs. It had been a long and drawn-out event; he drank too much to perform to the best of his ability, and I remained too intoxicated to accelerate the process. Vee waited patiently, stretching out alongside me, blocking any cold air that might penetrate the glass and curtain. Reaching for the bottle, I tossed down another glass of Sauvignon Blanc before succumbing again to oblivion.

***

Nick and I shared Sunday as a mutual day off. I busied myself cleaning before he even woke up. Nick's moods were impossible to predict, so I always concentrated on cleaning, fixing, or completing the things he'd most recently complained about. This method remained far from foolproof. Sometimes, no matter how well I'd cleaned, he chose to overlook my progress and yell about something entirely different that irked him. I never won.

Today, his mood wasn't too bad. He complimented the leftover ham I reheated for lunch. Between gulps of Mountain Dew and bites of cookies, he even told me the house looked nice. I wasn't sure if he meant because of the Christmas decorations or the cleanliness. I even got so brave to ask, during a commercial break from the football game, if he wanted to go for a walk with me.

"Aw babe, it's only the second quarter, and the score is pretty close. Maybe if it was later in the game and it was a complete blow out. But I'll tell you one thing I will do," he glanced at the wall clock, "I'm gonna switch from Dew to beer. Will you grab me a cold one the next time you come through?"

"Sure, sweetie." This was the Nick I'd fallen in love with—laid-back, cute, charming. I tousled his hair when I left the room and fetched him the beer right away, so I didn't forget later. I wanted this personality to stick around a while.

After popping the top off a dark bottle, sniffing the fresh release of barley and hops, and handing it to him, I asked, "Do you mind if I take Vee on a walk over at the park then?" From the back part of the kitchen, I watched Vee's ears perk up.

"Yeah, babe. Have fun."

I ran upstairs, excited to get out of the house. As much as I enjoyed solitude, Nick granted way too much of it the past few weeks. I embraced this opportunity to exercise and enjoy a crisp December afternoon. I layered myself in velvety long underwear and blue jeans, a tank top, long-sleeved tee shirt, and sweatshirt. Huge pink and black muck boots, my puffy teal coat, and purple fur-lined gloves completed my ensemble. A more mismatched entity probably never existed in this small town, but I'd stay warm.

The bedroom clock read 3:33 when I left, a number that stuck in my mind from the oddity of three threes. Plenty of time for a walk before it got dark. Once at the park, I started on the path by the tree line. I enjoyed the occasional falling snowflakes, leaving tiny puddles on my cheeks. The pine trees exuded a heavenly scent. Even the dank, cold water and mud smell from the river held a pleasant tang today.

Entranced by the beauty of this white solitude, I reached the trail's curve sooner than I expected to. Should I continue following this trail, or hike the same way Catherine and I trekked the other day? Despite my layers, I shivered while remembering the figures darting among the trees. But those had been hallucinations from sleep deprivation. I peered into the thicker trees across the parking lot, walking even further ahead, taunting the figures to reappear.

Nothing. This made me a little braver, but how could my walk remain pleasant if I stayed on the lookout for mysterious shadow figures that, in all likelihood, existed only in my imagination? Those thoughts forced me to retreat to the lake trail. A day without concocted images, and a day where Nick played nice, made this a day not to mess up.

A light, smoky blue dusk fell sooner than I expected. I had not yet made the turn to go back along the long side of the lake. The snow boasted a purplish hue while the trees reflected periwinkle. I shuffled along at an accelerated rate, remembering the clown in the car I'd encountered after dark. As of yet, I'd not caught sight of any other living being on this excursion.

As we rounded the lake, random snowflakes continued to drift to earth in intervals. After taking a few steps in this new direction, a sudden breeze picked up, filling my lungs with the pleasant woodsy scent from a nearby fireplace.

I walked as fast as my out-of-shape legs could manage against impending nightfall, but it engulfed both of us in silence. The quicker my stride, the more the wind whipped my face and snowflakes stung my already watering eyes. I wiped a glove across my eyes, then caught the runoff from my nose, wishing I had a tissue for excess snot removal. The thought of tissues and tissue-type paper led to the realization that I sorely needed a bathroom break. Not a feasible feat, I reasoned, until I caught sight of a soft, yellow glow ahead. The public restrooms!

I spoke to my dog to help forget about the urgency in my bladder.

"Of course, it won't be open, will it, Vee?" Back in Nebraska, park bathrooms are always closed throughout the winter months. Too few people frequented the parks, not enough to justify paying an employee for upkeep. And North Dakota parks, based solely on this one, seemed to be even less populated at any time of the year. Besides, unlocked and empty buildings were an open invitation to vandals and graffiti artists. There was no way this building would be available to the public.

I gave a tug on the women's handle. "Oh." Except that it budged. "All right, Vee. You can come in with me." I glanced around what little of the park I could see but, of course, a vacant expanse of nature greeted me.

Upon walking into the edifice, I saw a straight shot of a tan brick wall ahead, then a sink and two bathroom stalls. One was a regular stall, and the other handicap accessible. I chose the larger of the two so Vee could accompany me.

I used the facility, afterwards becoming nervous they had shut the water off for the winter. Despite the fact that my deposit would be anonymous, I didn't want my waste sitting here all winter long. A loud sucking noise cleared the bowl when I flushed, filling me with relief.

The yellow light extending from the ceiling crept under the stall door. Sliding the bolt aside, I detected more of a glow coming from the corner facing the exit door. Curious about the additional source of light, I stepped past the partial wall before flinging myself backward—arms spread, flailing, grasping stall partitions.

In the corner hunched a horrifying figure. Whether she crouched, or sat, was difficult to tell. I couldn't see her face because she tucked her chin into her chest. Long black hair spilled over her shoulders, covering what little of her face that might have shown. It hung heavy, greasy and unkempt, matching the state of her dingy, white gunny-sack dress. Her long, bony fingers grasped her knees from the bottom, clutching and pulling them into the rest of her body.

I wondered who or what this person was, why she was here, and if I needed to be afraid? Deciding she depicted a homeless person taking refuge from the elements, I edged my way toward the partial wall, my back pressed against it, inching along. If I left her alone, like most homeless people, she wouldn't harm me.

Three things happened simultaneously: I set my foot on the other side of the partial wall to beat a hasty retreat, the vagabond slowly raised her head, and I swallowed the bitter bile rising in my throat. Her eyes mirrored pools of white. Her mouth hung slack. She reached an imploring hand toward me, and I fled in terror.

CHAPTER 19

BACK TO THE GYM

ONCE ON THE OTHER side of the restroom door, I ran to the best of my ability in clunky snow boots. When I pitched forward, tripping myself up, I realized I still clung to Vee's leash. Vee nosed the side of my face that peeked out of the snow. I sat up, peering in apprehension behind me.

"Damn it, Vee! What the hell was that?"

Vee nudged me again as I pushed my hands on the cement under my butt to get up. I stared in accusation. "Why didn't you protect me? Dude," I slipped into 80s high school lingo, "you didn't even bark. What's wrong with you?"

Vee wagged his tail.

"That chick was messed up. I should call the police."

At those words, Vee smacked his head into the back of my knees. His ears turned to the sides and a hint of teeth peeked between his jaws.

"Okay, you're right. She wasn't hurting anyone, and the police would probably just kick her back out in the cold. Maybe I should tell Nick, though."

At this, I got a growl out of him. Vee did not care for Nick, but who could blame him? Not everyone shared my forgiving nature.

Unable to exercise much in recent months, I ran out of breath several times on the way home. Once there, I slid across the porch and banged into the front door. And some people didn't believe I was a klutz.

"Geez, Jen!" Nick hollered when I came through the door. "You tryin' to knock the house down?"

"Sorry. I just slipped. Don't worry, though. I'm fine."

"When are you gonna fix supper? I'm starving!"

I tried to gauge Nick's disposition. I'd been gone for an hour, but Nick downed a couple of beers during that time. Hanging my wet gloves and coat to dry, I pondered what I could throw together in short order. Once in the kitchen, I pulled out the rest of the ham, located some vegetables, and manufactured crunchy ham sandwiches.

"These sandwiches are genius. Dang, Jen. You're so creative."

I basked in Nick's compliment, my good mood restored. But my mind kept drifting back to the woman in the restroom. Sure, I could try confiding in Nick, but with what result? What would he think of me? He might forbid me to go to the park ever again. I certainly didn't want that. Perhaps I should confide in a friend.

* * *

Monday morning Catherine arrived in my classroom bright and early, as per her norm. She asked how I liked my Christmas decorations and told me she and her dad put up their tree on Sunday. I briefly let my thoughts flicker to Jason, flushed, and pushed those thoughts away.

Monday was also the first day to sign up for the Double Secret Santa I planned to sponsor the following week. I invited all high school students and staff to take part. The concept was new to the students and to me, as well. I created an exchange with a unique premise. Not only would each participant receive a gift from an unknown person, but they also gave a gift to an unknown person.

Students in my classes selected Spanish names at the beginning of the school year. They used that name plus a number for their Secret Santa name. For example: Rosa16. Staff members and students not enrolled in Spanish received assigned names and numbers. This way, those who shared a class with 5th period Rosa did not know if she was Rosa3, Rosa16, or Rosa45.

"Señora, you're crazy." Several students repeated throughout the day.

Each time I laughed with them and reminded them, "I prefer the word 'eccentric.'" But I recalled the images that haunted me, wondering if my students were right.

Nick texted me that afternoon, saying he was off to the bar with his friends for Monday night football and not to worry about supper. So when Alice Ann caught me after school and asked if I wanted to go out for a drink and a bite to eat, I jumped at the chance. Her husband was out of town on business, and she hated eating alone.

We agreed to meet at Shenanigans, one of her favorite restaurants. One of mine, too, as I'd loved the food I'd eaten there with Charles. Alice Ann flagged me down when I walked inside. The dimmer atmosphere smelled of savory meats and grilled vegetables. We ordered drinks, perused the menu, and spoke of troubled students. We both ended up ordering shepherd's pie.

While still discussing issues at school, patrons trickled into the restaurant. I recognized one of them. Charles escorted a voluptuous brunette. Interesting. Once seated, he scanned the room and caught me still staring. He gave a nod and a wave, but I turned away, embarrassed.

"Isn't that Charles Newman?" Alice Ann noticed when I became distracted from our conversation.

"Yeah. Umm, he's just someone I know from the gym."

"At the Homecoming Dance he looked like more than 'just someone you know.' You guys were fantastic on the dance floor. But then again, so were you and Catherine's dad. Too bad you're married, huh? All these hot guys practically throwing themselves at you."

"Yeah, too bad." I echoed.

"How is good old Nick, anyway?"

My eyes narrowed. "Fine."

"He's behaving himself? Helping around the house, staying out of trouble?"

"Sure. Why?"

"You can always talk to me if you're ever in trouble or have any problems you need to hash out with someone. It seems like you may not get out much, and I know it can be difficult to meet new people in this town."

"Okay. Thanks for the offer. I appreciate it."

Speculation crossed Alice Ann's features. Waiting.

I decided to broach the subject of the creepy apparitions that kept stalking me. "Well, there is something."

"Yes?" She put her hands on top of my folded ones. Her eyes peeled back wider, as if she thought she'd gain access to a long-kept secret. I didn't quite trust her eagerness, choosing to divulge minimal information.

"It's just, well, I've been taking walks at Leistikow Park, and I've seen some strange...people there. Are there many transients in Grafton?"

Alice Ann pursed her lips. "Well, it is a railroad town. Occasionally, I suppose, homeless people hop on open cars to travel. And we do have a river that meanders through the northern, overgrown part of town. Most of the river rats own or rent houses. But have I seen any transients? One or two in the past few years. I certainly don't recall there ever being any crime associated with homeless people. Why do you ask?"

"Oh, I thought I saw one there this weekend. On Friday there were a couple of people running through the trees off the walking trail, and then yesterday I saw a woman hunched in the corner of the restroom."

"Wait! Inside the restroom?"

"Yes."

"I thought they locked those up during the winter months."

"That's what I would have thought, too." Great. Alice Ann shot me a glance that contemplated how hard I'd hit my head when I suffered my last 'accident.'

"Maybe we should call the city about the unlocked building and let them deal with the woman if she's still there."

"Maybe." I echoed her again.

"As far as the people running around in the trees, that was probably just kids playing tag."

"That makes sense." Of course, Alice Ann offered a practical take on the matter, which I desperately needed. "With my imagination, I had Russian spies traipsing through the woods."

"Silly goose," she teased, but leaned in and lowered her voice. "Are you sure you didn't want to talk about anything else?"

The arrival of our mouthwatering food ceased the conversation. Whew. What had she wanted me to say? Was the entire world waiting for me to confess that my husband had anger issues, that he got a little rough with me from time to time? Well, it would not happen. Screw Alice Ann if that was the secret she intended to discover.

The creamy shepherd's pie melted on my tongue and slid down my throat. I'd never made this recipe but would love to try this winter. I closed my eyes in appreciation of this succulent dish and opened them, knowing someone watched. Not Alice Ann, whose head bent over her own steaming pie. Then who? Charles. My head whipped in his direction. This time I caught him staring, his hands folded under his chin.

His date gestured amicably, her jaw moving up and down as fast as a needle on a sewing machine, oblivious to his distraction. But Charles' personality dominated those around him. I stuck my tongue out at him, smiled, and turned my attention back to Alice Ann. I'd hear about this later.

We topped off our meal with Baileys Irish Cream Pie. To my relief, Alice Ann steered clear of confessions and admissions. We passed Charles' table on our way out. Once on the other side of the brunette, I looked at him over my shoulder and stuck my tongue out again. His eyebrows raised. I felt smug, but not sure why.

* * *

Tuesday evening, I worked my first shift at the gym since my hospitalization. Nakayla asked the person who worked before me to stay a little late and called me into her office.

She smiled at me. "Go ahead, shut the door. Please, have a seat."

Uh oh. Anything that began with "shut the door" couldn't be good.

"So, Jen, I haven't seen you since the day I took you home from the hospital. You look 100% better. How are you feeling?"

"Good." I admitted. "I'm getting more active all the time. Aside from some minor aches and a hitch or two, things are pretty good."

"Okay. But if it gets to be too much tonight, give me a call, and I'll cover for you."

"I appreciate the offer, but I think I'll be fine."

"Just keep it in mind. And hey, listen," she leaned across her desk toward me, "If you ever need someone to talk to, or vent to, I'm always here."

This sounded like a replicate of Alice Ann's spiel. I rose to leave. "Thanks again, Nakayla."

For the first couple of hours, I busied myself with reading email updates, looking over the new member list, and chatting with our members. A little after seven o'clock Charles strode in.

"Only time for a quick workout tonight," he mentioned while scanning his membership card. I presumed he said that to assure me he remembered we closed at eight o'clock. Funny. He hadn't mentioned anything about seeing me the night before.

At 7:36, Charles strode toward me again. "Were you celebrating last night?"

In the middle of counting my cash drawer, I tried to hint that he was distracting me, but he persisted. So, I answered with a question of my own. "No, were you?"

"The only celebrating that happened was when my airhead of a cousin finally left town. But hey, I thought you couldn't get away or weren't supposed to leave the house sin permiso."

"Nice gratuitous use of Spanish." Wry humor tainted my tone as I reached over the counter to high five him, except that he laced his fingers with mine and held on. "Nick went somewhere to watch the football game, so I thought I could get away."

192

I tugged at my hand, but Charles wouldn't release it. "Are you staying accident-free these days?"

"So far, so good." I pulled again, and this time he released. "I've been getting more exercise, taking walks in the park. I'm navigating better and trying not to be so klutzy."

Charles looked me in the eye. "I'm confident the more you get out of your house, the fewer mishaps you'll encounter."

I lowered my eyes, but he continued. "So, walking at the park...alone?"

"No, no. I have my dog with me."

"Big dog? Little dog? Is it worth its weight in protection?"

"Actually, he's great. He's a medium-sized, foxlike dog. The vet called him a dhole." I clicked on a picture of Vee on my phone, holding it over the counter for Charles to see. "This is Vee."

Charles peered at the picture of my dog. He took advantage of the proximity of my hand by wrapping one of his around mine, removing the camera with his other hand.

"How long have you had him?" Charles examined each finger as if he was a doctor checking my healing progression instead of a recent acquaintance.

"I, umm, he was a stray. He showed up right after my elbow got shattered."

Whether Charles wore gym clothes or casual dress clothes, there was no denying his tremendous sex appeal.

Nerves warring, I licked my lips while he continued his scrutinization.

"Does he help protect you from accidents around the house?"

"He tries." My eyes misted at the thought of Nick slamming Vee into a wall.

"Animal cruelty, as well," Charles murmured.

Heat from his hands flowed into mine and up my arm. I swallowed hard against a dry throat, trying to catch his eye. When he finished inspecting one hand, he held out his own—expectant, until my right hand settled in his palm. He repeated the process before curling my fingers into my hand and offering it back to me.

"Are you about done here?" Charles' voice smoldered. Although flattered and glad I wasn't the only one turned on, such reactions also scared me.

"Shortly. But then I have to get right home."

He muttered something to the effect of "Of course you do," when I turned on the overhead speaker to announce the gym would close in ten minutes.

I said goodnight to the two straggling members who had to get those last reps in before they could leave, and then turned my attention back to Charles.

"I have to do rounds now and make sure everything is secure." I fetched the hex key to lock the front doors.

"What? You? By yourself? All alone in this big old, haunted building?"

"No, it's not." I scrunched my forehead. My wild imagination started acting up, so I relented. "But since you're on the board, I suppose you could walk around with me."

"I'm positive Nakayla wouldn't mind."

Charles kept pace with me while I shut off machines, TVs, and lights, while checking to make sure all outer doors stayed locked and secure. He didn't touch me again until he walked me out to my car. Smoothing my hair down, he kissed my head, whispering, "Be safe, Shenandoah."

I got into my car and fastened the seat belt. Upon turning the ignition, I noted that my hand still shook; Charles' cautionary words affected me for multiple reasons. Be safe. That could be a tall order when living with someone like Nick. I felt safe with him. Most of the time. Still, I never knew what would set him off. Living with him made me understand the expression walking on eggshells.

I also worried about my safety when it came to the horrific characters I'd been seeing. Sure, my imagination ran on overdrive, but it never before conjured images this extreme.

And of course, my blossoming relationships with Charles and Jason caused me anxiety. Both men showed more interest than was appropriate, and it disturbed me that I shared their interest.

A rap on my car window brought a scream to my throat. I whipped my head to the left, froze in fear of the figure standing there, unclenching my muscles seconds later. With exasperation, I rolled the window down.

"Charles! You about gave me a heart attack!"

"Everything okay?"

"Yes, fine." I put the car in gear, waited for him to step back, and rolled the window up.

Be safe. That definitely included keeping my distance from this man. From all men. From all people? My mind raced.

Upon reaching my driveway, I caught sight of the most steadfast creature in my life: Vee. He was the first to greet me and the last to see me off when I left for school, my dearest friend and the one I could always count on more than anyone.

CHAPTER 20

Homicide Victim

WEDNESDAY AND THURSDAY MARKED days of statewide public-school testing in North Dakota. While I didn't follow lesson plans on those occasions, testing days at Grafton High School offered a whole new brand of exhaustion.

When I headed back to the gym Thursday evening, I found myself wishing I'd waited another week or two before resuming part-time work. I sat on edge all night, jumping each time the front door opened. But Charles never came. For some reason, disappointment settled like a cloak around my shoulders, weighing them down.

After making my closing time announcement and ushering what I suspected were the last few people out of the building, I began my rounds. This was nothing new for me. I'd done rounds a couple of times before I took my leave of absence, yet tonight things seemed a little spookier. I'd have to remember to offer Charles a cryptic thanks for giving me the impression this place was haunted.

I turned off the equipment on the second floor, jumping once when the heater clicked on and forcing air through creaky vents. Back on the main floor, I checked the short hallway then the darkened pool area, which always kind of creeped me out. Finally, I made my way to the locker rooms.

In the women's locker room, I picked up a towel, closed some open lockers, and paused. I heard the distinct sound of the elevator running. What the hell? Hair rose on the back of my neck. Deciding things looked good enough in here, I flipped the lights off. I raced to the hallway, casting a harried glance around.

"Hello? Who's here?"

No one was supposed to be on the premises. The elevator landed. The bulky door moved aside, but no one stepped off. Did that mean someone rode it to the second floor and sent it back down?

"Hello?" I yelled up the wide-open staircase. Not a sound from above. This contained the perfect makings of a horror movie. "Stupid Charles." I muttered, certain none of this would have happened had he not spread unsolicited rumors.

I scurried through the men's locker room, determined to finish up. I planned to call Nakayla on my way out, in case she wanted to investigate or call the police.

I left the men's locker room in slight disarray, running to the racquetball courts. Two bags of trash sat at the edge of the courts by the back door. That wouldn't fly. Lazy housekeepers. A glance back down the hallway assured me that no one stood behind me.

"Fine, whatever."

I pushed the left of the double doors open until it latched, grabbed the bags of trash, and stepped onto the short sidewalk that turned left alongside the building. The dumpster sat past the fire escape stairs and recycling bins.

As I turned, raindrops began to fall. Not remembering hearing about rain in the forecast, I hustled even more. Someone left one panel of the bin's lid conveniently open, and I didn't bother closing it. I ran back to the metal doors, realizing I hadn't detected any more sprinkles.

When I stood directly under the flat part of the fire escape, a fat raindrop splattered by my feet. Another big one landed on my left arm. Someone must've flipped a water bottle up there and it laid on its side dripping. I took a step back and sheltered my eyes with my hand.

Paralyzed, only a mere squeak emerged from my constricted throat. Positive this couldn't be real, I stared more intently at the body of a woman lying face down with her arm flung over her head. Her fingers stuck through the grates, dripping with blood. Vacant dead eyes stared down at me.

I began to hyperventilate. Another drop hit. I jerked my head to look at my arm. Ewww! A dead lady's blood landed on me. Dry heaves wracked my body until I realized a killer might lurk nearby. I bolted back into the building, pulling the door shut behind me. Although not sure this was the safest place to be, my car waited in the parking lot out front—a destination that became my all-encompassing goal.

Speed evaded my gene pool, and the hallway from back door to front never stretched out so long as it did tonight. At the first set of double glass doors, I grappled with the handle before obtaining a firm clasp. The second door pushed right open. I took one step into darkness and collided with another solid body. Determined not to be a victim, I flailed my arms, pummeling at the figure that sought to hold me.

"Jen! Stop for a sec. What is it?" An authoritative voice that I recognized and trusted commanded me to settle down. I clung to her upper arms.

"Nakayla! Oh my God! I'm so glad you're here! Call the police!" My urgent words rushed past her.

"Wait! Calm down. Tell me why."

What was wrong with her? Oh yeah, she didn't know. I'd show her.

"Come with me!"

"Wait! Jen! Did you get hurt?" Nakayla held my left hand and twisted my arm to better view the blood. "Jen! Your head is bleeding, too."

"It's not my blood!" I tugged at her wrist. She jogged down the hallway after me. I pushed the back door open with such force that it came careening back at me. Another shove and it clicked and stayed propped open.

"Look!" I pulled Nakayla outside and pointed upward.

"What are we lookin' at?" Caution bolstered her words.

"Well, I can't see. Where'd it go?" I began to hyperventilate again.

"Hey—whoa, settle down." Nakayla used a light on her phone to point toward the sky. "What are we lookin' at?" she repeated.

Suspicion settled over me like a buffalo-skin blanket. Could Nakayla be the murderer? Had she moved the body?

"The blood! This blood!" I pointed to my arm. "It's from the body! There's some on the cement, too." Pushing past her, I scanned the sidewalk for the sticky wet substance. Unable to locate it, I sensed sarcasm radiating from Nakayla. She kept her voice from sounding too condescending when she spoke.

"Jen, did you trip out here? Is that how you got scraped up? Did you...hit your head, by chance?"

I backed away from her. If I insisted on my version of events when no proof existed, I'd seem crazy. The only sane thing left was to apologize and move on. "Look... I'm sorry, Nakayla. That must have been what happened. Housekeeping left some trash bags by the back door, so I tried to help clean up. Sorry to cause problems."

"No, it's okay. Thanks for picking up another department's slack. I'm sorry you got hurt. I suppose you should fill out a workmen's comp form."

"No, I'm fine. My head is a little fuzzy. I think I want to go home now."

"Okay, if you're sure." She inspected my head, my face, my body. "But this is your only opportunity to file for workmen's comp. Once you leave property, you can no longer claim you sustained the injury here."

"Yes, I know. Thanks, Nakayla." I volunteered a weak smile.

"Hey, Jen!"

I'd reached the door and wanted nothing more than to vacate these premises once and for all tonight. I answered over my shoulder, "Yes?"

"If you'd like some time to recuperate, I can find someone to cover for you this weekend."

"That'd be great, thanks." I replied, half turning and walking out the first set of doors at the same time. I refused to let my feet linger, even if she thought of more questions.

I did not sit in my car brooding like I had on Tuesday night. Instead, I peeled out. The truth hit home. I really was losing my mind.

Upon seeing Vee's friendly and happy face when I got home, tears swelled in my eyes. When I closed the front door, a wall of water coated my face, dribbled down my neck, and soaked into my orange Sunset Gym polo. I flopped into the window seat, wrapping Vee in a fierce hug after he jumped up next to me. Burying my face in his fur, I let huge sobs consume me. Eventually I slid down to the pillow and drifted off to a dreamless slumber.

None other than Nick's voice woke me.

"What's the matter, babe?" I heard him croon in my left ear. "You forgot to lock the door, and you're sleeping downstairs? What's wrong?"

The yay, Nick was home collided with the shit, I forgot to lock the front door! in my brain. I'd been scared out of my mind, yet somehow, I'd forgotten to slide the deadbolt? That made no sense.

"C'mon, babe. Let's go to bed." Nick lifted me, blankets and all. I recalled the elbow accident when he lifted me and smashed my elbow. A twang of ghost pains resonated through my arm. I considered telling him about the incident at the gym, but decided I liked this happy Nick and didn't want to alter his mood.

Nick took me to our bedroom, laid me down, tossed the extra blankets on a padded chair, and covered me up with ample bedding. After a quick shower, he confused me by not demanding sex but cuddling instead. Moments later, soft snores echoed in my ear. I waited until his breathing regulated for a while before slipping out of the covers. Tucking the blankets around him, I kissed the section of his forehead where his hair fell to the side. Geez, I loved him when he treated me like this.

I pulled the blankets off the chair and descended back to my window seat, where Vee waited with the patience of a saint. This time I curled up and fell asleep immediately, Vee snuggled by my side.

* * *

Friday morning, I woke up rested but apprehensive about what today might bring. Would I become a murder suspect? Would a zombie woman drag herself into my sight? Or would some psycho stalk me? Although overly cautious, none of my fears were realized. I drove straight home after work and didn't leave the house once.

However, by Saturday, my physically fit body desired outdoor exploration. I recalled that so many of these images manifested after dark. Maybe if I went out in broad daylight, my mind wouldn't create such horrid images.

I occupied my morning researching new Christmas recipes to try. For Nick, I made a bacon, egg, and cheese brunch ring along with fresh-squeezed orange juice. His good mood from last night carried over, remaining until he left for work. I hoped it lasted a while, or even stayed permanently.

Even though I loved Nick in this light, my eagerness to go for a walk in the park surfaced as soon as he closed the front door.

"Dang, Jen. Calmate," I counseled, donning outerwear to face the winter afternoon. I thought the weather was manageable without ski pants since it wasn't too windy and the temp climbed above twenty degrees. Scarf, gloves, coat, boots, Vee with his leash, and I was set to go.

Once at Leistikow Park, we walked along the row of pine trees first, my favorite route. The part of the park I liked best was the arboretum; but I always thought I'd look silly walking through it to the north, then back on the return trip home. For that reason, I chose to start on this side, planning to finish by meandering through the arboretum. I saved the best part of the walk for last.

Other than a couple of cars driving past and a lone ice fisherman on the southern part of the lake, Vee and I explored the park by ourselves. Perfect. The way I liked it. I breathed deeply of crisp air, exhaling slowly, allowing all apprehensions to fade.

Today no shadows flitted among the trees. No clown babies peered at me from car windows. No homeless people plagued me. Only me, Vee, and the North Dakota landscape existed.

As I rounded the curve in the path, I spotted the wrought-iron swing that overlooked the lake from a distance. Today I used ample free time to visit and test it out. While I plodded through powdery grass, additional snow began to fall. The sound of the wind through the trees, the scent of pine needles—both fallen and still green on the tree—worked wonders.

Since the swing sat on the edge of the arboretum, name plates marked the trees leading my way there, but the winter landscape covered them this time of year. Passing some sort of fir tree and a clump of other trees with gnarled branches naked of leaves, I stood before the swing. With a waterproof glove, I swept aside fluffy snow. Once seated, I began to rock. At first Vee sat on the ground, the leash alternating between taut and slack. When I accidentally nudged him, he turned around and jumped up next to me. I shoved off, time after time; while it went nowhere near as high as a single pumper on a swing set, my stomach still expected that tremulous, fear-of-falling excitement. After several minutes, I slowed until the swing rested.

The world grew silent around me. I closed my eyes, inhaling the pine-infused air. Feathery ice crystals brushed against the skin on my cheeks before leaving trace amounts of moisture behind. Lack of sound directed my ears to strain for any miniscule noise. From my vantage point, the entire city of Grafton concealed itself in deep slumber.

Vee licked the occasional melting snowflakes from his nose. A blue jay scolded a blackbird for trespassing. An unknown critter scurried in the snow and brush, causing me to sit erect and peek over at Vee. He displayed no signs of alarm and uttered no warning growls, which calmed me down. Although...none of the creatures I'd seen before alarmed him, either. I turned to Vee.

A strong and amicable dog, years of intelligence shone behind his eyes. He projected a soothing aura. If he didn't sense a threat from the things we'd encountered, neither should I. They weren't dangerous, or they didn't exist. I shuddered, slipping off my gloves to bury both my face and fingers in Vee's fur.

"Either way, it's scary, Vee. Either I can see ghosts that aren't dangerous, or I'm conjuring images in my mind. Still, Nakayla did see the blood."

I sighed and stood, disgruntled that questioning my mental competency cut into my enjoyment of this perfect afternoon. My immobile posture allowed a chill to permeate heavy winter garments. Quick solution to alleviate the cold, get moving. I jumped off the bench swing. Vee's agile form landed by my side. We set off for the heart of the arboretum.

After a bit, we encountered the sidewalk path again and followed its curves. We weaved among trees that easily reached 50 to 75 feet in height. Vee and I rounded the first of a grouping of three large pines on our right when a flash caught my eye. Before I turned to identify the source, I was pulled into the trees by my right arm. I collided with an immobile object.

CHAPTER 21

A Sick Student

MY FLIGHT-OR-FIGHT instinct kicked in, as it had a lot in recent weeks. Was I being kidnapped? Was I about to be raped? Before any kick or squirm shook my body, the hard-bodied figure that held me spoke.

"Shenandoah, it's okay. I've got you."

The scream that I willed to erupt, wouldn't. Some part of my brain wondered why Vee wasn't growling and attacking my assailant. I mean, he'd stood up to Nick! Why wouldn't he wage war for me this time? I began a full body squirm.

"Shenandoah." The velvety voice smoothed. I began to hyperventilate. "Remind me again of your dog's name?"

"Vee!" I panted, squinting upwards.

"Vee, sit!"

I identified that authoritative voice, and the face it belonged to. "Charles, what...?"

"Did I surprise you? Did I frighten you?" His eyes darted wildly. I wondered if he'd been drinking, although I couldn't detect any scent of alcohol.

"All I've been thinking about is doing this!" Charles crushed his lips to mine, pulling me with more power against his body. Unable to escape, and not sure I wanted to even if my biceps obeyed me, I kissed him back. Vee's leash fell to the ground.

Charles smashed my lips into my teeth. His tongue forced its way into exploring every contour of my mouth. He almost acted as rough as Nick in an aggressive mood. But not quite. Charles was rough from passion. He wasn't a pissed off, spoiled boy, so the temper tantrum turned me on.

I kissed him back with more urgency than I'd ever kissed another being. His tongue and body responded in kind. My mind spun while he pulled me by the front of my coat, around to the side of a massive pine tree the city crew had trimmed to avoid blocking the sidewalk. He backed me in, not allowing our lips to part. I clung to him like a wanton woman.

My body tingled with desire. Fire danced through my veins, upping my body heat. Desperate to shed layers to ease excess heat and get closer to Charles, I pushed my body back to allow some room, pulled off my gloves and began unzipping my coat.

Charles realized we stood in plain sight of anyone who might walk through the park. Even though we hadn't spotted a soul, he expected unpleasant repercussions if someone identified us.

Thoughts of Nick discovering this escapade cooled my hormones. When Charles unzipped his coat and pressed his body up against mine, I cooled off a bit more. Not because I wasn't over-the-top horny, but because intimately touching the contours of his body made the situation all too real. I choked back tears and tried to pull away from him.

By this time, he maneuvered me to some trees even farther away from the common path. He glared at me.

"What? You want to back out now? You lead me on—me, virtually a stranger—and give me practically every sign that you want me to...that you want to have sex, and expect me to be okay with that?"

"I..." the flush that I'd already acquired deepened.

"You what?" he inquired. His eyes appeared menacing, and his mouth formed a grim line. "How do you even know you can trust me? I could be a recluse murderer, for all you know."

My eyes widened. I struggled, but to no avail.

"I'm not, of course. But do you see how trusting you are? How vulnerable, how scared, and yet how passionate? Would you have responded this way to anyone? Could any guy have had his way with you? What about your dog? Is she really any source of protection?"

"Vee does his best to warn me about dangerous situations." It pissed me off that Charles got the gender wrong and that he dissed my dog.

"But what about you?" he prompted. "What do you believe in? Do you trust everyone who claims to like you?"

"I..." Damn, words flew from my mind faster than a red-tailed hawk swooping in on an unsuspecting field mouse.

His tone and features softened. "Shenandoah." He lifted my chin with a finger to raise my gaze level to his.

"Why do you keep saying my name like that? Can't you just call me Jen like everyone else?" I blinked back tears that threatened to spill from my eyes.

"Of course, I'll call you whatever you prefer. Jen's a perfectly nice name, but Shenandoah is so beautiful." His gentle tone caved me. Tears collided with melting snowflakes, causing rivers to branch out across my cheeks.

"I think so, too." I sniffed, raising the arm of my coat to swipe at my nose. "And Vee must think you're a good guy, or he'd be having a fit right now."

We both looked around and spotted Vee rolling in the snow, shaking the excess away. He grinned and wagged his tail at us.

Charles pulled my head around to face him again. "Is there anybody in Grafton who Vee doesn't like?"

I hung my head in shame. How could I admit that the one person my dog bared teeth toward, on more than one occasion, was the man I shared a bed and a roof with?

"I think I know the answer. Doesn't that tell you anything? Shenandoah," he said in earnest, "can't you see what's right in front of you? An opportunity for happiness. A pillar of strength and safety. A man who's falling in love with you."

"No." I shook myself free of his grasp, and he let me. "C'mon, Vee! We need to get home."

Hvezda obediently trotted over. I picked up his leash and my gloves. Without bothering to fasten my coat, I pushed toward the sidewalk. A glance backward confirmed the tall, sexy, dark-skinned individual dressed in black, staring after me. Damn! If only it were easier. A niggling in my mind wondered how my life would have unfolded if I hadn't met Nick.

No! I didn't want to go there. He loved me. He did so much for me. He helped me get to this point in life. Which was where? The internal nagging continued. To the hospital? Almost dead? Free-flowing tears plopped in the snow, disappearing beneath my shuffling boots.

I shed my outer garments by the front entryway, ambling into the kitchen to concoct my hot chocolate specialty. Thoughts tumbled in turmoil over what I should and shouldn't want. To the outer world, I supposed that Nick and I lived an idyllic life; but behind closed doors, we were a mess. I resented this mess. I wanted more from our relationship and more for my life. However, sneaking kisses behind trees and under mistletoe violated appropriate protocol.

Propping the pillows against the pane nearest the front door in my window seat, I raised the blinds on the other two windows, sitting with a blanket pulled up to my chin. Vee settled between me and the biggest window, scooting my phone out with his back paw. I reached for it, planning to place it out of the way, when I noticed missed calls and missed texts.

The first text came from Catherine: "Señora, I tried calling you. Please call me when you get the chance."

The second text, also from Catherine: "PLEASE CALL ME!"

Alarmed, I noted three missed calls from Catherine's number and one voice mail. In her message, she sounded lethargic. She said that she felt weird, had trouble breathing, and thought she might have a fever. She added that her dad was out of town until late in the evening, and she was frightened.

My fingers tapped "Dial," but no one answered. Worried something awful had happened, I donned my coat and accessories haphazardly, located my keys and purse, and slapped my thigh for Vee to come with me.

Snow continued to fall, so I used my arm to brush the newly fallen couple inches off the windshield and hood of my car. Zero patience accompanied my wait at the end of the driveway for a vehicle creeping along as if this were the first snowfall of the year. Rolling various scenarios over in my mind, I kept my phone on the seat beside me in case she called back. It remained silent the entire way.

Vee and I tromped through fluffy snow. Once on the porch, I slid into the front door, punching the doorbell at the same time. I pushed back from the door and began pounding on it.

"Catherine!" I called through the metal door. Vee whined.

"Should we try the handle, boy?"

Vee barked once, jumping against the door as I opened it.

"Catherine?" My scared voice bounced off dark walls. "Catherine!"

After my recent visit, I remembered the first bedroom was not hers. I flicked on the hallway light and continued to the end of the hall. A common floor plan in ranch-style houses installed master bedrooms in the rear of the house, so I rendered a light tap on the partially opened door next to the guest bedroom.

I heard a rustling and took that as my cue to enter. Before I even flipped on the overhead light, I could tell that Catherine lay in the bed; a sickly funk hung heavily in the room. Rushing to her side, I could also tell that she'd fallen under the influence of a high fever. My fingers ghosted across her shoulder, pulling on it to turn her toward me. Heat seeped through her long-sleeved t-shirt. Her glazed eyes showed no signs of recognition.

"You poor thing!" I helped myself to supplies in the main bathroom. For what I couldn't find, I located in the master bath within Jason's room.

A typical mid-winter malady, Catherine suffered from a bad case of influenza. The ear thermometer revealed a temperature of 102.7, much too high for my satisfaction. I pulled off her covers, replacing her shirt and sweatpants with a tank top and shorts. A cold, wet cloth across her forehead began the active cooling process. Next, I soaked a cotton ball in rubbing alcohol, stroking it over her wrists and arms. I repeated this procedure until her skin cooled. I worked with a steadfast rhythm. If her temperature continued to climb, I'd escort her to a lukewarm bath. I didn't know if I could handle the task.

Twenty minutes later, Catherine's temperature dropped two full degrees.

"Catherine," I spoke again to see if she'd respond. Her eyelids fluttered, opening to register my presence. "Hey sweetie, how are you?"

Her eyes reflected gratitude. "Mrs. Adesco. Thanks for coming. I started feeling yucky, and I didn't want to be home alone. I'm so sorry I had to bother you."

"No bother," I assured her. "I was home alone, too. Do you think you could scootch up enough to drink a little water and take some Tylenol?"

"Sure." I knew she'd agree but hid my alarm when her teeth chattered during her answer. The onset of the chills. Another miserable aspect to having the flu.

After I medicated her and she sipped some water, I tucked the covers back around her. I found a quilt and another blanket in the hall closet. I sat and rubbed her back until she fell into a fitful sleep. I instructed Vee to hop up beside Catherine to help warm her. He understood the task at hand and stretched along her backside. I turned off the overhead light and clicked on a small table lamp sitting on her vanity.

"You stay there, boy." I commanded, leaving the door ajar.

I picked up the cell phone that I'd discarded with my coat when first entering the house. Catherine may have been reluctant to call her father, but I wasn't. I didn't know what city his business beckoned from, nor did I plan on encouraging him to hurry back. I considered myself capable of looking after Catherine. My intention was to put his mind at ease. If he'd tried calling to check in with her, he may have been worried.

The phone rang once on my end. "Hi, Jen."

I couldn't help but smile when talking to him. "Hey, Jason. I'm at your place with Catherine, but there's nothing to worry about. She's a little under the weather and wanted some company. I didn't know how soon you'd be home, or if you'd tried calling her."

"Is she okay?"

"She'll be fine. She's sleeping right now. Unless you have any objections, I'll stay here with her until you get home."

"No, yeah, that's great. Thank you. Thank you for doing this." Jason's words ran together.

"I'm happy to."

"Yeah, so, listen; I was just wrapping things up here, anyway. I can be home in about an hour."

"Jason," I could tell worry motivated him, "you don't have to hurry home on my account. I don't mind being here. I've got Vee with me and nothing to do at home."

Jason's voice softened and slowed down. "Okay. Thanks again for doing this, Jen. I'll see you soon."

I wanted to add the natural phrase "I love you" before I told him goodbye. That made me sit back for a moment. Did I love him? No, of course not. But I cared for him and his daughter.

I checked on Catherine again, told Vee he was a good boy, and reminded him to stay. Roaming into the family room, I took more time in registering my surroundings than on my previous visit. A picture of Catherine with her mom caught my attention. Light brown hair, similar to

Catherine's, cascaded around her face, and the same pale green eyes gazed upon the room. She was gone. Now I was here, taking care of her daughter. Not by her choice, of course. Not like my younger siblings, who were all adopted.

I enjoyed having a younger brother and sisters as I grew up, but I never understood how a mother, or even a mother/father combination, could abandon a child for someone else to raise. Where was the love? What about the sense of pride for the individual that they created? How could someone intentionally let go of their own flesh and blood?

I tried to imagine myself in some situation where necessity required me to leave a child of mine with others—and with a high probability of never seeing him or her again. Not a feasible option. Such an extreme circumstance remained incomprehensible to me.

CHAPTER 22

QUESTIONING ALL THE MEN

BY THE TIME JASON arrived, I'd checked on Catherine a couple more times before curling up with a book of the collective works of Poe and a cup of hot tea. The last time I'd peeked my head in on Catherine, she still slumbered with Vee licking her neck and cheeks. She'd be fine soon.

"Hi." I spoke in a low, calm voice to slow down his progression when he deposited his things over the back of the couch.

"Hey." He smiled and rushed over to me. For a second, I envisioned him bending to kiss my forehead. Dang! I carried this whole family fantasy thing a bit too far.

"How's she doing?" Jason's anxious eyes sought mine.

"She's much better, really. I think the Tylenol worked wonders. Her fever may even have broken."

"Great! Thanks, thank you. This was above and beyond the call of friendship." He pulled my hands together and shook them like one giant hand.

"It's exactly what a friend would do," I corrected. "Now go see her." I called after his retreating figure, "Oh, and Vee's in there with her. He's helping keep her warm."

Jason returned minutes later; all traces of anxiety melted from his face. "Thanks again."

This time when he walked toward me, he pulled me upright by my hands. I sensed a kiss was on his mind, and he didn't disappoint. But I had to resist, murmuring, "Jason, I can't."

He let my hands go and stepped back. "I know. At least before we had the excuse of the mistletoe. No relationship besides friendship is appropriate for us."

"This is true." I sighed, displeased. "But I do want to keep our friendship."

He also sighed. "Me too. Hey, are you hungry? Have you had supper?"

Jason admitted to leaving his conference before a group of them meandered toward local cuisine. Some planned to stay at the hotel again tonight, but he'd already decided to come home even before my call.

I confessed to not having eaten since lunch, reminding him I had no real reason to go home. I kept reading while Jason assembled some cold cuts and fresh fruit. While we ate, I mentally reviewed the events of the afternoon and the stories I skimmed through.

Since Jason and I coexisted as self-proclaimed friends, I decided to hurl some questions at him. I figured if he began regarding me with amusement or asking return questions that made me uncomfortable, I'd laugh them off. The wine we drank with supper helped loosen my tongue.

"Hey, Jason," he looked up and smiled. My heart leapt. That beautiful smile, formed by sexy lips, aimed at me. "Do you think that sometimes people get together for the wrong reasons?" When he scrunched his forehead I added, "Or that maybe they thought they got together for the right reasons, but then found out things were horribly wrong between them?" By my first question, I didn't want him assuming I referred to the two of us.

"Oh." Realization dawned on him. He regarded me thoughtfully. "I think sometimes we only share parts of our personality with certain people. Often, we open up more to the people we're closest to—family, loved ones, co-workers. In many cases, the things we share with those people are intimate—thoughts, emotions, hopes, and dreams."

"However," he continued, "Sometimes the worst in an individual is bared for those he...or she, thinks they own or can manipulate. Some people thrive in relationships, others deteriorate."

I couldn't look Jason in the eye while I considered his words. We both knew who I meant.

"But," my voice held sadness impossible for me to disguise, "hypothetically speaking, of course, how does one remove oneself from an unhealthy relationship? Wouldn't that be difficult?"

Jason's head bowed. "Yes, yes it would."

When he said nothing else, I pondered aloud, "I wonder how one would even begin such a process?"

Jason jerked his head up, and I swore I saw hope in his eyes. "I suppose," he contemplated, stroking his beard, "that the first thing the injured," he cleared his throat, "I mean interested party..." He looked from side to side at a loss for words. "The first step, I suppose, for a person who wanted out of a relationship, would be to admit to themselves that they really wanted to terminate it and know the reasons why. A confrontation might then occur, where the interested party would voice complaints. But reconciliation could occur if they made changes in the relationship. If not, the two parties could part ways."

"However," that word surfaced again, "In some cases a confrontation just might be too dangerous." He looked worried again. This poor guy gripped the shoulder restraints on an emotional roller coaster tonight.

"That's great advice!" I grinned at him.

"Really?" He sat back on the couch, relaxing his shoulders as he stretched his arms across its back.

"Absolutely. Hey, I was reading your collective short stories of Edgar Allan Poe and kept wondering, as I did back in high school, what it was that allowed him to create so many monsters? Was he really haunted? Was he insane? Was it his drug and alcohol consumption?"

"He did have quite an imagination, didn't he?"

"Do you think," I executed prudence while easing my way into this next round of questioning, "that all of his ghosts were imagined?"

"I guess that without being able to ask him personally, we'll never know. I've heard that another master of horror, Stephen King, always checks under his bed each night before he goes to sleep. Real or imagined, he appears to be haunted."

"I see what you mean. Can I now pose some even more hypothetical questions? I mean, these are extremely abstract."

"Go ahead, shoot."

"Okay. What if a person is being, say, plagued by monsters? Ghastly, terrifying monsters."

A slight wrinkle encroached on Jason's forehead. "You say plagued. Can you elaborate?"

"Stalked, intruded upon, bothered."

"Are they chasing you?" I looked at him sharply. "I mean," he amended, "the person. Are the monsters a nuisance or a genuine threat?"

"Hmm. Well, no, they probably aren't chasing anyone. They just show up when the person is alone, and they are so scary."

Jason must've been questioning my sanity, but he didn't look at me like he thought I purchased a first-class ticket on the crazy train. He waited a bit before responding.

"Monsters come in many different forms. Sometimes we even battle monsters within ourselves. If they're showing up all the time, they must want something. Does the person know what they want?"

"No!" I blurted. "This person has no idea. And the monsters look different each time. But no one else has seen them, and the one person who she tried to tell so far didn't believe her."

"Okay, the monsters aren't chasing anyone. They're just appearing. Do they seem lost, scared, like they need help?"

What? What was he talking about? What bizarre scenario featured monsters requiring help? And even if they did, why would they come to me for that assistance?

"So," he continued, "maybe this person should ask them. Approach them and ask what they want. Does only one monster appear at a time?"

"I believe so, yes."

"Perfect, then. Only one monster to deal with. One monster to question. What could it hurt?"

Hmm. Again, I kept my thoughts silent. What could it hurt?

I lifted my gaze to linger on Jason's face. So much about this guy screamed comfort and compatibility. When distraught, he was adorable. And when confronted with ambiguous, off-the-wall questions, he remained composed and logical.

"Great idea. I'll be sure to recommend it." Part of me wondered if Jason didn't think I used the monster metaphor in reference to Nick. "I'm going to check on Catherine again. Do you want to come with me?"

I crept over to the bed where she lay on her side with an arm draped around Vee. All signs of fever departed. Jason and I exchanged silent smiles.

Back in the family room, we selected a romantic comedy on Netflix and stretched next to each other on the couch, our feet resting on the coffee table, his right leg and my left leg connected from the hip all the way down to the foot. I loved the delicious fire that flickered and sent a slow burn along my leg, shooting tendrils of flames through the rest of my body. This burning intensified, deep and sexy, leaving me yearning with a desperation I didn't understand. Before the first plot point unfurled, we held hands; and by the time the movie ended, I couldn't even list the names of the main characters.

I didn't remember ever having felt this way about Nick. I never knew where I stood with him. One minute we'd be having fun, and the next he'd be yelling and hitting me. Rarely could I predict his mood with accuracy, although I constantly improved on determining potential sources of aggravation.

With Charles, the chemical reactions remained fiery and explosive—completely pleasant and always surprising. He was unpredictable, powerful, and enigmatic.

Jason represented comfort, practicality, and understanding. He escorted me to my car that had not managed to reach his garage this time. The snow tapered off. He assisted my departure by clearing fluffy precipitation from the windshield and hood. After I'd secured my seatbelt, he opened the driver's door, bent down, and gave me a quick kiss. Friends did that sometimes, right?

"Drive safely," he murmured, letting go of the door. When it latched, loneliness ensconced me. I couldn't believe the sadness involved in backing away from his figure, but at least Vee escorted me. I wanted to leave Vee with Catherine, but Jason insisted he come with me so I wouldn't be alone.

Shortly after eleven o'clock, my tires crunched through the snow in my own driveway. I pulled my phone from my purse to put it on the charger, discovering that I'd missed several calls. All from Charles. The most recent came twenty minutes ago, so I called him back.

"Shenandoah," he breathed into the receiver. Dang, but his voice oozed sex, especially when he uttered my given name.

"Hey, Charles. You called?"

"I'm glad you're finally returning my call, but where have you been?" Impatience interlaced his words. "I waited a while before I stopped over, then I kept calling. I didn't mean to upset you this afternoon, but I am trying to open your eyes to the world around you."

"I'm not upset, Charles. I'm beginning to understand."

"Well, I'm glad you're safe with this nasty weather. What compelled you to go out on such a night?"

His protective nature didn't bother me in the same way it did with Nick. "I went to take care of a sick student while her...parents were out of town. Her dad came home, and she's doing much better. But she really did need me for a while." It wasn't a complete lie.

"She's lucky to have such a compassionate teacher." The praise in his voice melted me inside.

"Thank you." I decided to make the most of the situation. "Hey, Charles? While I've got you on the line, do you mind if I ask you a couple of hypothetical questions?"

"Those are my specialty," he purred. "Fire away."

His answer to my first question, about the unhealthy relationship, instructed me to walk away and never look back. Also, to get protection—even a court order, if necessary. No doubt he concluded to whom I referred. I launched into the hypothetical monster questions, which he declined to take seriously.

"So... Monsters. Do you mean people who do evil things? People who seem like monsters? Is this basically your first question but asked differently?"

"No. I'm talking real monsters. Hideous, terrifying beasts. The kind they make horror movies about."

"Oh, my dear, sweet, Shenandoah. Those monsters aren't real. If we dream about them, they exist for a short while in our memories. But they're not real."

His words seemed to slight my fears, but I wouldn't let on. "So your answer—if I've got this right—is to not acknowledge their existence, thereby dispersing of them."

"Yes," he confirmed. "Unless the monsters are real people, in which case you seek help and protection. I am always here for you. You just need to tell me who the specific monsters are, and I'll drive them away. Your safety and happiness are a priority to me."

Charles hadn't kept the scenarios objective but turned them around about me.

"Okay, great answers. Thanks also for checking on me. I think I'm going to hit the hay now. Good night, Charles."

"Buenos sueños, mi amor."

Hmphf. Spanish to impress me?

That night, I couldn't get to sleep. I mulled over Charles and Jason's advice, plus I contemplated my feelings for them and reactions to their body chemistry.

When Nick came home, slumber still escaped me, which he took as an open invitation to have sex. Not that sex wasn't always on the table as far as he was concerned, but when conscious, I made his job easier.

Since he didn't fall asleep right away afterwards— maybe the barometric pressure from the storm kept us both up—I broached my questions with him. Although daunted by the risk, it seemed right to give all involved male parties a fair shot at my heart and at becoming my hero.

"Hey, Nick?" I rolled over toward him, tracing my fingers over his back.

"Yeah babe, what's up?"

"Can I ask you a couple hypothetical questions?"

He turned part way toward me with an irritated look on his face. "Can't you just ask me real questions?"

I couldn't back down. "Well, if they have to do with nightmares I've had, how could they be real?"

He relaxed a bit. "Okay, what then?"

I took a deep breath. "As you know, I saw that creepy kid in our backyard last month. The kid wearing a Halloween mask at Thanksgiving?" Nick nodded. "I've been having nightmares, and possibly hallucinations during the day. I can't seem to shake these monsters that keep plaguing me. What do you suggest I do?"

Nick rolled all the way over and massaged my arm. "It's okay, babe. They've got medication to help with that. With all the trauma you've been through, just call the doc and have him prescribe something. A little pill for a little peace of mind. Oh, wait! A little pill for a little chill." He smiled at his creativity. "Was that your only question?"

I gulped but continued. "I've got this student. And, well...this is my first teaching job. I'm not equipped to handle everything that gets thrown at me. So I've got this student who suspects her boyfriend's cheating on her, but every time she asks him about it he laughs and tells her how stupid she is. What kind of advice should I give her?"

"Babe, if the guy's sayin' she's stupid, then she is. Why would he lie? Tell her she needs to be more trusting."

"So, you think the guy's not cheating?"

"Not if he says he's not." Nick rolled over and thrust his butt out, almost knocking me off the bed. "You bitches are all the same. You don't know when to shut up and just believe what men tell you."

Plunk! Nick put me and the entire female gender right back in our places. I scooted out of bed and considered myself lucky he didn't choose to get physical.

Curled up in my window seat, I reasoned that I'd equally polled each of my candidates. I couldn't decide if the results surprised me or not. I also didn't know what next course of action to take, but one began to solidify.

For obvious reasons, I couldn't keep living in fear of running into monsters. Neither could I keep living in fear for my safety, even my life. I also could allow myself to have only one lover. Thinking back at the past 24 hours, I realized that I'd kissed three different men in one day. For God's sake, that made me a tramp!

I needed one man, no beatings, no monsters, and a safe place to call home. Heaven help me make the right choices to achieve these goals.

CHAPTER 23

THE FLU, ROUND TWO

SUNDAY MORNING, I AWOKE to gray skies again. This time, complete exhaustion tethered my body to the pillow. Not only had sleep eluded me, but it also denied me a decent rest when it arrived. I noticed with alarm that the hour hand already pointed past ten o'clock. I jumped off the window seat, amazed that Nick hadn't woken me yet. Breakfast needed whipping up, shopping done, bedding washed, the house cleaned. French toast heaped onto a platter and bacon sizzled on the griddle when Nick entered the kitchen.

"Smells great, babe!" He loaded some on a plate, poured the syrup and grabbed a cup of coffee. He scuttled off to the family room, popping back in for a few slices of bacon, which he wrapped in a paper towel. "Awesome feast, Jen. Great way to start my day off." He swatted me on the ass.

"Asshole," I muttered, hurrying to complete the necessary chores so I'd have time for an afternoon walk. Throughout the morning and early afternoon, a giddiness enveloped me. Never in my life had I gone on a hunt for monsters. In fact, I made every effort to avoid them.

While I spread fresh sheets across the bed, I considered the different apparitions I'd seen, the places where they'd appeared, and the times of day or night they'd manifested. Night at the hospital, night for the clown. Dusk for the homeless woman and the figures in the trees. Night for the bloody body. Late afternoon for the masked kid.

I'd felt presences in broad daylight. Unexplained shadows, strange noises, gusts of wind. And the same monster never appeared twice, nor had I seen one in the exact same location. So how did one go about tracking monsters?

Late in the afternoon, I hollered to Nick that a pot roast and potatoes baked in the oven, and I wanted to take Vee out for some exercise. I made sure to point out my personal benefit, keeping my ass nice and tight. Since he raised no objections, I bundled up and left.

"What do you think, Vee? Are we going to find us some monsters today?"

Vee looked up, happiness radiating from his gaze. He loved the fresh air and beauty of the park as much as I relished the outdoors and his company.

"Now Vee, if we come across something strange, I don't want you barking at it and scaring it off. At least, not right away. Now if it's someone who wants to mug me, then go right ahead. Obviously, I don't want to be mugged, kidnapped, raped, or murdered." I shivered.

Things Charles said yesterday about my safety seeped into my mind. But I led Vee on a leash for protection. Vee, who didn't bark at Charles, because he was one of the good guys. But Vee also didn't bark at any of the apparitions. So were my monsters good guys, too? Or did they materialize in my head, and Vee didn't even know they existed? What kind of convoluted imagination twisted through my head? I always perceived that it leaned heavily on the side of overactive, but then again, I'd also always known when things weren't real. I guessed that, whether real or perceived, I still needed to find a monster.

White-coated pines and an endless gray sky stretched ahead. Even the lake to my far left reflected a deep gray today. I skittered along the sidewalk. I hadn't seen a vision yet, but an unmistakable pull in my gut revealed the inevitability of encountering one.

Moments later, laying on the snow at the base of a pine tree, a hand waited. A small hand, like that of a child.

"Oh shit. Here we go, Vee."

I didn't like this at all, but I had to persevere in my experiment. Nearing the appendage, I honed in on more details. The hand belonged to a broken arm...of a doll! Not just any doll, but a scary one. A doll like my grandma owned when she was a little girl. The kind that stood about two feet high with eyes that opened when tilted upright.

This doll flaunted rosy cheeks, white plastic shoes, long, blonde curly hair, and a blue gingham dress with a white apron. She lay face up in the snow with her detached arm several inches above her head. She appeared innocent enough, but I knew better. No one placed a doll on fresh snow and left it when not a soul loitered in the vicinity. Besides, a sickening sensation inside me told me I found one of my...monsters.

As I stared, contemplating the doll, glued on eyelashes popped up to reveal glass eyes that matched her dress. Full, painted lips parted to reveal pearly white tiny teeth. The head turned toward me, eyes still open and toothy grin in place.

Now was the time. Time to quit running and face this new problem. A little doll versus a human with her dog. Internal pep talk complete, I eased nearer the lifelike toy. Although scared to close my eyes, I did. A lifeless, porcelain object couldn't drag its body through the snow. And for what purpose? To kick me in the knees?

"You're not real." I stated, but a quaver in my voice shook my resolution. "You. Are not. Real." I spoke aloud to dispel my fear and to make it disappear. But when I opened my eyes, one of the doll's slid into a wink then opened.

"What?" I screamed at it. "What do you want?"

Hurried footsteps sounded behind me. I spun to witness Charles sprinting my way. "Is everything okay? Did something happen to you?"

"It's just that I found this creepy doll." I gripped him by the forearms to support myself as I half turned. "Look at it. Isn't it messed up?" But when I rotated at the waist, I saw the same thing as Charles. Nothing. Not even an imprint where the doll rested in the snow.

"What doll?" Charles asked in all seriousness. "Did someone lose it out here in the snow? What a strange place to be dragging a doll. Did your dog spot it and try to dig it up?"

"No, no, it was on top of the snow. Its arm had been pulled off."

"By your dog?"

"No!" I pushed away from him, searching in desperation around the tree. It hadn't been a trick of my mind; it vanished when I closed my eyes, reemerging once I opened them again. It even winked at me! And it apparently moved. Had someone taken it away? Or—more horrifying than any prank—was it alive?

"Charles, did you see anyone else here?" I peered around for footprints, human or doll sized. Or even signs that something slid through the snow. Nothing.

"There's a guy ice fishing on the southwest corner of the lake. That's the only person I've seen so far. Except for the lovely lady in front of me." He amended.

Although grateful that Charles believed me and helped me look, I began to feel foolish.

"Maybe it was an animal. A rabbit or a squirrel? But then again..." a lack of tracks. He didn't need to say it. "Perhaps a bird?"

I agreed, unwilling to have him assume crazy should be my middle name. "I guess I'm just tired. I let my imagination get carried away. Weird." I shook my head in mock exaggeration. "Well, I suppose I should get on with my walk."

"Would you like some company?"

Since the doll and alleged danger disappeared, fear of recognition in public with another man by someone who might report back to my husband took over. A panoramic glance, this time for other humans, allowed my shoulders to relax when I didn't see any.

"For a bit," I conceded. "My husband is kind of jealous, and I don't think he'd approve." Vee and I started walking at a brisk pace. Charles easily kept stride. "How did you know when I'd be in the park?"

"This seems to be your favorite time of day to head out."

"That doesn't sound stalkerish at all!" I retorted.

"Hey." Charles caught me by the elbow and turned me around to face him. "I'm trying to show you there are other ways. There's another life."

"Another life aside from what? Do you want me to live the life of an adulteress?"

"I would tell you 'sorry' if I really was. But I'm not. You are a strong and passionate woman, Shenandoah. I want so much for you to learn that about yourself. By nurturing these characteristics, your potential in the world is limitless."

I opened my mouth to protest, but he pressed a firm finger against protesting lips.

"Let me be the one to teach you who you are." A request and a command at the same time.

My brain struggled with independence and conformity. I'd always wanted to fit in. Perhaps I'd gone about it all wrong. Or maybe the devil tempted me astray. If that was true, the devil had evenly chiseled lips, a body in peak form even into his 30s, and kisses that dipped my body in baths of molten lava.

On the other hand, if Charles was the devil, what sort of angel did that make Nick? No angel in my mind beat women physically and cut them down mentally. Perhaps the devil embodied Nick?

And if Nick was the devil, making Charles an angel, why did an angel tempt me so?

"It's complicated, Charles."

"Then let me be the one to uncomplicate things. Let me be the one to add adventure, love, and excitement to your life. Let me be the one to dispel fear and protect you. Just let me be the one."

Although an indisputable fact that my life couldn't continue on its previous course, I was reluctant to drop established certainties—Nick's volatile temper, my best friend, Vee, a house that I'd come to recognize as home. Two jobs, decent money, a couple of good friends. If I followed the instructions Charles provided and uprooted myself, what then? Foremost, I feared Nick's retaliation. With that shadow looming, I dared not run into the sunlight. This decision required prudence and patience.

"Let's just walk for today." I grinned at him and picked up the pace.

* * *

The following week at school grew hectic as the semester wound down. My Double Secret Santa began on Monday with many students and a handful of staff members shuffling in, leaving gifts on a table I'd prepared, and searching out their pseudonyms.

I participated, as well, except I knew who received my gift. One of the school's best wrestlers, a boy of Hispanic origin, walked to the table, tossed a gift down, and searched for his name.

"¡Ah, sí, jugo de naranja!" Hector seemed happy I'd chosen to get him a small bottle of orange juice, one of the items on his list of preferences. I smiled, happy to make the day better for a kid with a rough family life and who intimidated others like a boss.

At the end of that first day, several gifts remained on the table. Some participants brought gifts early and forgot to check back in. Others rushed to sports practices after school and lost track of time. Perusing the table, I found a Reese's peanut butter cup with María 7 scrawled in permanent marker across the top. María had been my Spanish name in high school, and 7 my favorite number. Yum. My mind cautioned against so many calories, but the pure bliss of peanut butter and chocolate provided instantaneous gratification after the work put into organizing this exchange.

Still savoring the flavors partying in my mouth, I spotted a tiny package on the back left corner of the table. Sra. Adesco, someone printed in neat, tiny script. Had some student brought a Christmas gift to me and been too shy to deliver it in person?

Sliding my finger under the tape fastening one side, I peeled the paper back, curious about the contents. I lifted the lid of the box to reveal a beautiful, hauntingly familiar pewter angel. The angel reminded me of my grandfather, but the angel's face—or lack thereof—was so similar to several faces I'd previously seen. Her eyes sunk into hollowed-out holes, and she had no visible mouth. She carried long-stemmed tulips.

At first, I thought Catherine left it since she'd been so concerned about me having an angel for my tree. But I'd shown her all my ornaments. Maybe she wanted me to own an angel figurine, as well? An inkling told me Catherine was not my benefactor.

Continuing to stare at the smooth curves, I couldn't figure out if it should scare me. This exquisite piece fascinated me. Were the creatures who stalked me trying to befriend me?

Nice thoughts switched to panic. How many creatures existed? Or was it one entity with access to gratuitous prank material? Why had I never seen the same goon twice? Still...my fingers caressed smooth pewter curves. What a nice gesture. Or an omen, a recess of my mind whispered.

The rest of the week at school sped by in a whirlwind of gift bags, giggles, and spies. Grafton High School allowed leniency on its no outside food or drink rule, which broadened gift ideas.

Friday morning before school, all participants met in my classroom to learn and reveal identities. Hector was so thrilled with the orange juice I provided all week that he gave me a surprise hug.

"Thanks, Señora! That OJ made my week. But let's be honest, aren't you glad that all these sniveling punks—especially the junior high kids—won't be constantly invading your room after this week?"

My mouth dropped open to protest, but before a response formed on my lips, he clapped me on the shoulder. "See you next week, Adesco." He sauntered past and disappeared down the hallway.

The kid who'd drawn my name for the week was a transfer student from Baltimore, who went by the handle "Toro Mapache." He'd adapted in a rough fashion to a smaller town, with a much smaller school system, and was rumored to share responsibility for some of the "wall art" in the downtown Grafton area. I thanked him warmly for the sugary delights he'd extended my way all week.

"Muchisimas gracias, Toro."

He proffered a nonchalant shrug, but satisfaction coated his face.

By the time 2:00 rolled around, our early out Friday time, fire licked my throat and pounding filled my head. I drove home, clinging to enough energy to get up my front steps and into the house. Vee's instinct dictated something was wrong when my affectionate embrace upon exiting my car became a hand to the head that slid off. He stayed by me and offered support as I tried to remove my coat and shoes.

The window seat greeted me. I collapsed into it, not even bothering to push aside the blanket. My body ached, wracked with fever, but I remained helpless. I wanted to sleep but couldn't. Behind closed lids, the anonymous gifts I'd received throughout the week kept appearing: the faceless angel, a second angel with her eyes closed and a brilliant silver star on her headband, and three different chunks of rock, which both science teachers assured me, fell from asteroids. One shone black with silver bits in it, one platinum with bright yellow jewels, and the other red speckled with black.

Who left me such peculiar presents? I fretted over this as I shivered and tried to finagle my way under the blankets. The faceless angel resurfaced time and again, but instead of holding flowers, her arms stretched out to me. She wanted to help me.

At one point, certain my eyes were open, I saw a life-sized version of my pewter angel hovering over me. She smoothed the blankets and tucked them in. With a wave of her hand, Vee understood to jump back up beside me. Vee wagged his tail and grinned up at the apparition until she patted him on the head. Much like every other creature that I'd seen in Vee's presence, he was not alarmed. I trusted Vee. I trusted him to protect me, and I trusted his judgment in character.

With the larger-than-life angel still looming, I allowed my eyelids to droop. Enough warmth spread through my limbs for the chills to subside and sleep to overtake me.

CHAPTER 24

Nick Gets Sick

I AWOKE TO A low growl from Vee. The front door clicked, and Nick stomped excess snow from his shoes.

"Damn," he said, cocking his head to look at me from another angle, "You look like hell."

"I think I have the flu," I croaked.

"Yeah, I think you do, too. Umm, everything okay?"

"Go to bed, Nick." I didn't want him around anymore than he desired my company at the moment.

I dozed in fitful slumber for at least twelve more hours. During that time, I remembered someone leading me to the bathroom where I relieved myself and splashed my face with water. I also recalled sipping water through a straw. Vee's presence was always there, always licking me, as if I was his poor, sick puppy.

My mind registered Nick leaving for work the next day, followed by my ringing phone.

"Hello?" my voice sounded strange, strained after a long period of nonuse.

"Hey, Jen. This is Jason."

Of course it was. My heart warmed at the thought of him.

"I've been wanting to call and check in on you, well, ever since Catherine told me you looked a little rough yesterday. But I tried, and you never answered your phone. Then I didn't want to get you in trouble for calling, so it's been killing me to know—are you okay?"

I responded in a gravelly voice, "I think I'm on the mend now, but I'm not sure how I survived the past day and a half. Must have been the same thing Catherine had."

"I'm absolutely positive that it was. I had it Tuesday, Wednesday, and Thursday, and was lucky to have Catherine around before and after school to take care of me. That was wicked stuff. Hospitals are getting a fair number of cases of dehydration and other complications from this flu virus. Did, umm...did Nick take care of you?"

On the verge of laughter, I decided that might come across as rude. Instead, I softened my reply, "No, just Vee. She's great at warding against chills."

"Do you mind if I stop over to make sure you're not still feverish? This is a tough virus to kick."

"That'd be fine. But," I hesitated, "I hope Nick has gone to work. I honestly think he left but don't remember for sure."

"Let me take care of the worrying. I'll find out before I come to your house."

I smiled. Of course he took precautions. After all, the picture of him with me severely ticked Nick off two months ago. While I wanted to believe in the goodness that I knew existed in Nick, I was certain he would kill Jason if he showed up at our front door. Then my husband would be in jail and the man—well, one of the men that I cared deeply for—would be dead. And Catherine would be an orphan.

I dozed off again, waking with a groggy head to a soft rap on the door. "Jen?"

"I'm here. C'mon in."

Noting my appearance, embarrassment flagged my cheeks red when Jason rounded the corner and spotted me lying on my side, propped on an elbow.

"Hey, Jason. I really think I'm doing much better. I should take a shower. I'm sure I look worse than something you'd find in a refuse heap."

Jason sat beside me on the window seat. He smoothed the hair from my forehead, laying a cool wrist against it. The fresh blush covering my cheeks had nothing to do with fever and everything to do with the man who made me a priority this afternoon.

"It would appear your fever has broken." His voice resonated a low timber, filled with compassion and some other emotion I couldn't identify. "You look charming, but if you'd like to shower, I'll wait here and fix you a light snack. You probably haven't eaten in over a day, have you?"

I shook my head.

Jason stood, offering to help pull me to my feet. He ruffled my hair. "Take your time. I'll be in the kitchen."

Nodding again, I grabbed the banister for support as I climbed the stairs. Each step was more laborious than the prior, I couldn't believe how much the flu taxed my body. I often felt this weak after... I brushed aside mental cobwebs. Oh yes. I often felt this way after an episode where Nick beat the living shit out of me.

While I showered, tumultuous thoughts about my troublesome relationships collided. My life, as well—a total disaster. I firmed up early New Year's resolutions. Always a pacifist, I preferred to let others duke out issues surrounding my life. Most of the time, I accepted the decisions they made. That's not to say I hadn't worked some things out on my own, but life seemed much smoother when others made choices I could live with.

However, continuing with Nick's abuse was not something I could live with. Literally. Deep inside, I foresaw Nick would kill me if things didn't change. I once thought a fresh beginning in North Dakota would improve his mood. However, the beatings had only increased in frequency and intensity.

The whole What would happen if I left him? scenario popped up again. The logical part of my brain wanted a plan in place. I recalled an assembly I attended in college where a middle-aged couple advocated Jana's Campaign. This helped me understand that leaving Nick might not be enough. Staggeringly high statistics showed far too many women were killed each year by ex-husbands and former boyfriends. I already stood for a tally mark on an atrocious list. I harbored no desire to become a death statistic, as well.

But I could no longer rely on friends, co-workers, or a pet to save me. I needed to make a choice and take action.

I joined Jason at the kitchen counter, confidence in myself boosted higher than it had been in a long time. He whipped up watercress sandwiches and herbal tea. With each bite, I sensed strength flowing into my body.

"Welcome back to the world of the living." Jason's grin caught me off guard and my heart lurched.

"Thanks for doing this. It's nice to have someone look after me." My hands encircled a Peace Garden State coffee cup, a welcome gift from the Grafton Chamber of Commerce, extracting heat from the warm tea.

Jason placed his hands around mine before looking me in the eye. "Any time. It's my pleasure." He shifted his gaze back to our hands. "You deserve to be cared for the same way you care for others."

Tears sprang to my eyes, but I held them back. Of course, he was right. That's what I'd been telling myself all along. Why continue to wait, hoping for what I wanted? Why not take charge of my life and get it now?

"So have you seen your monsters again?" His comment tumbled from out of the blue.

"Umm, well, yes. But only once. Or twice." I amended, unsure if I'd dreamt about the faceless angel, or if she'd actually set foot in my house. In all probability, I desired someone to take care of me so badly that my imagination conjured her from an inanimate gift I'd received.

"Did you talk to them?" Jason regarded me intently. It didn't appear—yet anyway—that he doubted my credibility.

"Well," I couldn't look him in the eye when I talked about this, "it was scary, but I tried. I guess I yelled instead of speaking, but I wasn't trying to be mean. I was really creeped out."

"Tell me about it," he murmured.

"I'm not sure I want to."

"Why not?"

I bit my lower lip. "You might think I'm crazy."

"Jen," he assured me, ducking his head and trying to look up into my face. "You've been through a lot, and I know you're still suffering. But believe me when I tell you I in no way doubt your mental state. Okay?"

Although I nodded, I doubted his words. "Well, last Sunday I went on a walk in search of monsters."

"And?" he prompted.

"I found one. It was scary, and I wanted to run, but I didn't. And then..."

"Did it chase you?" Jason's voice remained calm. He hung on my every word.

"No, but it winked at me. That scared me even more, so I screamed, asking what it wanted."

"Did it respond?"

"It never got the chance. Someone heard me screaming and came running to rescue me."

"Were you walking here in town?"

"No, I was at Leistikow Park. There hadn't been a soul around, and then he showed up."

"He?"

"Yeah, I think he was stalking me—or, at least, he led me to believe that he had been. Charles said he recalled when I liked to go for walks."

Jason scowled.

"This wasn't the first time it had happened, either. He surprised me once before on a walk."

The scowl deepened. "What did the monster do?"

"When I turned around to see who was coming, it disappeared. Completely. I mean, without even an impression in the snow."

"So it had been standing near you. Not hovering or flying."

I recalled the bizarre image. "It was laying beside a tree in the snow. And then, it was gone."

"Did you look for it?"

"All over. Charles helped me look. I know he thinks I'm a little cuckoo now."

Truth rang from Jason's response. "Well, I don't."

"Then yesterday, or last night... Oh, I don't know—some time when I was sick, I could have sworn one of them was here with me, in my house."

"Were you frightened?"

"A little. Honestly, I was too sick to be scared. Even if I had panicked, I couldn't have gone anywhere." My eyes fell on the pewter figurine. "It was a life-sized version of this." I thrust the angel at him. "Surely a hallucination brought on by fever."

Jason concurred. "That's highly possible."

"I imagined her taking care of me…like a mom…or an angel."

"Understandable. Luckily, I had Catherine as a caregiver. Did Nick even realize you were sick?"

"He knew." I slid off the kitchen stool. "He just didn't want to deal with it."

Jason muttered under his breath, something that sounded like "be a man." He stood and pushed his stool under the counter. Stepping beside me, he gave me an affectionate hug. Sexual tension simmered between us, but neither of us acted on it.

"I'm so glad you're feeling better." Enigmatic blue eyes bored into mine. "I worry when I'm not with you." He dropped a feather soft kiss on my lips, before backing away.

"Thank you." That's all I said, but it meant so much. It included an unspoken thanks for taking time for me, recognizing my worth and helping me battle my demons. When he left for home, a part of me went with him.

* * *

Nick's Christmas party was the following evening. They held it at the club, but catered the food and brought in a DJ, bartender, and cleaning crew. Happy hour began at four, and we arrived early.

By six o'clock, when they served our meal, Nick was already lit. He headed up the entertainment at our table, regaling all with antics from his high school days.

We'd barely finished eating when the DJ threw on the latest trending tunes. Nick stumbled when pushing aside his chair but didn't let inebriation keep him from the dance floor. He towed me after him, sending me into a spin once we reached the edge of the other dancers. After two fast songs, the smart-alecky DJ touted, "Now that I've got all you love birds out here, let's slow it on down a few notches."

Nick yanked my arm so hard I stopped short of a full-on body slam into him. "Oof—geez, Nick!"

"Aw babe, you know you like it rough." His arms that grasped my lower back slid down to my ass.

"Nick!"

"What's the matter, babe? You need a little more liquid relaxant?"

We swayed unsteadily throughout the song, and I worried about tripping and falling. After one slow song, we wandered back to our seats. He staggered and jerked me along behind.

I tried to fathom what was wrong. Nick got drunk all the time, but I couldn't remember the last time he'd lost control of his faculties in a public place. If he ever became that intoxicated, his next steps led him to bed where he collapsed. But we weren't home. He leaned back, his head and an arm flopped over the backside of the chair, one of his legs stretched out before him.

"Oh shit!" His body twitched forward, and he laid his head on top of crossed arms on the table. Several of his co-workers and their spouses shot sympathetic glances my way.

"Nick! What's wrong, honey? Are you okay?"

He turned glazed eyes toward me but said nothing. Also, not characteristic of Nick, who tended to become more vocal the more he imbibed. Placing a hand across his forehead, his skin flamed against my already warm wrist.

"Holy smokes! You're burning up!" I beckoned to one of his buddies, who came closer to assess the situation. "Do you think a couple of you guys could help me get him home? He's drunk, and he's got the flu."

Joe whistled to another guy. They assured me they could load him up in their vehicle and deposit him in his bed at home. My sole job consisted of holding doors open for them.

Once home, I scooted Vee out of the way, explaining the situation to him. A few minutes later two men escorted my husband, a combination of dragging and carrying, all the way to our four-poster bed.

"You want us to undress him, too?" one of them joked.

"I've got it from here, but thanks so much, guys."

"Sure thing, Jen. We'd do anything for you. And," the blond glanced at Nick's unconscious figure before waggling his eyebrows suggestively, "anything for one of your homemade desserts. Those scones, or whatever you whipped up for the moving brigade last summer, were out of this world!"

A shy smile emerged. "I think I could arrange for Nick to bring some to work next week."

The two men shuffled downstairs and back into the cold winter night. "Oh, hey!" I hollered at them as an afterthought. "You might want to tell Nick's boss that he might not be back in to work on Tuesday, or at least give him the heads up. This is a wicked flu bug."

"Will do!" they yelled back.

Trudging back up the stairs, I tried to make Nick comfortable. I debated taking the following day off from school but decided Nick was a big boy, capable of fending for himself. Besides, he hadn't lifted one finger to help me when I'd suffered in sickness. Vee held the same frame of mind, if his near-snarling stance from the doorway indicated anything. He never planned to bestow any of his magical healing powers on the man lying in this bed.

Much as I figured, Nick stayed knocked out while I taught school on Monday. That didn't bother me too much, since I gathered he needed sleep. What alarmed me the most was his temperature. I jumped into high-gear triage with cool washcloths and rubbing alcohol sponge baths. I also trickled some water from an ice cube between his cracked lips.

Within an hour, his temperature lowered substantially. I expelled a huge breath of air. What a horror if he succumbed to brain damage or even died on my watch.

I kept close tabs on Nick throughout the night. Well after midnight, I suspected his fever began to break. Restless sleep plagued him the rest of the night, and he barely acknowledged me in the morning. I tried to make him comfortable and left a cold drink and some saltine crackers on the nightstand. He boasted a low-grade fever when I left for school.

Optimistic that he might be showered and up and about when I got home, it surprised me to find Nick in bed scowling. It didn't take long for accusations and insults to fly.

"You left me home alone when I was so sick? What's the matter with you? And, oh—by the way—thanks, bitch. Thanks for not calling me in sick to work. Are you trying to get me fired? And I'm starving! Why don't you stop gawking and get your ass down to the kitchen to fix me something good?"

He flipped the plate holding crackers onto the floor. Staring at shards of porcelain and cracker crumbs covering the floor by our bed, I decided against my better judgment to stand up to Nick.

I brought my head up to meet his eyes. "I took far better care of you than you've ever done for me." He raised himself onto his elbows. "Oh, and do you mean call into work like you didn't do for me? Back when you weren't taking me to the emergency room for life-threatening injuries. Back then, Nick?"

My voice squeaked when he leaped from the bed and advanced on me. I hadn't thought he'd possess the strength to move that fast. He stood before me like a dangerous jungle cat.

When he prepared to take a swing, I turned to run. I stopped in the doorway at the loud thud behind me. Good. He was weak. I'd gone this far, so I decided to hurl one more comment back to him. "Fix your own damn food! I quit!"

I stopped long enough to grab my purse, keys, school bag, computer, and coat, then pealed from the driveway with more drama than my prudent self ever had allowed before.

But what to do? Where to go? My tense muscles clenched the steering wheel, tight enough I wasn't sure I'd be able to evacuate the vehicle. Driving on an aimless jaunt through town, I contemplated my situation. I couldn't go back home. Nick would not cool off any time this evening.

I made my way to the downtown area and parked in front of the large graffiti wall. I stared blindly at it for a while, fixating on one point, kind of like those auto-stereograms found in "Magic Eye" books. The longer I stared, the clearer an image of a purple-hooded figure became. When it beckoned me closer, I shook my head to break the connection.

I could not deal with any more monsters tonight.

CHAPTER 25

Sleepover

BACKING OUT OF THAT lot, I spotted Chez Brigitte. I parallel parked in front of the store, and the tension drained from several of my muscle groups when I walked inside. The eagle-nosed owner diverted attention from her current patron to glide over, welcome me, and thank me for returning. She said she'd give me some time to look and declared that she'd return momentarily.

I browsed for a bit, then collapsed on a pink chaise. Sure enough, the owner zoned back in on me. She remained perceptive as ever, figuring out that something distressed me and offering to impart advice if I'd share my story.

"Well," I gazed down at my twisted hands, wishing I'd taken the time to paint my nails before Nick's Christmas party. "For reasons I'd rather not say, I'm unable to return to my home for the next day or two, so I need a couple of outfits until I can revisit my own wardrobe."

Brigitte patted my knee like a loving grandmother. "Let's find you those outfits then." She stood in one fluid motion. "You're a schoolteacher, right?"

Two months later and she remembered. Small-town business. I nodded and watched in awe when she pulled out two size-eight outfits that complimented my hair and eyes. I swore I'd looked through those same racks and not spotted them.

"Wow! They're adorable. I'm not sure how I missed them. Now how much are they?" When I flipped the garments around to search for a price tag, Brigitte's hand deftly flicked the tags off, swooping down to scoop them up, crumpling them before my eyes.

"They're twenty dollars apiece."

"What? Are you sure?" Why destroy the tags if she spoke the truth? "Okay. I'll take them both."

"Of course, dear. I just wish I could help you more. You may want to head over to ShopMart to pick up any other necessities."

I nodded.

"Do you have some place to stay?"

My nod halted. I gave a quick side-to-side jiggle of my head, but added, "I'll figure something out. I'm a pretty resourceful girl." My weak smile didn't convince her, but she dropped the subject.

In a daze, I drove to ShopMart. I wandered aimlessly for an hour collecting toothpaste, socks, and a hairbrush. Once back in my car, I hoped I had what I needed. But I made a decision. Pulling out my phone, I dialed the exclusive number that made sense.

"Shenandoah, to what do I owe this privilege?"

My terse voice demanded. "Charles, are you at home?" I heard music and chatter in the background.

He changed to all seriousness. "No. But I can be. Give me five minutes."

"Wait!" He'd already disconnected.

Impatient fingers scrolled to find his number again.

"Yes?"

"This would be a whole lot easier if you gave me your address."

"Damn! Yeah, sorry. I'm on Western Avenue, just a few houses south of the Catholic Church. I'll be in my driveway waiting for you. Give me a five-minute head start, though."

"Sure." This time I disconnected first.

I waited a couple of minutes before beginning a slow crawl over to St. John's Catholic Church. A moment of panic seized me when a white pickup appeared on my tail one block past the high school.

"Nick!" I gasped but relaxed as the truck full of laughing high school basketball players passed me, using an illegal maneuver. I needed to get off the street and out of sight in case Nick came looking.

Charles lounged against his car, his arms crossed in front of him. I pulled up in his driveway and stoically walked over.

His frantic eyes searched my face and body for any physical signs of abuse, I assumed. The greeting confirmed that. "Are you okay? Are you hurt? What happened?"

"Umm, do you mind if we go inside to talk?"

"Perfect," Charles agreed. "Do you want to put your car in my garage? Would that be a wise thing to do?"

I nodded affirmation. "That's what Jason always does." No sooner had I uttered those words than I slapped a hand across my mouth. It was none of Charles' business what I'd done in the past, still I hadn't intended on revealing so much.

His eyes narrowed. "I'll open the door for you."

Once inside his 21st century house—modern suited Charles—he led me to his living room couch. "Would you like something to drink? Have you eaten supper?"

Nothing fazed me yet. Not thirst, not hunger. I supposed my body still registered shock. I couldn't believe that I stood up to Nick AGAIN. And the words I said to him! I needed to think things through with careful consideration before going back home.

"Shenandoah, tell me." Charles took both my hands in his, rubbing heat back into them. "There's a reason you called me."

Neither one of us could deny the electric surge that flowed between us. I sought to extricate my hands to diminish the flow. "Could I, by any chance, stay here tonight? Potentially tomorrow night, too?"

"Of course!" Charles tried to grab my hands again, but I stood up and moved away. "Has he hurt you? Are you in danger?"

"I'm fine. I'm just taking precautions. And nothing will happen between us if I stay here." My firm tone resonated and put him on the defense.

He stood beside me and sneered, "Is that what you tell Jason when you stay with him?"

Anger rose within me once more. It surfaced briefly at my house only hours ago, but that anger had been justified. Nick was an asshole. Charles was trying to help, and I hadn't supplied complete honesty. A deep breath suppressed my irritation. Sincere eyes turned to meet his hostile ones.

"Please? Can you help me?"

He sighed. "Of course. Sorry for my behavior. Are you hungry?"

Without waiting for my answer, he ordered a pizza with two side salads. By the time the delivery boy arrived, I hadn't regained my appetite. Nevertheless, I forced a few bites down.

Afterwards, Charles showed me a bathroom. The earth-toned geometric uniformity of this room amazed me. Every object except the toilet bowl displayed itself as a prominent square. This included large square tiles climbing halfway up the walls. A hint of masculine cologne lingered in the air, indicating that he used this as his secondary bathroom.

He opened the door to the bedroom across the hall. Everything in this room shone in cream or dusty rose.

"My sister helped me with some decorating when I moved in." Charles explained. "She wanted a nice place to stay when she came to visit."

"She did well." I entered the room but turned and placed an imploring hand on his arm. "He may try to find me. I mean, he didn't the last time, but I didn't stay away overnight. Also," I swallowed hard, "this time was a little different."

"How so?" Charles cricked his head to see my face.

"I talked back to him." My head bowed in shame.

"Given the circumstances, that may have been a dangerous move. But," he cupped my face in both his hands, "it's your right to speak your mind."

I jerked my head away from his hands. The intense heat between us bordered on insanity and invited me in. "I should go to bed now."

Charles acquiesced. "Let me know if you need anything."

"I will. Good night." I closed the door with resolve, leaning against it. I longed for a goodnight kiss I forbid him to bestow.

Before showering, I realized that my new purchases included no sleepwear. Steaming water somewhat eased the tension in my shoulders and neck. Wrapped in nothing but a plush towel, I crept across the hall back to my bedroom. I saw and heard nothing from Charles. He honored my wishes not to mess around this evening.

Thankful for clean undergarments, I donned those before redressing in the clothes I'd worn all day. It wasn't like they were sweaty, just slightly wrinkled. After a guilty pause while crawling into bed with dirty clothes, I laid down and pulled only half of the comforter over me. Taut muscles screamed until I used biofeedback techniques to relax them.

When my eyes gave way to slumber, I dreamed about one of my real-life nightmares—Nick. I hardly ever dreamed about Nick. So rarely escapable in reality, my mind enjoyed the break sweet dreams afforded. But not tonight. Tonight, he came at me full force.

In my dream I stood in our living room, smiling, waiting for Nick to walk into the house. Eager to share the good news that I was pregnant. When he entered the front door, he strode toward me. I thought he sensed the happiness I wanted to share. I remembered the odd movement he made to initiate a hug. His right shoulder dropped back. In two more steps, his fist flew right at my face. I saw black spots, determining from the loud crack that he'd broken my nose. But he wasn't through with me.

He picked up the fireplace poker and advanced again. I screamed at him to stop, to no avail. Nick jabbed the poker into every piece of flesh he reached. My leg, my arm, my leg again. Through my sobs, I heard a comforting voice calling me away from the attack and back to reality.

"Everything will be all right, Shenandoah. I'll take care of you now."

I fought my way out of the deepest nightmares I remembered. When my eyes flew open, I searched for the owner of the voice—Charles, of course, though it hadn't sounded like him. My irritation that he'd stolen into my room reconfigured as fear when I threw back the comforter and discovered no one in the room with me.

What the hell? Had I dreamed the voice, too?

"Shenandoah," the voice chanted.

I bolted to the door and down the hall. A pitch-black hallway impeded my progress, causing the doorknob from Charles' bedroom to jab into my gut. Wrenching his door open, I sobbed, "Charles!"

My freaked-out mind registered, even in the dim light, that he slept bare chested and barefoot, wearing nothing except pajama pants. By the time he reached my side, I felt silly. Apparently, my libido was a stellar force at stamping out fear.

"What's wrong?" Charles whispered. He hooked a hand under my elbow and pulled me into the crook of his arm. With his heady, masculine scent circling around me, words took a moment to form.

"I had a nightmare. And then I woke up, and someone was in my room."

"What?" Charles set me aside, picked up an object from the corner of his bedroom and ran down the hall. A gleam of light shone across to the bathroom door. After hearing a couple of muffled thuds, I walked down to join him.

"No one's here. I'll check the rest of the house. You sit tight."

I perched on a cream-colored chaise, reluctant to remain in the room alone, yet knowing he needed no deterrent during his inspection of the house. A minute passed. Muted sounds of doors closing indicated he'd made his way to the basement. A gust of campfire air settled around me, and I caught a whiff of burnt pine. Then I heard the voice again. "Everything will be all right, Shenandoah."

"Charles!" I shrieked. "Charles!"

I closed my eyes and covered my ears to block out all sounds. When strong, sinewy limbs encircled me, I screamed until Charles lowered my arms.

"I heard it again. The voice was here."

"There's no one in this house besides us. I checked everywhere and all the doors and windows are secure."

"Do you think he's outside?"

Charles pushed back the curtains on each window with the golf club he carried. "There's no movement outside." I recognized sympathy on his face when he set the club down and pulled me to my feet. "If there was anyone here, they're gone now."

I didn't believe him, and he knew it.

"Look, I can stay with you for the rest of the night, if you'd like." When my mouth opened in protest, he put his hands in the air in an act of surrendering. "Nothing will happen. Don't worry. I'm a man of my word. Plus, we both have to work tomorrow. A little shut eye would do us both good."

Pragmatic Charles made a point.

"Okay."

"Okay." He displayed excitement over my decision. "So where are we sleeping? Your room or mine?"

I thought back to his large room with doors leading, rationally, to an attached bathroom and walk-in closet. My smaller room seemed safer. "Let's stay here."

"Perfect," Charles replied. "Let me turn off a few lights..." He caught the fear in my face. "No, never mind. We'll light the lamp in here and turn off the overhead light. Don't worry, I won't leave you."

This time when I laid on the bed, Charles insisted that I lay between the sheets. He pulled the dusty rose comforter over himself and wrapped a protective arm around me. For a while I listened, intent on capturing the voice, or the sound of movement elsewhere in the house.

I also fought my baser instinct, which told me to take advantage of the ripped man whose six pack I swore I could trace perfectly through the blankets. The warmth of his body prompted me to slide one arm out from under the covers. The heat between us intensified when I interlaced my fingers with his. Damn. He'd acted so sweet, protecting me, yet the single thought crossing my mind involved jumping his bones.

Somehow, I fell asleep and woke to the insistent buzz of an angry alarm clock. My head jerked up before I remembered whose bed I slept in and why. During the night, Charles' hand moved from comforting protection to modesty violation. Done subconsciously or not, somehow his hand slipped up and under my blouse and cupped my left breast. A provocative fire threatened to consume me, so I pulled away and clambered out of bed.

"Your alarm's going off!" I yelled to break the sexual tension. Shit! Spending another night here without caving would constitute sheer hell.

The realization of our circumstances set Charles in motion. "It's okay. I'll get it. I set the alarm for six because I didn't know how much time you required in the mornings."

He disappeared, vanquishing the sleep-interrupting apparatus. Even though a new day dawned, the sky above was ominous. I didn't relish the thought of spending time alone. I dug through my shopping bags, shoved the door shut with my elbow, and dressed as if racing for first place. No voice intruded on my morning toiletries.

In less than five minutes I emerged, ready to get the day underway. Charles either did not possess Jason's culinary skills or he declined to use them for breakfast. He popped a couple of frozen waffles in the toaster and poured me some orange juice. Next he offered various flavors of coffee for his individual cup coffee maker. A vast selection awaited my vote, but I couldn't resist the glazed chocolate donut. He chose Mint–n-Mocha but brewed mine first.

Even though I'd already begun eating cinnamon waffles, my mouth watered as the chocolate coffee aroma infiltrated all air molecules in the conjoined kitchen, dining room, and living room space. Each breath I took resembled a powerful gulp, like I couldn't get enough. Was it too late to ask for one of these coffee makers for Christmas?

The week school began, I'd adopted the habit of arriving ahead of the required time. But this particular morning, I walked through the side entrance near my classroom over an hour early. This allowed me to catch up on grading papers. All day I looked over my shoulder and jumped when people entered my class in the middle of a period. A scream lodged in my throat when the phone rang late in the morning. I feared running into Nick when I least expected it.

I didn't think he would hurt me in a public place, and I certainly didn't expect that he'd hurt others, but he emanated a confrontational edge. After school, I asked the principal for an early dismissal to take care of some family business.

Once in my car, though, I couldn't decide where to go. I was not by any means ready to return to my house, although I wanted to drive by to search for Vee. Thoughts that Nick might still be home sick prevented me from doing so. Besides, Vee managed on his own during my hospitalization. It comforted me that he could fend for himself.

Charles gave me his spare key, but fear kept me from heading there without him. My destination became ShopMart. My goal, to locate concealing, non-sexy pajamas. My next stop, the supermarket. It didn't take me long to pick up ingredients for lasagna. A quick call to Charles told me he'd soon leave his office. He begged me to enter ahead of him and to make myself comfortable until he got home. I assured him I would and that I'd have supper ready for him.

Charles' house loomed as an ominous edifice before me, frightening even in late afternoon daylight. Pulling into the driveway, I tried to rationalize my fear. Yesterday

I stood up to Nick and walked out on him. I was terrified he would come after me and hurt me. I didn't want to be beaten any more. I'd suspected the voice in my room belonged to Nick.

The logical part of my brain reasoned that wasn't his style. He wasn't a haunt-behind-the-scenes kind of guy. He was more of a blunt, punch you in the face, get down to business brute. So, unless Charles played a trick on me—which didn't make sense as he hadn't even known I was coming—it required involvement by another party. But who else would've used my full name?

I let myself into Charles' house and began supper preparations. Continuing to fixate on the voice, I realized that I'd heard it before. I jumped and dropped a spoon when loud sirens wailed. These sirens hailed the emergency rescue units in town. Small towns like Grafton staffed first responders through volunteer rescue and firefighter personnel. More often than not, these services transported wounded and ill people to the hospital.

The hospital. That's it! That's where I'd heard the voice before. In fact, I shuddered, remembering the night of the wheelchair visitor. Back when I saw my first monster. Setting down the spatula, I slid the lasagna pan into the oven and settled in a high-backed chair at the kitchen island. I remained in deep thought when Charles entered the door minutes after five. If my monsters, formerly known as my pixies, offered assurance that things would be fine, maybe I should trust them. I longed to speak to Jason. His advice made more sense than anyone else's regarding this particular issue in my life.

Charles walked into the kitchen, slung his sports coat over the back of another chair, and gave me a hug and a peck on the cheek. Much like a man would, or should, do to his wife after work. How sad I kept experiencing ideal married life situations, but not with my own husband.

"Did you get through the day okay?" Charles appeared anxious. "Did he try to contact you?"

"No, but I was so nervous all day."

"Understandable. Do you think he's at work tonight?"

At my shrug he added, "I've got a private number." He put the phone on speaker and dialed the club.

"Grafton Country Club, this is Nick."

Charles prepared his speech in advance. "Sorry, man. Wrong number."

"No problem. Take it easy."

Had this good-natured banter come from the man who yesterday ordered me to the kitchen to cook his food? My mind, laden with guilt, acknowledged I should do just that, instead of making a meal for another man.

"Do you need to stop by your house for anything?"

"I'd like to check on Vee, but I'll wait until tomorrow after school. At least I know he's back at work."

After a supper Charles raved about, we relived childhood anecdotes over red wine. I shared stories of the odd blend of children my parents assembled through various adoptions. Charles, as the oldest son, carried on the family tradition of banking. His older sister still doted on him. She'd been the one who helped decorate his bachelor pad.

When I broached the subject about why he retained it as a bachelor pad, he replied, "There will always be plenty of women to date, and that's all I've needed so far. If the opportunity presents itself and I find myself needing more, beware to the woman on whom I set my sights. She just may find it impossible to escape me."

I couldn't tell if his words were meant to be romantic or chilling. I also noticed the way Charles kept eyeing my wine glass and offering refills. He'd given me his word to act as a gentleman, so I suspected he wanted me to ingest enough to serve as a sleep aid. The poor guy. Unless involved in a romantic interlude, he probably counted on eight to nine hours of uninterrupted sleep. This was his method of making sure I slept through the night.

Since fatigue crept over us from a full day and the events from the night before, we retired early. The arrangements we'd made previously suited both of us. Charles beat me in dressing for bed and snickered when I pranced in his guest bedroom wearing long-sleeved, red plaid flannel pajamas.

"Nice choice. Except," he sobered up a bit, "that when one knows what lies beneath, leaving everything to the imagination can be even more provocative."

Blushing, I sought extra refuge under covers. Whether from wine or exhaustion, I passed out immediately, even before Charles climbed onto the bed. I awoke to that obnoxious alarm clock and a delicious body wrapped around me.

"Good morning, beautiful." Charles kissed me behind the ear.

I sighed when he left the bed. Another perfect marriage moment. Charles adjusted the alarm since I proved myself a low-maintenance morning person. We ate a repeat breakfast of the day before and met at the garage door before heading to our respective jobs.

"Will you be here tonight?" he implored.

"I'll let you know." I promised. At his restraining hand on my arm I added, "I don't live here."

Mumbled words spilled from his lips, but he let me go. Before I shut my car door he warned, "I will come looking for you if I don't hear anything."

"Got it!" I grinned. "See you later." His words threatened my composure, even though nothing bound me to this man.

CHAPTER 26

GYM PARTY

I STILL WORRIED NICK might show up. My phone jangled mid-morning during my planning period. I panicked that confrontation time had arrived, so when Connie Chavez told me to come to the office rápidamente to pick up a bee-yoo-tee-fool delivery, relief swept over me.

"Gracias, Connie."

"Es de quién?" I heard her question as I pushed out of the heavy office door.

My mind raced on my way back to my room. A gift from Nick? Something from Charles? Surely not Jason. A bouquet of red, green, and white carnations awaited. I ignored the attached card and curious eyes, preferring to discover my benefactor in privacy. Elliott passed me in the hall.

"Oof, those are lovely, miss. Very festive for the holiday season."

"Thank you, Elliott. I love them." I loved them now, but my reaction might change once I learned the identity of the giver.

I hustled back to my room, pulling two small cards from the envelope. Nick's desperate scrawl made my breath hitch.

Jen—I'm sorry I love you. I can't live...

I flipped the card over.

...without you. I'm going crazy not knowing where...

I went to the second card.

...you are. Please come home. I love you. I...

And the back of that card.

...miss you. Love, Nick

Nick. Of course, he was sorry. He was always sorry. And of course, he missed me. The man stumbled around half helpless without me around to cook, clean, and organize his things. Pathetic. Him, for the way he treated me, and me for putting up with the abuse. And yet, he loved me. It wasn't fair of me to disappear. Sickness created a classic excuse. Could I hold his behavior against him? I'd acted in a reprehensible fashion, as well. Plus, he hadn't laid a finger on me recently.

By the time the next Spanish 2 class shuffled in, my face displayed a relaxed smile. I decided upon a course of action.

I didn't need to leave early because I memorized Nick's schedule at the country club. Before leaving school, I texted Charles that I was going home. I stopped at the store to purchase a pork loin, breadcrumbs, sweet peas, and ingredients to make a blueberry pie. As I pulled up to my house, an overjoyed puppy sprang off the porch. I responded with equal elation at seeing him.

"Vee!" I fell to my knees in the snowy grass by the driveway to hug the bundle of fur who collided with me. "Vee, I'm so sorry. I was in such a rage that I left without you. I'm glad you got outside, but did he hurt you?"

At his "woof" and prance and shake, I assumed he'd escaped problem free from the house and avoided Nick. I hugged him again. "I sure love you, boy."

At that, he nudged me over and began licking my face. Laughing, I got to my feet. "You are the best dog ever! I promise to never leave you here again if I'm planning to stay away for safety reasons."

Vee woofed in agreement and followed me in the house. Before long, succulent aromas wafted into all the rooms. I ate bites of supper while preparing the pie. I kept myself busy all evening, sitting down with a piece of pie shortly after nine o'clock.

A glance at my phone showed dozens of waiting messages. Most of them were from Charles, who was ticked off that I'd opted for my own home instead of his place. He kind of sounded like a jealous boyfriend, except for his worried statements. He could not protect me on this side of town, preferring to defend me from within his modern castle. I assured him things were fine. He made me promise to text if Nick manifested any aggressiveness. He promised in return to storm over here to defeat my foe.

After setting the phone down, I wondered if having another man beat up my assailant qualified as self-defense. If I held onto him as a retainer and used him if needed, did that count toward premeditated violence? I didn't know. I wished I possessed the independence and strength to take down Nick on my own.

The last time I'd run away, not long ago, I waited in bed for Nick to come home. This time, I waited downstairs. I started in my window seat, where I felt protected and safe, until I realized I'd place myself in a corner if Nick started throwing punches. I moved to a couch in the family room. From there, my odds at both slipping from his grasp and ducking out a door increased. Vee wouldn't understand, but I told him my plan, anyway. He laid on the far side of a recliner, close to the back door.

Through fitful dozing, I failed to hear Nick return home. The first sound that infiltrated my inner ear came from Nick's anxious voice.

"Jen? Oh, Jen. Thank God, I found you. I saw your car, but you weren't upstairs, and I thought...oh, never mind what I thought." He approached, smothering me in a bear hug. He pulled back, his eyes beseeching. "Please don't ever leave me again. You know I'm all talk. Sure, I can be an ass, but don't listen to that part of me. I need you here with me. I love you!"

Gulping back tears, I nodded. "I love you, too, Nick. I won't leave again."

Vee emitted a low growl, but Nick didn't hear it.

Nick hauled me to my feet. "Let's go to bed, babe." While he escorted me up the stairs, I recalled with gratitude that one of my evening chores included washing the sheets, stained with sweat from his fever.

Part of me expected rough, "I told you so" make-up sex, but Nick remained gentle. Afterward, I returned to my window seat.

The next morning gave me hope anew for improvement in our lives. Before I left for school, I kissed Nick on the cheek.

"Nick, I wanted to check with you. Tonight is our Christmas party at the gym. Can you get off work long enough to stop by and eat with us? Nakayla wants me to come, and she'd love to meet you."

"Babe," Nick drawled in a condescending tone, "I already missed a day of work this week. Besides, we're swamped with it being the Christmas season. We've got two parties booked at the club this evening." His voice hardened. "You can go for a while, I suppose. But no drinking and no dancing."

"Umm, okay." I gave him another quick kiss. "I guess I'll see you when you get home tonight."

When I arrived at school, I checked my phone. Sure enough, more messages from Charles. I shot him a short text telling him everything was fine.

Seconds later, he asked, Is Nick bringing you to the Christmas party this evening?

I replied with, No, he's scheduled to work.

But how convenient for him to pop in since the party's at the country club.

It's where? My mind reeled. Had Nick known this and played me? Well, I guessed this way he could keep an eye on me.

That evening, I chose to don the same outfit as I wore to Nick's party. This gathering was at the same location, but the guest list was different. Might as well get another use from such a pretty dress.

While confident in my appearance, I hated walking into places alone. I almost messaged Charles to meet me at the door when I arrived. My shy side emerged, but I pushed it aside to ask the hostess how to find the Sunset Gym Christmas Party. She instructed one of the servers who showed me to the stairs.

"Go to the bottom and take a right."

"Thank you." On to another room to enter all by myself. Time to put on my big-girl panties.

No one stood at the door to welcome guests as I'd expected. Instead, several of the 50-odd employees and their spouses or significant others stood around in small groups, drinks in hand, attempting small talk. I spotted Nakayla across the room mingling with a couple of board members. I waited a minute until I caught her eye, offering her a quick wave. To my surprise, she extricated herself from her companions and glided over to me.

"Hey, Jen! I'm glad you made it. How are you feeling these days?"

"So much better. Thanks. I'd love to work some over Christmas break if you need the help."

"We've already set the schedule," she apologized, "but if something comes up, we'll know who to call. In the meantime, you get one complimentary drink this evening. What's your pleasure?"

Nick told me not to drink, maybe for the sole reason he didn't want me spending the money. "White wine would be great."

"Sure thing."

She returned moments later. "Moscato okay?"

"Absolutely." I accepted the drink and downed a swallow before asking, "Our gifts for the exchange? Where should they go?"

"Right! Sorry. Of course, you'd want to put that down. There's a table over by the karaoke stand."

"Thanks, Nakayla." Karaoke I would have to avoid at all costs. My two previous performances required plenty of liquor beforehand. Not a situation I wanted to repeat in front of co-workers.

I placed a wrapped frosty, pine-scented candle on a table holding various assortments of gift bags and Christmas boxes. Originally arranged as a white elephant gift exchange, grumblings in the past led to a maximum of $10 per item. I didn't need anything, but I entertained the thought I might get a little surprise to make me smile.

Someone whistled, and Nakayla cleared her throat. "Take a seat, everyone! We'll eat, then we'll do introductions and play some games. Enjoy! Merry Christmas!"

I sat at the end of an eight-foot table. A vivacious redhead named Shannon sat next to me. Her excessively outgoing personality harnessed energy from attention, feeding on the laughter of others. Since her friends sat all around her and her husband—Michael, whom she adored—I only saw the back of her head during most of the meal.

The seat directly across the table from me remained empty until the servers wheeled in carts loaded with filet mignon and chicken cordon bleu. A breathless individual slid into that seat: Charles.

"Hello." I stammered. This man and I had shared intimacy not long ago, and I couldn't decide how to handle him.

He kept the conversation casual. I divulged several facts about my preferences and childhood and asked many of the same questions of him. We weren't supposed to know each other well, conversing for the sake of appearance. And while I never saw him signal the server, I suspected he was the party responsible for keeping my wine glass filled.

I hadn't caught sight of Nick yet, but they kept him busy at the bar. Introduction time arrived. Employees at a corner table began popping up, introducing their guests, claiming their department, and telling a fun fact about themselves. When Shannon's turn came, she went overboard describing hilarious character traits about family members. I didn't know whether to jump in when she paused or sit back and wait.

Finally, she turned to me, still laughing about her last anecdote. "You go!" She pointed at me with both index fingers.

I stood. "Well, I'm Jen Adesco. I work at the front counter, and my husband, Nick…" solid arms grabbed my shoulders from behind.

"Is right here," he completed for me. "Hey, guys! Sorry I couldn't join the party. We're pretty busy in the other room, and I'm working the bar. But I can tell you an interesting fact about Jen."

Oh shit, I panicked. This could be anything.

"If she wasn't a schoolteacher, she could easily make a living as a full-time gourmet chef."

My mouth dropped open. That was incredibly nice of Nick. I took my seat as Charles rose. I could tell Nick recognized him from the hospital.

"I'm Charles Newman, a board member. I'm alone this evening because my choice of dates had other plans. An interesting fact about me is that I'm a fencing master." As he announced his fact, his eyes stared straight ahead, boring into Nick's, who still stood behind me.

Nick stayed with us until all in the room had been accounted for. When Nakayla dictated directions for the gift exchange, Nick knelt down beside me. He began toying with my hair and spoke in a low voice. "I thought I told you not to drink."

"You did, but it was free. They gave us a complimentary drink."

"I said, 'no drinks.' How is your glass still full after an entire meal? You're really going to sit there and lie to me, telling me it's the same first glass?" He pulled steadily at a lock of hair he wrapped around his finger. "You'll leave and go home now."

"Nick, no," I pleaded. "I have to be here for the presents. I brought one, and it'll just be weird if I don't stay for that."

He curled hair around a second finger and yanked again. "As soon as it's over..." he cut off there, raised himself to his full stature, and smiled down at me and those in the vicinity. "No rest for the wicked. Merry Christmas, everyone!"

My fingers trembled when they touched Shannon's arm. "What were the rules? I missed them."

"Oh, they're just doing it the boring way. They put numbers on all the packages, then we'll draw numbers and pick up the corresponding gift. Ho hum. But then we get to start reindeer tag." She broke into raucous laughter and turned to poke Michael. "I'm comin' for you, Blitzen!"

I cast a weak smile at them. How predictable of Nick to ruin something that started out so sweetly. I couldn't even bring myself to look at Charles. When I glanced out from under my lashes, he no longer sat there. Twisting my head, I scoured the room for him. My eyes landed on his broad shoulders. He made his way among those taking part in the exchange, letting them select slips of paper and make their way to the table. He weaved in and out, eventually returning to me.

"Looks like there's one left. They saved the best for last. I hope you like your gift."

Hmm. Any particular reason he saved me for last? My gift alone remained. I held a small box covered in gold foil paper and tied with blue curled ribbon. The packaging alone yelled "expensive."

Nakayla's voice droned on behind me, listing the rules for reindeer tag. I fixated on the box. Blue sprigs of ribbon slid right off. The tape slit beneath my fingernail. With intrigue, I peeled back the paper and lifted the lid. A pair of sapphire earrings rested, nestled in cotton.

"They're so pretty," I said aloud.

Charles appeared behind me, hovering over my shoulder. "I'm glad you like them."

"Wait!" I spun around. "These are from you?"

"Well, of course. How else could I give you a gift that you'd be able to accept?"

I narrowed my eyes. "These aren't less than ten dollars, are they?"

"No, they're more like $830."

"What? Charles, I can't allow you to give me these. This is more than my husband even spends on me!"

"Hush now. Don't make a scene. Your husband may have spies in here. Now I'm going to pretend to admire your gift—which you definitely deserve—like I've never seen it before." Charles made a pretense of checking out the blue stones attached to silver studs.

"I have to go now." Not in the mood to make excuses or hand out explanations, I pulled my coat off the back of my chair and ducked out. Mercifully, neither Charles nor Nick tried to stop me.

* * *

Back at home, I rubbed Vee's head when I stepped from the car. Vee never let me down. I headed straight for the kitchen to whip up a cup of my comfort hot chocolate. I hadn't even pulled out all the ingredients when a muffled thud drew me toward the family room.

Squinting through the darkened room, I screamed when I made out a darker figure looming on the other side of the back door. It couldn't be Nick because Vee wasn't growling or running for cover. It had to be one of my monsters trying to get in. What did it want from me?

I trusted Veé's judgment and sickened myself with the cowardice I'd already displayed this evening. I stalked to the door with determination, planning to slam it back shut should I not like what I encountered. To my consternation, Charles grinned at me.

"Sorry if I scared you. I'm trying to keep this visit on the down low." He eased by me; our bodies practically flush. Every spot on my body that came in contact with his tingled with scorching heat. He took my hand and led me back to the lighted kitchen, where he spotted the jewelry box on the kitchen counter. He swept it into his hands and nudged the lid off.

"Please try them on for me."

Charles pried the earrings off the cushioned tab and placed them in my left palm. A couple of unsuccessful attempts after I'd removed the ones I wore to the party; I sought the bathroom mirror. Charles trailed after me, watching the reflection of my face.

Once firmly ensconced in my ears, he pressed me into the sink counter from behind and breathed in my ear. "Exquisite."

Evidence of his arousal burned into my backside. Holy shit, he made me horny, and this wouldn't do. He eased me around to face him. "I know he threatened you tonight. Do you think there will be repercussions when he gets home?"

"I'm hoping not." I found it difficult to breathe with my chest pressed to his.

"You don't have to live in fear. This isn't really even living. Shenandoah, you need to leave him for good. Not a day or two at a time, but forever. You need to file for divorce and get a restraining order. I spoke to the doctor at the hospital. He took pictures and has thoroughly documented every injury. No judge would deny you the right to get away from that scum."

Tears trickled down my cheeks.

"I can help you if you're afraid to leave him. What a Catch 22. Scared to stay, scared to leave."

"It's not just that, Charles. I love him."

His sigh of exasperation puffed his chest into mine. "Sometimes when you love things, you need to let them go."

I rolled my eyes, causing residual tears to trickle. "Ugh. I hate clichés."

Charles rubbed my lips with both of his thumbs. "You, my dear, deserve love that is fully reciprocated. I can give you that. Protection, happiness, love, security."

He kissed me hard on the mouth. Despite the way my body leeched onto this man, my mind still reeled with what he'd said. Even while I kissed him back, I knew he needed to leave.

A crash from the kitchen momentarily froze us in place. We scrambled to make things appear normal. Charles climbed into the shower, trying not to jangle the rings when he slid the curtain. I pulled the bathroom door most of the way shut behind me. With trepidation, I rounded the corner.

"Vee! What did you do?" Never before had Vee jumped up on counters, yet that appeared to be exactly what he'd done. The Reddi-wip can, and a spoon I'd placed next to it, rested on the floor. Vee stood over them, claiming complete responsibility.

"What the heck, Vee?" I walked over to him, contemplating the situation while I scratched his back, I bent to retrieve the objects. Charles peeked around the corner.

"Everything okay?"

"Yes. Vee just knocked a couple of things off of the counter."

"I apologize for my behavior. I shouldn't have hidden like a coward. But then again, we shouldn't have to be sneaking around. We need to be free to be together and love each other." He caressed my face. "I should leave tonight, but please think about what I've said."

I answered with nothing but a nod.

Charles pressed firm lips to mine. "Please be safe and keep in touch. I'll be out of town until the day after Christmas, but you can call me at any time. I will come back for you. Merry Christmas, beautiful. I wish I could be with you for the holidays. I love you."

Wistful eyes gazed into mine. He grazed my earrings with his knuckles and backed away.

"Thanks for the earrings. They are very pretty. I...I love them. Merry Christmas!" I called as he slipped out the back door.

Mercy, what a hot man. And also, off limits, which I believed Vee tried to point out. Upon my return to the bathroom, I admired the sapphire studs in my ears. Would Nick be able to tell their expense? He enjoyed pricey items, but he wasn't a jewelry connoisseur.

"I'm sure I can pass them off as cheap ShopMart knockoffs." I told my reflection, then caught Vee's eyes in the mirror. "It doesn't seem right to me, either. I'm just so confused trying to sort my life out. Is it too much to ask to be happy and fit in?"

Sighing, I went to bed, falling asleep despite my determination to wait up for Nick. A heavy body pinning me to the mattress woke me. I tried to scream, but the breath froze in my lungs.

"The drink was your downfall." A voice growled in my ear. "But I understand. I'm partial to liquor, myself. So, since you came home right away, like I said, you're forgiven."

"Thanks, Nick." I squeaked.

He rolled off me. "See? I'm not such a bad guy. But I am bushed, sorry babe." He slapped something with his hand—in all likelihood, his own ass. "You won't get a piece of this tonight."

"Good night, Nick."

CHAPTER 27

COLORADO

AFTER NINE O'CLOCK ON Saturday morning, Catherine called to remind me Grafton's annual Christmas celebration started this afternoon. Hectic testing schedules during the last week of the semester prevented any chance for us to talk before or after class.

"Of course, I remembered, Caterina," I assured her. "Nothing would keep me away. Where shall I meet you and at what time?"

"There's a tree and wreath auction at three o'clock on the west courthouse lawn. Would you like to go?"

"Sure. That sounds great."

"Dad said I could buy something this year, so I'm going with spending money!"

Her infectious enthusiasm sprouted an idea. "I think I'll bring some money, too. I could always use another Christmas decoration."

I couldn't wait to spend an afternoon and evening wrapped up in the Christmas wonderland Catherine promised. Nick rolled out of bed late, exhausted by his extra duties for numerous holiday parties. He ignored the chicken salad I'd made him for lunch.

"I'll grab a bite at the bar, babe. Gotta go!" A quick peck on my forehead and he ran out the door at 12:45.

I might have been upset, but I hadn't prepared my lunch yet, so I ate his. Settling on a couch in the family room, I chewed a piece of lettuce while deep in thought and flipped on the weather channel. For the holiday, we planned to visit my family first and next head to Nick's. From the looks of current radar, the potential for hazardous weather descended later in the week.

I arrived at the Walsh County Courthouse about twenty minutes until three o'clock, fearing parking might later become an issue. The lot to the left of the courthouse offered open stalls for convenience when loading purchases from the auction. I claimed one of those spots, figuring that even if I didn't buy anything, Catherine intended to. I anticipated helping her haul her treasure home.

Countless volunteers transformed the courthouse lawn and parking lot into a Christmas town. I couldn't even begin to count all the simultaneous events.

"Señora!"

Turning, I spotted Catherine hurrying to catch up to me.

"Over here, Señora," Catherine motioned me to follow her. "We need to register and pick up our paddles."

For not attending an auction before, she seemed to know the steps involved. My knowledge of auctions consisted of some guy getting excited and letting words fly from his mouth and stumble over each other. With less than fifteen minutes left before it began, we landed numbers 319 and 320. Unbelievable to think that many people showed up for a holiday auction.

At three o'clock on the dot, a man with a buckskin jacket climbed on stage and stood behind a podium. He banged a gavel like a judge and began his auctioneer rambling. Amidst his banter, and a couple of unintentional bids, we each ended up with marvelous decorations. I bid on several wreaths, but many of them exceeded an amount I intended to fork out. My winning bid gained me a green wreath filled with white gold baubles and bows, a perfect accessory for my front door.

Catherine selected a two-foot-tall white Christmas tree with pink and purple decorations. She hugged it to her side as we walked to my car.

"I love it because it celebrates the season but breaks with traditional colors." She glowed when she spoke.

"It's very beautiful and tastefully done," I agreed.

I pulled into Catherine's driveway with anticipation. Would Jason be here? So far, his name hadn't surfaced in our conversation.

"My dad's not here," she read my mind. "But he'll be meeting me for a wagon ride at six." She unlocked the front door and pushed her way in with her prize.

"I'm gonna set this up in my room. It might clash with the reds and greens in our family room. Go look!" she called over her shoulder. "I think me and dad did a pretty good job this year."

Upon admiring their creativity, I wished again my life could be like theirs. How refreshing to love the house you lived in and receive acceptance for your individuality.

I used the facilities before we headed back to the festivities. We observed glass blowing, tinsel weaving, and caricature artists, then joined the gingerbread house decorating. After, Catherine announced we'd better veer toward the back of the courthouse for wagon rides with Santa. I hadn't even realized darkness had fallen. I'd been too captivated by the sights and smells of Christmas.

Head swinging from side to side like a young child, I distractedly followed Catherine to the awaiting wagon. And to Jason. I restrained myself from falling into his arms. A longing to kiss and hold him clutched at me, but I settled for an amicable hug.

I thought it appropriate that Catherine sit between her dad and I on a bench, but she insisted otherwise. Of course, she wanted to sit by me, but she placed me in the middle. As soon as the heavy woolen blanket covered our legs, Jason's thigh contacted mine. Such intimate tangency turned me on, but diplomacy demanded I sit still with no outlet for my emotions.

Catherine chattered to her dad about the afternoon we'd passed together. Meanwhile, Jason's left hand disappeared under the blanket. After it squeezed my thigh, my right hand joined his under the blanket. We pulled gloves off of each other's hands and interlaced fingers.

After Catherine recounted all, she fell silent. I sighed. Pure enjoyment encircled me, from the clopping of horse hooves to the strong smell of hay, to the slight scratch of wool against my knuckles. My head dropped onto Jason's shoulder. Neither of us attempted to dislodge it.

All too soon the wagon looped around back to its original starting place. We disembarked and Jason howled in exaggeration to emphasize his hunger. A quick stop at Christmas Around the World yielded roast suckling pig, hot buttered rum punch, and a slice of Bûche de Noël.

At eight o'clock, the majority of attendees assembled to witness the lighting of the huge fir tree on the green behind the Spanish American War Memorial. Unanimous awe swept over the crowd. Immediately afterward, a kettle of unease settled in my gut. Something was wrong.

I tugged on Jason's arm. "I need to go home."

"What? Are you sure?"

"Yeah. I'm so sorry."

"Well, okay then. Let me walk you to your car, though."

I nodded. "Disculpe, Caterina. I need to head home. Enjoy the rest of the night with your dad and have a Merry Christmas!"

"Merry Christmas, Mrs. Adesco!" Catherine hugged me with all the vigor of an excited teenager.

"Honey, I'm going to walk Mrs. Adesco to her car. How about I meet you by the antler ring toss?"

"'Kay!" And she disappeared.

"So," Jason dropped into step beside me. "Any more monsters?"

I wondered about his obsession with them, but responded, "I think I saw one incognito today, and I think one of them talked to me during this past week."

"Really?" Jason's face mirrored his incredulousness. "What did it say?"

"Well, I was in hiding from Nick."

"Okay. Why was that?"

I couldn't look him in the eye because it still felt so wrong. "I talked back to him."

"And for that you ran away?"

"He wanted to hit me. He tried, but he was too weak from having been sick. So, I ran away. A voice kept reassuring me things would be fine. I can only assume it was one of my monsters because it wasn't Nick and it wasn't, umm, Charles."

Blue eyes narrowed, but Jason graciously said nothing about my choice of accommodations. Still, I owed him a small explanation. "I wanted to be where I'd impact as few people as possible, so I chose his place."

"So, you heard but didn't see anything."

"Right. Honestly, Jason, I was so freaked out that Nick was after me I didn't even consider it could be something else."

"And then today?"

"Among the ice sculptures, a Scooby Doo ghost-looking figure appeared to be barfing green slime. I actually saw it oozing from its wide-open mouth."

We reached my car. "Fascinating."

"Are you just saying that?" I couldn't prevent the skepticism. "You don't think I'm losing my mind?"

I caught a look of incredulity radiating from his face. "Not at all."

I appreciated his assurance and wanted to believe him. His interest in my apparitions bemused me. "Really, I do have to get going."

"Yeah, right. It's just..." he leaned in against my car, stuttering under the duress of apparent nerves, "I have a Christmas present for you. And I know I shouldn't have," he stood tall again, "and I didn't need to, but I did."

Rather than hand me a package, Jason pulled a solitary silver loop from his coat pocket. Without a word he sought my left hand, pulled off the glove, and slid the bracelet onto my wrist. Simple braided metal evolved into spheres on each end.

"It's exquisite," I breathed. "Thank you."

I leaned in and nibbled his bottom lip before smothering it in a kiss. How did he know it fit exactly to my tastes?

"Merry Christmas, Jen." He pulled me out of the path of approaching headlights and into the shadow of a nearby pickup truck.

As soon as the vehicle passed, I extricated myself from his grasp—an unwilling but necessary action. "Merry Christmas, Jason."

I opened my car door and set one foot inside when urgent lips whispered a passionate message in my ear. "Be safe. I love you."

When he turned away, cold winter air swirled at my side. I sank into the driver's seat in slow motion. Upon starting the engine, the urgency to get home returned. Could Vee be hurt? Was the house on fire?

Driving past the neighbor's hedge to turn into my drive, I saw Nick's pickup parked in its usual spot. "Shit!"

Nick never came home during a shift at work. Maybe his fever returned. Tense muscles made getting out of the car and ascending the front porch steps a difficult task.

Vee trailed me into the house but hung back while I investigated. Nick wasn't hanging out in the man cave, and he wasn't occupying the downstairs bathroom. Mounting the staircase, I heard a dresser drawer open and shut. No amicability showed on his face when I breezed through our bedroom door.

"Where the hell were you?"

"Hi, Nick. I, umm, I went to Grafton's Christmas festival. I would have loved to have gone with you."

"Why didn't you mention it or leave a note?"

"I'm sorry, but geez... Nick, it was only a few hours. I was with hundreds of Grafton citizens in a very public place."

"Whatever," he dismissed the situation with a shrug. "You need to start packing. We've had a change of plans."

"Wait. What?"

"Yeah, you'll need to call your parents and notify them of the change. Instead of going back to Kearney and Valentine, we're headed to Vail! My parents rented a condo."

Granted, I wasn't extremely close to my parents, but I enjoyed seeing them along with my younger siblings once or twice a year. Nebraska lies much too far south to travel there for a casual weekend jaunt. I looked forward to our visits on Christmas break and during the summer.

"But...my family's expecting us, Nick."

"They'll understand. I guarantee my family would be thrilled if yours invited us on an impromptu trip for the holidays. Now pack your bags. We'll drive to Fargo, get a couple hours of sleep at a hotel, and hop on the 5:05 flight to Denver."

"But Nick, can we afford airline tickets?"

"Covered by my parents. See? I told you, it's an offer we can't refuse. Now get ready. The sooner we leave, the more sleep we'll get."

I held my emotions at bay, working on autopilot. I'd already done all the laundry and readied the house for our absence during a few days back to Nebraska. I commenced packing. While Nick used the bathroom, I conducted a furtive search throughout the indoors for Vee. After setting food and water out on the back porch, I left the door propped, enabling him to vacate the premises.

I never saw him before we left, but decided he'd somehow gotten out. I comforted myself that he'd survive until I returned. Still, my heart hiccupped with a pang of worry as we pulled away from the house.

The dashboard clock read 10:02—much too late for me to notify my parents via phone of the bad news, and I would not text it to them.

Luckily, Nick possessed far better than my poor sense of direction. We pulled up to a Holiday Inn Express located adjacent to the airport in less than two hours. Nick left a wakeup call at the front desk. After a short elevator ride, I crawled into a king-sized bed, eager to resume slumber's sweet escape.

Far too soon, a cheery voice from the hotel office welcomed us to a great day in Fargo. I longed to tell her where she could shove her receiver.

With the holiday season, far more people than I'd imagined planned to fly from North Dakota to Colorado at this time of the morning. Calm weather prevented delays and turbulence. With the time change, the clock registered seconds after 6:00 a.m. when we landed. No hassles in the car rental line should have put Nick in a good mood.

However, any holiday seemed the perfect reason for Nick's inner grouch to emerge. Holidays when he didn't have to work were all the worse. Since it was not yet Christmas Eve or Christmas Day, unanticipated early animosity surprised me when it reared its ugly head.

Before, it had been too late; now it was too early to call my home, to let my parents down and break the hearts of the younger children. A couple of silent tears trickled down my face. He noticed.

"What?" Nick snapped.

"I really wanted to see my family. It's been a while. That's all."

"Oh, grow up. They'll always be there. Where else is your family going to go?"

"We used to move all the time during my childhood. They've slowed up a bit."

"See? They'll still be there."

"I know. But gosh, Nick, after our big move, I just wanted to check in with them. In person." A couple more tears of self-pity traced the tracks of the others, dropping onto my coat.

"Are you trying to make things difficult for me?" Despite the fact he drove a car west on Interstate 70 at 65 miles per hour, Nick's fist shot out and connected with my left cheekbone. Since I had no reason to expect it, the impact snapped my neck back. My forehead hit the passenger side window. Blackness, stars, and pain exploded throughout my head.

CHAPTER 28

CHRISTMAS

NICK'S SURLY VOICE PENETRATED my skull as he poked my arm. "I gotta take a leak, babe. If you need to go, now's the time. No more stops 'til we hit Vail."

I couldn't detect bladder urgency over the intense throbbing at intervals in my head and down my neck. My heartbeat in syncopation, first below my left eye, then on the right side of my neck, then the middle of my head. Often it didn't take turns but beat in counterpoint rhythm simultaneously in several places.

Since greeting Nick's family loomed in the near future, I decided to check out my injuries in order to develop a story. I struggled out of the car and squinted to find the gas station entrance. I caught the eye of an elderly man. He touched his face and distinctly mouthed the word, "Why?"

No answer emerged, so I shrugged. Once in the bathroom, I lifted my eyelids to the mirror, groaning at what I saw. Even the sound I emitted sent a new wave of pain pulsating from the neck up. I held my head between both hands, but to no avail. I peered through my right eye, spying a narrow slit where my left eye used to reside. A goose egg formed, causing the upper lid to puff up. Holy shit! The pain that wracked my head threatened to...

I barely made it to the toilet when a wave of nausea swept over me. I wretched violently, each time followed by an unbearable ache.

A rap at the door distracted me. "Babe? Are you okay? We need to get going. Can I get you anything?"

"Tylenol," I croaked. "And ice."

After suppressing additional dry heaves, I tucked my head down and shuffled through the filling station. I sensed pity in the looks cast my way and sought to avoid as many of them as possible.

A sensation to hurl again smacked me when I reached the car. I bent over and dry heaved a couple more times. Nick opened my door from the inside.

"Get in!" he barked. "This is embarrassing. But if you dare to puke in my car..."

I caught his drift. I'd end up unconscious or on the side of the road.

"Now here." Nick's voice gentled as he handed me a ginger ale with the top unscrewed, some generic ibuprofen, and a Ziploc bag full of ice. When I turned a questioning eye toward him, he explained. "They didn't have any small ice packs and the clerk could see you needed ice. She let me fill it from the beverage dispenser."

Lifting the bottle to my lips, I allowed effervescent bubbles to trickle down to my stomach. Relief massaged a distressed digestive system. I gobbled three pain pills, gingerly holding the ice pack where the most intense pain concentrated on my forehead.

Resting against the back of the seat and facing the window, I closed my eyes. Hot tears formed under puffy eyelids. This sucked. Not only had I been pulled away from my family, but I also got the shit beat out of me through no fault of my own.

"We're here!" Nick's cheerful voice provoked my head to respond with surging waves of pain. Damn it. Just when I finally reduced the ache to a manageable pang. Nick manhandled both of our bags to one side of his body and draped his other arm over my shoulders.

"Hey everyone!" he hollered when he pushed his way through the front door.

A chorus of voices responded.

"Hey, Nick!"

"Nick's here!"

"It's Nick and Jen!"

"Hey, guys!"

"Welcome to paradise in Colorado." This from Nick's dad. "Oh my God! What happened to you?" His voice boomed, and I suspected everyone in each adjoining condo heard.

"I, umm..." Crap, I hadn't gotten a story together yet.

"Stupid turbulence." Nick complained. "The fasten seatbelt sign clicked on when she was in one of those sardine-can bathrooms. As you can see, she didn't even have time to brace herself. Can we get some ice and then see our room? Jen should probably lay down for a while."

"I'll show them their room," one of Nick's nephews piped up. "It's just like me and Donovan's. It's got bunk beds!"

Oh yay. Well, I would take the bottom one if my feet even managed to get me that far. The little boy opened a door, and Nick eased me onto the bottom bunk. Before I lapsed into a prone state, Nick propped my head up with an arm. He produced a bottle of ginger ale and prompted me to take a couple of swallows.

"Get some rest, babe." He located a spot on my face that remained unswollen to plant a kiss. He met his mom at the doorway.

"I'll take it from here," she assured him.

"Hello, dear." Lucinda Adesco greeted me. She placed a large pill in my hand, plunked a straw in my drink, and held the bent end to my mouth. "This is for the pain." I obediently took the pill. Nodding hurt too much. "Would you like something to take off the edge and help you sleep?"

"Yes, please." I whispered.

Lucinda produced from her pocket another pill. "I thought as much. Sleep tight. I'll check on you later."

Several packages of ice wrapped in cloths encircled my head. The acute pain became muted. I tried to concentrate on counting how many pills I'd taken, debating on the safety of such an amount, when relentless sleep dragged me into its darkness.

* * *

I awoke in a fog several hours later, thinking dreams still ruled my subconscious. I didn't recognize any part of the room. I touched my distorted face but couldn't make sense of it.

I sat up, a half inch short of cracking my head on the bunk above mine that crossed its top like a "t." No dream. A dull pain throbbed in several locations on my neck, head, and face. This was my sad reality.

I eased myself into a standing position beside the bed, taking note that the pain minimally increased, nothing too drastic. I used the attached bathroom before wandering out to the central gathering place, a kitchen/dining room/family room combo area. The premises had been vacated. A note rested on the back of a flier for ski lessons, waiting for me on the dining room table. Lucinda's elegant script informed me they'd all gone to the mountain to ski and contemplated dining at the main lodge this evening. She mentioned the fridge was stocked with provisions, urging me to call if I wanted to join them for dinner. Otherwise, they'd bring food back to me.

A glance at the clock told me it was slightly after two. Shit. That meant after three at my parents' house, and they expected us for supper. Damn it! Time to place the phone call of disappointment. It's not like I'd never let my parents down before.

They, of course, expressed frustration, and wished I'd have let them know sooner. When I told them the trip came as a last-minute surprise, and about the turbulence that knocked me around, all was forgiven. They informed me that a skiing accident waylaid my sister, Arana, who wouldn't return home for Christmas either. Before I hung up I apologized again, told them I'd ship their gifts when I got back home, and promised to visit Nebraska during my school's spring break.

I returned to the bathroom to shower. Once done, I stood in the tiny room with three walls of mirrors and inspected my naked body. From the neck down, I looked pretty damn good. My skin bore the scars of various injuries and surgeries, most of them caused by Nick. My gaze rose to my face. With gentle fingers, I plied the puffy flesh that hid two scars which marred my face under this mess.

Once back in my bedroom, I grabbed my cell phone. I carried it with me into the bathroom, aiming the camera at my face. I took pictures from two angles to show the most damage. With a click of a button, I sent the pictures first to Jason, then to Charles. My caption for them read: Not caused by airline turbulence. Let them come to their own conclusions. They had no idea where my travels led me.

Charles would probably submit these to my file of bodily harm. Good. This was my way of making the statement that things would change. I now freely admitted to abuse and wanted to name the accuser. Soon, I needed to walk away for good. It had to happen, or he would kill me. This time, I was certain he'd given me a concussion. How long before a traumatic brain injury? All of my faculties concurred.

After dressing, I checked my phone. In the past ten minutes, it blew up. All sorts of messages from Jason and Charles. Some from Charles included:

This has to stop.

Are you okay?

Where are you?

And I'll hunt him down to the ends of the earth and destroy him.

Jason's texts contained a more subdued approach:

This has to stop.

He's not even a real man.

He doesn't deserve you.

What can I do to help?

And, Between him and your monsters, I'd choose the monsters every time.

I refused to answer any of their texts. Showing them would suffice for the moment. Two new men in my world said they loved me and offered me protection. So why had I vacationed with the one who proclaimed his love for me by violently knocking me around?

I sat on the couch in the living room and tried to plan my escape. But thinking made my head hurt worse. I settled for watching bustling ski junkies on the street below. Some loaded up to head to the slopes, while others unloaded to ready themselves for Vail's night life. After people-watching for over an hour, I dozed fitfully.

In my dream, an old man resembling the one I'd seen at the gas station in Loveland approached me. He touched his face and asked me why. When I didn't respond, his hand that hovered near his chin ripped the beard off his face. Horrible boils and pockets of pus revealed themselves. He didn't stop there. He scraped and pulled all the skin from his face until a gruesome deformity remained.

"Not so different from you," a hoarse voice whispered.

I awoke screaming as the light of dusk filtered into the room. The delightful scent of logs burning in a fireplace calmed my nerves. Until I noticed the electric fireplace. A jangling phone further startled me. The pulse in my forehead throbbed again. Locating the phone on the smooth marble kitchen counter, I chose to answer—half frightened it would be the faceless man talking to me again.

Lucinda's voice shattered the silence on the line after I answered. "Jen, darling, how are you feeling?"

"Hi, Lucinda. Not so good yet. I think I'll pass on dinner."

"We'll miss having you here terribly, but we'll be sure to bring you some tasty treats. I hope you won't be too lonely without us. We may be late getting back because we're planning to stay for the talent show."

"Lucinda?"

"Yes, my dear?"

"Do you have any more of those pain pills?"

"Absolutely!" She proceeded to tell me which cabinet housed them, pointing out that the sleeping pills sat on the shelf beside the pain reliever.

I thanked her profusely, pulling a can of Diet Pepsi from the fridge, then returned to observing the outdoor crowd. The throng thinned as the night got blacker. A beautiful curtain of snow lowered itself and coated the landscape. I shook my head to clear the image I swore I witnessed. Nope. She was still there.

A woman with long, gray, curly hair watched me. Her features seemed cloned from that old man. She stood at the corner of a building by the intersection of a street, staring at me with desperation in her eyes. Next, she began to peel off her face. In horror, I watched the entire process. Sunken holes in her face where eyeballs belonged, stared at my window and into my soul. She pointed at me, then back at herself. Next, she crossed her arms over her chest.

Was that hideous creature trying to indicate she loved me? I shook my head and backed away from the window. I checked the bottles of the drugs I'd taken to see if any of the side effects included hallucinations. No such luck. Creeping back to the far side of the window, I peeked out the curtain to see if she'd stayed. Not only did she stand in the same spot, but her head swiveled to face me straight on. This time she let her crossed arms slide down her chest until she pantomimed rocking an infant. She pulled one hand away and pointed at the fictitious baby, before pointing at me.

This was too much. My plans to wait up for the family vanished. I swallowed a sleeping pill, brushed my teeth, then returned to bed and slept through until morning. Even Nick's nephews didn't wake me in the morning with their clamoring around.

"Morning, babe." Nick's warm coffee breath flowed over my cheek and hung in a pool beneath my nostrils.

His hand crept over my side, flattened against my stomach, and pulled me back against his firm body. "Ready to hit the slopes today and show them how it's done?"

"I don't think so, Nick. My head still hurts."

"Aw, c'mon," he cajoled. "A little fresh air will perk you up."

I turned toward him to share the full impact of my distorted features. The time for open defiance loomed in the near future, but not yet. "I'm sorry, Nick, but it hurts."

Nick's face sagged in a slight frown. He opened his mouth to respond, but Damien burst into the room. "Didja hear, Nick? We're goin' ice skatin' this morning!"

"Oh, we are?" Nick rolled off the bed and scooped the youngster up, placing him on his shoulders. Damien giggled, loving his view from near the ceiling. "Then this afternoon we gotta go to Willy Wonka's chocolate factory with Grandma, and Grandpa's takin' the grown-ups to the booery. And tonight, we ski under Christmas lights!"

"Wha-a-a-t?" Nick exaggerated the word. "How can we do that?"

"It's for Christmas Eve, silly." Damien started bouncing on Nick's shoulders in his excitement.

Nick swung Damien down beside the bed. "Well, that sounds like tons of fun. Do you think we can talk Aunt Jen into going with us?"

"Yes! Aunt Jen, you have to come! C'mon Aunt Jen, get up!" he tugged at my blankets while yelling in my ear.

His voice pierced my skull, making me want to shove a wad of blanket into his pie hole.

Nick's dad, Romolo, appeared in the doorway. Stately in height, graying hair over a solid build, he carried excessive pride in his continued athletic prowess; I'd heard him brag about it several times in the couple of years I'd known him. He stood before us in wind pants and a sweatshirt. He instructed Damien to finish getting ready. Bending down, tipped his head sideways, and squinted into my face.

"Oof, Jen. Still feeling a little rough? It's too bad your face took the brunt of the blow during the airplane turbulence. Next time maybe don't order a drink during the flight, hmm?" He stood to leave.

"Good idea." I murmured. Whatever. This conversation didn't even matter, but the one between him and Nick after they left my room piqued my morbid curiosity.

"Feel better, babe. I'll check in with you later." Nick patted my leg and followed his dad from the bedroom.

He'd left the door open a crack. As the throbbing in my head slowed, what I heard next made me almost as sick as the day before.

"Come back here a minute," Romolo said in a hushed voice.

"What's up, Dad?" the obedient son asked.

"There wasn't any turbulence, was there?"

"Ahh, not really."

"Son, when you have to keep your woman in line, try not to mess up the face. Damn. She looks like shit! How many times have you ever seen your mom's face messed up?"

CHAPTER 29

The Monsters Speak

"**ONCE OR TWICE THAT** I can remember, but those were accidents. Oh!"

"They were accidents, son." Smugness clung to Romolo's words. "They were cases of my fists accidentally connecting with her face instead of somewhere else on her body."

"Dad!"

"You're a chip off the ol' block, son. Somehow, I messed up with Giovanni. He lets that bitch dictate his life. But you're like me. We keep our woman subdued. Remember, though: if you mess up her looks, all you've got left is someone who's good in bed. I mean, she's obviously good in bed, right?"

Nick emitted a nervous laugh. "Dad! Of course."

"Shit. Here comes your mom. Just keep in mind what I said."

Nick slid back into our room and closed the door. I feigned sleep because I didn't want him to know I'd eavesdropped. He kept silent for a while, then gently caressed my swollen cheek. Sheer willpower prevented me from flinching. The door latch clicked, followed by some rustling, and it clicked again. An aroma of peppermint mingled with chocolate interested me enough to peel back my eyelids to the fullest extent possible.

Lucinda sat with me, and Nick bailed ship.

"Here you go, sweetheart. The peppermint infusion in this hot chocolate will help with any lingering nausea." In a more hushed tone she added, "I'm so sorry this happened to you. Nick's dad let him be privy to a few too many of his, as he called them, discipline sessions. Of course, Nick got knocked around a bit, too, but it was always more about women being subordinate. Anyway, I'm sorry."

Her voice perked up again. "Meanwhile, to get you through the rest of this holiday venture, if I were you, I'd consistently use the pain and sleeping pills. You won't participate in the activities here, and sleep will take the edge off the pain. Hopefully, you don't have to go back to work upon your return."

"I don't work again until January third."

"Perfect. Now drink up and get a good rest while we're gone."

A weak smile emerged. "Thanks, Lucinda."

She returned my smile before ducking out of the room as a commotion occurred in the hallway. While everyone bundled up and readied themselves for the day's activities, I pondered my mother-in-law's situation.

Lucinda was a smart woman. She worked as a part-time accountant and kept a beautiful home for her family.

Despite her intelligence, she lived with a man who physically abused her. In fact, she recognized the signs of abuse so well she hadn't even asked about my predicament. She apologized. At a loss about why she remained in such a situation, I could not follow her example. If anything, I grew more resolute than ever about seeking a better future for myself.

Following Lucinda's advice, I drank the beverage she'd concocted while ingesting a sleeping pill. At one point, I got up long enough to look out the window to the slopes, watching the Christmas lights reflect off the snow. I took a leisurely shower and ate some soup that Lucinda left simmering on the stove. Another sleeping pill ended the least exciting Christmas Eve of my life.

* * *

"Hey babe, Merry Christmas." Nick had coffee breath again. I'd take coffee breath any day over booze breath.

"Do you think you're up to dressing and joining us for breakfast and presents?" Once again Nick played the part of the perfect, doting husband. I wanted to love him so much when he acted this way until I recalled his fists were the reason I was bedridden.

I begged to wait until the kids opened their presents before exiting our room, listening for the giggles and cheers to subside. Adult time finally began. Tissue paper already spilled from several gifts. Three unopened gifts piled in the upholstered armchair Nick ushered me to.

Giovanni and his wife gave me a gift card to a major bookseller chain. Lucinda and Romolo gave me some

Spanish novels to read in my spare time: Bodas de Sangre, Como Agua Para Chocolate, and El Diario de La Llorona.

Nick chose a more practical gift, more down to earth. He got me some exquisite gardening gloves, a trowel, and a hand-held rake. The gloves came equipped with purple rubber tips, and lilacs laced down the hands and around the fingers. A red background highlighted large purple flowers burgeoning throughout the garden tools. They were all gorgeous and high on the price scale, and yet, not what I wanted.

"Oh, Nick, they're so pretty." Considering the persistent throbbing in my head, I thought I took adequate measures to disguise my disdain.

"How clever," Romolo chimed in. "Nick's found a way to keep Jen productive even when school's not in session."

"Well, I didn't want her to get bored," Nick admitted. "And we Adesco men love to eat!"

"True!" Both Giovanni and Romolo agreed. Not long afterward, Lucinda announced brunch. She catered in cinnamon rolls and an egg, ham, and cheese casserole. Something like this, my mom and I would have stayed up late and gotten up early to achieve.

After that, everyone but me took to the slopes one last time. Nick and I projected our departure time for 6 p.m. to catch our 9:15 flight. I slept several more hours, showered and packed to go. We said our goodbyes, gave hugs all around, and despite my appearance, Romolo snatched his customary lip-on-lip goodbye kiss.

The ride back to the airport taxed me much less than the trip west. A good sign that my face and head were on the mend. Lucinda slipped me a couple more of those phenomenal pills, but I declined to take any during our travels. I preferred to maintain as many faculties as possible. Once arriving back in North Dakota, Nick opted to drive us the rest of the way home so we could sleep in our own bed. At 2:48 a.m. we rolled up the driveway.

Having slept the past three days away, even though a mallet knocked on my head from the inside out, exhaustion crept out of reach. Nick, on the other hand, exerted himself longer and harder than customary.

"I'm bushed, babe. Let's unload in the morning, or at noon, or whenever. Sometime tomorrow."

"My head aches a little less, and I've been sleeping a lot. I'll start the unloading tonight."

Doubt radiated from his face and tone. "Okay. Take it easy, though." Too tired to argue, he trudged upstairs.

Creeping back to the front door, I pulled open the inside one and saw Vee peering up at me through the screen. I pushed it wide enough to let him in, collapsing to my knees, burying my face in his neck fur. Voluminous salty tears matted his fur by the time I released him.

"Oh Vee, it was so awful. Look at my face!" The advent of fresh pain rocking through my skull indicated the need to calm down. Vee stared into my eyes, and I swore he understood exactly what I meant and what happened.

Instead of unpacking, I opted to cuddle with Vee on my window seat. He positioned himself so his tongue licked the lump on my forehead. I thought I'd prefer he work on my left cheek since visibility through that eye remained minimal. However, the longer I sat with Vee, his soft tongue lapping my injury, the less intense my headache. Somehow Vee located the spot to bring more immediate relief.

"What am I going to do, Vee?" But my friend didn't answer, only offering me comfort.

* * *

Even without a pill, I slept until almost noon. I unpacked the car, whipped up some pancakes, made sure that Nick got up, cleaned up the kitchen, and started some laundry. When Nick left for the country club, I breathed the proverbial sigh of relief.

First things first. I laid out on the dining room table the Christmas presents I'd received from the three main men in my life at the moment. The beautiful, jeweled earrings from Charles, the gardening gloves and tools from Nick, and the silver bracelet from Jason. Of what significance were these gifts to me? More importantly, what did they mean to the guys?

Nick expected me to stay out of trouble by growing more food to pamper him with more of my savory dishes. Charles expected me to wear his earrings. But why purchase such pricey jewelry? Was it his way of showing off how well he could provide for me? Jason gave me a simple bracelet. Nothing too expensive, nothing overly showy. A simple, beautiful, silver-plated bracelet. A token of our friendship and maybe more.

I stepped back and reconsidered the gifts. If I purchased one of these items, which would it be? My eyes drifted from one to the next. While the earrings appealed to my taste, blue being my favorite color, I would not buy them on a whim. Maybe if a special occasion arose, and my bank account boasted surplus funds.

The bracelet, a different story. I traced my fingers over the braided chords of silver. Sliding it over my hand, I enjoyed the sensation of cold metal encircling my wrist. Yes, I would buy this, and I felt comfortable receiving it.

Onto the gardening crap. Lovely, definitely. Something with a foreseeable use? Doubtful. I'd considered gardening in the past, but unlike my youngest sister, I had no burning desire to dig in the dirt and pull weeds.

I slid the bracelet off and placed it back on the table's veneer surface, then considered all three again. Was my preference of gifts also indicative of my preference in men? I didn't think so. Obviously, I'd married Nick. His gift should've meant the most to me. Then there was Charles. Extremely hot, very strong, undeniably protective. And Jason. A bit older than the others, exceedingly handsome, and with a daughter I adored. A ready-made family, but I wasn't looking to move into a situation like that.

I picked up all the gifts, took the gloves and tools to the closet by the back door, placed the earrings in my jewelry box, and eased the bracelet back over my wrist. I'd tell Nick my Secret Santa at school left it as a final gift.

After switching wet laundry to the dryer and filling the washing machine anew, I considered baking homemade bread. I boxed up gifts to send to my family, resolving to transport them to the post office the following afternoon. After the hectic travel schedule I'd endured, one day with no excursions from my house sounded heavenly.

The scent of cranberries and rising bread permeated the upper level of my house. Even though I'd set a timer, I wandered downstairs to check on it. I paused under the mistletoe, the odor of a burnt substance smacking me in the face. The bread!

Running to the oven, I pulled open the door. No, it was still soggy in the middle. The stove timer revealed twenty minutes remained before the first toothpick test. So why the smell of...why was Vee concentrating so hard on something in the backyard? Perhaps an unwitting rabbit hopped into our yard. I didn't think Vee honed the instinct to attack and kill adorable woodland creatures, but what else ensured his survival when we were gone?

I stepped alongside him, freezing in terror. An approximately eight-foot yeti stood three quarters of the way back on our lawn, not too far from the hammock. I couldn't see its left arm, and blood poured down the left side of his body, as if missing a limb. This wasn't fake stage blood, either. This blood oozed at intervals due to continual clot formation. Obviously another one of my monsters, and it was hideous.

I stared back at it for a few moments, before motioning it to come forward. Craggy brows hooded the eyes and fur ensconced its mouth, making any form of expression impossible to discern.

It plodded within a few feet of the house, halting once again. My spine tingled and my stomach knotted. I wanted to scream and hide in my bed under the covers, but the time had come. Walking to the door, I held it open, beckoning for the yeti to come inside.

Again, it ambled forward, but not in a threatening manner; rather, like an old friend come to visit. I stepped back when it reached the door, not only because of its huge frame but also because I didn't want it to touch me. A part of my brain registered that during this process no barks or growls emanated from Vee. He wagged his tail in greeting. Had the yeti and Vee been hanging out?

Aw, damn! A trail of blood and loose fur followed the beast across my floor and to the kitchen. It was so gross, and I would ensure every last bit of this nasty mess disappear or risk Nick's anger. At least we moved into the kitchen. I figured kitchen surfaces cleaned easier than any other in the house.

The yeti took a seat on a bar stool without my invitation. Poorly groomed but good mannered. I guessed a wild creature from the heart of Saskatchewan couldn't be expected to conform to all of society's standards.

A loud buzz from the stove timer made me jump and bang my elbow into a counter. Not wanting to turn my back on the visitor in my kitchen, I grabbed a hot pad and pulled the pan out without checking the inner consistency of the loaf. I moved across the island from my guest, the refrigerator door digging into my back. Here went nothing.

"What do you want?" My voice stayed firm, but my internal faculties twisted in a bundle of nerves. Let it come at me. It wasn't like I'd never been attacked before. This monster even lacked one of its members.

"Thank you for having me here." The pleasant masculine voice this monster emitted failed to match his ferocious exterior.

The incredulity of the situation forced a trembling into my voice. "But why exactly are you here?"

"I don't want to overload you with information, but I have a lot to share."

"What are you talking about?" Impatience strained my vocal chords. Once I recognized no imminent threat existed, other emotions unleashed themselves.

"You've noticed that I," he corrected himself, "that we've been trying to contact you for some time now."

"You, meaning all the monsters and crazy things I've been seeing?" This conversation plunged deep into the depths of surrealism, into a dream. I had to wake up.

"Yes. And before, we kept tabs on you without showing ourselves. You often detected our presence even then."

"How many of you are watching me?"

"There are just two of us."

"How can there be only..."

An insistent jangling doorbell interrupted our conversation.

"Maybe they'll go away." I shrugged.

Pounding on the front door and yelling ensued.

"He's not going away," the yeti informed me. "You'd better go answer the door."

Reluctance clung to my body like hundreds of tiny hands trying to hold me back. The yeti was right, though. It sounded like Charles, and if I didn't open the door, he'd contemplate breaking it down with brute force.

My hesitant steps halted when I neared the staircase banister. Turning back toward my guest, I thought I'd ask him to duck out back, but he'd already left. I cringed inwardly at the mess he'd left behind, but figured I'd create a plausible story if Charles barged into the house.

Charles stood holding the screen open with his shoulder. His upraised fists pounded on the slab of wood separating us, then dropped as his muscles unclenched. When his gaze focused on me, the tension knotted again. He raised his hands as if to cup my face, but changed his mind and lowered them. He must have been afraid he'd hurt me if he touched me. Charles clenched his fists at his sides and growled.

"I'll kill him. I will absolutely kill him."

I grabbed his fists, pulling him into the house. "I don't think premeditated murder is a charge you'd really want to face." This time, I reached for his face and cupped his cheek. "Thank you, though, for wanting to protect me."

Primal emotions exuded from Charles. His eyes glistened with intensity, emanating a feral heat that caused a thin sheen of sweat to form on his upper lip and brow. An act of violence had seriously pissed him off, and he appeared ready to answer that with more violence. I needed to calm him down.

"Is he here? What took you so long to answer the door? Why haven't you been answering my calls and texts?" He pushed past the hand I held to his chest.

Shit! I didn't care to explain all the blood in the house. My mind raced. I supposed I could pin it on Nick beating up the dog, or a stray dog ventured in?

"He's not here!" I called after Charles, who forged into the living room before making his way into the dining room. "Charles! He's at work."

"Then why didn't you answer the door?"

"I must have dozed off."

"My calls? My texts?"

"I was on vacation with Nick's family. It wasn't feasible to respond. Besides, I know what I'll do now. Things are going to change."

"Great." He breathed a huge sigh of relief. "Pack your bags! I'll call a lawyer, and we'll get an appointment set up this afternoon, if possible. At the very least, we can file a restraining order." Charles pulled out his cell phone, sending me a quizzical glance. "What?"

During his entire tirade, I hadn't moved. "I'm not going with you, Charles."

He shoved frustrated hands over his smooth head and laced them together behind his neck. "Of course you are!" He obviously saw no alternative. He turned away from me and began to pace, which led him to the kitchen.

"What's this?" I heard him shout.

I made my way to the kitchen the other way, past the staircase. A muddled explanation formed in my brain. I hoped it was plausible.

His expression when I entered the kitchen surprised me. Instead of gawking at a bloody mess, Charles stood with eyes closed over my loaf of cranberry bread, wafting its aroma toward his face with one hand.

"It's orange cranberry bread." I squeaked. How could he have missed... A cursory glance at the rest of the room revealed nothing out of the ordinary. How had that yeti cleared all evidence?

My mind flashed back to the park a couple of weeks ago when Charles interrupted my encounter with the doll. So one of two explanations fit. Either my monsters—otherwise known as my pixies—possessed magical abilities, or I was stark-raving mad. In true lunatic form, I retraced the yeti's steps all the way to the back door. Nothing.

"Shenandoah. It smells amazing. Do you care if I have a piece?" He came to stand behind me and peered out the door over my shoulder. "What are you looking at?"

"I was just wondering where Vee went. I hadn't seen him in a while." I surprised myself with the ease in which the lie popped out of my mouth.

I temporarily placated Charles with cranberry bread smothered in homemade apple butter and hot chocolate. On auto pilot, I convinced him to leave with the promise that I planned on getting help, and if Nick touched me again before I got out, I'd let Charles take over. He longed for an end game where he controlled the outcome of the situation. To be my hero and provide for his damsel in distress.

Before leaving, he kissed me long and hard on my unmarred lips. My legs swooned, and I leaned into him. With the small part of my good judgment that hadn't yet succumbed to hormones, I pushed myself upright and broke lip contact.

"Goodbye, Charles. I appreciate you stopping in to check on me. I'll touch base with you tomorrow afternoon when Nick goes to work—or sooner, if something happens. Meanwhile, I'm going to rest and try to speed along the healing process."

"Please don't leave my heart alone too much longer." Charles' dramatic air stemmed from a truth he believed. "We belong together, beautiful Shenandoah."

I smiled, closing the door on his retreating figure. Where the hell had he parked? On another block? He disappeared behind the hedge at the foot of our driveway.

I collapsed on my window seat and noticed Vee there, lying asleep on a mound of blankets. It always wore him out when he helped heal someone. Granted, he hadn't made all of my bruises fade away, but the persistent headache had relented. However, I'd roused myself a few hours ago, and already the day's activities exhausted me. Pulling my knees up to my chest, I rested my chin on them and closed my eyes.

Moments later, the doorbell rang. Would a yeti ring the bell? Far from an abominable snowman, Jason lounged against the doorjamb. Instead of bursting in and taking charge, he shot an easy smile at me.

"Hey, Jason."

"Hey yourself, beautiful."

I grimaced at his compliment. With no make-up and lumps on my face, I veered far from any beauty pageant contestant.

"May I come in? I brought sustenance!"

"You what?" I started laughing when he produced three boxes he'd sat on the painted dark-blue metallic chair beside the door. Our tan exterior and blue shutters made me fall in love with what I called our Holly Hobbie house. It reminded me of the one my mom treasured from her childhood. I stepped aside to allow him entrance.

"I brought food."

"No, I know what sustenance is. I'm just trying to understand why you brought it. Is this from your kitchen?"

"I just got off work and the magic elves took the night off. So, no. This is gooey Italian food from the pizza shop downtown."

I laughed again. Being with him was so easy. He wanted to check on me, yet he hadn't said anything about my puffy features. He walked ahead of me and set the boxes on the island in the kitchen. This room reverberated with action in a short amount of hours today.

Jason flipped open a box and scooped up a wedge of pizza heaped with toppings, with cheese stretching all the way down to its neighboring slices. He deftly snapped the cheese strands before bumping my bottom lip with this delectable invitation. Steam hit the roof of my mouth at the same moment my tongue collided with peppers, beef, and exotic cheese blends. Biting all the way through the soft crust, I closed my eyes in disbelief at the phenomenal combination of ingredients. Never had I tasted a piece of pizza so heavenly, and never had eating pizza seemed so erotic.

Jason turned the same piece of pizza around, taking a bite where I'd left off. He licked his lips to catch some sauce left behind. I let out a low moan at the sensuality of the movement of his tongue.

"I know." His eyes bored into mine with purpose. Dropping the pizza, he wiped his hand on a complimentary napkin before hopping onto the island and pulling me between his legs. His teeth nibbled on my bottom lip, caressed only moments ago by the Italian fare. I leaned in as close to him as I could, allowing him to envelope my mouth. By a mutual need to breathe, Jason broke our embrace, but I lingered next to him.

"Well, now we've gotten that out of the way—how are you? Does it still hurt a lot?" he asked, gazing at my face.

"Not as much as it probably should," I said, offering transparency in that aspect. "I actually think he may have given me a mild concussion."

A pulse ticked in Jason's cheek, but he held his silence, waiting for me to continue if I wished.

I bowed my head. "I know I need to leave. I'm making plans."

He tipped my chin up and implored, "Please don't let him hurt you anymore. Is there anything I can do to help?"

I lifted a tremulous smile to him. "Thanks, but I think I've got this covered."

"I hope so, Jen." Jason appeared shook up. "I don't think I could handle it if he hurt you again. My heart broke when you sent those pictures on Christmas Eve. I don't do well when good people suffer pain." He concluded.

"Rest assured, I'm not too fond of being the recipient, either." I pulled back and went to the refrigerator. "Should I throw a salad together to go with the rest of this?"

"That'd be great. But while you're doing that, I've got some questions for you."

"Oh...kay." Questions made me leery. I didn't want to divulge too much about my injuries or the actual beat-down scenario. I always tried to block those things from my head, at risk of wallowing in depression over my circumstances. He took a different route, though.

"So," he fiddled with the condiment tray in the middle of the island. "I've kinda got the picture on your home life. What about the monsters? Are they still hanging around?"

Why did he persist with his queries about my monsters? Although glad that he'd let me share my concerns about them, and grateful for his advice, I suspected him of assessing me for the proper asylum once I left Nick.

"Jen?"

I busied my hands chopping lettuce and carrots. "Yes, I did see something in Colorado. It tried to communicate with me via rustic sign language."

Jason grabbed my elbow and half spun me toward him. "Well, that's great—right? As soon as you know what they want, maybe they'll leave you alone."

"Only what if they want too much? Or if I can't give them what they want?" I thought back to the faceless woman in Colorado. Was she a fortune teller? Was she trying to foretell of a pregnancy? Did she mean to take my baby?

Patience bolstered Jason's reply, "Glass half full or half empty? I think we should always hope for the best."

"In my life, my mantra has been more like 'hope for the best but expect the worst.' That way, good luck is a pleasant surprise."

"Fair enough."

I dished up the salad and handed a plate to Jason, pursing my lips all the while.

"What is it, Jen? Did something else happen?"

I debated telling him about today's incident. What if he thought I was crazy? Oh right, if he already suspected insanity, that boat sailed long ago.

"I had a visitor today. It was about an eight-foot-tall yeti."

"You mean Charles?" he joked.

"How did you know Charles was here today?" My eyes narrowed, and I took a step back.

CHAPTER 30

Aliens

HE SIGHED. "I WAS going to tell you at the right moment, and it seems that moment has arrived. I called the club before Christmas to see when Nick would be back at work. I've been worried about you—apparently, with good cause. When I drove by this morning, I saw Nick's car in the driveway. I worked for a few hours, then took the afternoon off. Catherine is staying with her grandparents until after the new year, so I didn't need to explain anything to her.

"You haven't been answering your phone, so I had to reach you in person. Then I set up surveillance. Nick left for work. I waited quite a while to see if you'd leave or come outside. When you didn't, I contemplated approaching you, but then Charles appeared on the scene. His presence irritated me, and I wanted so badly to interrupt your time together.

"But I know how much time you spend with him is your decision, not mine. So I waited impatiently and was not heartbroken when he didn't stay longer. That took all my restraint, but I gave you some time alone before checking in. Oh! And I ordered pizza."

I released the breath I hadn't realized I'd been holding. "Okay." Stalked by men, by monsters, and by men who were monsters. So far, only one of the three caused me bodily harm. "So this yeti stopped by, and we had a brief conversation."

"Wait! It actually spoke?"

"Yes. Aside from missing an arm and being covered with blood, he was quite civilized."

Jason's mouth hung open.

"All he said was that he'd been watching me my whole life, and he had a lot to tell me. Then Charles showed up, and the yeti disappeared." We carried our dishes to the dining room table. "Why is it again that you are so interested in my monsters?"

"They just fascinate me. Do you think he'll come back tomorrow?"

"Well, I'll be here if he does."

"Do you want company?"

"Thanks for the offer, but I think I'll be all right."

"I'm sure you will, too."

We finished our meal over a light conversation about Christmas gifts we'd received.

"I couldn't help but notice," Jason's hand encircled my wrist, "you're wearing mine."

Warmth rushed to my cheeks when I admitted, "It's probably my favorite."

He brought my wrist to his mouth, bestowing a light kiss. My pulse jumped in response, and my body longed to follow suit. The look in his eyes and the electric heat emanating from his body expressed how our hormones jived in sync. Instead of caving to lust, or whatever other emotions lingered, we both stepped away from each other.

"You should get some rest," he murmured.

"We did get in late last night."

Jason helped me clean up the dishes and put away leftovers. I walked him to the door where he turned and kissed my swollen cheek.

"I do love you; you know." At my nod, he continued. "I will wait for you, and I'll support whatever decision you determine is right for you. Please answer the phone when I call you tomorrow?"

I pressed a quick goodbye kiss to his lips. As he trekked away from my house, I noticed his car was also nowhere in sight. Nobody wanted to be seen visiting my residence.

Even though the early evening sky pulled its black cloak over North Dakota less than a couple of hours ago, I contemplated heading to bed after disposing of the pizza boxes. Nick would throw an absolute fit if he suspected I'd ordered out instead of cooking supper myself. He'd flip out even more if he discovered an outside party purchased it.

I awoke in the middle of the night to excessively vulgar profanity, even for Nick, spewing from the master bathroom. Further curses ensued, and the sound of a fist hitting the shower wall made me jump.

Shit! Something horrible happened at work. I couldn't decide what was worse: me unknowingly ticking Nick off, or an outside source aggravating him.

This time, I wasn't responsible for his outrage. Had I been, I'd already be paying for it.

When Nick emerged from the bathroom, I peeked from under the covers to see an Apollo body draped in a towel topped by the head of an angered Zeus. The face wasn't pretty, and neither were his words.

"Damn it, Jen!" He flicked on the light. "I didn't get the promotion at work. I was due, but that bastard, Billy, got it."

Nick continued to rant about work for a minute or two; afterwards, in his sick pattern of transference, his anger turned toward me. He always found problems with something I'd done or hadn't done. This time he focused on his Christmas gifts. He'd wanted to wear a shirt to work that he'd gotten from his grandmother, and he still didn't see it in the closet.

In calm tones, I reminded him we hadn't unpacked last night, and I washed his new clothes today. His new shirt hung in the laundry room. He took a deep breath upon hearing the news, then lit into me about how I wasn't sociable on our trip. He called me rude, then upped the profanity. He knelt over me on the bed, like he was going to take a swing, but caught sight of my black eye. His shoulders drooped a little. He settled for pushing me out of the bed.

"Get out of here, you rude bitch. You are not sleeping in my bed tonight."

I wanted to quip back that I never did, anyway, but counted myself lucky to avoid his fists. Vee joined me outside the bedroom door.

* * *

I rose before light the next morning to begin deep cleaning the house. Sometimes even if Nick carried over his bad mood to the next day, the sight of me working hard to make things perfect in his house pacified him. Sure enough, when he descended the stairs and saw me dusting, the tight lines around his eyes relaxed. He even smiled.

"Now that's what I like to see. My wife, hard at work, keeping her man's house in tip-top condition. What's for lunch?" He took an appreciative breath. "It smells delicious."

I served us both blueberry scones and Eggs Benedict.

"Fantastic, babe!" Nick pulled my body flush with his, proceeding to execute a French kiss to the best of his ability. My heart sank when I realized it didn't measure up to either Charles or Jason's kisses. I'd turned into a tramp, comparing kisses between men despite my pitiful marriage. And yet, maybe this happened because I'd become emotionally detached from Nick. How could I love someone who hurt me so badly?

Nick broke the kiss, satisfied with himself. "Time to go deal with Billy."

"Oh Nick, no!" I no longer loved him, but still cared for him. To my knowledge, Nick saved most of his physical violence for me. I hoped he wouldn't attack a co-worker. "That's no way to get recognized for promotion."

"Relax, babe." He let a casual smile slip, a smile that used to melt me like butter. "We just need to hash some things out. And that kiss? There will be more where that came from tonight, so be ready."

Once he left, I gathered the boxes I needed to mail—one to my family, and one to my sister at her college in Maine. I also made a stop at the grocery store to replenish our fridge and pantry. My faithful dog joined me in what became the most popular room in the house. I ruffled his fur and teased him. "You're just here because you smell the dog treats."

In response, Vee put his front paws on the counter and nosed the bag containing the treats. I laughed at his jovial face and pulled the perforated tab from the box. One of these days I'd teach him to perform traditional tricks for these dietary supplements, but until that day I'd appreciate the flawless healing trick he performed.

I continued putting groceries away but stopped, pulling my head from the depths of the pantry. That smell, I caught a faint whiff of something burning. I recalled that smell. It weaved its way into my house yesterday, shortly before I spotted the yeti.

My stomach knotted. Ready or not, it was yeti time.

I peered out one of the back windows, but nothing seemed out of the ordinary. I contemplated withdrawing to the kitchen to assemble the ingredients for turtle brownies, when a large Cyclops doll with brown, braided hair popped straight up. My scream and backwards stumbling didn't rattle Vee. He waited, expecting this guest by the back door. Meanwhile, the creepy doll clung to the outer window frame. Was it waiting for a sign from me? Why hadn't the yeti come back?

With firm resolve, I nodded to the doll and walked to the back door. The doll jumped from that window, over to the next one, and landed on the screen door in some eerie version of Spiderman. Once there, she slid down to the porch.

There was no logical reason to be afraid of a four-foot-tall rag doll, yet my legs trembled. At least this monster didn't show up with an amputated bloody limb. I led her into the kitchen where she propelled herself onto a bar stool in a deft ninja move. My eyes widened. Talk about spooky. She occupied the same stool as the yeti, both of her stuffed feet dangling where his furry legs had doubled over. I fought to refrain from backing against the refrigerator. If she wanted to hurt me, she already would have done so.

I cleared my throat, but she spoke first.

"Thank you for letting me in." Her mature voice belonged to a woman, not a little girl, as I expected.

"What do you want from me?" A blunt question, but I needed it answered.

"As Aloska told you yesterday, we've been watching you and we have a lot of information to impart."

"Aloska? So, it's you and him. Just two of you, he said."

"Yes, that's right. My name is Teague."

"Those are interesting names," I mused aloud. "But how are there only two of you? I've seen so many strange things."

"I know this has been an unbelievable experience for you so far. The things I'm about to tell you will make no more sense than what you've already seen. While I assure you this is no Twilight Zone episode, it will take some time and consideration whether you choose to believe."

"Oh-kay." My mind registered three possibilities: I was dreaming, I was mentally unstable, or I was having a close encounter of the third kind. Whichever one, the doll's explanation might help me understand. "I'm ready."

"Have a seat, please." She gestured to a bar stool. "And keep an open mind."

I chose the stool furthest from her and announced to myself that I couldn't promise where my mind wandered. Not to worry. Once Teague began, I was enthralled.

"We're from a planet called Zelnoir. It's 33 billion light years away from Earth, but still in the same galaxy. Zelnoir has a similar composition to your Earth, existing in most facets as a utopian society.

"Zelnites, the inhabitants of Zelnoir, resemble humans and function in much the same way as humans, only with some enhanced features and various skills. Most notably, the sense of smell.

"We've kept Earth on a visitation cycle for hundreds of years, because we depend on Earth for the survival of our planet. The strange thing is," Teague leaned forward in earnest, "despite our similarities to humans, when we enter the Earth's atmosphere, we don't maintain our original form. We become," she gestured to herself from head to toe, "hideous creatures which terrify earthlings."

She paused for a moment, her regard intent. "What's more, our molecules don't maintain the same shape each time we enter the Earth's atmosphere. If a person were to encounter one of us, he'd never run into the same creature again."

Teague stopped talking to let her story sink in and to assess my reaction. I looked down at the counter because I couldn't concentrate with a raggedy Cyclops doll staring me in the face.

So, human-like beings alive on another planet... Not too far-fetched a concept in the grand scheme of things. Educational channels loved to tout the possibility of a parallel universe; that part, I found feasible.

As far as a utopian society—whatever. That might depend on the person giving the definition. Many forms of utopia existed. The enhanced senses, also credible. Didn't species everywhere evolve and adapt to their environment?

I even bought the idea that extraterrestrials had been visiting earth for who knew how long. Countless tales existed on the internet, in movies, in science-fiction books. Even ancient hieroglyphs depicted the existence of visitors from the sky.

Then the whole reliance on Earth matter arose. We possessed something essential for their survival. Again, a plausible notion if—for example—this other planet depleted its mines centuries ago. Weren't we in danger of exhausting several of our own natural resources?

So, it came down to the shape-shifting gig. Why wouldn't molecules transport and reconfigure in the same manner, or even basically the same way? What blocked these different creatures from manifesting the same original form? I couldn't wrap my head around such a far-fetched idea. It was the stuff of Hollywood movies, and ones I'd never seen before.

Glancing up and to my left, I jumped at the huge eye that leaned in and watched me. The doll eased back into an upright position when she noticed my discomfort. I squirmed. Nothing at all awkward about telling an alien you didn't believe her crazy tale. What if she pulled out a laser and vaporized me?

"I'm sorry, but I just can't comprehend the whole shape-shifting theory. The rest of it has threads of credibility. How do I know you're not making up a story to see how gullible I am? Is this some sort of reality TV program?" I looked around my kitchen in mock hopes of locating a camera, knowing all the while I wouldn't find one.

"Shenandoah," she reached out as if to touch me, pulling back at the alarm in my eyes. "I would never intentionally hurt you. You are safe with me."

Never intentionally. But if I resisted? So glad she put that clarification in there. "So, what do you want from me?" My voice bordered on hysterical.

The clang of the doorbell almost knocked me onto the floor. I halfway expected the doll to attack me, despite her claim to a peaceful nature—at least with me.

"Please think back to your childhood, your earliest memories. When you lay down to go to bed this evening, think long and hard."

The doorbell jangled again, and an insistent pounding began. Charles retained the sole privilege to ring with such persistence.

"We'll visit soon." Teague hopped off the bar stool, executed a mid-air somersault, and virtually flew to the back door.

If the information overload Teague gave me hadn't produced my headache, the racket coming from the exterior of my house did.

Despite his displeasure, Charles blatantly observed the cross look on my face. "I told you I'd get a hold of you!" I unleashed fury by way of a greeting.

Charles' swift lunge forward backed me into the house. "It's been three hours since Nick went to work."

"I'm a big girl, Charles, and you don't own me. It happens that I had company and wasn't able to contact you yet."

Charles' eyes glinted. "When you promise something, you should follow through, or risk upsetting others involved."

Emotions swelled within me. "What are you going to do? Hit me?"

Shock registered on his face when he realized what he'd said. He tried to hug me, but I fought off his embrace. "I'm fine, Charles. I told you I'd touch base today, and you can consider this my checking in—even though you actually did the dropping by. I'm trying to get my affairs in order, and it takes time. Trust that I know what I'm doing this time." At his doubtful look, I added, "Please?"

"Look, I'm sorry. I just love you so much, and I worry."

"I appreciate it." I scooted him back out the door. "But I have tons to work on, so if you don't mind?"

He turned his head back to secure a quick lip lock. Damn! He smelled and tasted so good. No! No more distractions. Time was slipping away if I wanted to begin a fresh start with the new year.

"Can I call you later?" Charles looked like a sad puppy, but cuter.

"Of course, you can." I gave a half-hearted smile, locking the door behind me. His doting affection covered me like a heavy quilt—comforting, but also borderline smothering. I'd do well to choose carefully before running headlong into any other relationships.

Right now, though, I needed to call Jason.

"Hey, you sweet thing," Jason drawled when I called his cell.

"Hi," I breathed.

"How've you been the past 24?"

"Well, let's just say I had another encounter."

"So, the yeti showed up again?"

"No, but Charles did."

"Was he invited?" a curious voice with no hint of jealousy.

"No. And he did not stay. What's the matter? You weren't stalking me today?"

"I didn't need to. I believed what you said."

Was there such a thing as too nice?

"Thank you for that. Today my visitor was a doll with one eye."

"What? That's cr..." his voice trailed off before he said the word.

"Crazy? I thought so, too. If that wasn't enough, the kicker is, she said she was an alien." I expected him to laugh or attempt the "c-word" again, but silence resounded.

"Did she say what she wanted?"

"No. She told me about her planet and its inhabitants. I guess she just wanted me to know."

Another pause on his end. "Do you care to share those details?"

"Maybe later."

"You're asking me to be patient again?"

"Yes. Please?"

"Jen," Jason implored, "patience is not one of my strong suits."

"You're better at it than you think." I disagreed. "Thank you! I love you!"

"I love you, too, Jen. Until tomorrow, then."

"Bye." I breathed. Although sad to end the call with him, plenty of chores needed tending before the following day.

I performed ritual tasks: making supper, baking dessert, doing dishes, and showering, but remained distracted the entire time. Instead of going to bed, around ten o'clock I climbed into my window seat with Vee and pulled the curtains back, hooking them on protruding nails, no longer fearful of a monster lurking on the other side of the glass. If I understood correctly, any monster would either be Aloska or Teague.

So, I began recounting my monster sightings. Could I remember them all? Doubtful. I was certain the number of females ranked much lower than the male monsters I'd seen, but how could I tell?

The armless doll in the park: female. Also, the faceless angel when I battled the flu. The homeless woman in the public restroom at the park. Most recently, the Cyclops doll. All the rest existed as Aloska. I learned their molecules got scrambled before each sighting, but I didn't know if gender swapping played a role in each reconfiguration.

According to Aloska, one male and one female alien stalked me. Why exclusively two of them? And why me?

I hugged Vee in a tight embrace and reminisced about my childhood. For eight years, I had lived as the sole child of William and Mary Decker. Although spoiled to some degree at home, they had limited my experiences in the outside world. To say my parents were overprotective was a gross under-exaggeration.

Even in grade school, they stifled my attempts at socialization. No one spent the night at my house, and I wasn't allowed to go to overnight parties until reaching the age of ten.

During middle school and high school years, they limited the number of dances, football games, and other events that filled in my social calendar. Mary monitored my clothing styles. It wasn't until college that I started learning about the world...and making bad choices.

I'd have preferred, when my parents became benevolent and opened our home to orphans, that they'd lay off the overzealous parenting but no such luck. Perhaps I was the jealous older sister who thought her siblings got away with murder; but sometimes they did.

However, interactions with my siblings happened in mid-to-late childhood. Teague said to contemplate my earliest memories. Nothing came to me, though. We moved so many times in my younger years that names, faces, houses, and towns vanished like the blur of the landscape in a moving vehicle. I remembered asking my mother once why I had to leave all the friends I'd made. Her explanation involved keeping me safe. She told me to consider it an adventure, so I'd put on a positive face and go on a new adventure every few months.

The consistent acquaintances I maintained were my pixies. I never saw them, but I knew they followed me on my treks around the yard and peeked in my windows. They constituted the unexplainable drafts of air that either cooled me off or made me shiver. They showed up at every house in each new town.

As I got older and started school, the moves slowed to once a year. When we adopted Arana, the moving slowed even more. After a couple more adoptions, we settled in Kearney, Nebraska.

I sank further into the pillows and stared out at the crisp, jet-black sky, punctuated by shimmering dots of light. Sighing, I smiled up at the twinkling lights that had been guiding men for centuries. I'd been taught my name derived from the Algonquian language and meant "Daughter of the Stars." How nice it would be to lose myself in the stars and to escape this hell of a life I currently called mine.

Continuing to stare at the stars, I imagined my body levitating, drawing nearer to their brilliant light. I heard a mass of voices, difficult to distinguish because of the multitude. Glaring lights made identification impossible. Two voices edged through the harsh environment, comforting me each time they sounded. I focused on those voices every chance I got.

"She's so beautiful!"

"Thank you. We agree."

"How are her vitals?"

"We've got her on oxygen."

"What is our estimated time of arrival?"

"Will she be okay?"

"I love her so much!"

"The oxygen is running low."

"How much longer?"

"The procedure can begin immediately."

"I love you, baby girl."

"Success!"

Rough hands grabbed at me and pulled me from the warm cocoon I'd settled into. It took my brain a moment to register that someone pressed pause on a beautiful dream.

"I thought I told you to stay awake and be ready for me!"

CHAPTER 31

True Identity

SHIT! IS THAT WHAT Nick told me before he left? It seemed so long ago that I couldn't recall.

"What has gotten into you lately that you can't even follow simple instructions?"

I forced my eyes open to prepare myself to deal with this onslaught.

With an arm around my waist, he maneuvered my legs around. My arms fell forward as he bent me over the edge of the window seat and began to remove my pajamas. Did he mean to rape me?

I struggled against him, fearing the sex would be rough and refusing to allow him to tarnish my favorite haven.

"You're right. You're right!" I screamed at him. "I forgot! Totally my fault. But let's move away from the front door and this open window."

Even though most likely no one would pass by at this time of the night, a single witness could land his ass in jail. He came around to my frame of mind and shuffled us, due to loose and falling garments, over to the ground-floor spare bedroom.

Somehow—either by accident or intentional—Nick bound my arms, rendering them useless. Rough didn't begin to describe the battery my stomach and inner and outer thighs took. I prayed the ordeal would finish quickly, willing myself to struggle and flinch as little as possible.

When he finished, I heard him mutter to himself, "Didn't mar her pretty face at all."

Nick clomped up the steps. When I heard the spray of the upstairs shower, I rolled around to disentangle my limbs. Dammit! This was not supposed to happen. My whole plan to avoid more pain failed, and now I suffered both internal and external bruising. Wincing, I hauled myself into the downstairs shower. Hot tears mingled with beads of hot water. Damn it. I stayed in the shower until the tears ceased.

I curled back up on my window seat and stared vacantly at the sky I'd gazed at with fondness hours before. My body ached and a hollow sensation permeated my core. Nick had stolen my essence for wanting to escape and my reason to keep breathing. Maybe I should let him kill me, after all.

Vee curled up next to me and gave my cheek a couple of licks. If only his capabilities healed a broken spirit. I came to the sad realization I might not succeed in planning my course of action. I'd let events play out according to Nick's will. Whatever.

By the time I fell into a dreamless sleep, gold and pink rays stretched across the night sky, eager to expose a golden ball of fire to a frozen land filled with cold-hearted people.

A few hours later, by divine grace, I peeled open my eyes and managed to prepare a meal for Nick by the time he emerged in the kitchen door.

My body clicked to auto pilot. I thought and felt nothing, going through the motions of cooking and cleaning. Nick had finally beaten me into submission. Once I ran out of obvious chores, I collapsed in a recliner in the man cave, staring at a holiday romance on the Hallmark channel. Vee curled in a ball at my feet.

An unexpected voice behind me didn't even make me blink. I distinguished the voice from all others. It was pleasant and kind.

"Good afternoon, Shenandoah. I hope you don't mind that I let myself in."

"No, that's fine," I said dully. I began to turn around, but a firm hand on my shoulder stopped me.

"If it's all the same to you, I'd prefer you stay facing forward."

I shrugged. Nothing mattered any more. "Is it because you're in a different body today?"

"That's part of it. Why don't you lean back in the recliner?"

I obliged. No longer did I carry even a trickle of fear for these monsters.

"Now close your eyes and listen to my voice."

The sleep I'd missed out on the night before longed to claim its territory. Staying awake posed a serious struggle, even in the presence of an alien.

"Do you know who I am?"

"Of course. You're Teague."

"Perfect. Now aside from yesterday in your kitchen, where else have you heard my voice?"

"It sounds like the angel who took care of me when I was sick. Was that you?" I executed a partial rotation before Teague reminded me to face forward.

"Yes, I was the one who took care of you. Well, Vee and I did."

"Yeah, I love Vee."

"I know you do. Or rather, we knew you would. That's why we sent him to you."

My hands clamped down on the velvety smooth gray arms of the recliner. "You brought Vee to me? Is he from your planet?"

"Stay seated, please." The voice reminded me. "Keep your eyes closed."

"Okay. But is that why Vee possesses healing powers?" This conversation amped my adrenaline, which brought me back to life. Some of my former spunk returned, and the world here and beyond held interest for me again.

"We did bring Vee to Earth but concentrate now. Fixate on my voice."

I focused on the agreeable pitch of a lovely voice, singing for me in an emotive Native American chant, and my mind floated in a fog. The longer she sang, the easier it was for me to sift through memories and dreams. Will she be okay? Teague visited me in my sleep—or was it a resurfaced memory?

"Were you there when I was born?"

The singing halted abruptly. Teague whispered, "Yes."

Wow! They had been aware of me for a long time. All of my life, apparently.

"So, am I important to you?"

"Extremely."

These one-word answers aggravated my mood, but at least the numbness dissipated. To feel meant I was alive, and I realized I did want to keep living. Stupid Nick for almost taking that from me. Stupid me for letting him affect me in that way.

"If I'm so damn important," I shouldn't swear in front of a virtual stranger, but this pissed me off, "why did you wait until I was practically a middle-aged woman before contacting me?"

"It's complicated."

Ooh. A two-word answer this time. "Yeah, so is my life."

I propelled myself over the right arm of the chair without returning it to its upright position. Whipping around, I encountered the most horrifying creature to swim the seas. Today Teague took the form of a practically decapitated mermaid, her head 90% upside down, attached by a bit of skin and sinew. Parts of her face and chest were poorly stitched with baseball threading. Green eyes glared daggers at me.

After the initial shock, Teague no longer scared me. I pretended she wore a costume. Graphic and ghastly, but still a costume. "Look, from now on I'm going to assume that every creepy thing I meet is you or Aloska, so you may as well just lay everything out for me."

"Very well," she acquiesced. "Storytime again."

The movement of her mouth in an upside-down position disconcerted me, so I flopped on the couch, leaving the back of my head for her to speak at.

"Our planet has a similar composition to Earth, the main difference being the atmosphere. It's got a much higher concentration of argon and a lower concentration of oxygen. This doesn't seem to be a problem for any of our vegetation or animals but poses huge issues for Zelnites.

"When we reproduce, the lungs of our young don't have the capacity or ability to grow and develop. If our babies aren't removed to a safe environment, it's impossible for them to survive infancy."

"That's so sad." More affected than I thought by such a loss of life, I bowed my head.

"It's tragic." After a long pause, she continued. "So what we've had to do is acquire a stable environment where our youngsters can mature at a normal rate. Somewhere they can develop in a healthy growth pattern. We chose Earth."

"You mean there are little alien babies running all around on our planet?"

"More or less."

"So, your kids are baby monsters. How do they take care of themselves?"

"Interestingly enough, as newborns, all we can see is their essence—the beauty and goodness within them. Years ago, we used to select their initial shell—the body they would first live in. Since time is so limited between the moment of birth and the transplant, we can't place them in a shell—even for transport. Plus, that would definitely cause a scrambling of molecules."

"If the timing is right, and it usually is, a mother gives birth en route to Earth. Then we use a precision tracking device we've perfected over the years. It hunts down host bodies for us."

My brow wrinkled and my mouth opened in protest. What the hell? They killed humans to raise their own children? I couldn't accept the murder of one innocent for the survival of another. I rose to my feet, intent on telling Teague to leave and to refrain from future contact.

She anticipated my reaction and appeared at my side. "Sit back down."

"We don't murder anyone," she lowered her voice, "unless we're forced to."

Her timber rose again. "Have you not heard stories about the reduction of SIDS in the past few decades? Infant mortality rates have decreased worldwide! Or have you seen the miracle recoveries of terminally ill infants, or read about the tremendous strength of a premature baby to survive? In most of those cases, it's us!

"We enable human families to stay together. Our tracking devices locate babies when their health is failing. We then deposit our children, and their lungs develop while they are raised among humans as humans themselves."

I sat on the couch, resting my elbows on my knees and my head in my hands. Alien benefactors to the human race, all the while using us to rear their own. No wonder kids sometimes acted so differently from their parents. It could also explain why some kids who even looked like their parents were convinced their entire lives that they were adopted. Bingo!

My head raised, and I sought Teague's upside-down eyes. "How long before their lung development is complete?"

"At least 20 years."

"Your kids grow up on our planet then. You don't even get to raise your own kids. Wow."

"Also, tragic." Teague's detached head bowed so low it dangled to her knees.

"Do they ever go back home with you? Or are they forever trapped here while your world dies out?" I didn't like stories without happy endings but couldn't figure out how this one might rectify itself.

A movement to the side of the room caught my eye. A hunchback with grotesque facial features lurked in the kitchen doorway.

"Aloska?" I wasn't sure why I questioned him. I already knew the answer.

"Much like your younger siblings, you, Shenandoah, were not born of your parents."

"That doesn't make sense at all. I wasn't adopted. I'm the only one they had, though. William and Mary are my parents."

Even as I said the words aloud, I began to doubt them. No, no, no! I squeezed my eyes closed, pressing my palms into them. Flashing back to the dream, I recalled both Aloska and Teague's voices. They were both present at my birth. Impossible!

A golden light filtered through miniscule cracks where my hands loosened their grip. I inhaled the odor of burnt wood combined with hot metal but couldn't figure out why since my monsters were already present and accounted for. Although I'd asked for the spilling of all truths, I hadn't counted on their overwhelming nature. Reluctantly, I sat upright and slid my hands across my eyes. When the pads of my fingers touched the tips of closed lashes, I knew the time had arrived to face my bizarre reality.

Before me stood a different couple than I expected. The male figure resembled a picture of a Celtic Norseman I'd once seen in a storybook. A blond beard and hair, they somehow appeared both scraggly and well-kept at the same time. Brown eyes were buried in a ruddy complexion, and his nose was a touch too large for the rest of his features. He wore a blue and black flannel shirt. The top two or three open buttons revealed a muscular chest. Blue jeans and hiking boots completed his attire.

His female companion stood at least a foot below him, with the features of a Native American princess. Long black hair fell to her waist. Olive-toned skin graced her features and set off eyes bluer than robin's eggs. She wore a cream-colored blouse and slacks a shade darker. An open green vest, black flats, and simple gold jewelry completed her outfit. She dressed as the epitome of a modern businesswoman.

These were my parents. A concept too overwhelming to wrap my mind around. I wanted to treat these guests well in my house, but I lashed out at them instead.

"What makes you think you can barge into my life after all this time? You couldn't have come sooner? My lungs were fully developed four years ago. Why do you even care?" I shrieked.

Teague and Aloska calmly took a seat on either side of me. They sat far enough away not to touch me, but close enough to envelope me in their aura.

Aloska sighed. "After several attempts to bring children back home at an earlier age, our society learned they cannot survive on Zelnoir until they've matured. By that time, a human mindset becomes ingrained in them."

Teague took over speaking. "When we try to contact our offspring, most of them run in terror because of the way we are forced to present ourselves. Most parents can only take a few futile attempts before their hearts break, and they give up. It's an arduous process, and rebuff is painful to the spirit. When parents recognize utter rejection, they let go. Their child spends the rest of his life wandering the earth as a human."

I jumped up to distance myself and to face them. "Let me get this straight. Several aliens freely roam this planet and no one, not even the government, knows about it?"

"No one," Teague added. "Not even the Zelnites in human host bodies. When they pass away of old age, neither they nor their family members are any wiser."

"But you do try to make contact?"

Aloska answered this time. "These days, it all depends. We've learned over the years how unreceptive Zelnite children can be. When they've grown as humans, adapted, and are healthy and happy, why would they want to believe? We monitor our children. We watch their physical and mental growth. We see them invest in relationships and life plans with other humans."

"Of course, we'd rather collect them and bring them home as soon as they're grown, but the fear factor is too great. Many parents opt to wait and keep monitoring their children. If a life crisis occurs—or their child becomes seriously depressed, or even terminally ill—they may choose that time for an approach. Even then, a great many are rejected. Knowing the odds are against them, many parents only attempt a handful of encounters. Those who see signs of encouragement persist."

Teague interrupted. "You see evidence of that in bookstores and movie theaters. Your best-selling horror writers tease their parents. Each reappearance fosters the fuel for a new monster in a new hit movie."

My jaw dropped. That made sense. Shame on those authors for manipulating their parents, such a typical human character flaw. Both Teague and Aloska fell silent.

They regarded me while I thought through this barrage of information. No hopes or expectations showed on their faces. They awaited my questions, and ultimately, my decision.

Would I need to decide today? My eyes narrowed at them. Surely not. They wouldn't expose all these facts and take all this time for me to make a rash decision.

"What happens when your children make the choice to return home with you?"

Teague leaned forward, encouraged by my question. "There are many ways we can arrange for your exit from this world. Usually, parents let their children decide. Some go hiking and are never seen again. That seems to be a preferred method. Others board cruise ships, but never get off. Some never show up for work. Some have even self-combusted. Whatever the method, they're all effective."

Unable to help himself, Aloska uprooted himself and scooted to Teague's side. "Life expectancy on our planet is 500 to 600 years. A Zelnite child takes with it the body it was given on earth. This becomes his or her 'home body.' It's the one most frequently lived in. However, as I told you the other day, we live in a utopian society. Part of that requires we switch shells on a regular basis. Our elders found this increases tolerance and lessens bullying and hatred. Life is quite pleasant. There are plenty of opportunities to further one's education, locate diverse entertainment, and maintain healthy relationships."

"I...yeah, okay." I noticed Aloska picked up Teague's hands and held them between his own. "No, no. What I mean is, I get what you're saying. Your story makes sense on so many levels. But I need some time alone to mull over what you've told me."

My guests leaned back against the couch, and their hands separated.

"Besides..." I began to see the ease in manipulating Zelnites. At length, when they allowed themselves to communicate with their children, they didn't want anything to jeopardize the bond they wished to resurrect and nurture. "You still haven't told me who you really are."

Easy smiles crossed their faces.

"We had to let you figure most of this out first." Teague said. She and Aloska stood. "We're your parents."

CHAPTER 32

Confronting Nick

I HAD NO IDEA what the protocol was for meeting alien parents for the first time after birth. I envisioned Teague leaning toward me in anticipation of a hug, so I walked straight into her arms, embracing her. Heavy arms settled around both our shoulders as Aloska enveloped us both in a huge hug.

I'd never been in a three-person hug—an awkward gesture, at first. The moment I relaxed my hold, so did my parents. My parents. I took several steps away from them as a realization dawned on me.

"The baby. The one who had this body. She died?"

Teague's head bowed. "It was a tragic accident involving an irresponsible babysitter. Your earth mother's heart would have been broken. We were pleased to assist and thrilled to find a host so quickly for you."

This felt wrong—me, living inside a dead girl's skin. I needed time to think. "I'm sorry. I really need some time alone."

"We understand." Teague said, walking to my side. She placed a hand on my shoulder, pushing the hair away from my face. "But we can't leave you alone for too long, especially now that you know."

"Plus," Aloska added, "We may be forced to intervene if that...that man dares to touch you again!" He trembled with multiple emotions.

Embarrassment flooded through me. They were here to rescue me. They'd tried to make contact because they knew my life was in danger.

"I'll be fine. I've got a great warning system. Vee, come!"

Vee remained by the foot of the recliner, head resting on his front paws during the entire revelation. He trotted to my side, adhering to the command, a happy tail wagging.

"I'm glad you like the pet we sent you." Aloska's voice remained gruff.

"I love him! I'm not sure I could have survived the past few months without him."

I escorted my newfound parents to the back door. Aloska put his hand on my arm, and Teague gave me an awkward side hug. They promised to stop by the following day.

I retreated to my window seat to ponder and to plan, immensely grateful Teague shook me from the funk that threatened to smother me permanently. I hugged Vee with a new resolve never to let emptiness consume me ever again. I deserved happiness. Teague and Aloska offered another option to achieve this goal.

But first things first. I needed to touch base with other worried parties before they showed up unannounced. I texted Charles that my situation remained safe; even though after last night, I longed to invoke a response from him. He'd said he would kill Nick, and at the moment, the thought of disposing of Nick brought me great satisfaction. Instead of hiring an assassin, I suggested we meet and talk the following day. This seemed to pacify Charles, who agreed to come over around five o'clock. Knowing him, he'd waltz in early.

Lying to Jason proved more difficult. I also told him I was fine and denied any visitors. I wanted to talk to him, but I might break down if I heard his voice. Even through the text, Jason sensed something disturbed me. He begged me to come over to his house. I remained adamant in my refusal. The tone of his texts relaxed when I promised he could come over the following day. I scheduled him at seven o'clock, my second appointment for the evening.

My plan fell into place, piece by precarious piece. I'd let Jason and Charles know that I'd walk away at midnight, New Year's Eve. To my knowledge, Nick had to work that evening. If for any reason he got the night off and wanted to go out, I'd either make an excuse or leave early. What I would need from them was availability, assistance if I got into a jam. If Nick came after me. If my car broke down. Whatever the case, I needed their willingness to help.

I thought I could pull it off all by myself, but I understood they longed for involvement. Plus, both claimed to love me, and I harbored feelings for them. As for my parents from this world, I supposed I'd contact them once things settled down. My new, make that original, parents? They tracked me my whole life. Doing it once again shouldn't establish an issue.

Until my departure day, I intended to gather the possessions I held most dear and pack them in my car for later. Nick would not hesitate to destroy my belongings, proving that on multiple occasions.

I fell sound asleep without eating supper. Blissfully, Nick did not wake me when he came home. My ordeal from the night before caught up to me. I slept a solid eighteen hours. Nick woke me before noon on Saturday morning.

"Don't you have anything better to do than sleep in and play mommy to that stupid mutt?"

"Sorry, Nick!" Flustered, the rapid movement caused my tender muscles to ache.

"Seriously," he persisted. "Don't you have anything better to do?" He pressed his arousal against me when I tried to slide by him. "You could 'do' me." His voice lilted, as in suggestion, but we both acknowledged an order when it crossed his lips.

"Nick, no," I whimpered. "I'm still sore from the last time."

"That's bullshit! Women's bodies are designed to take it as often as it's given to them."

I struggled, but to no avail. He threw me onto the stairs, flat on my back, and forced himself on me. With the previous bruises and tearing, his aggressive actions were more abrasive in order to have successful intercourse. I realized I couldn't escape, and my struggles ceased. When he pulled himself off of me, I crumpled to the base of the stairs.

"All right, bitch. I guess I'll make my own lunch. Damn! And the sex wasn't even that good."

Hatred for him glowed in my eyes. Could I stay three more days in this house? I eased tender muscles into the master bath. Afterwards, I inspected my body from every angle. Blood from new bruises pooled under the skin all across my back and the backs of my legs. Uglier, older bruises splotched my inner and outer thighs, my arms, and my stomach. I bled from the spot where he'd been the roughest.

That son of a bitch! Hatred bubbled through my veins. Revulsion born of repeated abuse by an asshole encompassed me. I needed a weapon stronger than my spirit and my words.

Damn. Without buying on the black market, state laws probably required a background check and a waiting period to purchase a small handgun. Too late for that.

I could always get a taser. Or mace. I racked my mind for a store to purchase either. My little brother once told me that in order to buy a taser, you had to first receive the jolt of one. He said it made you pee your pants. I would take a hard pass on that weapon. I wondered if stores even sold mace in a small town like Grafton. A quick check on Google confirmed ShopMart carried that product.

After Nick left for the club, I made a trip to ShopMart and to the grocery store. The entire process became cumbersome due to the ginger steps recent brutality forced me to take. I needed to whip up a meal and desserts for all of my anticipated company this evening.

The rest of the afternoon consisted of baking, learning how to spray mace, and packing treasured belongings. At 4:42 p.m., Charles stood at my door expecting entry.

"You're early." I commented, moving aside for him to enter. Despite attempts at normalcy, he noticed my pain. He caught me by the elbow before we reached the kitchen and turned me in a gentle maneuver toward him.

"What did that son of a bitch do to you now? I swear, I'll kill him!"

"Well, don't think I haven't considered how pleasant that would be."

"Dammit, Shenandoah, you were supposed to get a hold of me. You promised!"

I remained defiant. "Occasionally things happen too quickly for a proper response."

That calmed him slightly, but we both remained on edge throughout our dinner of scalloped potatoes, ham, green beans, and cranberry rolls. I had just poured coffee for the two of us when the front door banged shut. The stove clock claimed a time of 6:24.

"It's a good thing you've got dinner ready, babe. Because I am not in a mood to be messed with."

Instead of diving into the nearest shower to hide as he had a week ago, Charles sat his ground. His eyes hardened and his hands clenched the end of the counter.

Nick froze in the kitchen entrance, one shirt sleeve already unbuttoned and pushed up, the other one fighting his frustrated fingers. When the initial shock of another man in his kitchen subsided, Nick took command of the situation like the alpha male his daddy modeled for him.

"Who the hell are you?" he yelled. His voice lowered. "I know you. You're the asshole from the gym Christmas party that tried to get my wife drunk. You were at the hospital visiting her, too. Are you screwing my wife?"

The other alpha in the room raised his head in defiance. "She needs a friend, and I am happy to provide that service."

"You've been servicing my wife? You son of a bitch!" Nick advanced on him.

Charles rose. Although he stood a few inches shorter than Nick, he kept himself in superior physical form. "Are you going to use your fists to solve all your problems, boy?"

Nick's shade of red deepened at the insult. "Get out of my house!"

As much as I wanted to prevent Charles from getting hurt, I also accepted the limits of my abilities. I backed away from the two until I stood in the darkened dining room.

Nick knocked over one of the kitchen stools, sending a leg from that chair skittering across the floor. Positive the fight was about to begin; I closed my eyes. Instead of fists hitting flesh, a booming voice called out, "Hey! What the hell is going on here?"

Three pairs of incredulous eyes fastened on Jason. "I guess I'm glad I came early." He directed the comment to me.

"Jason, look out!" My warning came too late. Nick's fist connected with his jaw.

With two alpha males in the room, it surprised me that Jason made such a grand entrance. Even while rubbing his jaw, I expected him to back down and let Charles handle the situation. "I'm sure glad you punched me in front of witnesses. Now the record can state that I defended myself."

"Except," Nick corrected. "You're an intruder in my home. I'm defending myself." He took advantage as Jason examined his damaged jaw, sucker punching him in the gut.

Jason stumbled back at the same moment Charles flew forward. He grabbed Nick's arms from behind, trying to put him in a restraining hold—a wannabe boxer versus a master swordsman. I would have been entertained had I not been terrified for the safety of everyone present.

As one might've guessed, hand-to-hand combat trumped swordplay when no weapons were available. A well-placed elbow and a vicious uppercut freed Nick. Although outnumbered, he held the upper hand. And he hadn't even begun to pull out his psychopathic cards yet.

I cast a furtive glance around the room and did the only thing in my power to prevent more injuries. I screamed. I walked over by the refrigerator, my new favorite spot for confrontation, clenched my hands at my sides and screamed. Every time my scream died off, I gulped a deep breath of air and screamed anew.

Once the guys dropped their fighting stances, I shrilled at our visitors. "Get out! Get out of my house! Get out! Get out! Get out!"

"Jen, you don't know what you're saying!"

"Think carefully, Shenandoah. You need us here."

Triumph glowed in Nick's eyes. "You heard her—get out!"

Jason and Charles stared at each other. In unspoken mutual agreement they rushed Nick, knocking him to the ground. My scream pierced through the scuffle.

"Get the hell out of my house! Get out before I call the cops!"

"You tell 'em, babe!" Nick jumped up and joined me by the fridge.

At that point, defeat crossed the features of two grown men.

I solidified my mask of hostility. As much as they hated Nick, I believed they would respect my wishes. If the cops escorted them away, they'd be rendered powerless in a jail cell. If they left of their own volition, they'd offer potential to help if I needed it later.

Right now, all I required was for them to leave. If my big showdown with Nick was about to begin, it had to be me alone. Terrified to the deepest depths of my soul for this confrontation, I remained stoic before my audience.

"Out!" I glared at both of them. To my surprise, they retreated, looking back over their shoulders as they shuffled toward the front door. Nick stalked behind them yelling, "That's right, assholes!" He thumped his chest. "My house!" He slammed the door and turned toward me with malicious intent.

I gripped the door frame to the living room, my body partially hidden from his sight. Rage burned in Nick's eyes. He paced toward me like a confident jungle cat, positive his prey wouldn't run.

Think again! Turning heel, I skated across the hearth and ran into the dining room, flipping chairs over behind me. He stumbled and muttered an oath, but otherwise kept silent in his pursuit.

I looped back around to my window seat, pulling the curtains wide. Inching my back up against the side window, I brought my knees to my chest and held the largest pillow in front of me.

"Nick, we have to talk," I pleaded upon viewing his shadow from the kitchen doorway. "Things can't keep going on like they have been. You can't keep hurting me." My tone became firmer. "Do you hear me, Nick? This will not continue!"

Despite a steady build in confidence, I squeaked in fear when Nick rounded the corner. He lugged with him the entire wrought-iron fireplace tool set, complete with extra logs. He brought an entire arsenal!

"Did you hear me, Nick? This tough guy, physical routine is over! You will never hurt me again, or I will leave. Nick! Are you listening?" I shrieked.

His calm voice belied his displeasure. "What the hell were those guys doing here? Are you screwing around on me? You are, aren't you, bitch? What? Are you having orgies when I go to work? You whore!"

"Nick!"

I couldn't say I hadn't cheated. I'd kissed other guys, preferring their company over his. Maybe I deserve punishment, a recess of my mind whispered.

Tearing eyes away from his advancing figure, I glanced outside. Charles and Jason stood on the sidewalk along with two other figures. Aw, shit! The neighbors would witness this, too. But which neighbors? I noticed long, dark hair on the woman, who stood next to a robust man. Teague and Aloska. How humiliating for my birth parents to be privy to this sad aspect of my life, even if they'd claimed to have witnessed it before.

My gaze darted back to Nick, who rested a hand on the banister at the bottom of the stairs. He crouched a few paces from me, and that was dangerous territory.

"I should have known when you didn't want to give it to me that there were other guys involved. Evidently, I haven't been keeping you in line as much as I thought I had. Here's where the shit meets the fan." He paused, raising his voice. "I hate you! I hated that stupid chair of yours. I hate your ugly dog, and I hate this damn window seat you use as a bed. I'm done with all of it!"

He reached down to his right with both hands, hauling the entire wrought iron set up to his chest. Not certain what he planned, I deliberated on how to react. I watched and waited, ready to both defend myself and fight back at a moment's notice. He was easier to predict when he came swinging. Plodding steps halted a mere foot from me.

As I waited for him to drop his load, I regarded the potential weapons he carried. Instead of setting the entire ensemble down, Nick swung down, low to his right side, heaving it at me. His intent, to smash my entire body in a mangled mess of wrought iron and flesh.

The velocity at which such a contraption moved was incredible; its accuracy, as parts shifted, was not as impressive—and not as deadly for me. I stood on the cushioned seat, held my arms in front of my face, and braced for impact.

The textured object that grazed my arm must've been a stray log. The rest of the contraption collided with my view of the outer world from my favorite seat in the house. For a moment, I considered how pretty shattering glass sounded. When realization dawned, I turned into one seriously pissed off person. Pissed off alien. Hell, I didn't know.

Nick said he was done, but so was I. An anger born of a strength I'd never possessed coaxed me to grasp the poker from the shards of broken glass framing the window. It teetered precariously on the ledge. Damn it! A piece of glass sliced the back of my hand.

Rough hands pushed me from behind. By a miracle, I stopped my face from implanting on the jagged frame by slamming my left arm down. I kicked free from the hands, rolled, and fought to leave the alcove that no longer served as a refuge.

Something stronger than a hand clamped on my left forearm. Nick found the tongs, attempting to immobilize me. The forceps bit into my arm with relentless force. These teeth marks might last awhile. I realized we'd arrived at the point where normally I ceased to struggle due to the intense pain and hoped that he'd go easy on me.

Right. Because his fury would subside enough for him to see reason. Despite the intolerable pain and the satisfaction on Nick's face, I took action. Not known for my stellar upper body strength, I swung the poker with all my power. It connected somewhere above Nick's neck.

Three things happened at once: a splatter of Nick's blood slapped my face, the drop that landed in my mouth tasted warm and tangy; a petrifying, gurgling howl erupted from his lips; and the vice on my arm loosened. I scurried over to the stairs to discover that Nick wasn't on my tail.

He slumped onto the window seat, holding both hands to his face. Blood dripped from at least one orifice onto the cream-colored carpet. My gaze lifted for a second to the onlookers who advanced on the yard. It seemed like they wanted my attention, but I turned all of it back to Nick.

"You bitch," he rasped.

My heart beat out a crazy rhythm in my chest, along with the cut on my hand and on the indentations made by the clamp. For once, I advanced on him. I poked one of his hands with my weapon. The hand I dislodged from his cheek landed in a sticky puddle on the carpet. For the first time ever, I detected fear in his eyes.

"What's the matter, Nick? Cat got your tongue?" I edged closer, dragging the sharp side of the poker over his hand; a string of bright red bubbles rewarded my action. I needed to hurt him worse. He hadn't begged me to stop, and he wasn't crying.

I lifted the poker's tip until it hovered eye level to him. I wanted him to fear me. I needed him to question my next move. I dropped the poker straight down on that same hand. Nick winced. It wasn't enough. I pressed my weight forward onto the protruding rod. A squelch and popping noise followed, a sign wrought iron had penetrated his skin. I wiggled it around a bit, as I imagined nurses tortured me with needles when they drew my blood.

Suffer, sucker, my mind gloated.

And then my face met the carpet. Newfound self-confidence tripped me up. My intense concentration on administering pain distracted me, and I neglected to see his left-hand snake out and yank on my ankle. I shoved the poker into the hand that still held my leg. Nick tried to use my body to block the thrust, which somewhat worked. I ripped my pant leg before contacting him.

I peddled my feet to get away. Nick howled in frustration, pain, or both. I took a couple more jabs at any part of his body in reaching distance before stepping back to regard him. Nick writhed in serious pain, but he'd survive. I also couldn't count on him not catching a third wind and trying to attack me with ultimate vengeance. I needed him conscious to listen to me. I had to prove to him I won.

"Hey, jerkface!" I yelled at him.

His head lolled around to look at me, hatred emanating from his eyes.

"It's over, Nick." My level voice surprised me. "You're done hurting me. It shouldn't even have gone on this long. I'm calling the cops." I walked to the kitchen doorway, fumbling for my phone on the kitchen counter. As I prepared to place the call, Nick's condescending words cut through his heavy breathing.

"You're so stupid. Calling the cops will land your ass in jail, not mine. I'm obviously the victim."

"Dr. Bisbee and several others will be happy to attest otherwise. We've been building a case against you."

I detected worry in his face. "Aw, c'mon Jen. You know I accidentally get a little rough. I don't mean anything by it. I'll work on my temper."

I began dialing.

"Aw, hell, Jen. Whaddya want me to do?"

I punched the second number.

"Babe, you know I love you!"

CHAPTER 33

A Decision

BEEP—I PUSHED THE third number and a no-nonsense feminine voice greeted me through the receiver.

"911, what's your emergency?"

I stated my name and address, calmly informing them a domestic dispute had erupted. The operator reported she dispatched a squad car to my residence. She instructed me to stay on the line until help arrived.

With the final confrontation over, nerves ruled my senses while I awaited police back-up. Ever since I'd been pulled over for a taillight I didn't know burned out, cops kind of freaked me out. I kept a wary eye on Nick while the dispatcher periodically asked if I was still doing okay.

I sensed another presence in the room, assuming it was the police, forgetting I had not yet unlocked the door for them to gain entrance. Instead of the men in blue, Teague and Aloska walked over to me, accompanied by Vee.

"We're very proud of you. You've come a long way." Aloska said, draping a fatherly arm around my shoulders.

"Thanks." I uttered, and I meant it. "I think so, too."

Nick, who'd been silent for a while, screamed at me, "Who the hell are you talking to?"

I looked over a shoulder at my self-proclaimed birth parents, still catching a hint of campfire aroma when gusts of chilled night air evaded the room. Teague shrugged her shoulders, and Aloska shook his head.

Nick spewed some choice profanities and declared, "You're a freakin' lunatic! Absolutely crazy!"

But Nick couldn't see the visions that plagued me. Maybe there was more to this crazy business than...

A pounding at the door made me forget about the mind I might be losing.

"Mrs. Adesco? It's the police! May we come in?"

I skittered past Nick, climbing a couple of stairs to stay clear of his evil hands. Tony Wong entered first. His partner, Suzette, trailed him doggedly. A third officer, identified by his badge as A. Feldman, attempted to close the door in the small entryway where they awaited direction from me.

"You can just leave it open," I instructed A. Feldman. "It's not like the furnace can keep up with all the heat escaping through the gaping hole around the corner."

Nick's legs had folded under his body, but he'd allowed one to drift backward like a disjointed snake, causing Tony to stumble when he rounded the corner.

"This the guy?" he asked, standing upright and fumbling for his cuffs.

"That's him." Undisguised contempt massaged my words. "Feel free to call Dr. Bisbee to testify."

"Oh, we will." Suzette volunteered. "First, we'll interview these witnesses."

"Yes." Tony appeared irritated he hadn't spoken first. "Feldman, begin interviewing the witnesses while we take Mr. Adesco, here, into custody."

While Tony recited the MIRANDA rights to Nick, Jason and Charles let themselves in. The mass of people huddled at the base of our staircase, blasted by gusts of bitter arctic wind, seemed surreal to me. My beloved window seat's cushions lay in disarray, ripped and bloody. A gaping hole framed by jagged glass caused my stomach to lurch. I tasted a bitterness in my throat, and fought to swallow it down. Oh shit. I didn't want to puke in front of all these people. And on the carpet. Even though the carpet's best days had now passed.

I pushed past bodies to clear my head. Once again, Nick succeeded in taking something away from me that mattered. My window seat became my safe haven, my refuge after he destroyed my armchair. Still, after everything that transpired in this house, I doubted I would've stayed. It would be best to leave, anyway.

A. Feldman asked if he could use my dining room table to gather individual stories. I complied, mystified about why I wasn't going first. Instead, Charles sat perfunctorily across from him, intent on driving Nick's name into the ground.

The rest of us meandered in the living room. Or rather, my invisible parents, good friend, my dog, and I paced around. Jason walked straight up to Aloska and gripped his large hand with the confidence of a fellow ally.

"Wait. You can see them?" My eyes darted between the two men contemplating deception. "What do you do?" I asked Teague. "Become invisible when you want to? Are you trying to boost my self-image of mental instability?" The pitch in my voice climbed, despite an effort to control it.

Teague consoled me. "Honey, it's okay. It's a lot to handle all at once. Jason," she turned toward him and murmured, "Your parents will be happy you now believe."

"His parents?" my voice teetered on the brink of hysteria. "How do you know his parents?"

My own parents tried to shush me. A stern voice from the dining room demanded, "Everything okay in there?"

"Everything's fine." Good old, level-headed Jason. He waited until the four of us were alone again. "So, Jen," he stared at all three of us. "Are these, by chance, your monsters?"

I felt like a child caught in a lie. "Yeah, only they don't look so scary right now."

Teague resumed murmuring. "Jason's encountered many monsters, himself. Isn't that right?"

Jason nodded.

"But he chased his monsters away. I get the impression he's regretted it all these years. When you confided in him, he saw it as a second chance to ask the questions lingering in his mind."

I turned incredulous eyes on him. "Is this why you urged me to approach them? You wanted to know what they wanted as much as I did?"

"Okay, I'm ready for you now, sir." A. Feldman spoke from behind me.

"Don't worry," Charles assured Jason. "She'll be in good hands while you're helping put that bastard behind bars."

I raised my eyebrows at the couple before me. Teague put a finger to her lips, and they both stepped out of the way.

"Shenandoah," Charles breathed my name. Despite throbbing pain in several parts of my body, and the obvious mess that I'd become, the sexual magnet between us coaxed me next to him when he sat on the couch. "What you did tonight was both incredibly brave and incredibly stupid. I'm glad you finally turned that louse in. He doesn't deserve to breathe the same air as humans."

Noting the irony in his last statement, I wondered if I had the right to breathe this air. I glanced over to the fireplace where Teague and Aloska retreated, but they'd disappeared. I stood to look for them. Charles rose with me and gingerly tipped my head toward his.

I'd been through so much! At one time, all I might have desired was the chance to lose myself in his kiss. This time, I appreciated the hand on my shoulder that broke partial and then complete contact with Charles.

"Jen. Sorry to interrupt, but the unit is here. Officer Feldman says he'll interview you on the way to the hospital. Dr. Bisbee has agreed to meet us there."

In a display of emotion that put melodramas to shame, Jason exclaimed, "Geez, Jen! You could have been killed!" He held me at arm's length, quoting Monty Python in a British accent as the Black Knight, "But 'tis only a flesh wound."

I grinned. "It's true. I'll be fine."

Paramedics entered the room and guided me to the ambulance, despite protests that I could find my own way and even drive my own car. One of the attendants extended a hand, assisting me into the emergency vehicle. A fluttering curtain inside the broken windowpane reminded me that my home sat exposed to any marauding looters who might roam Grafton streets.

"Don't worry." The officer reassured me. "Someone on the force will board it up tonight."

During the short ride to the hospital, and after being admitted to exam room number one, A. Feldman questioned my relationship with Nick and the abuse he'd inflicted. I found the verbal degrading difficult to explain, so I stuck to the physical stuff. Sadly, the excessive amount of incidences clouded my memory. Throughout the interview I kept in mind that berating Nick, as much as I wanted to, lent a childish air. I needed to stick to reporting facts, as many of them as popped into my memory.

Dr. Bisbee was aghast when he moved aside the cloth gown I wore to give me a complete examination. Bruises from the other night glared from my body with a purplish-brown hue. Wounds from this evening crusted over but still oozed blood in a few spots. Nick's blood splattered in my hair, saturating the clothes I removed and heaped in a chair.

Upon completion of his inspection, Dr. Bisbee instructed Bryan Wright, the ER nurse, to clean me up before he administered a couple of stitches to my forearm. The harsh smell of hospital anesthetic assaulted my nose. Embarrassed at the scrub down under bright hospital lights, I tried to joke with the nurse. "I finally meet Mr. Right, and it's in the emergency room. Just my luck."

"Yeah, I've never heard that one before."

Okay, jerk—enjoy scrubbing dried blood. When my body felt raw from his ministrations, he pointed to a clean pile of clothes and ordered me to get dressed. Surprised to see my own clothes, I pulled them on with all the speed my stiffening limbs allowed.

Dr. Bisbee reentered and spoke comforting words while he sutured my arm. Before signing my discharge papers, he mentioned what I already knew—he approved that I'd turned Nick in. "I'm heading over to the jail now to work on a patient." He gave me a melodramatic wink. "I just might forget to administer a numbing agent before starting treatment."

I laughed and hugged Dr. Bisbee. "Thanks for believing in me."

The rest of my supporters mulled around in the ER waiting room. "I'm done," I announced to the group. "Thanks for bringing me new clothes to wear."

"Teague said you would need some. She also suggested I pack some extra things in a bag for you in case you didn't return home tonight. I should have thought of it myself. I hope what I brought is all right?" Jason seemed anxious to please.

"Who the hell is Teague?" I overheard Charles mutter to himself.

Eek! Jason went through my unmentionables. Besides those, he brought me a sweater, jeans, and my extra set of tennis shoes. "This is perfect, thanks."

Jason diverted attention by mentioning that Charles also helped at the house by supervising the covering of the window. My appreciative eyes caressed his face when I thanked him.

"Oh my," Teague whispered to my father. "Torn between two lovers."

"That's not what this is," I hissed.

Charles looked like he'd missed a private joke.

Aloska and Jason raised their eyebrows.

"Yeah, okay." Teague shrugged.

"Can I give you a ride somewhere?" Such a gentleman. I took Charles up on his offer.

"That'd be great. I'm going to stay at the American Lodge. I called while the doc practiced a cross-stitch pattern on my arm." I shot a meaningful look at Jason and my parents. I still had some questions and hoped they'd join me there. I said "goodbyes" meant as "see you soons."

When I'd consulted my phone to make the reservation, it had been close to eleven o'clock. That was the first time since Nick arrived at home that I'd realized how much time had passed.

Charles carried my bag to the hotel room and offered to stay with me. He swept the hair away from my neck and began kissing me there.

With reluctance, I pushed him to the hallway side of my door.

"As I told you before, I have a plan. I hadn't intended to execute it until the new year, but today's situation warranted that I move things up. I still need a bit of time. I promise you; I'll be in touch by New Year's Eve. All right?"

Charles agreed to my conditions but offered the name of a lawyer and the promise of never ending fidelity, devotion, protection if I chose him.

"My heart's still waiting," his lips earnest against mine. "I love you, Shenandoah." With no further words, he turned on heel and strutted away.

I sighed and leaned against the inside of the door. This entire procedure proved exceedingly difficult. First part completed. I made the break. The second big decision loomed. Which path to choose for my future? I couldn't afford to make another huge mistake, and I didn't want to move again. Where would I find stability?

Perusing the bag Jason packed, I found flannel pajamas and another change of clothing but no toiletries except my toothbrush, toothpaste, and hairbrush. About what I expected from a guy. Under a stream of hot water, the remaining pungent hospital odors swirled down the drain, replaced by the potent floral smell of mass-produced hotel shampoo. I'd already donned pajamas by the time my guests arrived.

Jason's eyes glowed, which I suspected meant that he'd been briefed on the details of his birth and what options his new life included.

"Who knew?" he asked, crossing the room to sit beside me on the bed. "Who knew two unsuspecting aliens would find each other here on Earth?"

Teague and Aloska smuggled Vee into the hotel. In a lazy stretch, Vee jumped from the doorway clear over to the bed and licked my face before laying down. My parents backed out of the doorway.

"Where are you going?"

"We'll let you have some time to talk to Jason." Aloska responded. "We'll be back shortly."

How considerate of them. Awarding Jason my full attention, I asked about his impressions and what he planned for his future now that the truth enlightened him.

"I'm meeting my birth parents tomorrow. Or more like today," he said after glancing at the digital clock beside the bed. "I'm grateful to have the opportunity to apologize for not trusting them when they tried to contact me. I've always felt badly about those incidents."

"And they told you the possibility of returning to their planet?"

"Ah, yes." He took my hands in his and studied them. "But that's no longer an option for me since I have Catherine to consider." He mentioned Catherine, but his eyes rose to mine as if to say, and you.

We spoke a little longer about Catherine and about the strange coincidences that shaped our lives. When my parents returned—it still seemed odd to think of them that way—Jason reclined against pillows propped at the head of the bed, and I arranged myself against him. Jason eased out from behind me and fluffed the pillows. His skilled yet tender kiss left me trembling for more. The room seemed to get colder when he moved away.

"Will I see you tomorrow?" he implored before leaving. "I'd love for you to meet my parents."

"How about I let you get acquainted with them first? On New Year's Eve, I'll throw a private party at my place for relatives and close friends. I'll text you the details."

Upon Jason's departure, Aloska and Teague ventured to the bed and sat down with me. Teague's black hair cascaded over my shoulder and across my chest when she hugged me. The aroma of pineapple infused with passion fruit calmed and reassured me, so I hugged her back. Speaking somewhere in the vicinity of my left ear, she asked, "Shall we make preparations to depart on New Year's Day, then?"

"Depart?" In my confusion, I inhaled several strands of Teague's hair and coughed them back out. "Sorry."

She didn't seem to mind spit mixing in her hair. I guess 24 years without the capability of holding your daughter made you more tolerant. "You are planning to come back to Zelnoir with us, aren't you?"

"Remember, Shenandoah, you've been wanting happiness—the very definition of utopia. You can forget all of your earthly troubles and create new and pleasant memories." Aloska reassured me.

"No offense," I didn't want to upset my parents, as I had no idea what they were capable of, "but even though I like you both and am growing fonder of you by the minute, I barely know you. I can't be certain that following you across the galaxy is what's best for me. I hope you can understand."

Teague massaged my temples. "My wish for you, my beautiful daughter, is to dream of life on Zelnoir this evening."

One last question tore from my lips before they left. "If I did decide to go with you, would I be able to return if I didn't like it?"

A furrow, so slight I almost missed it, formed between her brows then disappeared. "I'm sure it could be arranged, but it's not usually considered." She kissed my forehead and tucked the covers around me. "Sweet dreams, my love. We'll come to your New Year's Eve party and give you space until then."

They might even give me space after the party, I thought. The entire universe.

Vee curled by my side and we both slept until checkout time the next morning. True to what Teague told me, I dreamed of the world of my conception. A world that promised a life of happiness and little discord. A life meant for me to claim.

* * *

Random 2x4s nailed across the front of my house alarmed me when I pulled into the driveway. My beautiful Holly Hobbie house appeared to be a dilapidated mess.

The interior wasn't much better. I spent the entire day cleaning, baking, and thinking. That night, I slept in the extra bedroom upstairs where I'd located the star for the Christmas tree. It was one of the rooms Nick never defiled. Correction: one room he would never defile.

I woke on several occasions, certain each time that Nick was coming home, powered by his fury. With bags under my eyes, I spent the next morning packing. I wasn't sure how much I'd take with me, but I needed to move; hopefully, for the last time in my life.

After I forced down a couple bites of leftovers, I texted Jason and Charles instructions to arrive around eight o'clock for a late supper. I welcomed guests to bring champagne or other beverages, but my menu offered plenty of food.

Minutes before eight, an influx of guests arrived at my once perfect domicile. Had Charles been able to see Teague and Aloska, he would have charmed them with his wit and good nature. Jason arrived with his newly acquired parents in tow. Jody and Eleanor fawned over their son, much like any doting parents. All parental units observed and commented on the meal from the kitchen, while Jason, Charles, and I sat at the dining room table.

I'd never seen my parents ingest food before, so watching them rave over my succulent ham and perfect scalloped potatoes eased my mind about alien life on earth. I closed the meal down with a crème brûlée that

Jason noted the finest chefs in France would have trouble topping.

We poured the first round of champagne at 10:09 p.m. Instinct indicated everyone waited on me. This was "Jen's big decision night," and all parties believed they were still in the running. I'd assessed my future hundreds of times in the past couple of days, and always—ALWAYS—my mind steered me down the same path. Right or wrong, this decision remained my first option.

I made the first toast to friends and family, announcing I'd arrived at a decision for my future and would reveal it at midnight. Everyone seemed optimistic, certain I'd choose their path.

Two more toasts from others occurred before midnight, and we all enjoyed the effects of ample alcohol. We watched Ryan Seacrest count down the New Year. With glasses held high, we witnessed the ball drop in Times Square.

At exactly the stroke of midnight, Central Standard Time, I strode across the room, my intent never wavering. I pushed my body flush against Jason's, wrapped my arms around his neck, and kissed him with every intention of never letting go.

ACKNOWLEDGMENTS

To my mother and father, who inspired in me the love of words, reading, and writing.

To my children, who always supported my writing dreams.

To members of my writing group: Shelly, Adrienne, and Robin. Each one of you has made me feel like a world class author.

To my Beta readers who offered invaluable feedback.

To my students, past and present, who inspired names of characters.

To the city of Grafton, North Dakota, which offered the perfect setting, and Alma Public Schools, the YMCA of the Prairie, and Beatrice High School, for further setting inspiration.

To the staff members at the S.A.F.E. Center, who advocate for abuse victims.

To Mandy Melanson, from whom I learned so much, both as an author and as a person. Thanks for believing in me and what I could accomplish. To everyone at RhetAskew Publishing who helped form my words into a final masterpiece to convey issues I wished to address.

To my readers - I hope the characters in this book come alive for you.

To everyone who secretly wonders if they're in an abusive relationship - I urge you to reach out and talk to someone.

Anyone.

ABOUT THE AUTHOR

SHENNONDOAH RIVIÈRE is a full-time French, Spanish, and Speech teacher in a rural K-12 school. She also works part-time at a YMCA and for a seasonal haunted house.

When she is not working, she enjoys reading, writing, and acting in local theatre productions.

ShennonDoah writes poetry, short stories, song lyrics, and paranormal and science fiction novels.

WWW.RHETASKEWPUBLISHING.COM

Made in the USA
Monee, IL
08 November 2023